I0817694

The Anthology of IRISH FOLK TALES

VOLUME II

First published 2025

The History Press
97 St George's Place, Cheltenham,
Gloucestershire, GL50 3QB
www.thehistorypress.co.uk

British Library Cataloguing in Publication Data.
A catalogue record for this book is available from the British Library.

ISBN 978 1 80399 945 6

Typesetting and origination by The History Press.
Printed and bound in Great Britain by TJ Books, Padstow, Cornwall.

The History Press proudly supports
Trees for Life
www.treesforlife.org.uk

EU Authorised Representative: Easy Access System Europe
Mustamäe tee 50, 10621 Tallinn, Estonia
gpst.request@easproject.com

This book is dedicated to all Irish storytellers, past and present.

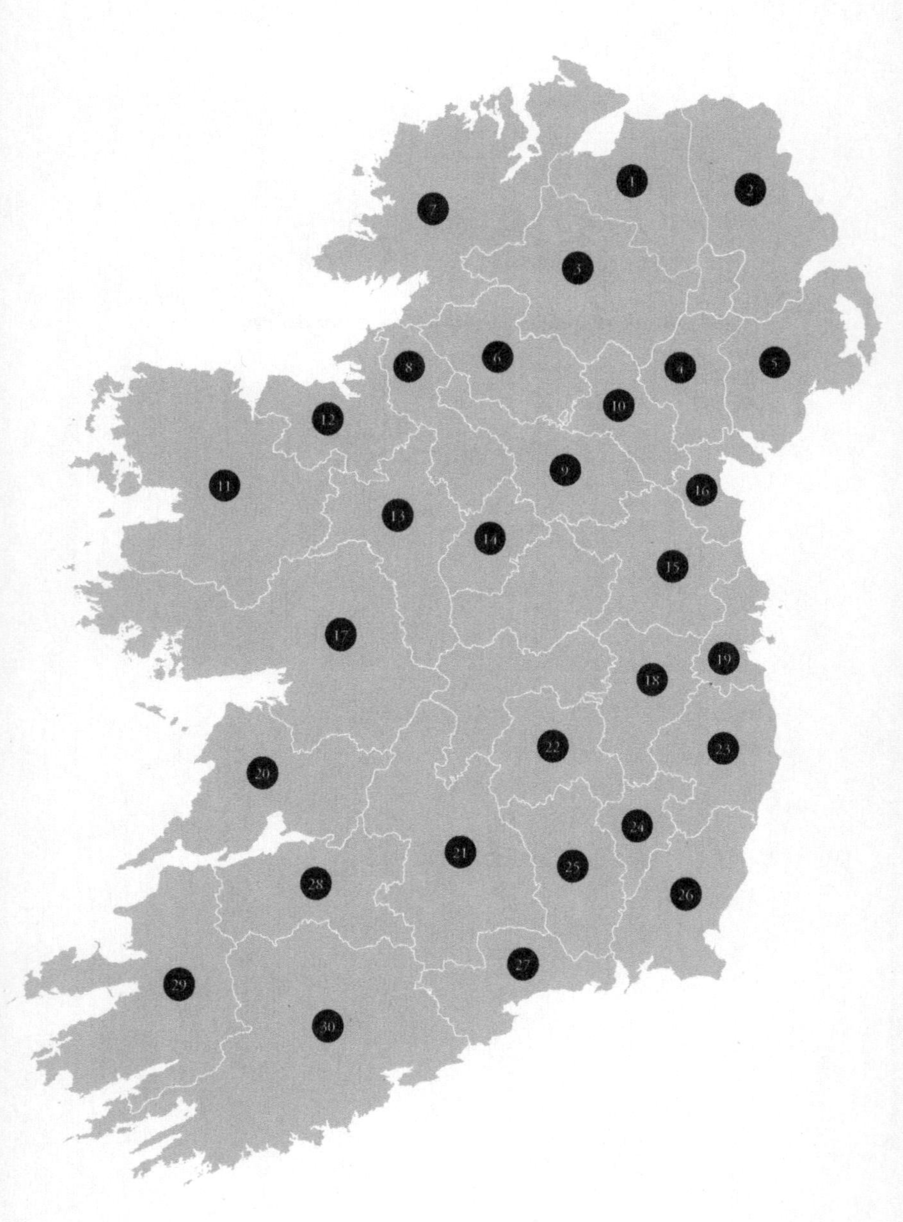
1
2
7
3
6
8
4
5
10
12
9
16
11
13
14
15
17
19
18
22
23
20
24
21
25
28
26
27
29
30

CONTENTS

DERRY

MADELINE MCCULLY

THE LOVESICK *LEANNAN SIDHE*

But like a lovesick leannan sidhe
She hath my heart enthralled,
Nor life I own, nor liberty
For love is lord of all.

From 'My Lagan Love'

Every county in Ireland has its own tale of the *Leannan Sidhe*, the fairy lover, and County Derry is no different. The story is told of a young man trying to withstand the romantic wiles of a fairy woman.

Hugh was an adventurous young man and wanted to see the world so, despite the pleadings of his parents, he set off. Well, he'd been travelling for about three years when he got word that his father was very ill and he set sail for home. Unfortunately, his father died before he arrived and his mother was beside herself with grief. He knew that he would have to stay at home. She was a good mother and he just couldn't leave her, so he set about trying to keep the farm going. To be a good farmer you need to have a love of the land, but since he wasn't a man of the soil at heart the farm began to get a bit run down. Within a year of his father's death his mother fell deeper into a decline brought on by melancholia, for she never got over the death of her husband.

Hugh took to the drink, and soon the farm suffered; crops weren't sown, fences went unmended and the house wanted the lick of white-wash. Sure, it broke his mother's heart to see her big son falling to pieces, and when she was dying she begged him to catch hold of him-self, to stop drinking and to find a wife.

Now, Hugh was a man of his word and he took his mother's dying words to heart. As her body was committed to the grave he made her a promise. He'd never touch another drop of drink, even when the other mourners were drinking after the funeral. When everyone departed to their own farms he walked around the place and took a good fresh look at it.

'Right enough,' he said to himself, 'it's a mess of the place. I'll put this to rights and maybe then I'll be able to find me a nice girl to marry.'

Now, like most places in Ulster, there are seven girls to every man, so you wouldn't have too much difficulty finding a nice girl. Hugh was a fine, big man and had a grand way with him, though he was unaware of his own good looks. Sure, wasn't he the finest looking man ever seen in County Derry? He had hair as black as the raven's wing, and eyes as blue as the sunlit sea. He was tall and broad of shoulder and under his tanned, windblown skin the powerful muscles rippled, having been built up from hauling in the nets filled with fish from the oceans of the world. Even the dissipation of the past year hadn't softened him up too much. All he need were the right clothes because, as his mother had often said, 'Clothes maketh the man.'

He began to clear the fields again for the planting and discovered that once he put the sea out of his mind he liked the land work. Still, at the end of the day it was lonely coming back into the house that had forgotten the touch of a woman. After a particularly hard day clearing the far field of rocks and trying his hand at building a stonewall, he resolved to do the final thing that his mother had asked of him, and that was to find himself a wife.

Knowing that there was a big fair on the Monday at the beginning of August he went into Portstewart to buy himself some decent clothes. Coming out of the tailor's shop he stopped as if struck by lightning, and indeed it was lightning of a kind, for didn't he spy the most beautiful girl he'd ever laid eyes upon.

Oh, her hair was like a fire glowing in the sun, her skin was white, and on her cheeks were freckles sprinkled like gold dust. Poor Hugh was besotted at first glance, and as he made his way over to her he wondered if this lovely creature had a husband already. When he reached her side he looked down and she, catching his glance, looked up. Sure, wasn't that the truth of the saying, 'It was love at first glance?'

Didn't they chat as if they'd known each other all their lives, and as the sun began to set in the sky and the market emptied, he asked if he could walk her home.

'You can,' said she, 'but only as far as the bridge, because my father will be waiting near there, and he warned me not to have any truck with strangers.'

Hugh would have walked to the ends of the earth with her, but as they neared the bridge she stopped. 'No further, Hugh, and thank you.'

Hugh stuttered out the words, 'Can I call on you, Kate?'

They arranged to meet, and as the summer dipped into autumn they were as deeply in love as any young couple could be. When she decked herself out in her best clothes and went out of an evening, her father suspected that there was a man in the offing. Now, an elderly man depending on a daughter to see to him in his old age gets a bit obstreperous and selfish when a young man is in the offing. He determined that he would put off any man courting Kate, but he didn't let on to his daughter what was in his mind.

'Will you marry me, Kate?' Hugh asked her one night, and her smile lit the heavens, for wasn't she as besotted with him as he was with her?

'Aye' she answered, 'but you'll have to square it with my Da. Come round tomorrow night and see him.'

As Hugh was walking over the mountain road on the way home that night, a wind whistled up out of nowhere and he knew right away that it was no ordinary wind. His mother had warned him about the *Leannan Sidhe*, a fairy woman of great beauty wanting to carry off handsome young men who were betrothed to another. It was said that once she got her eye on a man he was going to be tortured by her presence until she finally ensnared him. So Hugh pulled his cap down until it almost covered his eyes and kept his head down too, looking only at the road. Didn't he know that any man, looking into the fairy lover's eyes was doomed to follow her forever?

Well, that *Leannan Sidhe* came to his side and wrapped the wind around him like a blanket, and he had to battle against it to move an inch along the way. She pulled and she hauled, but he would not raise his eyes, and eventually she tired of the struggle and let go of him. When the sound of the wind disappeared he looked around and didn't he catch sight of her on the hill, and she was burying something under a gallan rock (a standing stone). He took note of the spot and hurried on home, determined that the next day he would see what she had buried.

The dawn broke and Hugh rose, pulled on his clothes and went to the hillside, knowing that the fairy lover would not come out in daylight. He pushed the rock aside, for it was powerful heavy and there, underneath it, was a bag made of the softest leather. He looked around, lifted the bag, and it was heavy. When he undid the string he couldn't believe his eyes for the bag was chock-full of gold coins, bright as the leaves of the buttercups growing in his field. All sorts of thoughts were going through his mind, but the main one was not to tell anyone about his find. He would provide Kate with any treasure she asked for when she was his wife.

That night he dressed in the fine suit the tailor in Portstewart had made for him and went to ask Kate's father for her hand in marriage. He noted that this farm was as neat as a new pin, that the cows were well fed and content, and the outside of the house was newly whitewashed, unlike his own.

'Well,' he thought, 'with my gold I can fix up my farm and Kate will never want for anything.'

Kate was waiting for him at the door. 'Me Da's in a right 'aul mood and he'll try to make you lose your temper. Now I'm warning you, hold onto it, for it will do us no good for you to lose it.'

He nodded and she brought him in. Her father was sitting in front of the turf fire and he neither rose nor took Hugh under his notice at all. Hugh went forward with his hand out in greeting.

'Hello Mr Logan, I'm pleased to meet you. Here,' he said, 'Kate told me that you smoke the pipe, I brought you a couple.' He held out the clay pipes and Kate's father took them, looked at them then threw them on the hearth, where they smashed. Hugh stood with his mouth open and Kate's eyes beseeched him not to retaliate. He stepped back and squared his shoulders.

'I've come to ask for your daughter's hand in marriage, sir,' he said, his voice was strong with passion.

'What! If you think that I'd let my daughter marry a ne'er-do-well like you, you have another think coming. You, with not a halfpenny to your name, your run-down farm and dirty house and no cattle. You, who drank like a fish of the sea that you sailed on and drove your poor mother into her grave. How dare you think that you would make a suitable husband for my Kate? Get out of my sight and don't come back!'

Before he could stop himself, and forgetting what Kate had said about not losing his temper, Hugh retorted.

'I've got plans sir, and gold aplenty, more than every man in this parish put together, and I can tell you that Kate would never want if she marries me!'

'You! Where would you get gold when you're scarcely scraping a living out of that dung heap of a place you call a farm?' By this time, Kate's father was on his feet and pointing to the door. 'Come back here when you can prove it. Until then, get out!'

Kate took Hugh's arm and he could see the sheen of tears in her eyes. Outside Hugh held her in his arms. 'I'll be back and I'll show him. Don't worry. We'll be married by Advent, I promise you.'

Hugh went on his way home, all the while debating in his mind about showing the gold to Kate's father, but sure, wasn't the love of his life worth it? He was so deep in thought that the cloying wind was on him before he had a minute to compose himself. But just in time he remembered, and when the *Leannan Sidhe* started her pulling and hauling again he was able to resist her. Aw, but he knew she was angry and that it wasn't the end of her trying out her wiles on him. He was fair exhausted by the time he arrived at his own wee house.

That night he stayed up and scrubbed the place from end to end. He blackened the pots and painted the crook over the fireplace and even whitewashed the side of the chimney. Once he started he couldn't stop, for if Kate's father agreed to let her marry him he was going to bring her back to the cottage the day after to have a look at her future home. In the morning he took every bowl, cup and plate from the dresser and painted the wood a lovely bright blue. He rummaged in the big cedar chest at the back of the room, where he knew his mother had stored her linens, and there he found the nicest curtains and tablecloth.

By the time he had finished he was ready to go to Kate's house, and he set off with the bag of gold in his pocket. The old man refused him entry and Hugh went to the wall outside the cottage door and spread the gold coins along it. With three steps that were almost jumps Mr Logan was at the wall, fingering the gold.

'I won't ask where you got it young man, but,' and at this point he slapped Hugh on the back, 'you can marry my daughter when the house is fixed up and the farm running well.'

Hugh blinked, 'that's too long a time.' He reached out and took Kate's hand. Her father stared greedily at the gold and thought.

'I'll tell you what, young fellow, I can have your farm fixed up in no time because I have strong workers. I can start you off with a herd too but I'd need to hold onto this gold for safekeeping. Would you trust your future father-in-law to do that, hmm?'

Hugh was so overjoyed that he and Kate could marry soon that he agreed, and true to his word her father did everything he said, although between you and me, he didn't have to spend but a fraction of the money. Every time Hugh enquired, Mr Logan had another wee job to do with the money, and the wedding was a grand excuse. When the couple married, the people came from miles around to celebrate the union, because country folk love nothing better than a wedding to get them all together. And what a wedding that was, with not a penny spared. If they wondered about the transformation in the farm they didn't pass any comments.

When the jollification was over the young couple snuggled down in their own bed, but before there was any funny business, a strange sound came to the window. It chilled the heart of the young man, for he knew that it was the accursed *Leannan Sidhe*.

'What's that, Hughie, darlin'?'

'It's only the wind, my love,' he said and he lulled her to sleep with his kisses. The same thing happened many times after, but always Hugh gave the excuse that his house was higher up the mountain than her father's and the wind was only to be expected.

All went well until Kate received word that her father was ill.

'Of course you'll have to go down to see him, and if you need me I'll come.'

'Who'd look after the farm, Hugh, if you go? Don't worry.'

He brought her to her father's and was relieved that he wasn't too sick.

'I'll be home by next week,' she promised him as she kissed him goodbye, and on his lonely walk home he began to hear the rustle of the wind, and it grew louder and louder and then he felt the grasping fingers of the fairy woman pulling at him and trying to carry him away, but he kept his eyes downturned, as always, and after a long time she left him with a fearful loud moaning of wind.

That night, although Hugh was exhausted by the tussle and pulling of the *Leannan Sidhe*, he took a long time to fall into a fitful sleep, tossing and turning restlessly in bed. The rattling of the wind on the window disturbed him, and still half-asleep he went to check that it was closed. When he opened the curtain without thinking there she was, staring at him with eyes as dark as the bog pools and her long hair glistening like the setting sun, and he was enthralled. With no more than a whisper he followed her to the Other World.

What seemed to him to be a day later, but was actually seven years to the day, a strange thing happened in the sky. He watched the light gradually fade and a dark circle crept across the sun. When the earth became as dark as night he turned away with a strange sense of foreboding and stumbled. His hand touched a cold object, and when he raised it, he saw that it was a horseshoe. Now we know that iron or salt keep the fairy bewitchments away, and it was a strange stroke of fate that his hand fell on a horseshoe. When the sun's light returned he was still grasping the horseshoe, and he was standing at the hollow of the hill near his house.

He walked down to the farm, wanting to get it ready for Kate coming home. Little did he know that he had links in the Other World for he had no recollection of what had happened to him. Sure, isn't that the way it is with the fairies, their time is not the same as ours.

When he reached his house everything looked different. He peered in the window and there was his wife Kate, putting a scone on the griddle. When she moved back he saw a man sitting on Hugh's own chair, rocking a cradle by his side, and in it was a baby. Hugh pushed on the door and knocked and pushed again but it wouldn't budge an inch to his pushes. When his wife finally opened it he could only stare at her, so beautiful was she that he wanted to pull her into his arms and never let her go.

'What do you want, old man?' she asked. He opened his eyes wide in shock.

'Kate, don't you know me? I'm your husband, come back.'

'Away with you, old man. You're not my husband. He was the most handsome man in these parts. Look at you, you wizened, filthy man! Away with you!'

She moved to shut the door on him and he caught a glimpse of himself in the mirror opposite. She was indeed right. The face that looked back at him was old and wrinkled with a grey tangled beard that hung to his waist.

But worst of all, behind him shimmered the image of the *Leannan Sidhe*, as beautiful as before. Her eyes beguiled him again and she pulled him away and that was the last that was seen of the two of them forever.

And Kate had had to stand the brunt of her father's anger when he opened the bag of gold and found only the withered leaves of the buttercups in place of the gold that was left. He maintained that Hugh had stolen it back and had run off, for Kate's father was not a man who believed in the fairies.

Shiela Quigley was one of the great storytellers of Ireland and this is a version of one of her stories.

BROGEY MCDAID AND THE WEE FOLK

Now, you might have heard the likes of this story before but I'm sure there have been some changes in the telling because my great-aunt told me that it was the honest truth. All I can do is pass on what my great-grandfather said when he told it to my great-aunt. Since neither is around to dispute it, I'll relate what I remember, for I was just about twelve years of age when I first heard it and reality and fantasy sometimes merge.

Ah, these forty long years I have travelled
All by the contents of me pack.
Me hammers, me awls and me pincers
I carry them all on me back.

(From 'The Cobbler')

There was a journeyman shoemaker who travelled around the country making shoes, and it was a bitterly cold day just before Christmas 1830 when Paddy Joe McDaid, nicknamed 'Brogey', (after the Irish word for 'shoe', '*brogue*') arrived in a wee place a few miles outside of Derry. Journeymen of all kinds relied on the people to give them lodgings. Sure, it was the tradition in the country areas never to refuse a bed to anyone.

This man knocked on the door of a nice wee cottage and when Maggie McLaughlin opened the door it's no word of a lie that his heart leapt and it was nearly like a blow to his chest, for she was the loveliest girl he had ever laid eyes upon.

'Come in out of the cold,' said she. ''Tis a bitter day.'

He needed no second bidding, and didn't she offer him a place beside the hearth in front of a big turf fire with a sup o' tea and a lump of soda scone in his hand.

'Take off your boots, if ye have a mind to,' said she, 'for it's wet through they must be with all that tramping the byways.'

When Matt, her father, came in from the barn, Brogey and Maggie were getting on like candle wax and a wick and Matt was right glad to see the smile on his daughter's face, for she was getting on for thirty and no man on the horizon. He nodded to himself too, since Maggie had never invited a man to shed his shoes before. It was for that reason that he gave Brogey a mighty shake of the hand and chatted with him while Maggie put out the supper.

Now, Brogey was an honest man and he saw that the soles were hanging off Matt's boots, so he offered to fix them for him by way of thanking Maggie. For poor folk didn't have the money to spend on boots, and half the childer in the country were running around in their bare feet anyway.

It must have been love that made Brogey settle down, for he never moved on, and wasn't he right glad during the hard winter that his time tramping as a journeyman shoemaker was over. He and Maggie made plans to tie the knot as soon as Lent was over. And what a wedding it was! Matt sent out word to the whole townland and not a one refused except the 'oul skinflint of a cobbler from over the hill. Sure, they weren't a bit surprised, for the man must have heard about Brogey's great skills, and he was afeard he might set up and do him out of the little bit of business that there was.

Matt moved to the lower room and Maggie and her man had the upper room in the house to themselves. The two men worked together companionably and fixed up a place in a wee room attached to the house for Brogey to start a shoemaker's shop.

'Maybe you could even make saddles, bridles and the like for you're a talented man with the leather,' said Maggie's father, 'and sure, if the trappings for the horse fail we're a bit stuck to have them fixed, for that cobbler doesn't know one end of a horse from the other.'

Mind you, that cobbler made some sort of shape at mending the boots for the local farmers, but he wasn't good enough for the gentry who went to Derry or Coleraine for their footwear.

Now, Brogey took great pride in his work, but it's hard for a man to start up and attract customers at the beginning. Soon though his expertise was broadcast around the countryside. 'Sure, he can make a pair of boots from scratch as well as fix up your auld ones!' was the news. No matter what kind of shoe or boot a man, woman or child wanted, Brogey could make it. The local women were delighted, because on the *ceilidhe* nights it was the custom to dress up, and a nice pair of shoes added class to the outfit. The men began to notice that the soles of their boots lasted longer too because he used only the best of leather. After a while, some of the gentry came to have their shoes and boots made too.

The cobbler began to lose business, for not only was he not good at his trade but he was an auld crabbit man who was often the worse for wear through his drinking of the porter, and would as soon eat the nose off anyone who complained as look at them.

Everything was going grand for the young couple until one night Brogey's workshop went on fire and he and his wife Maggie were lucky that it didn't spread to the house. The locals gathered around and formed a bucket chain, and soon the fire was put out but the shoemaker's room was burnt out and the leather unusable. Only the iron lasts on which he fashioned the shoes and nailed them together were saved. Maggie was distraught, for wasn't she expecting their first baby? I have to say that there were rumours flying around about the cause of the fire, but as Brogey said, 'What's done is done and nothing will change it.'

'Sometimes', my grandfather said, 'an ill-wind blows something good, for didn't the people around set to and built a place onto the house for Brogey to carry on his business? And it was much better than the wee room he had before, for hadn't it a grand big window facing the road so people could see the lovely work he did. There was only one thing wrong, they didn't have the money to buy the quality of leather that he wanted, and the cobbler wasn't about to let him have any of his.'

Brogey went to bed that night, keeping his worries to himself, but he couldn't sleep. He got up and made his way into the workroom and looked around. All he could find were some small pieces of leather in a bag, and to pass the time he made up a wee pair of shoes. Sure, doing a good job, even if it's on tiny shoes that would fit no one, gave him some satisfaction, so he set to and made another pair. Both pairs were too small for even the tiniest feet, but he was satisfied that he had little shoes to put on display to show off his skill. He put them neatly together and admired his own work, knowing that the shoes had been fashioned without the use of even one nail. For some strange reason his worries had gone and he was ready to do whatever it took to earn a living for Maggie, himself and the baby. He went back to bed and slept like a man with no concerns.

It seemed as if he'd only been asleep for moments when he was shook awake, 'Brogey, Brogey, wake up. Come and see what's in your room.'

He dragged himself out of bed and followed his wife out to the workroom. When she opened the door he couldn't believe his eyes. There, sitting on the table was one of the nicest hides of Moroccan goat leather that he had ever seen. He touched it, felt it and even smelled it and he knew that he had never seen the quality of it before.

'Maggie,' he said, his voice almost breaking with emotion, 'we have the best neighbours that God could give a man. Now we'll go and thank them, for this is the best day of our lives.'

They went to the first neighbour, but he didn't know what they were talking about.

'Sure I didn't do that, Brogey. I would have if I'd had the money but I didn't. Maybe it was Barney,' he said.

The couple went to Barney, but he knew nothing either and sent them on to another, but no one seemed to know anything about it. Puzzled, they walked back to the house and when Brogey went into the room again he noticed the two pairs of tiny shoes were gone.

'Maggie,' he called, 'did you move two wee pairs of shoes I made?'

'Indeed I didn't. Sure, I don't interfere with your work, Brogey,' she answered, and went on making the breakfast.

It wasn't long before people started to come into the shop to ask Brogey about the leather. Soon a bit of a crowd gathered, and the talk went round and round, but it was only when he mentioned about the wee shoes that they looked at one another.

'Sure, if it wasn't one of us it must have been the fairies,' Matt said, and that was the general consensus. 'Imagine fairies coming to help out,' they were saying with excited, babbling voices.

'What you need to do,' said Barney, rubbing his chin and stretching his neck, 'is make another wee pair or two to thank them and leave them here on the table, and if it was them then they'll be back.'

With that they all left and Maggie looked at her husband. 'D'you believe all that nonsense?' she said.

'Well now, Maggie, maybe it's not nonsense but if it is all I'm out is a few wee bits of leather.'

Maggie tut-tutted and left him to work. All day he cut and sewed and never put an iron nail near the tiny shoes, for fairies don't like iron at all, and he did the finest job he'd ever done in his life. He examined them and couldn't find a flaw anywhere.

'Ah,' he thought, 'I could do the same work on other shoes if I had enough leather and I'd be the happiest man in the world.' Before the words were fully out of his mouth he had the strongest desire to cut out the makings of a shoe from the new goatskin. He smoothed it out on the table, felt it for thicker parts that needed skiving but he had no need to spend time on that, for it was the smoothest leather he'd ever felt. By the time Maggie called him in for his dinner he had the first lady's shoe made and oh boyo, it was grand! Right after his meal he went back to the workroom, and by the time he'd finished it was nearly midnight but on his window shelf he placed the most beautiful pair of moss green leather shoes ever seen in the country, if he wasn't mistaken.

That night he slept like a baby with a full stomach, and in the morning he couldn't wait to see if the wee shoes were gone. He rushed into the workroom and on the bench was another beautiful skin of leather in a rich dark brown. He searched around the bench but the little shoes were gone.

'So it was the fairies! I knew it!' He held the leather to his nose to inhale its rich smell, and there underneath, on the table, was a tiny bell. When he lifted it, it rang with a sweet, tiny tinkle and begod when he looked up a lady had just entered the shop.

'I couldn't help but see those beautiful shoes in your window. May I try them on please?'

He turned his back while the lady slipped off her boot and tried on the first shoe, for a man doesn't look at a lady's ankle. 'Oh, the other one please, this fits like a glove!' A few moments later, when he turned around, she was walking the length of the shop with the moss-green shoes on her tiny feet.

'Oh, sir, these are exquisite. I must have them. I must! I simply must!'

Sure the bell tinkled again and another lady came in. Her face fell in disappointment when she saw the shoes on the first lady's feet.

'Oh, I so wanted those lovely shoes. I'll pay you more. How much are they?'

Before he could answer, the first lady said, 'Ten guineas, sir and they're mine.'

'I'll give you fifteen!'

'Twenty!'

'Twenty-five!' The bargaining went on and he stood there with his mouth agape.

At fifty guineas he held up his hand. 'Ladies, I will make another pair, slightly different of course, so you will both be satisfied.' He pondered about accepting the price but Maggie, on hearing the commotion had come up behind him.

'Fifty guineas it is,' she said and accepted the gold coins.

When they left he turned to his wife. 'That's a desperate high amount to pay for a pair of shoes,' he protested.

'Sure they can well afford it and don't forget that all our neighbours gave from their substance when they helped us, because none of them have much in their pockets. So we can share our good fortune, for without them and your good work we wouldn't have any.'

The pattern continued and ladies came and went, each buying shoes and passing on praise by word of mouth. The men followed the example and it seemed that every gentleman in the county was wearing high boots, made of the finest pigskin or goatskin. When a baby boy was born to Maggie, Brogey thanked God, for life couldn't be any better. But he began to have niggles of conscience about so much good fortune coming their way and not spreading it around as much as they should. Brogey, being an honest man, sat talking to Maggie one night after the baby went to sleep. He broached a subject that was giving him the tingles of guilt.

'Maggie, my love,' he started, 'I've had all this good fortune and I was passing by wee Jack's cobbler shop and it looked awful run down. You know I never meant to put him out of business, but that's the way it looked. I'm of a mind, and I hope you'll agree with me, that maybe

I should go to him and offer him a goodly amount of money to let me buy over the business.'

Maggie looked up from her knitting but didn't say anything for a moment. She looked a bit anxious. 'Well, what do you think?'

'I think you are a good man and I'm a lucky woman. We've more than enough to do what's right. So go tomorrow and do what you've said. Now come on to bed.'

That night about midnight, he made his way to the workroom and what did he see but one of the wee folk sitting on his table trying on the tiny shoes that he made every day. He wasn't a bit shy and he sat down at his workbench and watched him without saying a word.

'You'll be thinking that it's time our swapping came to an end, aren't you?' said the wee man, stroking his beard and looking at him with sparkling eyes.

'Aye, along those lines, I was,' Brogey answered.

'Well, sir, let me put it like this. You've shoed every man, woman and child in this fairy kingdom, and right glad we are for you're the only man who made us shoes without nails. For you know that the iron isn't a good omen for us and that's a fact. We'll go now, but we'll make you a promise afore that. If you ever need help for yourself, your family or your neighbours, just leave your window ajar and we'll come. And if we need more shoes we'll let you know too.'

Brogey nodded. 'I don't know how to thank you. You've made us all very, very happy and we'll not forget it.'

'What goes around comes around,' said the wee man, 'Ah, would you look at that?' He pointed to the wall and Brogey looked up and saw nothing. When he lowered his eyes again the fairy was gone, and on the bench was a pile of beautiful leather skins of all colours, enough to last him for his time.

Now, you'll be wondering if he ever saw the fairy again, and sure he did. He needed their help again after the night of the Big Wind on 6 January 1839 but that's another story for another time.

And that's the story as my great-aunt told it to me and just as I told it to my children. Sure, how are they to know about the wee folk if we don't tell them?

ANTRIM

BILLY TEARE & KATHLEEN O'SULLIVAN

MARTHA CLARK AND JOHNNY BRADY

No one remembers when 'once' was, or precisely what time it was upon, but that is when this all started, one person telling the next person, telling the next and so on, year in, year out, and that is enough to let you know that what happened was a brave time ago – upon someone's time.

There was a neat wee woman called Martha Clark and she lived in a neat wee porter lodge at the foot of the Lady Hill, which belonged to a big estate, Redhall. You will maybe know that that's down near Ballycarry.

Martha was not married. She was a shepherdess and she owned a few sheep – twenty in all – and she used to keep the sheep penned out the back of the porter lodge. Now, the thing about Martha was, she was a wee bit deaf.

One morning when she got up and looked out of her window, she saw that every one of the sheep was gone. There was not a sheep to be seen. When she went out, she discovered that the gate had broken, so all the sheep had got out that way. Now, she had a good idea where they had gone to, so she set off, along the Magheramourne road, until she came to the Burnside Loaning. She went along the loaning, passed the oul' wa's, and she saw a man ploughing a field. This man's name was Johnny Brady.

It so happened that Johnny was a wee bit deaf too. It was never known how Martha lost her hearing, but the way Johnny lost his hearing was legendary. It seems at one time he had been one of the best poachers about Ballycarry. He used to do most of his poaching around the lands belonging to Redhall. Redhall was owned at that time by a man called Pottir and he did not like poachers one bit.

Pottir had lookouts and gamekeepers keeping an eye out for poor Johnny day and night, and every time they caught him, they'd take his weapon and rounds and his catch, and they would send him on his way, with a boot up the backside for good luck. It got that bad that Johnny could not afford to buy cartridges, so he started to make his own. In fact, he more or less built his own shotgun too, and it was said that because his gun was crudely made and in those days there was no ear protection, this is what had made him go a bit deaf.

A poacher's day starts early, but Pottir himself would never be up out of his bed until about nine or ten, so he did not often see Johnny. When he did, he did not recognise him, as Johnny would disguise himself as one of the gamekeepers. Johnny took great delight in having sport at the landowner's expense. One morning, he saw Pottir coming towards him. So he broke his gun and hid it down the back of his trousers.

Johnny cupped his ear and Pottir bellowed, 'Well, my man, what are you doing up at this time of the morning?'

Johnny said to Pottir, 'Indeed sir, I was going to ask you the same.'

Pottir answered, 'If it's any of your business, I am out to get an appetite for my breakfast.'

Johnny said, 'Indeed sir, I'm out to get a breakfast for me appetite.' And he sauntered off to do just that, with a smile on his face.

Another morning, a game warden caught Johnny red-handed, poaching trout by the Burnside Burn. He had two trout in a pail. But, he told the warden that the fish were his own pets and he was just letting them have a swim.

'Nonsense!' shouted the game warden.

'It's true,' said Johnny. 'Surely it's not against the law for me to let my pets swim here, is it? You see, I put them in for a swim and when I whistle they come back to me.'

'I've *got* to see this,' said the game warden.

So Johnny tossed both trout into the river.

'Okay, now let's hear you whistle for your trout to come back to you.'

'Trout?' said Johnny, once he'd got rid of the evidence. 'What trout?' And he took off like a hare, leaving the game warden on his knees, staring into the river.

Johnny had great craic at the expense of the keepers of the game. One morning, when he had bagged himself a brace of pheasant (that's two), he ran straight into a warden. The warden asked, 'You, my man, have you got pheasant in that bag?'

'I have,' says Johnny, 'and if you can tell me how many I have, I'll let you have them both.'

Too silly to heed the broad hint, and after much brow furrowing, the warden guessed, 'Three?'

'No, just the one,' said Johnny, and continued on his way.

It was later, on that very same morning, that Martha Clark saw Johnny ploughing and asked, 'Johnny, have you seen my sheep?'

Johnny did not catch what she had said. He thought she was asking him what he was doing, so he just pointed at the furrow the plough was making. Martha looked at where Johnny was pointing and assumed he was telling her where her sheep had gone. So she said, 'Thanks very much Johnny.' And she climbed over the fence, set off up the field and over a wee hill into a small valley … and there were all her sheep. Martha counted them: two, four, six, eight … the whole lot, all twenty of them, were there, but one wee lamb had a broken leg.

She said, 'Oh, you poor wee cratur you.' She gathered the lamb in her arms, cradled it, and carried it back down the field. Of course, all the sheep knew her well and followed after her. So when they got back down to where Johnny was standing, Martha was thinking to herself, 'it was awful kind of Johnny to tell me where me sheep went, so I think I'll give him this wee lamb as a present. It's got a broken leg, but he could fix it up with a splint.'

She said, 'Johnny, I'm going to give you this wee lamb as a gift.'

Of course, Johnny did not hear what she had said. All he saw was, there stood Martha, with a lamb cradled in her arms, and the lamb had a broken leg. He thought that she was accusing him of breaking the lamb's leg.

Johnny said, 'That's absolutely nothing to do with me. I never broke that lamb's leg. Go on, take it away out of here.'

Martha could see Johnny was not best pleased, but because she did not hear what he said, she thought he was cross and saying that he did not want the lamb, but he wanted one of the bigger sheep. She said, 'Indeed you are *not* having one of the bigger sheep; you'll take this wee lamb, or nothing at all.'

Johnny insisted, 'I had nothing to do with breaking that lamb's leg, you can clear off. Take it away out of here.'

And they started to bicker, neither hearing what the other was saying. A whole row started, and the noise of the two of them shouting and bellowing at each other eventually attracted the neighbours, who came out and gathered around to see what was going on.

It wasn't long before the local peeler came up from Whitehead on his pushbike. When he heard the row, he got off his bike. 'What's going on here?' he asked, making his way through the crowd to where Johnny and Martha stood yelling and gurning and ranting at each other. 'Look,' the policeman said, 'if you don't stop this rowing right away, I'll take the both of you into custody and you'll be up before the judge in the morning and you'll be done for breach of the peace.'

But of course Johnny and Martha never heard a thing he said, and carried on exchanging insults. So he arrested the pair of them and took them both down to the police station in Larne. Martha carried her wee lamb with her.

The next morning, they were up before the judge. At that time, it was a judge called Jackson. He was known to the criminal fraternity of Larne as Santa Claus Jackson, because he was full of good will and always saw the best in people. But, in the strangest turn of fate, Judge Jackson, the wise, learned, always lenient man, was also just a wee bit deaf. Not only a wee bit deaf, but a bit short-sighted as well. It did not matter what was presented in court, he just judged the case on the facts, as *he* thought best.

This morning, Judge Jackson had Johnny and Martha, with the lamb cradled in her arms, standing before him. Each of them was explaining to him their side of events. He did not hear a word of it.

What he saw in front of him was a man and a woman, and the woman was holding, in her arms, what looked to him like a baby. He got it into his head that this must be a couple looking for a divorce. Eventually he said, 'Tell me this, how many years have you been married?'

Martha did not hear what he'd said properly and just caught the words 'how many'. She thought the judge was asking how many sheep she owned and answered, 'Twenty your honour.'

'You mean to tell me,' said Jackson, 'you've been married twenty years and now you have this beautiful little child, and you are up before me looking for a divorce? Go home the two of you and live together in peace and harmony.' With that he got up and left the court, leaving Johnny and Martha without a clue what was going on.

Martha asked the policeman, 'What was it he said?'

The policeman shouted into her ear, 'He says you've to go home and live together in peace and harmony.'

Martha said, 'But we're not married.'

The policeman yelled again, 'Well you'd best go and do something about that.'

And that's how Martha Clark and Johnny Brady came to be married. And do you know they lived for many a happy year, according to Judge Jackson's ruling, in peace and harmony. The reason being, they never heard a word the other said.

MONTERLONEY: A RURAL REMINISCENCE

The savage loves his native shore,
Though rude the soil, and chill the air;
Then well may Erin's sons adore
Their isle which nature formed so fair.

James Orr (1770-1816)

It would be hard to find a warmer welcome on a cold day than at Aunt Lily's hearth, Monterloney, a good place to hear and share some of the stories, family history and folklore of this beautiful place.

The farmstead at Monterloney, on the Magheramourne road, County Antrim, home to the Humes, can be found on maps from 1832. They were farming people, with the daily preoccupations of harvest and survival that went with the lifestyle.

A very simple record of community events has been preserved through the poetry of Billy's granda', William Hume: the characters, the new houses being built in the area, the deaths of neighbours, and the emigration of members of the community to Australia and Canada.

A song he wrote on the importance and purity of the local waterways brought William Hume special notoriety. He was a farmer, and although maybe not as famous as the foremost Ballycarry weaver poet James Orr (who is known as the Bard of Ballycarry; his work is said to be comparable with Robert Burns), William was known as a folk poet, writer, singer of songs, fiddler and local entertainer on the concert scene in the 1930s and '40s. The song he wrote was 'The Mutton Burn Stream'. An edited version was recorded by an international performer, Richard Hayward in 1978 and it even featured in a film called *The Luck of the Irish*.

The Muttonburn Stream

I remember my young days
For younger I've been.
I remember my young days by the Muttonburn stream.
It's not marked on the World's map,
Nowhere to be seen,
That wee river in Ulster, the Muttonburn stream.

And it flows under bridges, takes many's the turn,
Sure it turns round the mill wheel
That grinds the folks' corn.
Then it wimples through meadows,
And it keeps the land clean.
Belfast lough it soon reaches, the Muttonburn stream.

Oh the ladies from 'Carry,
I oft times have seen,
Taking down their fine washing
To the Muttonburn stream,
No powder or soap used,
A wee dunt makes them clean,
It has great cleansing powers, the Muttonburn stream.
And the ducks like to swim in it,
From morning till 'ene
Sure they dirty the water,
But they gets themselves clean.
I have seen them a'diving
Till their tails were scarce seen,
Waddling down at the bottom, of the Muttonburn stream.

And it cures all diseases,
Though chronic they've been.
It will cure you of fatness,
It will cure you of lean,

Oh it acts on the liver,
The heart, lungs and spleen,
It has great curative powers, the Muttonburn stream.

Oh the secret it's out now, a long secret it's been,
How the jaundice was cured by
The folks round the stream,
They boiled up the water,
Put in essence bog bean,
All gives way to the power, of the Muttonburn stream.

Oh I used to go a partying, at night when no seen.
For they aye gye guid parties,
That lives round the stream.
Coming home in the morn time,
Feeling oh so serene,
Sure I slipped and I fell in, the Muttonburn stream.

William James Hume

When the song was recorded, because slight adjustments were made, some discrepancy arose about authorship. However, about a mile away was a lady called Susan Hay, a neighbour and friend of the Humes. She was a 'go to' character for local lore and history, and is on an old BBC recording, speaking about hearing William sing his composition when she was young. Susan was in no doubt that the words were his. She is supported in this by extensive family and academic research.

The plain verses, composed by farmworkers like Willie Hume, or weavers and craftsmen, tell of everyday folk. A fiddle was to appear on the Aldfreck Banner to denote William Hume's musical talents. The banners were used at the annual Broadisland Gathering.

Billy's maternal uncle, Tommy, was Granda' Willie's son. For the first few weeks of his summer holidays, Billy made his way from home, along the lane and through Redhall Estate, to see Uncle Tommy on his farm, on the highest point of the townland of Aldfreck. It was roughly a one-and-a-half-mile walk. Named Monterloney, the farm was known amongst the family as The Homeplace, in reference to where Billy's mother and siblings were born and brought up. It had no electricity. They used candles, oil and Tilley lamps and had outside 'facilities'. They had no television either, just battery radio.

Monterloney was a magical place for a boy, with its amazing views over Larne and Belfast Loughs, Islandmagee, beyond to Scrabo Tower in the County Down, Galloway, the Solway hills, the Mourne Mountains and, if the light was right, away off to the Isle of Man.

Uncle Tommy (Thomas Hanna Craig Hume), being the eldest Hume male, was left the farm when Willie died in 1948. Tommy farmed it all his life after the death of his father. Even as a small boy, Billy could see his uncle's contentment in doing so. Tommy had a Zen quality. Very calm always. He used to make the boy feel important and useful during his holidays.

Billy worked with him, getting the grass cut and turned, even when the little lad knew he was more of a hindrance at times. Tommy would sit his nephew on the mudguard of his Ferguson TE20 tractor when he was driving around the open fields. Billy could steer it that way and Tommy would sit back, smiling, seemingly idle, with his arms folded.

Then there was the old reaper with cast-iron wheels. Instead of horses, Tommy used the tractor to tow it around.

There were so many corncrake in the field that Billy had to run ahead of the reaper, shooing them away. It was dangerous. Not many young lads today would do it, what with health and safety regulations. The birds could fly, but ran and ran, unwilling to leave their nests or their young.

By the time he was ten or eleven, Billy worked on the hay, bundling it in ricks, to put on a thing called a slipe. After that, they started baling. The bales reminded young Billy of giant Weetabix. Nearby, farmers cut the silage. In those days, molasses or treacle was added, and the heavy, sweet scent drifted. Billy liked it; others found it sickly. Silage now is gathered by machines and sealed to stop it rotting.

Tommy's big old rough-haired terrier was called Teddy, or Ted. To make his wee nephew laugh, his uncle would ask, 'Well Ted, what would you like for your tea, loaf or soda?' The dog's woof sounded as if Ted was asking for loaf.

Excitement came one day in the shape of a bicycle. Billy's cousin Isabel had a bike she had outgrown and Tommy fixed it up for Billy. It was the first bike he had ever owned and Tommy showed him how to ride it in the lane. Uncle Tommy looked ancient to the lad, with only a few teeth left in his long thin face. Billy never imagined him doing anything as youthful as riding a bicycle, but he would never, ever forget his training.

Duffy's Circus sometimes came to Whitehead, but, after seeing Tommy riding a bike, Billy knew there was not a trick cyclist in it that would have outclassed his uncle. He sailed in circles with one foot on the saddle and the other leg stretched out behind, leaning over to steer it. Then he seated himself and turned around to pedal himself backwards, sitting on the handlebars. Then he stood astride the front wheel. Billy was amazed. Tommy must have learned this in his youth and it never left him.

Another thing Tommy could do was barrel walk, and he taught Billy to roll a barrel along, walking on the top of it. The boy was so delighted when he mastered it. There was a wee girl he wanted to impress and he took the barrel over to the front of her house and away he went, up and down. But it was a big old metal oil drum, so it made a terrible noise thundering along, and the next thing her mother was out, shouting, 'William, go home!'

He didn't let it deter him. He went another day, with what he hoped would be a more musical offering, and went up and down serenading outside her house, with Brahms' Lullaby on recorder. Again, her mother was out, shouting, 'William, go home!'

Living on the farm with Tommy was Oul' Aunt Maggie. In 1926, Willie Hume's wife, Agnes Craig of Ballyboley (Tommy's mum/Billy's grandma), died giving birth to her seventh child. Maggie Smyth, Agnes' half-sister, a spinster woman, stepped in to help on the farm and 'care' for Willie and his offspring. There is a notion that she did this with some resentment, perhaps blaming Willie for the death of her sister. It seems she never finished chastising him, and occasionally tore up his writing and poetry. Billy was wary of her, as 'a bit of a tartar', and he and Tommy sometimes hid, to avoid the inevitable scolding.

There were breaches in the storm clouds that made up Aunt Maggie's mood. She would give Billy small bits of change, for sweets, when he went with Tommy for errands in one of the old cars.

Aunt Maggie also displayed a softer side in caring for the youngest child whom her sister had left behind, Hubert. It appeared to some that the tenderness she felt for the boy fulfilled a need in her. He had a deformity of the spine, weak chest and was often poorly. Some observed that Hubert may have been a little more robust but for her overprotection of him. He remained her 'baby' into his adulthood. This being the case, young Billy never knew if his Uncle Hubert actually had special needs. He remembers playing endless games of draughts with him. Hubert could also do intricately carved fretwork.

As Hubert got older, he spent winters in hospital, in what were known as the 'extra wards'. These were like old army Nissen huts, where he received care and Maggie got respite. He died in his forties.

So, formidable as she was, Aunt Maggie had enough to cope with and always kept things on track. She loved to cook for the family. One of Billy's favourites was a hearty dish of pinhead oatmeal, onion and bacon fat, called 'Scad the Beggars', or 'Mealie Crushie', served with boiled spuds.

Oul' Aunt Maggie spoke Ulster Scots, known as 'the hamely tongue'. In recent years, Ulster Scots has become identified as a discreet regional language, with organisations seeking to research, conserve and develop its use. Maggie would warn her nephew to get home 'afore dallygan', meaning before daylight has gone. Or, in describing the actions of a certain person, she might say, 'Ha, him oot scungin' the country wi' the wuttericks aboot his feet.' In this, she was talking about a man staying out late, with weasels around his feet, meaning he was in bad company. For 'yes' she would say 'faith aye'. A vest was a 'simmet' and a pullover was a 'ganzi'.

In later life, Tommy met, courted and married Lily, someone, aside from Oul' Aunt Maggie, to share his life with. In time he had a son, David.* Aunt Maggie lived on with the new family, as there was the old cottage, as well as the subsidy house that William Hume built in 1929. Farmers then were given assistance for such buildings through the government.

It marked an end of an era for Billy. Uncle Tommy had different priorities, and Billy's mother felt he should not spend time on the farm during the summers any more. So, as he got older, Billy worked on local farms to fill his time and earn a little money.

Lily still lives on, hale and hearty, in The Homeplace, warmed in winter by her cosy log fire, warming others with her generosity and stories.

---

* Dr David Hume is the founding chairman of the Ballycarry Community Association in 1990 and co-founder of the Broadisland Gathering festival.

TYRONE

DOREEN MCBRIDE

THE GHOSTS OF LISSAN HOUSE

County Tyrone is undoubtedly beautiful, with a varied landscape and a strange haunting atmosphere. One can almost feel the presence of the souls of the dead who have lived, and loved, there in the past. Many respectable people have, over the ages, reported seeing ghosts in circumstances that cannot simply be dismissed.

Thanks are due to Dr Neil Watt, for the following tales about the ghosts who haunt Lissan House.

Lissan House dates back to the early seventeenth century. It was owned by the Staples family, who were planters. It is in the heart of an ancient area called Glenkonkyne, a densely wooded district thought to have been used for religious ceremonial purposes in the past. It was once ruled by the O'Neills, who were the Kings of Ulster and as a result it embraces the cultures of both planter and Gael.

One of the owners of the house, Sir Robert Ponsonby Staples, was a well-known painter. Many of his drawings and sketches may still be seen in the property.

Sir Robert was an eccentric who believed many of the ills of his generation were caused by wearing shoes. He thought they interfered with 'healing magnetism' coming up from the earth and insisted people walk about the house in their bare feet.

In the mid-nineteenth century, Sir Thomas Staples inherited Lissan House. He had a very beautiful wife, Lady Katherine Staples, known as handsome Kitty Staples. She loved music, spending money and entertaining but unfortunately she was unable to have children. Her husband died years before she did and the heir to the property was a nephew of her husband, Nathaniel Staples, who lived in India. When dilsy Lady Katherine and Nathaniel Staples met, it was hate at first sight! They simply could not stand each other so when she moved out of the house she took all the furniture, light fittings and doors with her. Her nephew was left with nothing but a worthless, empty shell. She's not a happy ghost because her action annoyed the other spirits haunting the house. They loved their old home and were furious with her. It is said her action led to a reversal in the fortunes of the Staples family. They lost a lot of money and no longer have the high place in society they once held.

A well-known artist painted a portrait of handsome Kitty Staples in her prime. When she died it was given to her god-daughter and eventually ended up in an auction. The Lissan House Trust bought it and hung it up on the drawing room wall. The minute it was put in place Nathaniel's portrait fell off the wall. There was no reason for this as it was hung on secure wires and the hooks on the wall were intact. The dislike they had for each other on earth must be continuing through eternity!

Hazel Radclyffe Dolling, the last member of the Staples family to live in the house, died, aged 82, in 2006 and had many strange tales to tell about the ghostly goings-on in her home. Certain parts of the house suddenly become cold, the heavy footsteps of an invisible man or a small child's sobs might be heard and sometimes it is possible to smell lavender and rose petals. One house guest saw a group of noisy children playing in the hall. She wondered who they were and walked towards them to ask, but they skipped off down the hall and then vanished into thin air.

Dr Neil Watt, who once managed Lissan House, insists he did not believe in ghosts until he went to work in the house in 2013. He has since changed his mind because of his experiences! The first was when he was working during the first Christmas after which he'd been appointed as curator. He'd gone into the garden and collected holly and ivy to be used as decorations. He'd been working for a long time and became very hungry so he phoned his sister and asked if she'd bring him a Chinese takeaway. She is a medical doctor, a very sensible, down-to-earth, practical person. She agreed, bought a takeaway, drove up the drive and parked her car in front of a drawing room window. She entered the house, looked at Neil and said, 'Why didn't you tell me you had company? I'd have bought two takeaways.'

When Neil said he was alone she replied, 'You're joking! I saw a podgy young man, dressed in tweeds, standing beside the piano, chatting away to you.' There was nobody there!

Once when Neil was working in the ballroom he heard a dog barking at his feet, a distinct 'Woof! Woof!', the type of bark a dog gives when it wants to be taken for a walk. He was intrigued and did something he thought he'd never do. He asked a medium to come in. She looked at Neil and said, 'You're fond of dogs, aren't you?'

'How did you know?' he asked.

'Because two dogs, a red setter and a terrier, are running around your feet!' she replied.

One of the ghosts in Lissan House caused a bad atmosphere around Lady Staples's bedroom. Both Neil and the chairman of Lissan House felt an unreasonable urge to get out whenever they went into that room! One night the burglar alarm sounded. The chairman came to turn it off and check the premises. As he approached Lady Staples's bedroom, he was suddenly tossed to the ground and hit the skirting board, so Neil and he decided to ask a medium to visit to find out what was happening. She said Alexander Staples, the founder member of the family, loved his old home and was protecting it. He was taking especially good care of Lady Staples's bedroom and was standing, shouting obscene language them. She said, 'The best way to deal with a ghost is to face it. Whenever you feel Alexander's presence talk to him. Tell him you are only looking after the house, you love it too and it needs attention. You're not going to do anything harmful.' Now when Neil goes into Lady Staples's bedroom to carry out basic maintenance he talks to the ghost and feels a right eejit while doing so! But it works!

The last owner of the house, Mrs Dolling, used Lady Staples's bedroom as a guest room. Women who slept in there often reported hearing footsteps. Sometimes a lady, dressed in a gold dress, wearing boots and carrying a doll and a candle, came into the room and tried to set Lady Staples's bed on fire! Perhaps that's why the ghost of Alexander Staples protects it?

Photographers and people walking in the garden often see a little girl, aged between 11 and 12 years old, looking out one of the windows on the top floor. Photographs have been taken of what must be a ghost because there's nobody there! That little girl is very shy. She has never appeared for a medium, although she has often been spotted peeping round corners or hanging over the bannister.

One night when Neil and one of the trustees were setting up a piano in the ballroom they heard two ladies laughing. Neil went on an errand to the far end of the house and, while he was away, the trustee heard chit-chat behind him, yet there was nobody there.

THE FINTONA RAILWAY

I am grateful to the late Tom McDevitte (Barney McCool) for telling me about the Fintona Railway and making me laugh so hard I felt sore for days afterwards. Like Tom, I am really sorry it has closed. It would have made a marvellous tourist attraction. I am also grateful to the staff of Castlederg Library and to Christine Johnston of the Library of Emigration at the Ulster American Folk Park for being so helpful and providing a lot of information. Dr Nevin Hamilton, Florence Chambers and George Beattie were also helpful in this regard.

I have a confession to make. I'm not sure if the Fintona Railway should be called a railway or a tram. It was originally thought of as a railway, then, over time, it metamorphosed into a tram.

Perhaps in Ulster's Counties, today cannot be found
A place so void of changes as this cosy little town.
If Cromwell should revisit it, 'twould seem the same today
As when he placed his cannon on the top of Liskey Brae.

John Donnelly, 1926

Fintona's name is derived from the Irish '*Fionntamhnach*', meaning 'the fair watered land'. It's a very pretty, small rural town about 8 miles south of Omagh. In the 1830s, it consisted of one main street, which was about half a mile long, with a few side streets coming off it. It had five small water-powered mills, a brown (unbleached) linen market, a monthly fair for cattle and pigs and a weekly market on Fridays, which mainly sold oatmeal. In spite of its small size, Fintona had twenty-eight spirit shops! Apparently the spirits flowed over to such an extent that they resulted in frequent riots! The town was a social outlet for a wide area. A road, which was finished in 1829, passed through Fintona and linked it with Enniskillen and Omagh. It was decided to build a railway to Fintona in the 1830s because it would be very useful for transporting wood. The Londonderry and Enniskillen Railway opened a branch line to Fintona on 5 June 1853.

Once it was agreed that a link between Fintona and the main line would be useful, a committee was set up. It decided that railway lines should be laid along the track because hauling heavy loads along rails is much easier than transporting them along the rough paths acting as roads in the region at the time.

There was considerable debate over the type of power that should be used. It must be remembered that this was in the very early days of railway history, shortly after the invention of Stephenson's steam engine. Most of the committee members treated Stephenson's 'newfangled steam engines' with suspicion. Even the dogs in the street knew they were unreliable, prone to breaking down and that they could explode. Eventually it was decided that the most reliable source of power was horse power. They bought a large Clydesdale horse and christened it 'Dick', thereby establishing a tradition. All the horses used on the

Fintona Railway were called Dick. It didn't matter what kind of a horse it was – a mare, a gelding or a stallion – its name was Dick!

People were very class-conscious during the Victorian age. You were expected to know your place and stay in it! To do anything else was considered disgraceful behaviour. This class consciousness posed a big problem for those behind the Fintona Railway. How were the first- and second-class passengers going to be separated from the common working classes? The solution was simple: build carriages with an upper storey and charge a premium for sitting in comfort, sheltered from the weather, in the lower storey. As a result, the first railway carriages on the line looked more like a stage coach than a railway carriage! First- and second-class passengers sat inside designated carriages. Third-class passengers sat on the roof. It was very dangerous because of overcrowding. The driver was perched on the roof edge and could be pushed off and fall to his death. Horses can be unpredictable, so there were many other types of accident on the line and some of them were fatal.

The 'Dicks', who succeeded each other, were stabled overnight in a long shed. Little is known about the early Dicks but the last one was a gelding, looked after by the last driver, Willie McClean, who treated him like a member of his own family. Dick recognised Willie's footsteps every morning and used to whinny as they approached. Nobody could handle him like Willie. By the time Willie McClean was appointed in 1922, the design of the carriages had changed considerably. They now looked like a tram, not a stagecoach. Horse-drawn streetcars had been designed in America and were introduced in Belfast in 1872. Their design influenced the Fintona Railway so Willie had a coach that looked like city trams of the day, except that it had two compartments and could be pulled by one horse. Willie didn't have to perch perilously on the roof. He enjoyed working on the line until 1957, when it closed.

Eventually the strict classification by class was dropped and passengers could sit wherever they liked. There was one occasion when that caused difficulty. Most of the regular passengers had got on and chosen their seats when a crowd of gypsies arrived. Gypsies travelled around the countryside in caravans, so basic cleanliness, without a proper water supply, must have been impossible for them. They were odoriferous, to put it mildly. The regular passengers got off and complained to Willie, who dealt with it with his usual aplomb. He announced, with a perfectly straight face, 'Will all passengers in the back end of the tram please come up to the front because the back end is not going.' Surprisingly enough, that worked! The gypsies made sure they were in the first carriage and the other passengers got into the second.

Around 1947, a young lad called Jack Griffin worked as a boy porter on the line. One morning, when he arrived for work, there was no sign of either Dick or Willie. Eventually he discovered Willie in a small shed with Dick, who was lying on the ground. The poor horse was obviously ill. 'Will you help me get Dick up?' asked Willie. Jack did and they managed to get Dick to walk very unsteadily down to his stable, where he lay down again. A horse has to be really ill to do that, so his behaviour was a very bad sign. Willie noticed Dick kept looking down at his side and he said, 'I think poor Dick's in pain. He could have indigestion.' He mixed about a pound of Epsom salt and got Jack to help give it to Dick. It did no good, so they sent for Ernie Johnston, the local vet, who mixed a foul, black concoction, which looked like tar, in a basin. It took the three of them to get it down Dick's throat. 'There,' said the vet, 'that'll fix him.'

Willie replied, 'On top of what I've given him.'

'What did you give him?' asked the vet. When Willie described what he and Jack had shoved down poor Dick's throat, the vet shook his head and remarked, 'Poor Dick'll never get over that! You might as well give up and close the door on him.'

'When the vet left, Willie said, 'Here, Jack, come give us a hand. I'll no' close no door on old Dick. We'll ring him.'

They got Dick up and took him into the yard, where the process of ringing began. (To ring a horse, it is walked round and round in a circle.) The poor animal was very reluctant to move so, while Willie ringed Dick, Jack encouraged him to keep going by hitting him on the rear with a whip. After some time, the horse's sides began to heave and his stomach began to rumble. 'Look out, Jack!' warned Willie. Dick let fly, producing enough to fill a wheelbarrow, and there was a stench that is recorded to have been smelt all the way from Fintona to Dromore! Dick seemed better immediately and ate a hearty meal. He was back at work the following day. Willie blamed the trouble on Dick having eaten hayseed.

According to Nevin Hamilton, Dick never moved quickly! It took him ten minutes to cover the length of the railway line and people could walk it in eight! Sometimes passengers paid the penny fare, got fed up with the speed at which Dick was moving, got off and walked the rest of the way!

It is easy to laugh at the original builders of the Fintona Railway for not seeing the advantages of a steam engine over a those of a horse, but then the past has an insidious way of affecting the present.

Today the standard railroad gauge is 4 feet 8.5 inches. That is derived from the original specifications for imperial Roman war chariots. The Romans were organised, efficient people. They ensured that all their chariots were standardised by having the same wheel spacing. Roman war chariots were drawn by two horses working side by side so the initial ruts were the same width as two horses' backsides.

Imperial Rome built Europe's first long-distance roads, including those in England. When coaches replaced chariots, they had the same wheel spacing. A different one would have caused the wheels to break when travelling for long distances over the original ruts.

People who built tramways used the same jigs and tools they had originally used for building wagons, so they had the same original wheel spacing. That resulted in the same gauge being used for railway lines throughout the British Isles because the same workers built both types of vehicle (Ireland had another rail gauge as well as the standard one).

Wagons used in America were originally built by workers from the British Isles. They have the same wheel spacing for the same reasons and so does the US railway system.

Space shuttles sitting on their launch pads have two large booster rockets, called SRBs, made by Thiokol at their factory in Utah. The SRBs are shipped, by train, from the factory to the launch site, where they are attached to the sides of the main fuel tank. The railway from the factory to the launch site has a tunnel through which the SRBs have to pass. The engineers would have liked to make the SRBs larger. They were inhibited by the size of the tunnel, which was built using the ancient Roman measurements. Thus, what is arguably the world's most advanced transport system is based on the width of two horses' backsides, as measured by the ancient Romans thousands of years ago! As a result, I feel it would be unfair to blame those behind the Fintona Railway for not seeing the advantages of a steam engine over horse power.

ARMAGH

FRANCES QUINN

LIVED ONCE, BURIED TWICE

This type of story is associated with many areas. I heard this story in brief from individuals in both Armagh and Lurgan and each one insisted it was from their homeplace. I felt compelled to find the truth of the matter. Reports in the Armagh Gazette *(1924) revealed all for 'Lived Once, Buried Twice'. However, a different story of long ago retold in the* Lurgan Mail *(1 April 1988), unfolded the story of Margery McCall who lived in Lurgan.*

The present story is from Redrock, an area about 4 miles outside Armagh City. The cemetery there is reported to contain a great deal of rock under the surface – with the result that graves weren't always dug down the statutory six feet – which proved too much of a temptation for one would-be grave robber.

There was a fairly young woman living in that area, a Mrs Lister. She was happily married with two children. Since she was a strong, young woman, everyone was shocked when she fell ill suddenly and, deteriorating rapidly, in a very short space of time passed away. There was great dismay at her dying 'before her time' and the neighbours greatly pitied her bereft husband and children. She was duly laid out and the coffin was placed on four chairs below the only window in the room. All the mourners who waked her commented, as they inevitably do, on how well she looked and how she looked in death just as she had in life – down to the redness of her lips.

Those who laid her out had tried to remove a lovely diamond ring from her finger but as it proved impossible it had to go with her to the grave. Amid great anguish she was finally buried in Redrock cemetery and her husband and children returned to a house that felt very empty indeed.

That evening, after their servant man had tended to the horses and cattle and eaten his supper, he slipped off under cover of darkness to the graveyard. He was carrying a kitchen knife, for, like everyone in the household, he knew about the diamond ring. Once in the graveyard he took a shovel and dug out the newly filled grave. His task was not so onerous on account of the grave being shallower than average because of the rocks underneath the surface.

When he prized open the coffin there lay the diamond ring, sparkling in the light of his lantern. He hoped he could haul it off the finger but after a strenuous effort he felt he had no more time to lose and he resorted to the knife. As the blade cut into the skin, the 'corpse' stirred and Mrs Lister opened her eyes to see someone leaning over her with a knife.

'Leave me alone! Leave me alone!' she spluttered, trying to understand what was happening and then she cried out loudly as she realised the danger she was in. The servant was alarmed. A hard-headed man, he had not expected to encounter anything as ghoulish as a corpse rising up to protest his crime. It was too much and he fled, never to be seen or heard of again.

The bewildered corpse was surrounded by darkness apart from the light of the servant man's lantern, which he had left behind in his haste. The poor woman could think of nothing else except to try to get out of the pit she was in and to reach some hopefully 'normal' world above, for it was hideous to find herself in what seemed to be a coffin. She lifted the flickering lantern and, by balancing herself shakily on the wooden side of the coffin, she was able to place it on the damp ground above, but clambering out of the pit was a different matter. A shroud is not the ideal garb for night-time climbing so when she reached the top of the pit she found herself dirty and shivering amid the tombstones in the graveyard.

At least she knew where she was then, so, covered in mud, she stumbled on bare feet towards the gate and down the road towards a glowing light that she figured was her own home. Shaking with cold and fright, hunger and weakness, and in a state of great confusion, she tapped weakly on the lit window of her house.

When her husband drew back the curtain he was greeted with the ghastly sight of a woman who bore a passing resemblance to the wife he had buried that afternoon. Greatly alarmed, he called the servant woman and when they opened the door his wife, filthy and with bleeding feet, collapsed into their arms. Between them they got her inside and upstairs into a bath of warm water to clean and warm her ice-cold body.

The doctor was summoned to attend to her. One can only imagine what his thoughts were when he was called out to someone he had pronounced dead. The patient lay ill in bed for some weeks afterwards but, to the surprise and delight of all who knew her, she emerged fully recovered at the end of it all.

Mrs Lister went on to bear several more children and she lived to a ripe old age. When she finally died, her headstone was inscribed 'Lived Once, Buried Twice'.

The facts of this account come from a descendant of the woman who worked in the Lister's house at the time. Indeed a sensational event like this would not be easily forgotten and the happy ending would ensure that it was passed on like a family heirloom.

What the servant man had attempted in that case was not so very unusual even in the present day. Grave-robbing, especially for jewellery, is widespread and has gone on for millennia. Of course it has been legitimized in cases where the plunderers are termed 'explorers' and the plunder 'museum artefacts'!

DRAIN JUMPER

Perhaps there was something in the water in County Armagh that encouraged the jumping gene, because I came across this instance of an unusual ability in The Portadown Times. *It was written by 'The Chief' who was both founder and owner of the paper, and a local historian.*

In a different part of County Armagh we are told that the church at Mullabrack jumped across the road! Of course we're tempted to think of miracles but in this case it was nothing as interesting as divine intervention but rather road developments. The surrounding area is redolent with famous names. This Church of Ireland church was associated with the Culdees (*céile Dé*: companion of God), a semi-lay religious order back in the eighth century. Though in this case they think there may be seventh-century remains of the original structure lying beneath the much renovated present-day church.

The rector of this church from 1849 to 1859 was Lord John de la Poer Beresford, brother of the Primate Beresford. He was much liked by his parishioners and quite unconventional. He obviously enjoyed mixing with the locals because he was very fond of an old beggar woman who was over 100 years old. She had evidently been quite athletic in her day because she could still jump drains! When Beresford met her, he would give her a shilling for performing such a feat. He once invited her to jump over a straw rather than take on the task of a drain to prove herself. She was so offended that she tried to leap the nearest flax hole instead, but in her zeal she miscalculated the width and fell in. She might have drowned had Lord John not been there to pull her out.

He took her back home with him where she got dried out and was entertained by his wife, Lady John, who gave her fresh clothes to wear. This unexpectedly brought about the end of her jumping days. She told the disappointed Lord John that she wouldn't jump any more drains because she didn't 'think it seemly for her Ladyship's duds to be cuttin' such capers.'

DOWN

STEVE LALLY

THE RAPPAREE: REDMOND O'HANLON

A shepherd that lives in Slieve Gullion
Came down to the County Tyrone.
And told us how Redmond O'Hanlon
Won't leave the rich Saxon alone.
He rides over moorland and mountain,
By night, till a stranger is found,
Saying, 'Take your own choice to be lodging
Right over or under the ground!'

(From 'Redmond O'Hanlon' by Patrick Joseph McCall)

It's said that the first of the legendary English 'highwaymen' were royalist officers who 'took to the road' when they were outlawed under the Commonwealth. These were men familiar with the relatively newfangled pistols, which gave them an advantage over their victims, armed only with swords.

Perhaps because they concentrated on the wealthy, the highwaymen became popular heroes. No one, except the victims, grieved when the dukes and lords were held up with the immortal words, 'Stand and deliver, your money or your life'. In fact, some of these infamous highwaymen such as Dick Turpin, James Maclaine and Claude Duval held a celebrity status.

Here in Ireland we had our own legendary highwaymen known as 'rapparees' and 'tories' (*Toraidhe*). Both names are of Irish origin, the former meaning 'plunderers or destroyers' and the latter signifying that such outlaws who committed these heinous crimes were 'hunted' or 'wanted men'.

These men were products of the confiscation of lands from the native Irish. These dispossessed landowners were, to say the least, vengeful and many of them, like their English counterparts, were trained in the art of war.

They took themselves to the nearest woods, bogs or mountains, and honed their martial skills in order to bring down the unwelcome foreigners.

There was no mercy shown to these outlaws; they were pursued, hunted down and shot when captured. Their heads carried off to obtain rewards that were offered by the English rulers. Official documents state that this was a thing of weekly, sometimes daily, occurrence.

Of all the Rapparees of Ireland, the most famous, was Redmond O'Hanlon (*c.* 1620–25 April 1681). His name and his deeds are still vividly remembered today in the counties of Louth, Armagh, Monaghan and of course County Down. The writer William Carleton made him the central character of his 1862 novel *Redmond Count O'Hanlon: The Irish Rapparee*. But Carleton's story is mainly fiction, smattered with facts and loosely based on O'Hanlon's life.

O'Hanlon was one of those 'noble fugitives' driven into rebellion and transgression by English policy in Ireland. He was the chief of Orior, in County Armagh, claimed to be hereditary royal standard-bearer north of the Boyne. He was the son of Loughlin O'Hanlon, rightful heir to Tandragee Castle, now home to the popular snack food 'Tayto Crisps'.

In 1653, under the Parliament of the Commonwealth, the O'Hanlon lands were taken from them and the family was sent to Connacht, where they received a small pittance of land. At the Restoration in 1660, Hugh O'Hanlon petitioned to have their lands restored, but this was in vain.

Redmond O'Hanlon, probable brother of Hugh, took to the hills, vowing 'vengeance, black and bitter' against the 'Horde of Undertakers' that now held the best lands in Ulster. Many other dispossessed Irishmen flocked to his banner. Amongst these men were Protestant landlords, militia officers, and even Anglican and Catholic priests, who would work as informal members of his gang, giving him inside information and casing places for him to raid.

For twenty years he kept the settlers in the counties of Louth, Armagh, Monaghan and Down in terror. Many of the big farmers were paying him regular contributions for protection from all other tories. A letter from the era states that O'Hanlon's activities were bringing in more money than the king's revenue collectors. He was as shrewd a businessman as he was a bandit.

According to letters by St Oliver Plunkett, O'Hanlon increased in public favour as the colonial militia who were sent to capture him spent more time looting and pillaging the peasantry than actively looking for him. Those who did come across him did not live to tell the tale. It seemed that none would oppose him either through loyalty, admiration or fear.

It is said that O'Hanlon was never outwitted, except for one time by a country lad who was servant to a merchant shopkeeper in Dundalk, County Louth. This merchant had a debt of a couple of hundred pounds owed to him by another merchant in Newry, County Down. The Dundalk man wanted the money, but Redmond O'Hanlon held the country between Dundalk and Newry and so no man with either money or valuables would dare pass through that way.

The servant lad who worked for the Dundalk merchant had often heard his master complain and moan about the fact he could not get his money, so he offered to go to Newry to collect the debt. The master had perfect faith in the youth's honesty and integrity, but would not hear of such a dangerous and insane proposal.

But many months passed by and the young man's self-confidence and eagerness for adventure kept growing and in the end his master consented to his undertaking the dangerous mission.

He supplied the boy with pistols and ammunition, but to his surprise the boy insisted on taking an old slow-going grey nag, instead of the best racehorse in the stables. The youth set out and in less than half an hour he found himself winding his way through the craggy trails of the Fews Mountains. He was in no hurry and he whistled as he went, for he wanted to be seen. He travelled a long distance without meeting a single soul, kept company only by the wind rustling the leaves on the trees, the sound of his horse's hooves trudging below him and the occasional cry from a wild animal or bird.

He was beginning to fear that his plan might fail, when he heard the sound of thundering hooves, and soon saw the notorious Redmond O'Hanlon dashing towards him. He was mounted on a magnificent black stallion. The boy feigned fear and even made a weak attempt to gallop back home on the old mare, but in a moment O'Hanlon was beside him.

He asked the lad who he was, where he was coming from and what the purpose of his journey was. The boy answered all these questions frankly and truly and with every expression of great innocence. Then he confidently told his interrogator that there was just one thing he was afraid of, and that was being robbed by Redmond O'Hanlon.

The stranger assured him that he would protect him from this danger and having asked the boy when he expected to return, the boy told him with every show of confidence.

The youth was then given free passage and made his way to Newry, where he got the money for his master. Before returning, however, he got two or three pounds changed into copper, which he carried in a large leather bag, holding the remainder of the money secretly on his person. Then he proceeded to make his way home and, as expected, he encountered O'Hanlon again at the appointed meeting place.

On learning that he had got the money, O'Hanlon demanded the cash at once. The poor boy pleaded hard, but in vain. O'Hanlon produced his pistol and uttered the words, 'Stand and deliver, your money or your life'. At last, with an air of desperation, the boy shouted, 'Well, it shall never be said I handed you my master's money', and so saying, he flung the leather bag across a high hedge (some say a high wall).

The coins jingled as the bag fell and O'Hanlon dismounted his horse with ease, impressed by the lad's courage and yet totally deceived by his apparent naivety. No sooner had he crossed the hedge or wall, the boy slipped from his old mare and jumped on O'Hanlon's powerful stallion and was off like the wind. Behind him he left a bewildered O'Hanlon with a useless horse and a bag full of coppers.

In William Carleton's novel, *Redmond Count O'Hanlon: The Irish Rapparee*, he mentions this story and claims that O'Hanlon's horse was put into a livery in Dundalk and advertised. O'Hanlon never claimed him, but instead wrote a letter (unsigned) to the lad's master, stating that the horse's owner made a present of him to the 'young rogue' in reward for his cleverness and ingenuity. Carlton also states that O'Hanlon could never tell the story without laughing heartily and 'wishin' he had the trainin' of the lad'.

O'Hanlon's escapades and adventures continued for a brave few years after this incident. But things were to take a turn for the worse for the outlaw. O'Hanlon had an undying hatred for Anglo-Irish landowner Henry St John, who had been granted the traditional lands of the O'Hanlon clan. This hatred deepened when St John began evicting O'Hanlon's clansmen in large numbers. A private war between the men and their forces raged. The first major casualty of this war was St John's nineteen-year-old son, who was killed by the O'Hanlon gang on 9 September 1679. Outraged by this, James Butler, 1st Duke of Ormonde, the 'Lord Deputy of Ireland', ordered the assassination of Redmond O'Hanlon.

The duke's warrant was issued to Mr William Lucas, a planter and militia officer from Dromantine, who in turn recruited Arthur 'Art' MacCall O'Hanlon to carry out the assassination. Art was Redmond O'Hanlon's foster brother and close associate but was of a treacherous and avaricious nature.

According to the Revd H.W. Lett, who wrote about O'Hanlon in the 1898 edition of the *Banbridge Household Almanac*, when the order for his death was brought about, Redmond assigned two bodyguards to be at his side at all times, these were Art O'Hanlon and another member of the gang, William O'Shiel.

On the day when O'Hanlon met his death, Monday 25 April 1681, it was O'Shiel's turn to keep watch outside an abandoned cabin, where he was resting. Inside, Art sat beside him. The place was described in a pamphlet printed in Dublin in 1681, as being near 'Eight-Mile-Bridge', now Hilltown in County Down. There had been a fair at the 'Bridge', which is now known as Banbridge, and Redmond was there to intercept traders coming back and rob them.

At two o'clock in the afternoon, as Redmond lay asleep, Arthur O'Hanlon discharged his blunderbuss into Redmond's chest and then fled the scene. Lett states that when William O'Shiel heard the shot he ran into the cabin and found his leader still alive. As he lay dying, Redmond asked O'Shiel to cut off his head as soon as his 'fastly-ebbing life should be over'. This was to prevent the sport, triumph and gruesome displays of his enemies. As soon as the breath left his body, O'Shiel complied with this grim request and ran from the cabin holding his leader's head. Another source F. Mac Poilin, writing in 1936, stated that O'Shiel hid the head in a disused well close by. The decapitated body was later brought to Newry and men were sent to search for the head.

A military search party subsequently recovered the head and it was taken to Downpatrick Jail in County Down. As was the custom at the time, O'Hanlon's head was put on a spike outside the jail for all to see. Other accounts state that parts of is body were put there too, like some macabre exhibition. According to folklore, O'Hanlon's mother travelled to Downpatrick and composed a lament upon seeing her son's head spiked over the jail.

After this cowardly and treacherous deed, Art O'Hanlon received a full pardon for his previous misdemeanours and £200 from the 'Duke of Ormond' for murdering his leader. William Lucas, the planter and militia officer who had recruited Art and arranged the killing, received a lieutenant's commission in the British Army.

'Thus fell "The Irish Scanderbeg", who considering his means, and the circumstances he lay under, and the short time he continued to act, did more things to be admired than "The Scanderbeg" himself', stated Sir Francis Brewster. This 'Scanderbeg', to whom O'Hanlon is likened to, was the King of Albania, whose story reads like that of 'Jack the Giant Killer'. He was known to have cut fully armoured men in two with one swipe of his sword.

There are many stories, debates and speculation about where Redmond O'Hanlon's body found its final resting place. Revd Lett states he is buried in the parish of Ballymore in an old graveyard called Ballynaback, situated between Tandragee and Scarva, County Down. Another source states he is buried in the 'Conwal Parish Church Cemetery' in Letterkenny, County Donegal. And many believe his body is buried somewhere beneath the road from Poyntzpass to Newry in County Down. The Poyntzpass Gaelic Football team is called 'The Redmond O'Hanlons' in his honour.

There is a great belief amongst locals that the ghosts of O'Hanlon and his gang still haunt the scenes of their wild career. And tales are told of a 'Headless Ghost' roaming the lands around Hilltown in County Down.

BLACK DERMOD

This story was recorded in the Banbridge Almanac *of 1880 by an anonymous writer. It is a powerful and beautiful County Down folk tale and wonderful addition to this collection. The story was also known as 'The Half-Brothers'. The original was somewhat disjointed, so I took it upon myself to piece it together. I hope you enjoy it.*

The county of Down is a district renowned for its varied picturesque scenery and general interest. It is a pleasant spot for a summer ramble that could not be easily found elsewhere. No matter whether the traveller's taste prefers the rugged scenery of the uplands that border Dundrum Bay, the grandeur of Strangford Lough with over 360 inlets, its ruined castles and powerful currents. No matter if one may travel in pursuit of pleasure, health, pilgrimage, information or the picturesque and antique splendour of round towers, ancient buildings or Druidic remains and other archaeological treasures so common in the county, no one will be disappointed.

This story features one such rambler and his experience that is surely one of wonder in the magical county of Down. I know very little of this character, only that Ireland was the birthplace of his mother's race. It is not specified where he himself was living at the time; one can only assume it was the mainland of Great Britain as he states he paid numerous visits to Ireland for hiking or rambling excursions on its shores. He was stopping off to visit some friends in the village of Rostrevor, which lies at the foot of Slieve Ban, and this is where his story begins.

One morning our rambler left to go on a walk with his friend Charlie Vernon, whom he was staying with. They crossed the Bay of Kilkeel and began a trip around the coast to Newcastle. They intended to rest for the night and make an ascent of Slieve Donard, the Monarch of the Mournes, the next morning. In the evening they amused themselves by strolling about the beach, watching the fishing boats that lay at anchor in the bay with their sails flapping lazily against their masts, while their owners got ready to tempt the dangers of the deep.

Whilst admiring the boats, the rambler's friend gave a startled cry and pointed towards a narrow ledge that jutted out from the side of the mountain overhanging the sea. On the precipice two men were engaged in a violent struggle. One of the men stumbled and ended up hanging, suspended over the raging sea. He was holding on with only one hand and was reaching out for assistance with the other. His opponent walked towards him and brought his boot down hard on the poor man's hand. He fell screaming and the dark waters swallowed him up below.

According to the narrator of this tale, he and his friend ran as fast as they could to get a boat and save the drowning man. But they were stopped in their tracks by an elderly gentleman who happened to be the parish priest of the area and introduced himself as Father Michael. 'Ah Sirs!' exclaimed the old man, 'It is of no use; the struggle that you have witnessed was not between mortal men. Every year, on this day, the same tragedy is played out again and again'. As you can imagine the two young men were confused and disbelieving of this statement. The old priest asked them to sit down on some large stones near them and calm themselves, and he would tell them of this tragic tale.

Father Michael began, 'You see, this all began twenty-five years ago, when two brothers struggled on the brink of that abyss. Afterwards the one who hurled the other into the sea committed suicide, and since that time, on the anniversary of his death, the villagers have been terrified by the sight that you have just witnessed'. By this time a number of fishermen had assembled around Father Michael and the two walkers, and all wholeheartedly agreed with what the priest said. The old priest then asked the two ramblers to dine at his cottage and even offered to be their guide up the mountain the next day. He promised them that he would tell them the whole story of the apparition during their walk. Of course the two men accepted without a second thought. They ate tasty bacon and cabbage at the priest's house and even partook in some of his stash of the 'Rare Auld Mountain Dew', better known as 'Poteen'. Father Michael was a kind and educated man with a wealth of knowledge about the area and the mountain range. He was a dignified and vigorous-looking character with a shock of grey hair that sat on his head like a wiry bird's nest. His face was well etched with lines and a pair of spectacles framed deep knowing eyes that sparkled with wisdom. They left his abode happy and content and the following morning met Father Michael there, again waiting for them, ready to ascend the mountain.

The ascent of Slieve Donard is a gradual one of about 4 miles, climbing nearly 3,000 feet above sea level. There is a mountain path winding up the rock-strewn slopes and scattered bog-land. To the left of the mountain lies Ardglass and Strangford Lough, which Father Michael pointed out was part of the story he had promised to tell his companions. At last they reached the summit and, throwing themselves on the grass, they gazed long and earnestly on the surrounding landscape. Near the summit they saw the ruins of two buildings that the priest identified as being the cell and oratory of St Donard, a disciple of St Patrick, who once made his home on the mountains; and here the peasantry assembles on the patron saint's day to do penance and pay their devotions. Here, sitting at the foot of the ruins, Father Michael began his tale.

He pointed towards one of the mountains and said, 'You see, gentlemen, the mountain that stands on the south-west, divided from Slieve Donard by that narrow vale and stream? It is called 'Slieve Snaven', or 'The Creeping Mountain', because a portion of it can only be ascended in a creeping posture. As you can see, it resembles some old fortification, very high, over-hanging and detached, as it were, from the eastern side of the mountain. After the rain a stream rushes from the western side of the rock, shooting from the top and falling in a large cascade to the beach; to the east of this fall there is a vast natural cave, with an entrance nearly as wide as the cave itself. This chamber is lined with ferns, grass and beautiful mountain plants and is inhabited by many hundreds of hawks, jackdaws and owls. At the far end there are some crevices through which light penetrates, and if you climb up through a narrow passage on the left, to the top of the rock, you will arrive at one of the most beautiful, magnificent and romantic spots that can well be conceived'. Father Michael stood up for a minute and took a swig from the bottle he had brought with him and then offered it to his comrades, who accepted happily. They were all happy and content, enjoying the calmness and serenity of the situation. Father Michael sat back down and continued his story.

'One summer evening over twenty-five years ago two lovers were seated there side by side. The young man was called Carrick O'Farrell and the young woman was called Nelly O'Hara', when the priest said this girl's name his eyes glazed over and there was a sorrow about him. He began again, 'Everybody loved Nelly O'Hara; she was the prettiest girl in County Down, a county noted for the beauty of its women, I'll have you know,' stated the old priest, smiling. 'At a dance everybody was ready to fight for the honour of shaking a foot with her; indeed rival wooers did often finish by breaking each others heads in revenge for their own broken hearts, till at last it was well understood that the only one Nelly was ever going to be interested in was young Carrick O'Farrell. He was the son of a small farmer who lived near Kilkeel, he was a fine lad, who could hold his own and could handle a blackthorn-stick with the best of them. One by one they retired from the contest, and the little world on the Down coast accepted that he was the chosen suitor.

But everything was not all roses and love, for Nelly's poor father, Denis O'Hara, had met with many misfortunes. During the early part of the potato famine, he had become security for a poorer neighbour, who had since failed, and the little money Denis had saved soon disappeared. The rent, which up to this period had been punctually paid, fell into arrears; his landlord, a stern and harsh man, who had no compassion for his tenants, threatened to turn him out of his farm. Ruin seemed to stare Denis O'Hara in the face. Then, for the first time in his life, he was forced to do something that would take the light out of his beautiful daughter's eyes, the one thing he loved more than anything else in the world. He refused his consent for her to marry the one she loved, Carrick O'Farrell.

Poor handsome Carrick was not the eldest son; his father had been twice married and had two children. Carrick had an older half-brother called Dermod, he was a morose and menacing character and he was strongly suspected by the villagers of being the cause of several wrecks that had taken place around the time. False lights had been used, and the vessels were lured to certain destruction among the treacherous rocks that studded the shores of Strangford Harbour. Although there was no solid proof of the culprit, rumour pointed to the dark, sombre man who answered to the name 'Dermod Dhu', meaning 'Black Dermod'.

Black Dermod was one of the many suitors who had been rejected by Nelly, but unlike the others he had not given up all hope. He advanced small sums of money, from time to time, to Nelly's father, and when he found out that Denis was in dire straits and in need of financial aid, he once more began to urge his position of Nelly's suitor. The father soon consented, but Nelly, who despised and feared Dermod as much as she loved and worshiped his half-brother, declared that nothing should tempt her break her promise to Carrick.'

Father Michel stopped and looked at his two companions and asked if he was boring them with his story. They both replied that they were intrigued, even enchanted and urged him to carry on. The priest solemnly nodded and continued with his tale.

'Well as we know, the constant dripping of water will, in time, wear away a rock; and at last Dermod swore that if Nelly did not marry him, he would send her father to prison. She knew the shame would kill her father, begged for a month's delay, and promised to become, at the end of that time, the wife of the man who would pay all her father's debts and prevent him from being turned out of the home of his forefathers.

Nelly arranged to meet her lover Carrick at the place that Father Michael had pointed out to comrades earlier that day. This spot had long been their meeting place, but now the gloomy mountain seemed to frown upon their fortunes and love, casting a shadow over their happiness. Their situation was bleak, but there was still a chance that Carrick could solve their predicament. Nelly had bought them time by asking for the month's grace. That meant that Carrick could call in a favour that may save them. He would have to go to Dublin to meet a man whose yacht he had saved from wreckage on the rocks, as it was following the false beacons left by his cruel half-brother. They parted sadly and Nelly prayed as she had never done before that her lover would be successful in his task.'

Father Michael propped himself up and excitedly told his companions how Carrick had saved the yacht.

'A few months previous, Carrick had spotted a beautiful cutter-yacht, with the stars and stripes flying at her masthead. She was the property of an American gentleman called Mr Winthrop, who was making a tour around the coastline of Ireland. He was accompanied by his daughter Kate and a party of friends. They had docked a few times around the coast and climbed the Mourne Mountains and taken many of the walks round about. But about a week after the yacht's arrival she was caught up in a terrible storm and, it being night time, the crew on board could not make out where the harbour was. Black Dermod had placed burning beacons along the rocks, hoping that the boat with its wealthy crew and bountiful cargo would be smashed and he would benefit from the spoils. The roar of the wind and the billowing waves had the young Kate Winthrop terrified. She was screaming so, that her shrieks could be heard above the waves. As the vessel seemed doomed to certain destruction, a fishing hooker passed under her stern and a voice was heard hailing her. A rope was thrown and a man hauled on board. He sprang to the wheel and just as the man at the look-out cried "Breakers Ahead!" he roared his command: "Haul your starboard braces! And ease off to port!" Well the sailors rushed to obey and the yacht answering, her helm swung round and entered a narrow channel with breakers on both sides of it. For a few minutes, which felt like an eternity she held her course, and then her passage widened and, like an ocean bird, she rounded the point and reached the open sea. The worst of the danger was over and after a while the gale and tempestuous waves slackened. The cutter was safely anchored in Strangford Harbour; those on board owing their lives to Carrick O'Farrell were in deep gratitude to the young man.

Mr Winthrop was by no means ungrateful to the young man; he offered him a farm back in America. But Carrick preferred to stay at home and there was no way he would leave without Nelly. He knew that she would not desert her father in his troubles. However, Mr Winthrop told him he would give him time to reflect upon his offer, and said he would be staying in Dublin for the next few months and would write to him on his arrival.

So with this in mind, Carrick made his way to the capital city to meet the kind American and tell him of the terrible predicament he and his beloved Nelly were in. When he met Mr Winthrop and told him all, without hesitation Winthrop gave him enough money to not only pay off old O'Hara's debts but leave Carrick himself enough to start afresh. Winthrop then offered to bring Carrick back to Dundrum on board the yacht; telling him the whole party wished to be present at his wedding, and that he still hoped to persuade him to cross the Atlantic with his new bride. The cutter made a quick passage and was soon anchored in the bay. Carrick thanked his friends and made his way towards Slieve Donard. Before he would go to Nelly's cottage he was determined to climb the hillside and look once more at the old meeting place where they had parted so sorrowfully a few days before.

Well he did so and was met there by none other than his wicked half-brother, Dermod Dhu. "So you have returned then?" said Dermod, mockingly. "Yes and with great success!" shouted Carrick. "I have returned just in time to prevent the villainy you have plotted. I have the money to release Dennis O'Hara."

"Liar!" roared Dermod.

Carrick replied with a light, satisfied laugh as he turned and began to descend down the cliff. Hoping to take him at a disadvantage, Dermod sprang up at him and seized him by the throat. The two brothers were equally matched in regards to height and strength, but the younger brother's clean style of living gave him advantage over his insalubrious brother. As they struggled they drew closer and closer to the smooth and slippery edge of the cliff that fell down to the cruel sea below. Dermod was getting weaker and was about to beg for mercy, when all of a sudden his brother's foot caught in the tangled fern, and they fell with poor Carrick rolling over the edge of the cliff. Staring death in its hideous eyes, Carrick clutched at the tough, short bushes on the brink of the cliff edge. For a few awful seconds he looked up at his brother. Calmly his brother walked forward, raised his foot and brought it down hard on Carrick's hand. With a cry of "Cain!" upon his lips, Carrick lost his grip and fell to the sea.

As the waters closed around him, his whole life came back before his eyes: the memories of his true love, Nelly and their first meeting, and his promise to her to return. The frowning face of Black Dermod came between them; and then the dark waters sank in his ears and mouth and all remembrance faded; with the voice of his beloved Nelly calling to him, consciousness left him.

The end of the month came and Dermod claimed his bride. Nelly had heard nothing of her lover, the officers were ready to take her poor father to prison, and she allowed herself to be led to the little village church by the man she detested and who, unbeknownst to her, had murdered her one true love.'

Father Michael paused from his story and asked his companions, 'Was she to blame? Was she false to her love? Ah! How many innocent young girls have been sent as victims and sacrifices up the altar, to save some father or brother from disgrace! Surely the misery of such martyrdom is a sufficient punishment for the heartaches they have caused. Who will try to judge, when a girl has to choose between her lover and her kindred?' The young men agreed with the old priest and there was a sorrow in their hearts as they beckoned Father Michael to continue.

On he went, describing how the chapel was decked out with all the mockery of gaiety, flowery garlands were twined round the pillars, roses were scattered on the path as the bridal party entered that holy place. Among the spectators was Mr Winthrop and several of the gentlemen from the yacht, who quietly took their places without causing surprise, as one of the sailors had informed the villagers of their wish to witness the ceremony. The bride appeared with her father, surrounded by her family; she was pale and trembling. The weight of heavy sorrow seemed to have added years to her young pretty face. Dermod advanced to her, and the priest was about to commence the service, when from among the strangers dressed as a sailor, Carrick stood up and stepped between the bride and groom. He held Nelly's hand and facing his brother said, 'I have come to claim my bride'. With a blasphemous yell of hatred, Dermod rushed from the church as Nelly fell fainting into her lover's arms.

The wedding ceremony continued, only with Carrick as the groom. A boat from the yacht had rescued him as he was sinking for the last time. The shock of it all had brought on a fit of illness that confined him to bed for several days. But Mr Winthrop's personal doctor had taken good care of the young man. There was now a great joy in the air as all the lads and lasses danced merrily that evening in the old barn at O'Hara's farm; and before the yacht left Ireland, Nelly consented to go to America with her new husband.

In the New Country, fortune followed Carrick and he became one of the most opulent in the Far West. Nelly adored her husband and, surrounded by her many children, she lived happily as the day is long and almost ceased to think with any regret of her home in Ireland.

Two days after the wedding took place; the body of Dermod Dhu was washed up on the shore at the foot of the mountain from where his brother had fallen. And ever since on the anniversary of his death, the restless spirit of Dermod Dhu returns to go through the crime that doomed him to destruction.

The old priest stretched himself and, standing up from his hard seat, explained, 'That is why you saw that struggle; it was the ghost of Black Dermod, damned to relive his treacherous act for all eternity in the Mountains of Mourne'.

The evening was drawing near and the sun was sinking behind the distant hills as the three men slowly descended the mountain together. And as the wind whistled above their heads they thought they could hear the howls of Dermod Dhu, forever trapped in a moment of madness amongst the Mountains of Mourne in the County Down.

FERMANAGH

DOREEN MCBRIDE

THE REMARKABLE ROCKET

This is one of Oscar Wilde's stories. I have included it because Oscar Wilde was educated, as a boarder, in Portora Royal School, Enniskillen.

I am indebted to my good friend Sheila Lahiffe, who, many years ago, arranged for me to stay at her family home in Dublin. There I had what Americans refer to as 'a blast'. We exchanged stories and Sheila's sister, Mary, gave me a book of fairy tales by Oscar Wilde. I was entranced by it and have been a fan of Oscar Wilde ever since. I have retold this tales in my own words. It is a story with a moral, although he himself wrote, 'It is a very dangerous thing to tell a story with a moral'!

The whole country was in an uproar and everyone was excited. Their prince, who was tall and handsome with hair like fine gold and large, dreamy, violet eyes, was getting married. It was like a fairy tale. His fiancée came from Finland. These were the days when it was part of the Russian Empire. She arrived in Ireland in a beautiful sledge shaped like a lovely golden swan. She lay on white silken cushions between the swan's folded wings. The sledge was drawn by six reindeer and she wore a soft white ermine cloak that reached right down to her tiny feet and a tiny cap made of silver tissue on her head. Her skin was as white as snow. Of course people in Ireland don't see snow often and if they do, it usually doesn't stay around for long so they said, 'The princess is beautiful. She is just like a white rose.'

When the prince saw the princess he fell immediately in love.

'Your picture was beautiful,' he said, 'but you are ten times more beautiful!'

The princess lowered her eyes modestly and blushed.

A young page boy standing beside her said, 'She was like a white rose, but now she's like a red rose.'

The whole court was delighted and so was the king. Everybody went around saying, 'Red rose, white rose, white rose, red rose.'

'That page boy has a lot of sense,' said the king. 'Double his wages.'

As the page boy was never given any wages, that made no difference to him at all, but everyone in the court said, 'What an honour for the page boy! His wages have been doubled.' And the page boy was delighted to know he'd been honoured.

The marriage ceremony was magnificent. The bride and groom walked hand-in-hand up the aisle together under a purple velvet canopy embroidered with little pearls. They were so happy and so much in love they could hardly keep their eyes off each other.

After the ceremony the prince and princess sat in the middle of the top table and drank out of a crystal loving cup.

'Ahhhhhhh,' said the court. 'See how much they love each other. The cup has stayed as clear as glass. If false lips touch it, it turns cloudy.'

The wedding breakfast lasted five hours, after which there was a ball. The bride and groom danced the rose dance together and the king was so pleased he played his flute. He was a terrible flute player. He didn't have one note of music in his head. He only knew two tunes. He kept forgetting which tune he was playing and getting mixed up. He made a terrible squeaky noise but he didn't know that. He was the king so nobody dared tell him.

It was dark when the ball ended and everybody went outside to watch the firework display. The little princess was very excited. She'd never seen fireworks. The king ordered the royal pyrotechnist to be in attendance in case anything went wrong.

The princess turned to the prince and asked, 'What are fireworks like?'

'They are like the Aurora Borealis,' replied the king, who always answered questions meant for other people. 'They light up the sky. Frankly I prefer fireworks to stars because you know when they are going to appear. You are in for a treat, my dear, because fireworks are as delightful as my flute-playing.'

A great stand had been put up at the end of the king's garden and as soon as the royal pyrotechnist had put everything in place the fireworks began to talk to one another.

'Oh look!' cried a little squib. 'What a beautiful garden. Just look at all those yellow tulips. They're gorgeous. I'm so glad I've had the opportunity to travel. Travel improves the mind and does away with prejudices.'

'You stupid squib,' sneered the big Roman candle. 'The king's garden is not the whole world. The world is an enormous place. It takes at least three days to see it properly.'

The Catherine wheel had been attached to an old deal box when she was young and had suffered from a broken heart,

'The world is any place you love,' she said sadly. 'Unfortunately poets have written so much about love they've killed it. Nobody believes in it any more. And I don't blame them. True love suffers and is silent. Romance is dead.'

'Feel your head,' said the Roman candle. 'Love and romance never dies. They go on for ever, like the sun, the moon and the stars. The prince and princess are truly in love. That love will be everlasting. I heard it from the brown paper I shared a drawer with. He knew all the latest court news.'

The Catherine wheel was one of those sad people who think if you repeat something over and over it eventually comes true, so she shook her head.

'Romance is dead. Romance is dead. Romance is dead,' she sighed.

A sharp dry cough was heard. Everyone looked round. It came from a tall, superior-looking, supercilious rocket. He was attached to the end of a very long stick. He always coughed before he spoke. He believed that attracted attention and added gravity to his words.

'Ahem! Ahem!' he said and all the fireworks stopped to listen – all, that is, except the poor Catherine wheel who was still shaking her head and murmuring, 'Romance is dead! Romance is dead!'

'Order! Order!' shouted a cracker because he thought that was the right thing to say. He wanted to be a politician and had studied parliamentary procedure.

'Quite dead,' whispered the Catherine wheel before falling into a deep sleep.

As soon as there was perfect silence the rocket began to talk in a slow, distinguished manner.

'The king's son is very lucky to be married on the day I shall be let off. If it had been arranged beforehand it could not have been more fortunate for him, but then those of royal blood tend to be very lucky.'

'Oh dear me!' said the little squib. 'I thought it was the other way around and we were to be let off in honour of the prince's nuptials.'

'You are probably being let off to honour the prince and his charming princess, but I – I am different. I am quite remarkable. My mother was a famous Catherine wheel. She was 3 feet across and danced quite beautifully, achieving nineteen pirouettes before she eventually went out. Each time she turned she threw seven pink stars into the air. She was made of the best of gunpowder.

'My father was of French extraction and a rocket like myself. He flew so high people thought he would never come down again. He was a kindly being so when he saw all those anxious faces looking up into the sky he decided not to worry them and descend. He made a stupendous descent in a shower of golden rain. The press wrote about him in very flattering terms and the *Court Gazette* said he was "a triumph of Pylotechnic Art".'

'"Pyrotechnic Art" is the correct term,' said a Bengal light. 'I saw it written on my canister.'

'I said "Pyrotechnic",' said the rocket in a very cross tone of voice. 'I am never wrong so you should know not to contradict me. It is extremely bad manners to contradict. You should know better.'

The Bengal light felt put down so began to bully the little squibs to show he was still a person of some importance and a force to be reckoned with.

'As I was saying,' continued the rocket. 'As I was saying … What was I saying?'

'You were talking about yourself,' replied the Roman candle.

'So I was. I knew I was talking about something very interesting. I always find conversations about me extremely interesting, don't you?'

The Catherine wheel began to snore.

'Just listen to that,' complained the rocket. 'I'm being interrupted yet again. I hate being interrupted. It gets on my nerves as I'm a very sensitive, highly strung soul.'

The cracker turned to the Roman candle and whispered, 'What's a sensitive person?'

The Roman candle bent over the little cracker and whispered in her ear, 'A person who because he's got corns himself goes and treads on other people's toes!'

The little cracker couldn't help it. She laughed and laughed and laughed.

'Pray, what are you laughing about?' asked the rocket, who was annoyed.

'I'm laughing because I'm happy,' smiled the little cracker.

'Happy! Happy!' exclaimed the rocket. 'You've no right to be happy. It's very selfish to be happy. You should be thinking about others. You should be thinking about me, the remarkable rocket. I'm always thinking about me and I expect everyone else to do so too. That is called sympathy. It's a virtue I possess to a high degree. Think, for instance, what a tragedy it would be if something happened to me so I did not go off tonight. The prince would never be happy again. Neither would the princess. Their whole married life would be ruined. As for the king, he would never get over it. In fact when I think about the possibility of that situation I am moved to tears.'

'If you want to go off tonight you'd better keep your gunpowder dry,' said the Roman candle.

'That's right,' said the Bengal light, who had recovered his sense of self-esteem and was feeling better.

'Common sense!' sneered the rocket. 'You forget I am a very remarkable rocket, very remarkable and very uncommon. Anyone can exhibit common sense, if they haven't any imagination. I on the other hand have been gifted with a vivid imagination. I never think of things as they are. I always view them in a different light. As for keeping myself dry! Huh! You obviously do not appreciate my emotional nature. It is fortunate I could not care less. I am sustained by my sense of superiority. I have a big heart. None of you lesser mortals have hearts. Here you are, laughing and feeling happy when the prince and princess have just been married. What foolishness!'

'Why can't we be happy?' exclaimed a small fire balloon. 'It is a very happy event. The young couple love each other. Their hearts are full of joy. When I soar up in the air tonight I'm going to tell the moon and the stars all about it. You'll see them twinkle with happiness when they hear about our beautiful bride.'

'What a trivial view of life,' sniffed the rocket. 'If that's all that can be expected from you, you must be hollow and empty. Don't you realise the prince and princess could go and live in a far-off country and have a beautiful little son, with violet eyes and spun gold hair like his father. That poor little boy could be drowned in a river. What would you feel then? It doesn't bear thinking about. The thought is too dreadful to contemplate. The loss of their only son. I'll never get over that.'

'But they're only just married,' protested the fire balloon. 'They haven't had time to have a son, never mind lose one. They are happy. Nothing bad has happened to them.'

'I never said they had a son,' replied the rocket. 'I just said they might have one and they might lose him. If they did lose a son there would be no point in talking about it. I hate people who cry. The thought of their loss has me very much affected.'

'You are very affected,' said the Bengal light. 'In fact you are the most affected person I've ever known.'

'And you are the rudest person I've ever met,' replied the rocket. 'Understanding my friendship with the prince is quite beyond you.'

'But you don't even know him!' growled the Roman candle, who was beginning to feel annoyed.

'I never said I knew him. If I knew him I probably would not be able to be his friend. It is a very dangerous thing to know your friends.'

'The important thing is to keep yourself dry,' said fire balloon, who was very sensible.

'That may be important for you,' sniffed the rocket. 'But I shall weep if I so choose.'

He burst into tears, which flowed down his cheeks, along his chin, down his body and along his long stick to the ground, where it nearly drowned two little beetles, who were thinking of setting up home together and starting a family.

'You must be very romantic,' sighed the Catherine wheel, 'because you cry when there's nothing to cry about.'

The Roman candle and the Bengal light were annoyed and shouted, 'Humbug! Humbug! Humbug!' They were very practical people who, whenever they objected to anything shouted 'Humbug!'

It was a beautiful evening. The moon appeared to be smiling and it shone in the sky like a huge silver shield. The stars twinkled with joy, the air became scented by evening primroses and white lilies. Music sounded from the palace and the prince and princess danced beautifully together. The flowers stood on their tiptoes and peeped in through the windows while nodding their heads in time to the music.

Ten o'clock struck, then eleven, then on the stroke of midnight all of the courtiers came out onto the terrace.

'Let the firework display commence,' ordered the king.

The royal pyrotechnist bowed low, called for his six attendants, who each carried a flaming torch at the end of a long pole.

The effect was magnificent.

'Whizz! Whizz! Whizz!' went the Catherine wheel as the little rockets danced around. 'Boom! Boom! Boom!' went the Roman candle. The Bengal light made everything look scarlet, the Fire Balloon cried, 'Cheeriooooo!', as he soared upwards, dropping tiny blue sparks as he went. 'Bang! Bang! Bang!' went the crackers, who enjoyed themselves immensely. Everyone had a great time except the rocket. His gunpowder was so wet with his tears he could not go off. His poor relations, to whom he'd never speak without sneering, shot up into the sky, making wonderful showers of golden fire, and he just sat there, looking more supercilious than ever.

'I must be reserved for some really grand occasion. Perhaps the birth of an heir to the throne?'

The next day the workmen came to tidy up. The rocket felt pleased.

'This must be a deputation. I will receive them with the dignity becoming my station.'

He looked more superior than ever, stuck his nose in the air and frowned to give the impression he was thinking about something very serious. The workmen took no notice until they were going away, when one of them caught sight of him.

'Look at this!' he cried. 'Here's a bad rocket.'

He threw the rocket over the wall into a muddy ditch.

'BAD ROCKET? BAD ROCKET?' said the rocket as he whisked through the air. 'That's not what the man said. That's impossible! He must have said "GRAND ROCKET". "BAD" and "GRAND" sound very much the same. In fact they often are the same.'

He fell head first into the mud.

'This is very uncomfortable,' he said. 'It must be some fashionable watering place. A spa, that's what it is. I've heard fashionable people talking about going to a spa to help their nerves and goodness knows what. Considering the company I've been forced to keep I could do with a relaxing break. My nerves are completely shot to pieces. I have been placed upside down to reverse the effect of gravity on my brain. That should do me a power of good.'

A little frog, with a green mottled coat and bright intelligent eyes, hopped over to him.

'Hello,' he said, 'and welcome. I see you're enjoying a mud bath. There's nothing quite like mud. It's good for the blood, you know.'

'Ahem! Ahem!' coughed the rocket.

'What a wonderful singing voice you have,' exclaimed the frog. 'It's very like a frog's croak. Will you join us at our glee club tonight? We make the most musical sound in the world. The club's held in the duck pond near the farmer's house. We begin when the moon rises. The sound we make's so entrancing everybody stays awake to listen. Why only yesterday I heard the farmer's wife say she couldn't get a wink of sleep because of us. It's wonderful to be so popular.'

'Ahem! Ahem!' said the rocket. He was annoyed because the frog spoke so quickly he couldn't get a word in edgeways.

'Yes! You have a wonderful voice,' said the frog. 'And I do hope you will come and join us tonight. Now I must go and look for my six beautiful daughters. I'm afraid the pike, who's a perfect monster, will make a meal of them. Goodbye! It's been a pleasure talking to you. I must say I've enjoyed our conversation.'

'Huh! Conversation indeed!' snarled the rocket. 'We did not have a conversation. You did all the talking.'

'I like to do all the talking,' replied the frog. 'It prevents arguments and saves time.'

'I like arguments,' said the rocket.

'Arguments are vulgar. Everyone in society knows that. Now I really must go. I see my daughters in the distance.'

And with that the little frog hopped away.

The rocket put his nose in the air and said in his usual supercilious fashion, 'You are an annoying, ill-bred person. It's very irritating to find somebody who talks about himself all the time when I want to talk about myself. That is sheer selfishness on your part. Selfishness is a detestable characteristic, especially when exhibited to one of my temperament. I have a sympathetic nature. You should follow my example. I am a very important person. Don't you realise that yesterday the prince and princess got married in my honour? Of course a provincial, like you, would know nothing about what goes on at court.'

A large, bright blue dragonfly was sitting on a nearby bush.

'There's no point in talking to him,' she said, 'because he has gone away.'

'Well, that's his problem. I am not going to stop talking to him simply because he has gone away. I like to hear myself talk. I am such an excellent conversationalist. I often have long conversations with myself and I am so clever sometimes I do not understand what I say.'

'Well, then you should lecture on philosophy,' said the dragonfly as she spread her lovely, gauze wings and soared up into the sky.

'How foolish of her not to stay,' said the rocket as he sank a little deeper into the mud. 'She has wasted a marvellous opportunity to have her mind stimulated and improved by the brilliance of my thought. However, I don't care one iota. I understand that genius such as mine is rarely appreciated by the lower classes.'

After some time a large white duck, with yellow legs and webbed feet, came up to him. She was considered a great beauty in the duck world because of her waddle.

'Quack, quack, quack,' she said, 'you're a very peculiar shape. Were you born like that or did you suffer a serious accident?'

'You are obviously something of an ignoramus,' replied the rocket. 'My shape is considered to be most elegant in refined circles. However, I will excuse you. You obviously do not move in high society so have never been given the opportunity to know better. I can fly up into the air and come down in a shower of golden rain.'

'A fat lot of use that is,' said the duck. 'It would be different if you could do something useful, like plough a field or pull a cart like a donkey or even look after sheep like a collie dog.'

'My good creature,' said the rocket in his haughtiest tone of voice, 'I can see you're a person of the lower orders. A person in my exalted position is never useful. We have accomplishments and that is more than enough. I have no sympathy whatsoever with any kind of industry. I maintain work is something done by people who have nothing else to do.'

The duck had a peaceful nature. She never saw the point in arguing with anyone.

'I suppose we all have our own ideas and opinions,' she said. 'Anyway I hope you come to live here.'

'I will not!' cried the rocket. 'I find this a very tedious place to be. It lacks the attributes of both society and solitude. It is merely suburban. I shall probably go back to court where I will make a sensation.'

'I thought of entering public life,' remarked the duck. 'There are so many things that need to be reformed. I took the chair of a committee and we passed resolutions condemning everything we didn't like. It didn't have any effect that I could see, so I gave up in disgust and went back to domesticity.'

'I am made for public life,' said the rocket, 'and so are all my relatives. We excite attention wherever we appear. When I eventually go off I will be a magnificent sight. Domesticity distracts the mind from the higher things of life and causes one to age rapidly.'

'Ahhh!' sighed the duck, 'The higher things of life. How wonderful! That reminds me, I'm hungry. I must go and find something to eat. Quack! Quack! Quack!'

With that she waddled over to the stream.

'Come back! COME BACK!' yelled the rocket. 'I have a lot to say to you.'

The duck paid no attention and disappeared from sight.

The rocket murmured to himself, 'I'm glad she has gone. She had a very middle-class mind. I should be careful of the company I keep. I would not want to be contaminated by the middle classes.'

He sank further into the mud and began to think about the loneliness of genius.

Suddenly two little boys appeared. They ran down the bank carrying a kettle and some sticks.

The rocket thought they must be part of a deputation and looked dignified, which is particularly difficult when you're standing on your head.

'Oh look!' cried one of the little boys. 'An old stick. I wonder how it got here? It'll do for our fire.'

'OLD STICK! Impossible!' said the rocket. 'He must have said "GOLD STICK". That is a compliment. He must mistake me for one of the court dignitaries!'

The little boys lit the fire and stuck the rocket on top before lying down on the grass and closing their eyes.

The rocket was very damp so it took a long time to dry out. Eventually he went on fire and became very excited.

'I'm going off!' he cried as he made himself stiff and straight. 'I'll go higher than the sun, higher than the moon and away up past the stars. I shall go so high that –'

Fizz! Fizz! Fizz! Up he went! Straight into the air!

'Yippeeeeee!' he yelled. 'I could go on like this for ever and ever! What a great sensation! I am a great success.'

The sun was shining brightly and nobody saw him.

Then he felt a curious tingling sensation in every pore of his body.

'I'm going to explode,' he thought. 'I will make a great noise that will be the talk of the court for at least a year and I shall cover the world with stars.'

BANG! BANG! BANG! His gunpowder was tremendously loud but nobody heard it.

Swoosh! The stars inside him burst into the sky and cascaded towards earth in a cloud of golden rain.

And nobody saw them, not even the two little boys, who were still lying in the sun with their eyes shut. All that was left of the rocket was an old stick. It fell down to earth and hit a goose, who was taking his afternoon stroll along the riverbank.

'Goodness!' said the goose. 'It's raining sticks!'

'I knew I'd create a great sensation,' gasped the rocket as he went out.

THE COONEEN GHOST

Thanks are due to the staff at the Westville Hotel, Enniskillen, for being the first to tell me about the Cooneen ghost and to Robena Elliott in the Enniskillen Library for telling me the story in greater detail.

The entry in the 1911 census of Ireland for Cornarooslan, County Fermanagh, records that Mrs Bridget Murphy, her son James (21) and her four daughters, Anne (18), Mary (16) Bridget (12), Catherine (7) and Jane-Anne (3), lived in the townland, but the entry hides a dark secret. The family were soon to be plagued by a poltergeist, which became known as the Cooneen ghost.

The Murphys moved into an isolated farmhouse in 1913. It was a comfortable, thatched cottage that had belonged to people called Burnside. They sold it to the Corrigan family, who passed it on to the Sherrys. The Sherry family were the first family to experience poltergeist activity. They only stayed there for one night and were so terrified they moved out, kept quiet about their experiences and six months later sold the house to the unsuspecting Murphys.

The ghost first made itself known to the Murphys shortly after Mrs Murphy's husband Michael fell out of a cart and was killed. At the time the death was thought to be freak accident but, in retrospect, people wondered if Michael's death had been the work of the ghost.

James went out to a ceili in a neighbour's house shortly after his father's death while the rest of the family enjoyed a quiet night at home. Mrs Murphy and Anne were sitting chatting beside the turf fire and the youngest daughters were in bed.

Suddenly they heard the children screaming in terror and a loud tapping on the walls and heavy footsteps.

At first Mrs Murphy and her daughter were not worried. They thought someone was playing a joke on them. When James came back home the three of them searched the house from top to bottom but found nothing. That was the beginning of the nightmare.

After that, the poltergeist made regular appearances. It began with occasional knocking on the front door. When members of the family went to answer it they found nobody there. There was a room above the house, which was used to store hay and was accessible by an outside stone staircase. Heavy footsteps were often heard coming from it, but, yet again, when one of them went to investigate there was nobody there.

Mrs Murphy invited her neighbours round to see if they had the same kind of experiences. They did, as did Cahir Healy, the MP for the area, who said, 'I simply could not believe what I was seeing.'

Eventually the family went to two priests, their own parish priest, Fr Patrick McKenna and Fr Peter Smyth, CC Cooneen, to see if they could help. The two gentlemen didn't see or hear anything. At a later date two other priests, Fr Coyle, a young curate at Maguiresbridge, and Fr Eugene Coyle CC, also of Maguiresbridge, came and attempted to help.

Fr Coyle said, 'I stood in the children's bedroom and watched bedclothes on an empty bed rise and fall as if someone was lying there. I felt a cold, evil presence, then pots and pans suddenly flew off the dresser onto the floor. On another occasion Fr Smith and I were standing side by side downstairs when we heard a crash coming from the storey above. I can't really describe what happened next. It felt as if a terrific blast of cold air rushed between us. We both felt it. It was very strange because it didn't disturb our clothing. We saw the ghost grab cups and saucers off the dresser and smash them on the floor. It snatched the bedclothes off the sleeping children and flung them across the room. At times the bed lifted several inches off the ground before falling back down again while mysterious shapes appeared and disappeared on the walls.'

Other observers heard the Cooneen ghost snore or make noises which appeared to come from far below the ground. It could hiss, whistle and make a sound like a kicking horse. It could also tap out tunes – its two favourites were 'The Soldier's Song' and 'Boyne Water' – and reply to questions by tapping out answers.

Neighbours came to sit with the family at night and they all experienced the ghost's activity. Mrs Murphy moved the children's bedroom to the end of the house, but the ghost followed them. A respectable neighbour heard a noise coming first from one side of the children's bed, then the other and then from under the bed. This was followed by a scraping noise along the bed. The bedclothes rose gently as if 'a dog or a pig was hoking in it.' He asked the little girl if she felt anything.

'Yes, I can feel something pressing down here,' she said as she put her hands on her tummy.

Fr Coyle was given permission to perform two exorcisms in the house. They didn't work. The ghost continued to make sheets rise up off the beds, throw cups and plates around the room and issue deafening groans which appeared to come from upstairs. It seemed to be jeering at them.

The Murphys were terrified. They had hoped Fr Coyle would be able to get rid of it. To make matters worse the neighbours began to ostracise them. Rumours were rife, including one saying the ghost was that of a pensioner who had been murdered in the house.

Another rumour held that James Murphy had found a book in a forest near Cooneen called *The Legions of Doom* about the practice of satanic rites, how to contact demons and so on and that he had developed an unhealthy interest in the spirit world. He was supposed to have raised a demon. So it was said the Murphys had brought the entity on themselves. It served them right, so it did!

The malicious stories were the straw that broke the Murphy family's back. They decided to leave Fermanagh and emigrate to America. They were relieved when they left their old home because they thought they had left the ghost behind. It was not to be. Halfway through their voyage they discovered it was still with them. Passengers complained about tapping and banging coming from the Murphys' cabin. The noises became so bad that the captain paid them a visit and demanded the family stop making such a racket. He didn't believe in ghosts or poltergeists, refused to credit what they told him and threatened to put them off ship if they didn't stop creating such an obnoxious noise.

The ghost continued to haunt the Murphys when they reached New York and they were forced to move house five times. It didn't leave them until 1915.

Was the Cooneen ghost the first ghost to cross the Atlantic in an emigrant ship? Was it the first Irish-American ghost?

DONEGAL

JOE BRENNAN

THE BEE, THE HARP, THE MOUSE AND THE BUM-CLOCK

I love this story from Seamus McManus, the well-known Donegal storyteller, featured in his collection Donegal Fairy Stories, *published by McClure, Philips & Co. in 1900. It is a deliciously funny tale of Jack's woes and triumphs, reflecting the humour of the North West. McManus collected and published so many wonderful stories. I have met a number of people who remember, as children, gathering around the pump at the top of Mountcharles village, to listen to McManus telling stories when he was home visiting from the US.*

Once there was a widow who had just one son named Jack. They lived happy and well with their three cows that provided admirably for them. But alas hard times crept across the land and fell on Jack and his mother. The crops failed and hunger stared in the door. Things got bad for the widow and for want of money and for want of necessities she made up her mind to sell one of the precious cows.

'Go over to the fair in the morning Jack and sell the branny cow,' she said.

'Ah mother, are things so bad that we have to let the lovely cow go?' said Jack.

'They are, I'm sorry son, but you're not to worry your head. Just make sure you get a good price for that fine beast.'

In the morning the brave Jack was up early, had what little there was going for breakfast, took a stout stick and turned the cow onto the road. Jack marvelled at the multitude on the road heading to the fair. Soon he found himself surrounded by people and animals and enjoyed the merriment all around him. He observed the various cows on the road and looked favourably on his own branny cow that looked strong and healthy compared to some of the others.

Now when he entered the town he spied a great crowd gathered in a ring in the street. Curious, Jack made his way into the middle of the crowd. His eyes widened to saucers when he saw a man in the middle with a wee harp, a bee, a mouse and a bum-clock* in his hands. When the man put them all on the ground and whistled, the bee began to play the harp, and the mouse and the bum-clock stood up on their hind legs, took hold of each other and began to waltz with great elegance.

And as soon as the harp began to play and the mouse and bum-clock to dance, there wasn't a man or a woman that didn't begin to dance. Indeed everything in the fair, pots and pans, the wheels and reels, began to dance as well, jumping and jigging all over the town. And Jack and the branny cow were as bad as the next.

There was never a town in such a state before or since. After a while the man picked up the wee harp, the bee, the mouse and the bum-clock, and put them in his pocket. The men, the women, Jack and the cow, the pots and the pans, wheels and reels, that had hopped and jigged, came to a sudden stop. A great racket went up in the air as everyone began to laugh as if to break its heart.

As the crowd started to drift away the man turned to Jack.

'How would you like to be master of all these fine animals?' he asked.

'Why,' said Jack, 'I should like it fine.'

'Well then how will you and me make a bargain for them?'

'I have no money I'm afraid,' said Jack.

'But you have that fine cow,' the man replied. 'I will give you the bee and the harp for it.'

'Oh but my poor mother is at home with a terrible sadness and sorrow on her,' said Jack. 'And I have this cow to sell and lift her heart again.'

'And better than this she cannot get,' said the man. 'When she sees the bee play the wee harp she will laugh as if she never laughed in her life before.'

---

* *A bum-clock is a Dor beetle.*

'Aye that she would and it would be grand to behold,' said Jack.

He made the bargain. The man took the branny cow and Jack started for home with the bee and the harp in his pocket. He was full of excitement and desiring to see that laugh on his mother's face he skipped home in jig time.

'Oh Jack, you're a sight for sore eyes,' said his mother in welcome. 'And I see you've sold the cow.'

'That I have mother,' said Jack.

'And did you do well?'

'Indeed I did and did very well mother,' said Jack.

'So how much did you get for her then?'

'Oh it wasn't money I got for her at all but something far better.'

'O Jack! Jack,' cried his mother, 'what have you done my son?'

'Just wait till you see mother, and you will say that I have done very well.'

Jack took the bee and the harp out of his pocket. His mother nearly fainted at the sight and was speechless. Jack set the bee and the harp on the ground, began to whistle and the bee began to play the harp as soon as he did. His mother let a great laugh out of her and she and Jack began to dance. The pots and pans, the wheels and reels began to jig and dance over the floor too and indeed the house itself hopped about also. When Jack picked up the bee and the harp the dancing all stopped and his mother laughed on for a long time. But when she returned to herself her mood switched in jig time and a dark cloud swept over her.

'Jack you're a foolish silly fellow,' she said with anger raging across the room where laughter had danced only a short time before.

'There's neither food nor money in the house and now we have lost one of our good cows,' she said. 'You'll have to go to the fair tomorrow and take the black cow to sell.'

Jack was up early and headed off to fair with his mother's warning to 'get a good price for her' ringing in his ears. He made his way to the fair ignoring all the hustle and bustle on the road. But as soon as entered the town he saw a big crowd in a ring in the street.

Said Jack to himself, 'I wonder what they are looking at?' his curiosity ablaze.

He pushed himself into the crowd and saw the wee man from the day before with a mouse and a bum-clock. He put them down on the street and began to whistle. The mouse and the bum-clock stood up on their hind legs and got hold of each other and began to dance. As they did there wasn't a man or woman in the street who didn't begin to jig also, and Jack and the black cow, and the wheels and the reels, the pots and pans, all of them were jigging and dancing all over the town. Indeed the houses themselves were jumping and hopping about and such a place Jack or any one else never saw before.

When the man lifted the mouse and the bum-clock they all stopped dancing and settled down, and everybody laughed heartily. The wee man turned to Jack again.

'I'm glad to see you again. And how would you like to have these animals?' asked he.

'I should like to have them very much only I cannot,' said Jack.

'And why is that Jack?'

'Oh I have no money,' said Jack, 'and my poor mother is very down-hearted. She sent me to the fair to sell this cow and to bring home some money to lift her heart.'

'Well if you want to lift your mother's heart I will sell you the mouse,' said the man. 'When you set the bee to play the harp and the mouse to dance to it, your mother will laugh as if she never laughed in her life before.'

'A kind offer indeed but as I say, I have no money sir to buy your mouse,' said Jack.

'Sure that is no issue Jack, I'll take your cow for it.'

Poor Jack was so taken with the mouse and had his mind so set on it, that he thought it was a grand bargain indeed. He gave the man the cow, took the mouse and started off for home. When he got home his mother welcomed him.

'You sold the cow Jack,' said she.

'I did that,' said he.

'Did you sell her well?'

'Very well indeed mother.'

'And how much did you get for her then?' asked his mother.

'Sure I didn't get money for her but great value I got,' said Jack.

'Oh Jack! Jack! Whatever do you mean?' she asked.

'I will show you that,' said Jack as he lifted the mouse out of his pocket, and the harp and the bee, and set the whole lot on the floor.

When Jack began to whistle the bee began to play, the mouse got up on his hind legs and began to dance and jig. Well Jack's mother gave such a hearty laugh as she never laughed in her life before. It made Jack's heart sing with delight to see such a sight and to know he had done the right thing. To dancing and jigging herself and Jack fell, the pots and the pans, the wheels and reels began to dance and jig all over the floor, and the house itself jigged too. And when they were tired of this Jack lifted the harp, the bee and the mouse and put them into his pocket. He delighted to watch his mother laugh for a long time. But when her laughter died away her mood changed in jig time and she got very down-hearted.

'You are a stupid, good-for-nothing fellow indeed,' said his mother. 'We have neither money nor meat in the house and here you have lost two of my good cows and now I only have the one left.'

She ordered Jack to take her last cow to the fair the next day and to make sure to bring home money to her 'to lift her heart'. He promised her he would and went to his bed with a stomach that growled as loud as the raucous in the house earlier.

Jack was up early and on the road to the fair with the spotty cow. When he arrived in the street he saw a crowd gathered in a ring. Of course Jack's curiosity wasn't going to allow him to walk on. He pushed his way into the crowd and there he saw the man he had seen on the two previous days. This time he held the bum-clock in his hand and he put it on the ground and started to whistle. As soon as he did the bum-clock started to dance and as before the men and women, the children in the street, Jack and the spotty cow all began to dance and jig along with the wheels and reels, the pots and the pans, and the houses themselves.

When the man lifted the bum-clock and put it in his pocket, everybody stopped their dancing and broke into a hearty laugh. The wee man turned and saw Jack.

'Well Jack my brave boy,' said the man, 'you will never be right fixed without the bum-clock, for it is a fancy thing to have.'

'Och but I have no money for such a thing,' said Jack.

'No matter for that, for you have a cow and that is as good to money to me,' he said.

'But I have a poor mother who is down-hearted at home and she sent me to the fair to sell this cow and raise some money to lift her heart.'

'Oh but Jack this bum-clock is the very thing to lift her heart, for when you put down the harp and the bee and mouse on the floor and put the bum-clock with them, she will laugh as if she never laughed in her life before.'

'Well that is surely true and I think I will swap with you,' said Jack.

So Jack gave the cow to the man and took the bum-clock himself and started for home. His mother was glad to see Jack home.

'I see you have sold the cow,' said she.

'That I did mother,' said Jack.

'And how much did you get for her?'

'Sure I didn't take any money for her mother but great value I did get for you,' said Jack.

With that he took out the wee harp, the bee, the mouse and the bum-clock, and set them on the floor. He began to whistle and the bee struck up the harp and the mouse and the bum-clock stood up on their hind legs and began to dance. Well Jack's mother laughed like she had never laughed before in all her living days. The wheels and the reels, the pots and the pans, went jigging and hopping over the floor and the house itself went jigging and hopping likewise. When Jack lifted up the animals and put them in his pocket, everything stopped and his mother laughed on for a long time after. But when she came to herself again and saw what Jack had done, a black anger descended on her.

'Now we're without money, food, or cow!' she thundered at him. She scolded him heartily, then sat down and began to cry.

Poor Jack, when he looked at himself he confessed that he was indeed a stupid fool entirely. He wondered to himself what he could do for his poor mother. He went out along the road thinking on what he could do when he met a wee woman who greeted him; 'Good-morrow to you Jack,' said she, 'and how is it you are not trying for the King of Ireland's daughter?'

'What do you mean?' asked Jack.

'Didn't you hear what the whole world has heard, that the King of Ireland has a daughter who hasn't laughed for seven years and he has promised to give her hand in marriage, and give the kingdom along with her, to any man who will make her laugh three times.'

'If that is so,' said Jack, 'it is not here I should I be.'

Back to the house Jack went and gathered the bee, the harp, the mouse and the bum-clock. He put the lot in his pocket and headed for the road.

'And where are you off to now boy?' she asked.

'Mother it won't be long till you get news from me,' he said.

'Ah Jack what foolishness has gotten into you now?' she said.

'I told you I got value and value you will get,' said Jack and he said goodbye to her.

When he reached the castle there was a ring of spikes all around it with men's heads on nearly every spike. He didn't like the look of this and no mention of it had the wee woman made.

'Whose heads are these?' Jack asked one of the king's soldiers.

'Any man that comes here trying to win the king's daughter and fails to make her laugh three times, loses his head and has it exhibited on a spike,' said the soldier. 'These are the heads of the men that have failed so far.'

'A mighty big crowd,' noted Jack.

Then Jack sent word to tell the princess and the king that there was a new man who had come to win her hand. In a short time the king, the queen, the princess and the whole court came out and sat on grand chairs of gold and silver in front of the castle. Jack was ordered to come forward and undertake his trial.

Jack put his hand in his pocket and took out his menagerie and the harp. He gave the harp to the bee. He tied a string to one and the other, took the end of the string himself and walked into the castle yard with his animals behind him.

When the king and queen, and court saw poor ragged Jack with his bee and mouse and bum-clock hopping behind him on a string, they fell into a roaring of laughter that was loud and long. And when the princess lifted her head and looked to see what they were laughing at, saw Jack and his paraphernalia, she opened her mouth and let out such a laugh as never was heard before.

Jack dropped a low curtsey and said, 'Thank you my lady. I have one of the three parts of you won.'

Then he drew up his animals in a circle and began to whistle. The minute he did the bee began to play the harp, the mouse and bum-clock stood on their hind legs, took hold of each other and began to dance. With that the king, the queen, the court and ragged Jack himself began to dance and jig, and everything about the king's castle, pots and pans, wheels and reels and the castle itself began to dance.

The king's daughter, when she saw this, opened her mouth again and let out of her a laugh twice as loud as the one she let out before. And Jack in the middle of his jigging, dropped to a curtsey and said, 'Thank you my lady, that is two of the three parts of you won.'

Jack and his menagerie went on playing and dancing but try as he did Jack couldn't get the third laugh out of the king's daughter. The poor fellow realised his big head was in danger of ending up on a spike.

Then the brave mouse came to Jack's help and wheeled round on its heel and as it did so its tail swiped into the bum-clock's mouth and the bum-clock started to cough and cough. When the princess saw this she opened her mouth again and let out the loudest, heartiest and merriest laugh yet.

'Thank you my lady,' said Jack dropping another curtsey, 'I have all of you won.'

Jack stopped his menagerie and the king took him and his animals into the castle. A clatter of servants descended on Jack, washed and combed him, and dressed him in a suit of silk and satin, with all kinds of gold and silver ornaments. He was then led before the princess. And true enough she confessed that a handsomer and finer fellow than Jack she had never seen and she was very willing to marry him.

Jack sent for his mother and she was brought along for the wedding which lasted for nine days and nights, every night better than the last. Each night Jack brought forth his menagerie and set the whole place to dancing.

Jack smiled at his mother and said, 'I told you they were value and value we have now.'

GHOST LIGHTS IN RAMELTON

'Ghost Lights in Ramelton' is a retelling of two stories I heard from Mary and Willie Montgomery in Ramelton, great-grandparents to my children. A wonderful kind couple, full of devilment, their home had been a ceiling house before the arrival of television, and they always had a story to tell. 'Fairy Wandering' in my Donegal Folk Tales *was also courtesy of them. It is lovely to remember them in this collection.*

There was a woman who lived in Ramelton by the name of Aoife and if you had mentioned any of these events to her, she would have laughed. She was a religious woman and had no truck with superstitions or belief in anything other than God and mere mortals who walked the world like herself. She was a good Christian-living woman who didn't let alcohol pass her lips and tried to keep bad words about others firmly behind her. She went to church every day and was good to her neighbours.

Now her husband, Packie, was somewhat different in character. He led a good life, went to church every Sunday and was there to help his neighbours at the drop of the hat he kept firmly perched on his head, except when it rained. When asked why this was so, he promptly replied, 'Sure I wouldn't be sitting in the house with a wet cap on my head would I?'

Unlike his wife he was partial to a wee drop once in while and then his tongue was somewhat looser.

Despite his Christian values he was prone to a bit of poaching, especially in the River Lennon. Now you might think this was somehow contrary to his beliefs but in his view of the world he wondered 'how any man can claim to own a river when it is constantly flowing and moving from one place to another!'

Occasionally he would walk the fields in search of rabbits to vary the plate at home. His wife never commented on the fine salmon that he put on the table but her demeanour when rabbits were produced was somewhat different. Now this was not down to a different view of the rabbit over the salmon but more to do with the company he kept when out lamping.

These so called 'good boys' were fond of their messing about the town and even more fond of the poitín that was cooked up in the hills.

'Where are you off to at this hour?' Aoife asked him.

'Ah sure, I'm just going for a bit of a stroll with a few of the boys,' he said.

'Ha. A bit of a stroll indeed,' she snapped. 'Would this stroll involve Patsy or Johnny?

'Aye, I think they'll be along,' he said.

'Well don't come back here drunk.'

On one such occasion the boys were up in the fields around Aughnagaddy House. They were out lamping for rabbits and as it was a clear night the temperatures had fallen so they had a wee drop to keep the chill off.

'We've being going around and around for ages,' complained Patsy some time later, 'and we've got nowhere.'

'I'm telling you the house was just over there,' said Johnny pointing.

'We've been over that way and it's not there,' said Patsy.

'I think we've been wandered, boys,' said Packie.

'Ah, don't be stupid man,' said Patsy and Johnny. 'You don't believe in that sort of nonsense.'

'Indeed I do. Many's the story I've heard of people been wandered by the good people,' said Packie.

'That's just the drop speaking,' said Patsy.

'Well how else can you explain the fact that we've been wandering around here like fools for God knows how long?' demanded Packie.

'We've just missed a gap in the hedge or something,' said Patsy.

'Well look at that branch there with my handkerchief on it,' said Packie. 'We've passed that branch four times now. We're just going around in circles.'

'What is your handkerchief doing there then?' said Johnny.

'I put it there when I thought we had been wandered,' said Packie.

'Ah you're just having us on with your handkerchief and wandering nonsense,' said Patsy.

'It's a fact and the best thing we can do is stop here till the good folk lift the wandering,' said Packie.

Just then they saw a light moving a short distance away.

'What's that?' said Patsy.

'I don't know,' said Packie, 'but will you look at the poor dog. It's frozen in terror and his hair is standing on end.'

'Quick, hide,' said Johnny.

The three of them fell to the ground and held the dog tight. They peered through the hedge as the light drew closer. There was no sound but they could see it was the window of a carriage on its way up to the house.

'That was close,' said Patsy.

'Ah, we must be closer to the house than we thought,' said Johnny.

'But why was the dog so scared?' asked Packie.

'He wasn't the only one,' said Patsy. 'You look like you saw a ghost.'

'Did you not feel it when that carriage went past?'

'Feel what?' said Johnny. 'And what carriage?'

'A terrible chill,' said Packie.

'And what carriage are you talking about?' said Johnny. I didn't hear the sound of any carriage.'

'Exactly. It was a ghost carriage I tell you,' said Packie.

'Ah don't be ridiculous. You've had too much to drink. First the wee folk wandering us and now ghosts,' said Johnny.

'I felt it too,' said Patsy.

'What?' said Johnny.

'Never mind your bravado Johnny,' said Patsy. 'I can see it in your eyes that you felt it too.'

'Well maybe there was something a bit odd about it,' said Johnny.

'I'm getting out of here,' said Packie. 'Look you can see the lights of the house now.'

The three friends headed away from the house and out onto the main road. As they stepped out they nearly crashed into Mickey.

'Where are you going like a crazy thing?' said Packie .

'It's yourself Packie,' said Mickey. 'I heard the sound of you coming and I thought it was that carriage coming back again.'

'What carriage?' said Patsy.

'I was coming down the road there on my bike when I see the two lights of a carriage coming up the road, a sight you don't see too often these days,' said Mickey. 'And because it's so dark I got off the bike and got into the side of the road. But the blasted thing came charging at me and knocked me into the ditch. It took me ages to crawl out of it with the bike on top of me.'

'How do you know it was a carriage?' Johnny asked him.

'I saw the lights,' said Mickey.

'We saw it too,' said Packie.

'We saw something,' said Patsy. 'But we didn't hear anything.'

'It was that carriage,' said Packie. 'We saw the light from within but it weren't a natural thing I tell you.'

They all headed down the brae towards the town. The first house they came to was Packie's.

'Don't be annoying that wife of yours with your stories,' Patsy warned.

'Sure she won't believe a word of it anyway,' said Packie.

He went inside to be greeted by a suspicious-looking Aoife.

'You're home early and not a rabbit in sight,' she began, but stopped when she saw his face. 'Good God, what happened?' she said. 'You look like you've seen a ghost.'

And with that he told the whole of the curious incidents of the night.

'Too much drink, that's what it is,' Aoife declared.

'And what about Mickey,' said Packie. 'Your own cousin and him coming home from work.'

'Ah, he's always imagining things in the dark,' she said.

'It's true I'm telling you Aoife.'

'Aye, true like that story you told me about the fish earlier today,' she said.

'That was the truth.'

'You expect me to believe that a salmon knocked Patsy out cold and then flapped back into the river.'

'Well where else did it go?' he asked.

'The fool let it go.'

'He did not,' said Packie. 'I thought I saw the keeper just after we hauled it in. It was huge. I said 'run'. I went one way and when I looked back Patsy was struggling to his feet with the fish. I went and hid myself and waited. I didn't see any sign of the keeper and guessed I must have imagined it so I went back to find Patsy. And there he was lying flat on his back where I had seen him last but no fish. He had a right bump on the side of his face.'

'Ah, get out of it you with your auld stories,' said Aoife.

Now about a week later Aoife was coming out of church after evening mass when she met her friend Maggie.

'Do you fancy a wee walk Aoife?' said Maggie. 'It's such a lovely night.'

'Aye I would,' said Aoife. 'I'm in no hurry home as Packie is out with the boyos.'

They headed up along the Letterkenny Road. They chatted away as they walked with nothing to disturb the night other than the hoot of an owl.

But suddenly they both cried out and stood stock still. They felt a terrible chill creeping over them. Then they saw it, two carriage lights approaching at great speed. They knew they should step in to let it pass but they were frozen to the spot in terror. Then the two lights came on top of them and passed on through. Neither of them could speak nor move for some time.

'What was that?' whispered Maggie at last.

'I don't believe I'm saying this but I think it was a ghost carriage,' said Aoife. 'I laughed at poor Packie when he told me they had seen something like it last week.'

The two women turned on their heels and headed home. By the time they arrived Packie was sitting in his chair by the fire.

'What's happened to you?' he asked. 'You look like you've seen a ghost.'

'Well God forgive me for not believing you last week,' said Aoife. 'But I wouldn't have believed it if I hadn't seen it with my own two God-given eyes.'

And from that day on she wasn't as quick to dismiss Packie's stories, but she rarely spoke of what she herself had witnessed that night.

LEITRIM

SUSIE MINTO

By folk tales, we usually mean old stories that have been passed on, often with a strong element of invention, yet also with a ring of truth to them. However, sometimes the line separating what is a 'made up' tale and what is a story about something that more than likely happened is hard to place. When studied closely, most things could have taken place, so when is a story only a folk tale and when is a story not a folk tale?

The two stories that follow involve people and places that are recognisable, even verifiable to an extent. They have a place in Leitrim's (and Ireland's) political and religious context at the time of their happening, and I have used my collector's licence to offer them for posterity and possible further inquiry and study.

The first story is about a man who was probably wrongly hanged and whose last words led to a legacy of an unusual healing charm.

JACK BIRCHALL

It is said that 'truth is often stranger than fiction'. What follows is a glimpse into the fascinating account of a poor labourer, Jack Birchall, who was wrongly convicted of murder and hanged at Roscommon in 1829. Two 'threads' of evidence provide peculiar proof of his innocence: one, a manuscript held in Trinity College Library and the other, literally, a length of the rope that hung him. For almost two centuries, that fatal rope has brought healing to thousands of people touched by it and this, in its own way, has convinced all who heard the story that Birchall was an innocent victim of perjury.

So who was Jack Birchall and why should this story stand out so strongly in folk memory? The surname is recognisable to this day in Drumshanbo. The Protestant owners of the Blackrock Estate on the outskirts of the town were originally Lindsays, until the last of the Lindsays married Toby Birchall, also a Protestant. The subsequent estate owners were known as Lindsay Birchall. It is believed that Jack was the son of Henry, who in turn was an illegitimate son of either Toby or Robert Birchall. Toby was known for his 'extra mural' activities.

Jack Birchall was about twenty when his life was cut short when he was found guilty of murdering Thomas Cox, the manager of the Arigna Ironworks, a crime he denied. On 23 February 1828 a group of men attempted to steal gold which Cox had received to pay his English workforce at the Arigna Ironworks. The men approached Cox's house in the middle of the night and called out to him. The moment Cox raised his bedroom window and put out his head, he was fatally shot. Cox's quick-thinking sister put the gold into a crock of cream, resulting in a fruitless search by the robbers when they subsequently ransacked the house.

Two men employed at the ironworks – Tom Glynn, the night-watchman, and Jim Beirne, a teacher and private tutor – swore that Birchall was very much involved in the shooting of Cox. Both men were implicated in the robbery/murder but needed to construct an alibi to save their own lives. It was their questionable evidence that finally convicted young Birchall.

At the time of his conviction, Birchall lived in a small house with three brothers and a sister. His siblings claimed that their brother was at home asleep at the time of the murder, but this was over-shadowed by the compelling, sworn evidences of Glynn and Beirne. However, it took three trials before Birchall was convicted. At the third trial the judge was one of the best judges of his day: the Hon. Baron Smith. Handing down the sentence of death, on Friday, 7 August 1829, Smith was said to have pronounced the sentence 'in the most pathetic strain'.

On the day of his execution, 10 August 1829, outside the new Roscommon Courthouse, twenty-year-old Jack Birchall professed his innocence to the crowds and said from the scaffold: 'As I am an innocent man, bring home the rope that will hang me for it will have a cure in it.'

A friend of Birchall's, John Morrison, heard Jack's plea and, after the hangman's grim work was finished, asked for a length of the rope. The story goes that, on his way home, he stopped for a rest in the house of a woman who had a terrible ulcer on her leg. He remembered the piece of rope in his pocket and offered it to the woman, as nothing prescribed previously had managed to make her well. She accepted his offer. A few days later, Morrison was in the neighbourhood and called in to find out how she was faring. Remarkably, there was an improvement and he applied the rope to her ulcer several more times in the coming days and weeks and she fully recovered.

It is here that the rope takes on a life of its own. It has been passed on through the Morrison family, who lived in the Gowel area, east of Leitrim village, for two centuries. Hundreds, if not even thousands, of people have made use of its curing properties, and the thinnest remnant of that well-used hangman's rope still remains to this day. Those who believe in the power of cures have no difficulty in seeing this as sufficient evidence of Jack Birchall's innocence.

However, a local historian, Des Guckian, from Dromod, County Leitrim, felt compelled to delve more deeply into Jack Birchall's case, and, after piecing together all the available evidence in newspapers and court proceedings, he published his definitive account in 2012 under the title *Not Even a Sparrow Shall Fall: The Cruel Fate of Jack Birchall.*

While Des Guckian was researching the story, a local history lecture in Carrick-on-Shannon in 2007 came to his notice. It was delivered by Professor Roger Stalley of Trinity College Dublin and was on the work of Daniel Charles Grose, an English topographical artist, engraver and author who travelled all over Ireland and who had lived nearby in Annaduff for a number of years and died in Carrick-on-Shannon in 1838. In 1991, Professor Stalley had published Daniel Grose's *The Antiquities of Ireland: A Supplement to Francis Grose*, a hitherto unpublished work. In his talk, Professor Stalley referred to illustrations which Daniel Grose had done around the Arigna area and to Grose's 'Writing an account of the murder of the manager of Ironworks and the wrongful hanging of a young man for it'. Des Guckian found the manuscript at Trinity College Dublin. It was the final piece of evidence he needed to prove Birchall's innocence. The manuscript told that, on his deathbed a few years after the trial, Tom Glynn confessed that it was he who had shot dead Mr Cox and then framed Jack Birchall.

Des Guckian sees a much bigger political drama being played out through this case than the mere activities of some local would-be-robbers in Drumshanbo. He refers to the national political back-drop of 1798 when local yeomen and rebels, supported by the French, clashed strongly in that area. Referring to the obvious sectarian divide in the period 1828–29, Guckian states in his book: 'The subsequent capital punishment of Jack Birchall and the far more lenient sentences given to the other accused may well be explained by reference to the nasty bigoted way in which the smaller but state-backed Church of Ireland and the larger and emergent Roman Catholic Church locked horns in deadly combat just at that very time of the Catholic Emancipation struggle around the years 1828–29. The Protestants had recently begun a new evangelical movement called "The Second Reformation" and one supposes that to support the cause of an "illegitimate" might not have been "politically correct".'

The *Roscommon and Leitrim Gazette* and other unionist papers decried the murder and demanded a conviction. The more obviously guilty men had the backing of influential priests, such as Daniel O'Connell's friend and supporter Fr Tom Maguire from nearby Drumkeerin. The Catholic accused, through the influence of the priests, ended up with lesser sentences.

I'll end this tale of the unfortunate Jack Birchall with some words from a ballad, 'Burchall's Lamentation', which is still known in the Mount Allen area, west of Drumshanbo and close to where he lived:

Burchall's Lamentation sounds through all the nation,
His father's desolation I mean to let you know;
Drumshanbo, Keash and Leitrim, it grieves me for to leave,
When I think of those false traitors who have sent me to my grave.
Tom Glynn did all he could, he was fond of human blood;
Three Assizes there he stood, till at last he ended me,
Now I am going to die upon the gallows tree,
I'm as innocent of Cox's murder as the child upon your knee.

This story has been retold with permission from Des Guckian, author of Not Even a Sparrow Shall Fall – The Cruel Fate of Jack Birchall. *A copy of his book may be purchased by writing to him at Des Guckian, Dromod, County Leitrim, Ireland.*

FRANCISCO DE CUELLAR

This story is about a Spaniard whose remarkable story of survival in Ireland in the late sixteenth century was penned by himself on his return to Spain. The letter he wrote came to light long after he died, and it is documented in many sources in Ireland. His original letter is now a treasured item in an academic archive in Madrid (and was viewed by this author in 2014).

When the great Spanish Armada set out to try to overthrow Elizabeth l of England in 1588, the plan was foiled by a combination of thwarted attacks, re-routing the return voyage to Spain of the 130 ships, storms in the North Sea and shipwrecks. More than twenty-four vessels were wrecked on the coasts of Ireland and altogether about fifty ships did not make it back to Spain.

When the storms off the north-west coast of Ireland struck the ships, some of the ships anchored close to the coast to try to sit out the worst. But the severe weather battered them and pushed many of them on to the rocks. Most of the occupants of the stricken ships were lost at sea and, for those who survived drowning, worse was yet to come. The local Irish, as well as the hundreds of locally-garrisoned English soldiers, wasted little time in massacring any survivors they laid their hands on. Bodies were stripped of wealth – many had gold coins sewn into their clothes and valuable jewellery round their necks.

In the most extraordinary of circumstances, verging on the completely miraculous, one particular sea captain survived the storm, survived several beatings and attacks from both native Irish and English troops, and even survived a second storm when he finally secured passage for the journey home on a ship that was headed for Antwerp. The reason all this is known now, with incredible accuracy, is that not only did the amazing survivor write down his awful adventure, but aspects of it were also passed down through both the oral and written sources of North West Ireland.

His name was Francisco de Cuellar and his name is very well-known in the areas around north Leitrim and Sligo where he found some refuge, even while his life continued to remain at great risk. De Cuellar was born in the mid-to-late 1500s. He was in the army that conquered Portugal in 1581, he sailed in the frigate, the *Santa Catalina*, to the Strait of Magellan and was in Brazil expelling French settlers.

Extraordinarily, he had been sentenced to death just before the storm struck for the crime of breaking out of formation. For whatever reason, the sentence was not carried out and, when the disastrous storms rose up, it was every man for himself. The ship he was on was driven on to Streedagh Strand off the north-west coast of the present County Sligo.

De Cuellar managed to escape the sinking ship and was advised by the scarce few helpful people he met to head for the castle of Brian O'Rourke of Breffni in the mountains of what is now north Leitrim, where some survivors were already in safe refuge. He stayed some time there, leaving once with a group of fellow sailors to try to get on board a ship that was still intact, but they failed to make the connection and many of the people he travelled with on that perilous journey to the ship were also murdered on the way.

He returned to O'Rourke's stronghold and remained there some time before moving on to the territory of the MacClancys, probably at Rosclogher near Lough Melvin. When news came of a huge army of English heading for MacClancy's castle, the Spaniards, including de Cuellar, offered to defend it whilst the Irish went into hiding. The courageous Spanish had nothing to lose but their lives and they had survived this far by the wiles of destiny.

The English besieged the castle for many days, until a snowstorm forced them to retreat. When the MacClancys returned, they were grateful beyond words and de Cuellar was offered MacClancy's daughter in marriage as a thank you. He declined and shortly afterwards, in the thick of winter, he and a group of Spaniards went on their way again. Some say they sneaked away from the castle, so as not to offend their host.

The next place of refuge was with the Bishop of Derry and a safe passage to Scotland was found for de Cuellar and other Spaniards who had arrived earlier in the north of Ireland. In Scotland, another long wait was necessary – this time of several months while he waited for the Duke of Parma to get him a safe passage to Flanders.

Within sight of the harbour a Dutch fire attack caused de Cuellar's ship to be lost and once again he survived by clinging on to wreckage, finally managing to complete his journey home. But de Cuellar's war services were far from over and to the end of his life he continued to be involved in siege after siege.

How and when he died is not known, nor if he had any children. It is likely that he died in the early 1600s.

Of his supporters in Ireland, O'Rourke was hanged in London in 1590 for treason, among his alleged crimes being his support of the Spanish survivors. MacClancy was captured in 1590 and beheaded.

Postscript

The original letter can be found in the Real Academia de la Historia (The Royal Academy of History) in Madrid: https://www.rah.es.

References to aspects of the story can be pieced together from several internet sources. Background notes and parts of the letter are in this online archive: https://celt.ucc.ie/published/T108200/index.html.

CAVAN

GARY BRANIGAN

BRICÍN THE SURGEON

Many people will be forgiven for thinking that brain surgery is a modern invention; I know I certainly did. There is no doubt that it will surprise a lot of people to learn that well over 1,000 years ago such procedures were being carried out in the present-day border parish of Tomregan, between the counties of Cavan and Fermanagh.

Located in the ancient kingdom of Bréifne, the area of Tuaim Dreacuin was a famous district of learning, having, as it did, an ancient university that contained three colleges within: one for Brehon Law, one for History and Poetry, and one for Classical Learning. Among its celebrated staff was a professor known as Bricín, a highly respected saint, a distinguished scholar, and an outstanding surgeon. His fame spread far and wide, and many came seeking advice and assistance for the various ailments they suffered from.

One day, Bricín was teaching in class when there was a great commotion outside. A carriage came thundering through the gateway and he could hear the panicked shouts of men saying, '*Cá bhfuil Bricín?* Where is Bricín?'

He came rushing out, asking, '*Cad é an fadhb?* What is the problem?'

Barely able to talk from exhaustion, the men were just able to utter, 'Battle … Uloira … hopelessly outnumbered …'. Bricín walked around and, looking into the carriage, immediately recognised Cennfaelad, one of the chieftains of Ulster. Cennfaelad was in a bad way, with a large axe protruding from the top of his head and blood streaming from the wound and running down his face. The prognosis was not a good one at all.

Bricín called to two of his students. 'Prepare the operating room,' said he, and to another two, he said, 'Take the chieftain and prepare him for surgery.' Bricín then went and washed his hands in the stream and collected some healing herbs that he needed for the operation.

Telling the soldiers that he must not be disturbed, he worked long and hard on Cennfaelad. First, he controlled the bleeding and then slowly and carefully removed the axe from his skull. It was only at this point that he was fully able to see the full extent of the damage. Bricín set about removing the damaged tissue with his specialised scalpel and repairing what remained with his other tools.

After two days straight, the surgery was completed. Bricín placed a thick layer of healing herbs over the wound and bandaged up Cennfaelad's head. He gave strict orders for the chieftain's undisturbed rest and convalescence at the university. During this time, Bricín tended to him day and night, and slowly Cennfaelad regained his strength and came out of his coma.

Save for a slight twitch in his left eye, Cennfaelad had fully recovered. His memory was completely restored and he was infinitely grateful for what Bricín had done for him. He developed a keen interest in studying at the three colleges of the university, and following through on this, went on to become one of its most distinguished scholars and poets. Cennfaelad produced three famous works, on law, Irish grammar and contemporary history.

ST PATRICK AND THE IDOL OF CROM CRUACH

I have long been fascinated by the Killycluggin stone, which sat between two rivers in the very historic and ancient place within the present-day County Cavan area known as Magh Slecht.

Magh Slecht loosely translates from the old tongue as 'Plain of Prostrations' and is believed to point to the area being a place of worship of the old gods and the old ways.

Although the original stone now sits in pieces in the excellent Cavan County Museum in Ballyjamesduff, there is a replica of how the stone may have looked set at the side of the road near Ballyconnell.

It is believed that this stone represented the pagan Crom Cruach, known as the Irish Sun God and the god of all gods. This fairly unassuming carved stone was covered in precious gold and silver and positioned in pride of place within a circle of twelve idols. It was worshipped by the native Irish.

The legend of Crom Cruach is a dark and sinister one. The ancient texts of the Metrical Dindshenchas claim that the people worshipped the god by offering up their firstborn child in return for a plentiful harvest in the coming year. The children were brutally killed by the established process of smashing their heads against the stone, which represented Crom Cruach, and their blood was sprinkled around the base.

One day on the eve of the new year festival of Samhain (forerunner to the present-day Hallowe'en), the High King Tigernmas had travelled with his court in procession from his royal seat at Tara to the idol of Crom Cruach at Magh Slecht in order to worship him. Whilst they were prostrating in deep devotion to their deity, their druids were preparing the sacrifices to be put to death.

St Patrick and his disciples were watching the proceedings from a nearby hill and just before the forced slaying of the innocent, he reached out the Bachal Isu, or staff of Christ, which miraculously reached from the neighbouring hill with such force that the Crom Cruach stone collapsed, falling forward with its head symbolically pointing towards Tara.

St Patrick then came down off the hill with his brethren and, taking a sledgehammer, smashed the stone, causing the Devil within to emerge with horrific growls and roars. St Patrick then struck his staff on the remaining rubble of the idol, and banished him to hell. The twelve idols surrounding Crom Cruach were then swallowed up by the earth.

The original Killycluggin stone in Cavan County Museum is in fact the same Crom Cruach, and its shattered appearance is testament to the pivotal role it played in the conversion of the local pagans.

MONAGHAN

STEVE LALLY

JOHN O'NEILL AND THE THREE DOGS

This is a fantastic tale from Monaghan collected from the 2005 Tydavnet Journal. *It is truly a spellbinding tale.*

A long time ago, near the mountains of Slieve Beagh (*Sliabh Beagh*) that straddle the border between County Monaghan and the counties of Fermanagh and Tyrone, there once lived a widow and her only son John. They lived on the Monaghan side of the mountain and were very poor and knew not what to do to keep themselves from starving.

They really didn't want to sell their only faithful cow, but they knew that if they were to stay alive, they would have to.

On the fair day, John set out with his cow before him.

When he reached the town, he met a man with three dogs.

'How much do you want for the cow?' John was asked.

'Twenty pounds,' said John.

'I can give you something worth much more than that,' was the reply.

'What is it?' asked John.

'My three dogs,' replied the man.

'And what use would your dogs be to me?' said John.

'Well,' was the reply, 'here is Speed. He can run so fast that nothing can catch him. Not even the wind can move so fast. Then there is Guess. He can tell you what you are thinking and inform you of future events. And this here dog is Strength. He is so strong that nothing can resist him. He is so strong that he can snap iron bars with a stroke of his paw.'

John stood in amazement.

'And now,' said the man, 'isn't that a fair exchange for your cow?'

John agreed without hesitation and they separated, one with the cow and the other with the three beautiful dogs. John now felt that he could not, without the cow or the money, return home to his mother, so he was determined to set out and seek his fortune.

With his three beautiful dogs in tow, he headed towards a forest. It was a cold winter's evening and darkness was about to fall like a black sheet over him and his dogs. John reached the forest and found shelter under some tall trees. He thought about having a wee sit-down, but in the distance he saw a light flicker in a castle, so he followed the light.

He made his way to the door of the castle and knocked. He could hear heavy footsteps approaching. The door swung open and all he could hear in a huge bellowing voice was, 'Who is there?' He was terrified because what he saw was the stuff of nightmares. Before him was a giant, a huge figure that made poor John freeze on the spot. He could feel the dogs pulling on the leads, trying to make their escape. He explained to the giant that he was tired and needed a room for the night.

The giant said, 'Yes, you can come in because you will taste delicious as breakfast in the morning.'

John continued to walk in, followed by his dogs. The dogs somehow made him feel protected.

The giant said, 'Where do you think you are going with those?'

He demanded that John leave them outside, but John said he would not enter without them.

The giant was angry, but when he heard a snarl from Strength, he soon changed his tune and said he could bring them in.

The giant, John and the dogs entered the dining room and began to eat the feast before them. John was delighted and, being a poor boy, he would never have seen such beautiful food and treats. John demanded that the dogs be fed at the table. The giant said they could be fed outdoors, but again he changed his mind after John persisted.

After they had eaten, John said he needed to rest and asked the giant if he could be brought to his room. The giant said yes, but he said he would need to put the dogs outside first. John again demanded that the dogs be treated exactly as he was.

The giant gave in to his wish once again. They entered the most luxurious room John had ever seen. He climbed up on the big bed and up jumped the dogs behind him. One at his head, one at his side and one at his feet.

John and the dogs had a peaceful night's sleep and awoke refreshed and ready for the off. The giant asked John if he would like a tour of the castle before he went. The giant said that if he agreed, he would need to tie his dogs up first. John agreed this time and he left the dogs behind to go and look around the castle. The castle was magnificent and John was so impressed.

When they had almost finished the tour, the giant turned to John and said, 'You have seen all of my rooms but two. One is private and you cannot enter, and the other you can. Come and you can have a look.'

The giant opened the door and what John saw filled him with deep terror. Right in the middle of the floor was a huge block covered with blood and an axe beside it on the floor. On the walls hung the bodies of dead men.

'What do you think of this?' asked the giant. 'I am sick of your cheek and demands. This is where it ends. You will join these men very soon.'

He smiled at John and said, 'Kneel down, sir, and I will cut your head off. I don't think you will miss it as it's nearly useless.'

John asked to be left alone for a few minutes so he could come to terms with what was about to happen and the giant agreed. When the giant returned, John lay down and the giant cut his head off.

John was buried the next day. Guess, the dog, caught wind of what was going on and said to the other two dogs, 'Do you know what happened to our master?'

'No,' they said.

'Well, the giant cut his head off and now they are on their way to bury him.'

Guess told the other two dogs that there was an enchanted well in the forest that had healing powers and if they got to it, the healing water would be able to restore their master to life.

Strength hurled himself against the cage that the three dogs were locked inside and, without exerting much effort, the three dogs were set free. Off to the forest they went in search of the healing well. They found the well and Speed immersed himself in the water and ran back to the castle as fast as he could.

By this stage, the procession had reached the graveyard. Just as they were about to lower John into the ground, Speed came out of the forest as quick as a flash.

The dog said, 'Open the coffin so I can see my master one last time.'

The giant said it was too late to do that. The gravediggers lowered him into the ground and began to cover the coffin in clay. Just then, out from the forest came Strength. He seized the giant by the neck and demanded that they open the coffin. The men did what the dog said and opened the coffin. Speed jumped in and rubbed himself all over the wound on John's neck. Guess entered the coffin and did likewise. Lastly, Strength jumped in and because his coat was shaggy and held more water, he rubbed his master's neck as best he could and to everyone's amazement John woke up and got out of the coffin.

John demanded that the giant walk back to the castle and take him to that horrible room with the dead bodies hanging on the wall. He told him to kneel down so he could cut his head off. The giant agreed, but said that he hoped he would allow him to have one last request. He asked if he could enter the private room and John agreed.

After a short time, the giant returned and kneeled down and allowed John to cut his head off. The giant was buried the next day in the grave that had been meant for John.

John was anxious to know what was in the private room. When he entered, he was surprised to see a beautiful girl sitting in an armchair. He looked at her and asked her why she was there. She told John that she was a princess and that one day while she was out in the forest a thick black fog had descended. She said that when the fog had lifted, she had no idea where she was. She was lost and on her own and frightened. The giant captured her and brought her back to the castle. He kept asking her to marry him, but she wouldn't and kept telling the giant to let her go home.

John asked her what the giant had asked her when he entered the room. The girl said that the giant told her about the enchanted well that could bring people back to life. She also told him that the giant said he was going to be beheaded and that she was to go to the healing well, fetch some water and bring him back to life. She reassured John that she was not going to do such a thing and that she couldn't care less about what came of him as long as she was free.

John asked the princess what she wished to do now.

She replied, 'I would like to go back to my people.'

So the next morning, John instructed Guess to help guide them back to where the princess belonged. Together with the other two dogs, Strength and Speed, they made their way to where the princess had once dwelled. The journey was long.

When they reached their destination and said their goodbyes, John took one last look at the beautiful princess and then embarked upon the long journey back to the giant's castle, which he now took for his own.

Some time passed, until one morning Guess spoke to John and said, 'Do you remember the princess?'

John replied, 'Yes, how could I forget her?'

Guess told him that she was in terrible danger, that a ferocious lion was going to come down from the mountain and devour her unless they saved her. Guess went on to tell him that the butler from her castle promised that he would save her (because she had promised to marry her rescuer), but he would not because when the day came he would be too cowardly and he would let her be killed.

On the day the lion was to appear, John and the three dogs made their way to where the princess dwelled. When they eventually arrived, there were droves of people gathered outside to witness the happenings.

The princess was sitting next to the butler, waiting on the lion, and John and the dogs could tell from her face that she was terribly shaken and frightened.

The butler did not have an air of confidence, as expected. He looked far more afraid than the princess herself.

Just then the lion came from the mountain. He meant business. His jaws were wide open, ready to attack, and his eyes were firmly set on his prize. The crowds gasped in sheer fright and terror at what was about to happen.

When the lion pounced on his prey, the butler ran away and hid. Strength leapt up onto the lion and caught him by the throat. With one bite, he killed the lion and the creature fell dead on the ground. The crowd gasped once again, this time with utter relief for finally the princess was free. Just as the lion fell to the ground, the butler appeared again and stuck his sword into the lion, claiming that he was the one who had killed him. His intention was to make it look like he was the hero, so he would be the lucky man to marry the princess. As the princess had fainted with fright when the lion had pounced, she could not tell who had saved her and so the date for the marriage was set.

She did not love the butler, but accepted that it had been him who had rescued her and so she felt that she had no choice but to take his hand in marriage.

The wedding day arrived and this time the crowd was full of laughter and joy. Even John and the three dogs were present, but John stayed at a distance, for his heart was sad and low. He was about to witness the woman he was falling in love with marrying another man, knowing he was not the right person for her.

Just before the marriage, the princess was thinking and happened to look out of her window. Strength was sitting outside. His presence brought everything back to her and she was able to fill in the gaps and remember exactly what had happened on the day she had been rescued. She remembered the lion, the butler running away and the dog stepping in. So the princess demanded that she marry the owner of the dog and not the butler, who had pretended to be brave. What use was a man who pretended to be a hero? Anyway, she did not love him, so her heart was not true.

The butler, still lying, protested that he *was* the man who had rescued the princess, but Strength held him tight until he finally told the truth.

John and the princess married that very day and they lived happily ever after in the castle.

One day, while John and the three dogs were walking through the forest, they came by a block with an axe.

Strength said to John, 'Cut my head off.'

John was shocked and refused.

The dog said, 'If you don't, I will cut yours off.'

John said, 'I would rather that than have to kill you.'

Just as Strength was about to kill John, Guess stepped in and put his paw on John's neck. Guess told John to arise and do as Strength commanded. He told him not to be afraid and said that he would be surprised by what would happen. Strength knelt down and put his head on the block and, with closed eyes and a heavy heart, John cut the head off one of his most faithful friends.

When John opened his eyes, he saw that Strength had turned into a beautiful prince. He commanded John to cut the heads off the other two dogs, Guess and Speed. John did what he was told and they, too, turned into beautiful princes.

John gasped in astonishment.

They then told John the full story. They had been subjected to magic by the ghastly giant and taken away from their father, who was the King of Oriel. They told him how they wished to return to their father. They thanked John for his friendship and loyalty and for never giving up on them. They waved him and his new wife a sorrowful goodbye and off they set in the direction of Slieve Beagh. They were never seen again. But they say that on moonlit nights you can hear the sound of howling from the three dogs carried on the night wind.

THE WILDE SISTERS

This is a well-known story from County Monaghan about the tragic lives of Oscar Wilde's two half-sisters.

This is the heartfelt inscription on the gravestone that was erected for the half-sisters of Oscar Wilde, who lost their young lives tragically in a fire in County Monaghan in 1871.

You can visit this grave, if you wish. Just a short distance south-west of Monaghan town, on the road to Clones, there is a signpost which reads 'Drumsnatt Church of Ireland'. To the rear of this small country church is the grave where the two sisters were laid to rest a long, long time ago.

The sisters in question, who lost their lives in a fire in a nearby manor house, were the half-sisters of the Irish poet, novelist and dramatist, Oscar Wilde, who was born in Dublin in 1854. Oscar was only 18 when his half-sisters died, but loss and heartache were already known to him. Five years before the tragic event, when Oscar was just 12, he had lost his younger sister Isola, who died at only 10 years of age, after a bout of fever, at the home of her aunt, Margaret Nobel, in Edgeworthstown, County Longford.

Isola's death had a traumatic effect on Oscar Wilde and he was said to have been inconsolable for months afterwards. When he died in 1900, his possessions included an envelope containing some strands of his beloved sister Isola's hair, with the inscription 'My Isola's Hair' penned on the envelope.

Oscar had just gone to Trinity when his two half-sisters died and it is said that his grief was not at all on the same scale as when his younger sister passed away. This is most likely because he knew them less since the girls were only his half-sisters. Some sources argue that Oscar may not have known them at all, because Emily and Mary may have been kept secret.

They shared the same father – Sir William Wilde of Dublin. Despite the fact, however, that their father attended their funeral, it is believed that he was terribly grief-stricken and heartsick, having to bury two more of his children.

The *Northern Standard* was the only paper in the area to report the tragedy, in a brief obituary in its 25 November 1871 issue. Their deaths had been discreetly kept from the Dublin press. The *Northern Standard* reported that Mary died on 8 November and that 'Emma', by which name Emily was better known, died on the 21 November. Normally something so tragic would have been more widely publicised, but it was obviously kept under wraps to preserve Sir William's reputation.

According to Julian Hanna (2015), in his essay 'Death by Fire: The Secret of the Wilde Sisters' in the online magazine *Numéro Cinq*, the first published account of the story appeared in a biography of William Wilde by T.G. Wilson in 1942.

Emily and Mary Wilde were living in County Monaghan and were being looked after by a relative, a Revd Ralph Wilde, rector of St Molua's, Drumsnat, who was the brother of their father.

The night of the fire was Halloween night. A party had been arranged to celebrate All Hallow's Eve, or *Samhain* in Ireland, and because the girls were popular with the local people, they were invited to a ball in a manor house called Drumaconnor House. The man who owned the house was Mr Andrew Reed, a local bank manager. This house still exists and is still known by the same name. Currently it serves as a B&B, just off the Monaghan–Clones road.

After the other guests had gone home, the two girls remained for a while longer and a gentleman took one of them for a final dance around the floor (it is said that the gentleman was Mr Andrew Reid, the host of the party), but as they glided past the open fireplace, her crinoline caught fire. Her sister ran to her rescue and in the hysteria her sister's dress also caught fire. Those in attendance tried to smother the flames by wrapping garments around both girls and some stories say that those who remained at the ball carried the girls out and rolled them in the snow.

Local historian Eamonn Mulligan, co-author of '*The Replay*': *A Parish History* (a history of the parish of Kilmore and Drumsnat, published in 1984), explained that in their efforts to conceal the whole tragic episode and to shield the person of Sir William from further adverse publicity, the family name of the Wilde sisters was actually altered to read 'Wylie' in several later reports, particularly in two reports written by the coroner for the county, Mr Alexander C. Waddell, who was clearly influenced by the stern request from Sir William Wilde that no inquest be held. Instead, an inquiry was held, to be followed by a second inquiry, but no inquest. Both of the coroner's reports are quoted in full by one of County Monaghan's leading historians, Mr Theo McMahon, in the 2003 edition of *Clogher Record*, of which Theo was editor of several years. The second of the two reports is somewhat similar in content to the first. It reads as follows:

> On Wednesday 22nd November 1871 the death of Miss M Wylie, daughter of Sir William Wylie, was reported to me as resulting from very serious injuries caused by her clothes accidentally catching fire from those of her sister Miss L Wylie on the night of 31st October in the house of Mr Reed of Drumaconnor. In accordance with the report I attended the residence of Mr Reed where she had been an invalid since the painful occurrence. From all the circumstances of the case, same as those attendant on the death

> of her sister, I did not consider anything further necessary than a careful inquiry into the facts, which showed that everything possible was done to preserve the life of the deceased.

Crinoline dresses were fashionable during that period and they caused the deaths of many young women. It is easy to imagine how the tragedy occurred. So simple: in moments, the atmosphere would have changed and panic would have set in. It is also easy to understand why her sister ran to help. Her kindness and selflessness caused her to die also.

The crinoline is a woman's large petticoat that has come in and out of fashion since the early nineteenth century. The original garment was made from very stiff horsehair fabric that kept the fashionable hoop skirts of the 1800s in their proper position.

In 1864, the *New York Times* reported that almost 40,000 women throughout the world had died because of crinoline fires. I read about how dangerous crinoline was in an article on the *Vintage News* website (2016):

> As fashionable as the crinoline was, it became one of the most dangerous articles of clothing ever known. It was highly flammable, any women who witnessed the flames were unable to help for fear of their own skirts catching fire. It is reported that in Philadelphia, nine ballerinas were killed when one brushed by a candle at the Continental Theater.

The deaths of Emily and Mary are still very much spoken about among the people of Kilmore/Drumsnatt parish and the people are extremely grateful to Eamonn Mulligan and Father Brian McCluskey, co-authors of '*The Replay*', and to leading historian Theo McMahon for researching the subject in such depth as their work will help keep the story alive for future generations of folklorists and historians in north Monaghan and beyond.

Julian Hanna states that the aftermath of the tragedy was, if possible, even more gruesome than the terrible accident itself. He is of the opinion that to die on Halloween night would have been merciful: instead, the young women lingered on for days and weeks at

Drumaconnor. He goes on to say that the sisters remained in the house, as was the custom at the time, where they were treated for the severe burns they had both suffered. Mary, the younger sister who had tried to help, died first, on 9 November. Her death was kept a secret from Emily, who was also near death, to spare her the shock; nevertheless, three weeks after the accident, on 21 November, Emily also died.

Hanna writes about the local legend of the 'woman in black' – thought to be the girls' mother – who visited the graves regularly for twenty years after the tragedy. I have heard this from several people in Monaghan. Oscar Wilde also used to tell the story of a woman in black. Wilde, who was still a teenager at the time, recalled an unknown woman's visits to his house during his father's last illness. The woman would come into the house and kneel by William's sickbed, while Oscar's mother stood by, watching without interfering, apparently aware that her husband and the woman, who shared a tragic bond, had loved each other deeply.

I heard from one source that the 'woman in black' would travel by train from Dublin to Monaghan and make her way to the girls' grave, say a prayer and return to Dublin. It is said that she wore a black veil and would not speak if approached by someone.

MAYO

TONY LOCKE

AN GORTA MÓR

Ireland has suffered the devastating effects of famine many times during her history. The Great Famine, or *An Gorta Mór*, is the most important event in modern Irish history and the actions of the government of the day compounded its effects. The failure of the potato crop was unprecedented and led to the deaths of more than 1.5 million people and mass emigration on a scale never seen before or since. It was a time that most Irish people rarely talk about. Some remember it as a famine; however, others still refer to it as 'The Great Starvation' for when there is food enough to export there should be no famine.

God sent a curse upon the land because her sons were slaves.
The rich earth brought forth rottenness, and gardens became graves,
The green crops withered in the fields, all blackened by the curse,
And wedding gay and dance gave way to coffin and to hearse.

(Anon., 1849)

FÉAR GORTACH

'*Féar gortach*' means 'hungry grass'. This is a patch of dead grass that pops up where someone has died violently, according to some, while others say it happens where someone has died of hunger specifically. There are those who suggest that it's a spot where a corpse has lain on the way to its final resting place, or even where they still lie, covered by grass, a reminder of the famine. There are even those who say that it may be a fairy curse. Whatever the reason, the grass becomes a predator.

Have you ever been walking down a green grassy *bóithrín* (the Irish term for a small road with room for one cow) on a bright sunny day when you were suddenly overtaken by a hunger so strong you almost passed out? Believe me, it's happened and a good Irishman would immediately know why and what to do. Anyone who walks or passes over the *féar gortach* in Irish, will suddenly become hungry beyond reason, even if they have just been well fed. Those who live near patches of such grass have been known to keep extra food on hand in the case of afflicted travellers knocking on their door. No other side effects are known.

Sometimes you might even hear some of the older folk say, 'The *féar gortach* is on me', meaning they are feeling very hungry. When we were young children we were told to always have a biscuit or a piece of bread in our pockets when going out for a walk just in case the *féar gortach* came on us. However, if you didn't have a biscuit you could always suck on a shoelace.

As an adult when I visit somewhere like the famine village over in Achill, I place a piece of bread and pour a little of what I have to drink onto the ground as an offering to the spirits of the place.

THE *FEAR GORTA*

When we were children we were told the story of the *Fear Gorta* or the 'Man of Hunger'. He was a tall thin man dressed in black, raggedy clothes. He travelled around County Mayo, going from place to place, village to village and town to town during times of famine. It was said that when he knocked on your door you had to welcome him as you would a stranger and offer him a little food and drink even though food was extremely hard to come by during the famine. For this reason many would hide behind closed doors, some would deny him any food or drink and some would even chase him from the door. For these people there would be no hope; they had sealed their fate – death by starvation.

Those who spared a small piece of potato or a drop of milk, even if that was all the family had, or those who genuinely had nothing except the offer of a welcome hand would be thanked by the *Fear Gorta* for their generosity. He would then politely refuse their offer and take his leave of them. However, before he left he would say, 'Because of your generosity and your honest welcome today you will be truly blessed. Neither you nor your family will ever die of the hunger. Tell no others of what has passed here but from this day forth your pot will never be empty, your jug will never run dry.' In the morning the woman of the house would go to the pot, where she would find a great big potato, more than enough to feed the whole family, and a jug that was brimming over with fresh, creamy milk. It would be the same each morning and the family would survive the famine.

Ireland has traditionally been known as the 'land of a thousand welcomes'; however, I wonder how many of us would welcome a stranger to our door today with an offer of a hot meal and a warm drink?

THE WHITE TROUT OF CONG

About 2 miles west of the village of Cong in County Mayo there is a cave known as 'The Pigeon Hole', or 'Poll na gColum' in Irish. A popular destination for tourists and walkers, the cave can be accessed by a steep flight of limestone steps. Once inside the cave, you will be struck by its size and the river running through it, which at times can be mistaken for the cry of the banshee. The walls are covered with bushes and ivy and this is where the pigeons nest, which is what gave the cave its name. In Irish folklore, the Pigeon Hole is the home of 'The White Trout' or 'The Fairy Fish', which avoids bait and evades capture.

The legend of the 'fairy trout' concerns two young lovers who were engaged to be married. One night the young man was ambushed and murdered and his body was thrown into the nearby lake. The young girl was heartbroken because he meant the world to her and she fell into a deep depression, slowly pining away. Eventually she wandered off and was never seen again; some say she was taken by the fairies. Shortly after her disappearance, a white trout appeared in the local lake. People had never seen such an unusual fish and soon rumours began to spread about the fairy fish. In Ireland, the belief in fairies was very strong and superstition was rife, so the fairy fish was given the greatest respect because it wouldn't do to upset the 'little people', as the fairy folk were called.

As the years passed, the people never bothered the trout and it lived quite happily, doing whatever it is that fish do. One day, a soldier heard the story of the white trout and decided to catch and eat it. Eventually he caught the fish and took it back to his house, where he attempted to cook it. He soon realised that this was no ordinary fish; no matter what he did, it just would not cook. He flipped it from side to side and tossed it over and over in the frying pan but to no avail. The soldier wasn't going to be beaten by a fish, so he decided to eat it anyway. He put it onto a plate and just as his knife touched the skin of the fish, it let out a scream, jumped of the plate and fell to the floor.

The soldier stood, mouth agape, as the fish transformed into a beautiful young women. Holding out her arm, she pointed to where the soldier's knife had cut her skin. She spoke to him and told him that she was waiting for her one true love to return. She demanded that he give up his evil ways and return her to the lake. The soldier was shocked and, shaking with fright, he told the woman that he was very sorry and that he would renounce his wicked ways, but how could he take a beautiful woman back to a lake and just throw her in? The woman then told him that she would transform back into a fish and that he could take her to the underground river within the Pigeon Hole because the river fed the local lake, so no one would see him and he would be safe. She then transformed back into a white trout. The soldier quickly picked her up, ran to the Pigeon Hole and placed her in the river. As soon as she entered the water it turned blood red for a moment as the cut on her skin quickly healed.

It is said that to this day at certain times you may see a white trout swimming in the lake or the river deep within the Pigeon Hole. Look closely and you will see a red mark upon its side. Some people say it's the mark of a knife cut and some say it's where she was burned in the soldier's frying pan. As for the soldier, well, he changed his ways and never ate fish again.

SLIGO

JOE MCGOWAN

THE SHIP-SINKING WITCH

Fishing was poor along the Sligo coast when news reached there of great catches of herring across the bay in Bruckless, County Donegal. This was the nineteenth century and there was no dole then, or State subsidy; you got nothing for nothing. Fishermen had small plots of land, where they grew their own food, but they still needed cash to pay the landlord and to buy the few essentials that could not be grown: tea, sugar, tobacco, flour.

It was usual for seafaring men to take great risks: it went with the occupation. It wasn't that there was any such thing as choice in employment. There were no jobs. You took a penny where you got it. Craft were frail, equipment patched and barely serviceable. Bruckless was a long way from home, but the men made their boats and nets ready, said goodbye to their families, and set sail.

When the Mullaghmore men got to Donegal, the herring fishing was as good as they had hoped. The weather was fine and they worked all through the night, landing their catch in the mornings. Each day, an old woman came and asked the men for herring. They knew her as Biddy. She had very little money, but gave whatever few pence she could. When she had no money left, however, the Donegal fishermen refused to give her any more fish.

But it was not because they were miserly. Fishermen worked close to nature and the primal elements. They held the sea in reverence and fear. Care was taken not to offend spirits that, although unseen, were ever watchful. Taboos were rigidly observed: to stick a knife in the boat's 'taft' or mast invited bad luck; meeting a red-haired woman on the way to a fishing trip was an evil omen; bread went unbuttered for fear of bringing misfortune; whistling was forbidden as it 'whistled up the wind': 'there'd be "a bad smell off ye" if ye whistled in a boat. Ye could play music or sing, but there'd be no whistling'.

To give goods away without receiving anything in return, they believed, was to 'give away your luck'. There was no question of taking a chance with such things. Luck, good or bad, meant success or failure, poverty or survival; the belief ran deep in the orthodoxy of rural communities. In their life's cycle many forces, mysterious and unpredictable, sinister and benign, were at work. Customs, pagan or Christian, endorsed by generations of experience, were sacrosanct. They protected against evil and the unknown. No, they couldn't just give the fish away; they had to get something in exchange.

Any small amount would do, but the poor woman had nothing. Nothing at all. Evening after evening she came to the boats and each time she was turned away. Eventually she was given fish by the crew of a Streedagh, County Sligo boat, who took pity on her. Taking the gift, she went off up the road, threatening those that refused her that they would have cause to remember their meanness. There would be a story to be told soon, she threatened.

The Streedagh fishermen lodged in the same house as the Donegal men. When they went out to shoot their nets the next evening, a Donegal boatman unintentionally donned a sweater belonging to a man named Bruen from Streedagh, County Sligo: a happy mistake that would later save his life.

The next day, Friday 12 February 1813, started just like any other day. A rosy dawn broke bright and clear over the Bluestack Mountains and Barnes Gap as the fishing fleet finished their night's work. Preparing for her revenge, the old woman watched from a cabin window on a hill overlooking the bay. She filled a milk pan with water and, placing a wooden bowl to float on it, she asked her daughter to keep watch from the window and tell her what she observed. Staring at the pan with a fierce concentration, the old woman splashed the water about in the vessel, causing the bowl to dance about.

'What do you see?' she asked the girl.

'Oh, a breeze has sprung up, mother,' she replied.

The old woman continued to agitate the water. 'What do you see now?' she asked.

'The breeze has turned into a gale,' the daughter replied. 'The men are reefing the sails. The boats are in big trouble.'

The witch, for that is what villagers later claimed she was, continued to cast her spell while questioning her daughter: 'What do you see now? Are they still afloat?'

'Yes, mother, but some have sunk and others are trying to make it to land.'

She continued to dash the water about in the pan until the girl told her mother that she could no longer see the boats. Crying out in delight, Biddy ceased her stirring. The storm abated but the fleet was completely wrecked. Some were swamped at sea, while others were driven ashore and broken to matchwood on the rocks. The old woman's words had come true. Most of the Donegal boats were lost and their crews drowned – except for the man who was wearing the Streedagh man's jumper. He came safe from the old woman's curse and lived to tell the story.

It's a remarkable tale, but is it true? Newspapers of the day do indeed carry accounts of the tragedy. It happened at Bruckless, County Donegal on 12 February, 1813. According to these reports, no accurate estimate of casualties is known. The approximation of forty-five men drowned, leaving 'thirty widows and one hundred and two orphans,' is regarded as conservative.

What caused the sinking? Was it a natural disaster, a vindictive act precipitated by the old woman's curse, or a mere coincidence? Who can say? We do know that tales of ship-sinking witches are nothing new. Approximately 1,500 years ago, the Greek play *Alexander Romance* described a similar ship-sinking rite performed by the Egyptian pharaoh Nectanebus. Perhaps this was a secret formula handed down from the ancients; a practice, like so many others, that is now lost.

When news of the Bruckless drowning reached Mullaghmore, families feared the worst. Villagers lined the shore, anxiously scanning the sea for sight of the absent boat. They lit fires on the cliffs at night to guide the fishermen home. Hoping against hope that their men would return, they prayed for a miracle but steeled themselves for a tragedy.

We can only imagine the jubilation of the watchers when word eventually went out that the Mullagh boat was sighted beating against the wind and waves as she made her way home. Hard pressed and storm driven, the crew couldn't make it to the harbour and were forced instead to head for shelter. They beached their craft at *Trágh Ghearr*, south-west of the peninsula under where Classiebawn Castle now stands.

Watchers lining the shore counted seven men on the boat as she sped along the coast behind the hill known as *Cnoc na Taoisigh*. They were relieved to see that everyone was safe, but surprised to see a woman sitting at the helm, alongside the skipper on the 'stern taft'. This created something of a stir. Maybe one of the men had met a woman over there and there might be a wedding in the offing! When they went to help the fishermen draw their boat to safety, they found only seven men, but no woman. The fishermen shook their heads when they were asked about the stranger on board. No, there were only seven men on the boat at any time. There must be some mistake. No, there was no woman. The enquirers shook their heads in disbelief. Sure hadn't the whole village seen her clearly with their own eyes as the boat went by the headland?

Following the incident, villagers discussing the strange visitation speculated that the woman they had seen in the boat was the spirit of a dead relation, guiding the fishermen safely home from the drowning tragedy – or perhaps a woman of the *sidhe*, who took the boat and crew under her protection.

The mystery of the extra passenger has not been resolved to this day. The individuals who witnessed the incident are long dead, the details barnacled and dimmed with time. The story itself barely survived. It was passed on by the recollection of one old man of the village; passed on faintly through a fortuitous 'echo-harbouring shell' of memory.

The story has another curious twist. Some time after this extraordinary deliverance, the fishermen and their relations made a pilgrimage to a place known locally as *Dostann na Bríona* near Classiebawn Castle. There they left a 'wee crockery jar of whiskey' as an offering and a thanksgiving. Why? To the uninitiated, *Dostann na Bríona* looks like nothing more than a hilly outcrop. To whom or what, then, was the offering made? There was no church there, nor even a ruin, so we can be certain it was to no Christian god!

'People used to go to the Fairy Rock, or *Dostann na Bríona* as some call it, for lots of reasons with bottles of whiskey and *poitín*,' Thomas, an old man of the village, once told me.

It was a regular thing, long ago. The offering was left at a small round hole at the top of the rock in thanksgiving for a blessing or at set times like Hallowe'en. They used to pour the whiskey on the ground or break the bottle and let the liquid soak into the soil. Whatever the reason it was done it's an enchanted place. Anyone'll tell you that! There was this fella one time brought a bottle of *poitín* up and he was having second thoughts about pouring it out. Begod wasn't it knocked out of his hand before he could think!

Quare things happened there. There was this fella one time delivering a keg of *poitín* to Classiebawn. 'Twas a nice day and he was taking his time. When he was going up past the Fairy Rock, he sauntered over to the door to have a close look at it. He got an awful hop when he heard a voice saying to him, 'Pssshth! Give us a drop of what you have with you there.'

He jumped back and made for Classiebawn as quick as he could. Before he got to the top of the avenue, the keg fell and smashed on the ground.

As it spilled on the ground, he swore he heard a laugh and a voice saying, 'Good enough for him!'

Thomas took a long pull out of his pipe. Looking at me thoughtfully for a minute, he ventured an opinion: 'Don't ye think he'd be as well if he had to take the cork off it and give them a taste? I'm thinking if he had, he'd still have had the *poitín*!'

SODEN'S GHOST

Old fishermen seemed to have an endless supply of stories from times past. One of these was often told by Jamesy Charlie Gallagher about the ghost of the landlord and priest-hunter Soden from Moneygold. He recalled how a demon spectre had wrought great mischief when the Mullaghmore boats were out fishing herring at night. He and his fireside listeners marvelled at the priest who, following appeals from the frustrated fishermen, banished the devilish presence to Bomore Island's bleak and barren rock.

Soden had gone raving mad following a confrontation with the local curate, a Fr Rynne, following which 'he ate his own flesh and nothing could be done with him'. Jamesy explained:

> The priest was saying Mass above along the river there at Grange, near where the Tech is now. Soden was the landlord in Grange; he was living where Kilfeather's shop is now. Someone informed on the priest, as there was a price of £5 on their head then, that there was a crowd of them saying mass up at the Mass Rock. Soden sent the yeomen out right away, arrested the priest and brought him down. I heard me father at that hundreds of times, that oul' history. When he tried to sign the warrant to execute the priest he wasn't fit, he went clane mad, the priest was never executed.

Following Soden's descent into insanity he was locked in a disused Revenue Police barracks in Grange, County Sligo. Later known as Lang's Shed, it had barred windows and doors but was demolished around 2004 to make way for a new housing estate. The Loughlin family from nearby Caiseal, charged with his care, fed him his meals through the bars. Because of his violent nature, his food was delivered at the end of a pitchfork. Once a week they tied him to a lone blackthorn tree in a nearby field, 'in order to scrape the lice off him'. The tree still stands.

Soden lived for about a year after the incident. Following his death, reports went out of a 'huge black dog with fire coming out of his mouth' seen at Hood's Gate near Soden's property. At night, people went around by the fields rather than pass the spot. In the daytime, passers-by hung rosary beads on the handlebar of their bicycles for protection. Horses pulling sidecars or traps reared up and stood trembling when they came to the haunted spot. It happened to the O'Connors of Moneygold, but thankfully Mrs O'Connor had the presence of mind to say a prayer: 'Go on, in the name of God', she said to the horse, upon which the horse calmed down and went ahead.

Locals called on Fr Rynne to do something about the spectre, upon which he exorcised the unquiet spirit to the open sea a few miles away. The phantom dog disappeared following Fr Rynne's intervention – but that wasn't the end of it. The following winter fishermen from Mullaghmore went to the priest with a strange story. Something – they believed it was Soden again – was interfering with their nets and tangling them as they fished herring at night. Could he do something to help them?

The priest went to the seashore and, performing the exorcism again, banished the tormented and tormenting demon to the bleak and barren Bomore Rock, 10 miles out to sea. Legend has it that his ghost still resides there but is allowed to return to the mainland once every seven years.

There are those who will testify that they have witnessed the homecoming. On a calm summer's day, with no living thing to be seen, or enough wind to stir a leaf, they have heard noises like 'a herd of elephants or horses' crashing through the woods on the old Soden estate. They believe it was caused by the phantom landlord making his way to his old haunts from where he was originally banished.

'A ghost is compelled to obey the commands of the living', W.B. Yeats once wrote. 'The stable boy up at Mrs. G----'s there met the master going round the yards after he had been two days dead,' an old countryman told him. The lad said, 'be away to the lighthouse, and haunt that; and there he is far out to sea still, sir. Mrs. G---- was quite wild about it and dismissed the boy.'

For those who felt they had been wronged, the placing of a curse on their oppressor was the only resort left to the persecuted of those harsh times. There are many examples of harm coming to tyrants by mysterious means; in this instance, the priest was the avenging agent.

According to a recent report in the *Irish Times*, exorcisms are still performed today and, furthermore, the Catholic Church is introducing new rites for expelling demons. An exorcism is a ceremony of prayers in which a priest, with the approval of a bishop, casts out an evil spirit, calling on it aloud to leave a person or place. Speaking from Rome, Cardinal Jorge Arturo Estavez confirmed the modernisation, affirming that, 'demons are fallen angels as a result of their sin, and they are spiritual beings with great intelligence and power.'

Father Malachai Brendan Martin, author and priest, stated that, 'Exorcisms can be extremely violent. I have seen objects hurled around rooms by the powers of evil. I have smelt the breath of Satan and heard the demon's voices – cold, scratchy, dead voices carrying messages of hatred'.

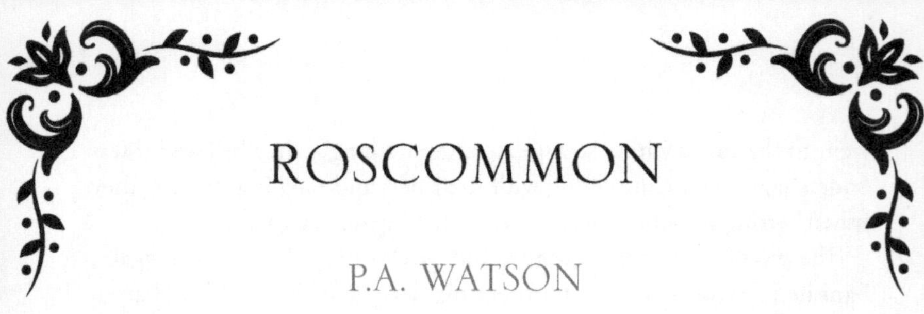

ROSCOMMON

P.A. WATSON

THE PRICE OF A PRIEST

A whistling woman or a crowing hen calls the Devil out of his den, and everybody knew that hearing either a whistling woman or a crowing hen indicated serious trouble for the family concerned. But if both happened at the same time, that could only mean catastrophe for the family or indeed, for the whole village.

Mary Dolan seemed to be a normal little girl growing up but just when she turned sixteen she started whistling well-known tunes. As they were getting ready for pre-dawn Mass at the rock, Peg, her mother, heard her one morning; she was crestfallen. She blessed herself with holy water, she sprinkled and blessed the girl and then attacked a surprised Mary verbally, in a vicious way that Mary never thought her mother was capable of.

'What harm is it?' she asked in all innocence.

'What harm is it?' said her fuming mother as she sprinkled more holy water. 'Your father must be turning in his grave. It's the devil, that's what it is and it will bring bad luck on you and all the family, so don't ever dare do it again.' Mary said she meant no harm; it was only a bit of sport but if it bothers that much she would not do it again. The mother was doubtful; she had seen this malady and its consequences before but she never thought it would come to her own child. Then she heard it, a strange weird off-key sort of crowing sound. It was not an ordinary 'cock-a-doodle-doodle-do' but more of a 'cock-a-draca-doodle-dy'. Her heart jumped, she turned snow-white, she broke into a cold sweat, it couldn't be but it was, a crowing hen. This and the whistler!

'We're doomed,' she cried. Peg looked out to see where the accursed hen was. She was standing on one of the two cut-stone peers that her son Matt had recently erected. She told him he should never have taken the stones from that bloody Norman Castle. There was never anything there only mayhem, murder, disease, devastation, destruction, and fierce, fighting factions forever forcing ordinary poor people to die for causes they often scarcely understood. No wonder the place was left desolate for the wild creatures to inhabit. There could be no luck in the stones from there anyway, but to steal them at night, what was Matt thinking? Now look at the trouble they were in.

'Oh God help us!' she said, wringing her hands. She knew when Matt told her that a weasel had spat at him from the castle wall. She knew when the weasel followed Matt home and killed six hens that night. She knew when Matt broke the weasel's head with a blackthorn stick that no good would come from it. Of course, the Devil from hell made sure that the weasel did not kill the hen that was going to crow. Maybe the weasel was the Devil. Now the Devil had his way. 'Oh God, his Blessed Mother and St Joseph help us,' she wailed.

When Matt came home he met a very angry mother, who castigated him for getting notions of himself. Nothing would do him but two cut-stone peers and an iron gate like the gentry.

'We were better off when we had the heap of manure outside the front door hiding the house and giving bailiffs and landlords the impression that we lived in shit, had nothing and knew nothing. Just because you broke a few horses for Crofton, Coote and Mahon does not make you a gentleman. Just because you gelded a few horses and none died does not make you a gentleman. Just because you won a few steeplechases does not make you a gentleman. Just because you have an understanding with the gentry that you are Roscommon's most knowledgeable horseman does not make you a gentleman.'

'Whoa, whoa woman, what are you talking about?' asked Matt as soon as he could get a word in edgeways. Just then, the hen flew on to a peer and started to crow.

'Now you know,' said Peg. 'That hen will be the death of you and that's not the half of it, Mary is whistling,' she said, bursting into tears. He took her shaking, sobbing body in his arms and just held her tight.

'There, there,' he said, for he could think of nothing else to say. The double whammy shook Matt, leaving him speechless. He was not easily shaken, for, so far, he had made a great success of his life and that was not easy when dealing with the land-grabbing tyrannical English and their Redcoats doing their dirty work. He had lived by his wits always, but he could think of no solution to this unearthly problem. If it was only the hen he could pull her neck and dump her on someone else's land to get rid of the bad luck. Better still he could take her to Mahon's land and pull her neck and bury her there so that no bit of bad luck would stay with him or his family. But his darling little sister Mary whistling at the same time, that made a whole new situation and he did not know what to do. However, he did know that any injury he inflicted on the hen, that same thing might happen to Mary. He was the oldest and, since his father died many years ago, he was the man of the house. He would ask his cousin, the priest, for advice and divine intervention if possible.

'Here, take this,' said Matt as he handed his mother his money pouch, containing a great number of sovereigns. 'Both of you go to the Mass Rock by the fields and don't ever come back here. There's enough money there to get you both to America and set you up well there. I will stay here and do what has to be done.' The mother nodded, hugged him tight, whispering in his ear, 'God bless you Matt.' She took the bag in one hand and Mary by the other hand and both disappeared into the night.

Thirty years before, although the handy woman had to be rushed the hundred yards from one house to the other to birth the first cousins within the hour, they were a decade apart. Peter Pious Dolan came quietly into the world at three minutes to twelve on the night of 31 December 1749, while his cousin Matt arrived kicking and screaming one hour later on 1 January 1750. Peter Pious had to be severely slapped on the bottom to get him to cry enough to clear his lungs; he seldom cried again and was always quiet and studious. Matt, on the other hand, was wild and flamboyant from the very start. Their fathers, who were twin brothers, were unalike in every way and this was repeated in their sons who were born in different decades.

As they grew and attended the same hedge school, the 'loving enmity' that was always evident between their fathers was again manifest in the cousins. This difference was made worse by Matt who always referred to Peter Pious as 'old man from the last decade, too old to laugh or play'. Peter Pious's gentle retort was always the same: 'There's no manners on you, Matt Dolan.'

At school, to which they walked barefoot 3 miles daily together, they were both bright children. The schoolmaster was glad to have such talent and while he always had Peter Pious tagged as a priest; Matt was full of devilment and had to be verbally and often physically disciplined. During his time at school every insect, creepy crawly, flying creature or furry little animal from the parish also attended at one time or another, much to the annoyance of the girls, the amusement of the boy's and the anger of the master, and Matt was always responsible. But for all that, he was the life and soul of the school.

On the way home in the evenings, Peter Pious walked at a steady pace, with little interest in his surroundings. They did not carry books except a work copy concealed inside their clothing, as their schooling was illegal activity. Unlike his cousin, Matt was fascinated by everything he saw and he either examined it, jumped on it, threw stones at it or, if it was edible, bit it or stole it altogether. In harvest, no apple, plum, gooseberry or pear was safe and even a cake left outside on a window to cool could be minus a bite. In winter, raw turnips and even potatoes could suffer. Nobody begrudged them, as priests were scarce and there was promise in the cousins.

At that time, people had very little land and it was not unusual for some to graze the side of the road with some quiet animal that would not stray. Tim had such a pony and he lived half a mile from the two scholars. One morning, Matt jumped on the grazing pony and rode it bareback to within a hundred yards of the school, where he dismounted and abandoned the steed. Peter Pious was horrified as he ran behind foretelling all sorts of imminent trouble. Nothing untoward happened. The pony headed for home but as there was better grazing here, he took his time. In the evening, the boys caught up with him a mile from the school. Matt mounted the animal again and persuaded

Peter Pious to ride behind him, holding on to Matt for dear life. After several days, Tim found out what was happening but he was not bothered, only asking that the pony would be left to him on market day. So thereafter, they rode to school, four out of five days. Matt was a natural horseman and jockey but, over a few years, even Peter Pious became a proficient jockey. This would prove very useful in later life.

When they finished school, Peter Pious was smuggled out to the continent where, fourteen years later he was ordained a priest. Meanwhile, Matt had made a name for himself as a gifted horseman, who could break any young horse perfectly so he would never stop, stag or throw his rider. When he started winning point-to-point races, the gentry took notice and Mahon, Coote and Crofton were quick to give him commissions to buy promising young horses for them. To this end, he travelled to fairs over several counties and got a bit richer than his neighbours, so much so that he thought it appropriate to clean up the front of his house and build stone peers with an iron gate. He had arrived.

Two years before this, Peter Pious had returned as a priest-on-the-run. On a very wet January day, Matt was at a fair in Roscommon and, as always, he was busy with everyone wanting to talk to him. If it was not gentry on horseback, it was some poor farmer looking to have a horse examined for wind, bots, stop, stag, curb, halt or mange. He worked free for the peasants but the gentry would pay through an increased price for their next horse. When a scraggy-looking poor bearded man with a stick quietly asked Matt to get him a horse and Matt looked him in the eye, he recognised Peter Pious. He kept his cool.

'Be walking outside the town in an hour and don't speak to me unless I have a spare horse.' Peter Pious shuffled off and no one noticed.

'Jump up there,' said Matt, an hour later, as he handed Peter Pious the reins of his spare horse. 'You're a horse dealer from Sligo coming to my house for the night, if anyone asks.' As stonewalls had ears, they rode in silence.

Very soon Matt had arranged lodgings in safe houses and given the horse to the priest. That horse would be kept on different farms and would always be neglected-looking and dirty in order to look like a farm horse.

Some time before that, Crofton's daughter was getting married and, of course, she would arrive at the church in a coach-and-six. Now, Crofton had a pair of black horses, each with four white legs, like socks that he used for his buggy. He commissioned Matt to scour the country for four similar horses to make six for the marriage carriage. Matt travelled widely from Meath to Dublin to Cork and back through Clare and Galway. He got the four white-socked horses much to the delight of Crofton and the profit of Matt.

He also got another young horse for himself. This one he thought would be a winner. He was black colt with a white star on his forehead. Matt trained him, groomed him, named him Flyby and won every race on him. He was famous and unbeatable.

At that time, there was a £5 reward for a dead priest but the gentry and the soldiers, mostly, did not enforce this. However, the law was there and a certain Captain Mathews was determined to do his duty and rid the county of meddling priests. Many were convinced that he was a descendant of Cromwell; otherwise he could not be so vicious. He got wind of the arrival of Peter Pious and thereafter he led four-soldier-patrols throughout the area night and day.

Matt decided that Peter Pious was in danger and needed a faster horse so that, if it ever came to a chase, the priest could outrun the Redcoats. The next steeplechase he competed in, he fell at the first jump and lost the race. Not only that but he announced that his shoulder was injured and that he would not race again for a long time. The real reason for this was that he had found a horse that looked like Flyby, but of course he was just ordinary and would never be a winner. Matt groomed him exactly the same as Flyby and pretended it was the same horse. Meanwhile, he cut Flyby's tail, hid him in a wood to get scruffy-looking and painted his white star black. A few weeks later, Peter Pious was riding the camouflaged Flyby.

Matt's fears were well founded. One dawn, just as the priest was mounting his horse after Mass on the rock, Captain Mathews and his three minions came galloping. While the ragged congregation scattered among the rocks, Peter Pious mounted Flyby and they went like the wind. The Redcoats confidently followed but, after a mile, the priest was nearly out of sight so they gave up.

'Blimey, the ruddy priest's 'ose is magic then,' said Ray, the private from London. Mathews hit him a vicious back hander with his whip across the face, knocking him from his horse.

'You stupid bloody fool, you're talking the same stupid superstition as the filthy peasants. Get on your horse and don't ever let me hear you or any of His Majesty's soldiers speak such nonsense again.' As they rode home a very angry captain vowed to himself that the rogue who misled the fools would not best him again.

After his mother and sister left to go to the Mass rock, Matt got the bucket and went to the well for water. By the time he arrived back he felt faint and, leaving down the bucket of water, he sat on the windowsill to catch his breath. Matt and his mother knew that he had to drown the crowing hen at dawn. What his mother did not know was that Matt had been feeling bad for a few days, that yesterday he had been coughing up blood and that last night he got a bad fit of coughing and a lot of blood came. For the first time in his life he felt weary, and he was hot and sweaty as he sat there in the predawn.

Peter Pious decided that in future all Masses would be celebrated two-hours before dawn so that he and his people could get home under the cover of darkness. He should have anticipated that the captain would expect just such a move. On the very night that the trouble had arrived at Matt's door, just as Peter Pious was finishing his next Mass, they first heard and then saw the outlines of horses coming fast. The priest jumped on Flyby and galloped away. The people scattered. The soldiers followed Flyby. Just as Peter Pious was passing Matt's house, the crowing hen fluttered onto the peer to crow. The horse swerved throwing the priest over the wall on the far side of the lane. He banged his head and blacked out. The horse stopped with his reins dragging on the ground, just as Matt arrived out from where he sat and picked up the reins. The soldiers arrived round the corner. 'Shoot!' shouted the angry captain. Matt and Flyby fell dead.

When the priest awoke he heard talking from the far side of the wall.

'It's bloody Matt the horseman,' the captain was saying, as he lifted Matt's head by the hair. When he dropped the head with a thud the priest knew that his cousin, friend, tormenter and wonderful benefactor was dead. Through tears he held his breath.

'That's why we couldn't catch the bugger. Look, it's Flyby with his star painted. Matt, the bastard, was the priest all the time. Who would have thought? Well, the meddling, conniving bastard is dead now. Fire the house, as I want to erase everything that the two-timing Matt stood for. Now the beggars will know who's the boss and who runs this God-forsaken country.' While the three soldiers were setting fire to the house the covetous captain searched Matt's clothes for the gold that he felt Matt should have. Disgusted, he kicked the corpse. When the thatch was ablaze he said, 'Nothing more for us here, mount up.'

After they were gone the sad and grateful priest gave the last rites to his Matt.

'Thanks for everything,' he whispered, 'especially my life.' Then he crept away.

Among the people of the parish and the whole county there was consternation and unrest.

A few days later, when word of the night's happening reached the powers that be, the gentry were concerned and disappointed but a little sad for the loss of Matt who they genuinely liked, not just for him, but for their own stable of horses. They were also baffled as to how Matt could have led a double life so successfully, laughing, joking, riding, training and dealing by day and doing his illegal priestly thing by night. It was a pity, they thought, that a man so talented was not one of theirs. They were also concerned by rumours of reprisals. There were none, as Fr Peter Pious told the people that, in his opinion, Matt had died a martyr and was now a saint. Matt's mother and sister made it to America where they joined those who had gone before and Matt's gold gave them all a head start.

When the fire started, all the hens fled cackling and fluttering across the fields where they were soon devoured by the grateful foxes. Perhaps the full foxes were crowing to their friends about it!

Captain Mathews and the four soldiers were sent back to England. Thereafter, while priests were still officially banned, in practice they were tolerated and Fr Peter Pious ministered to the people for fifty years, the last few after Catholic emancipation in 1829.

He never did hear about the whistling girl or the weird hen.

And what did the peasants say of Captain Mathews? 'May his cat eat him and then, may the Devil eat the cat and then, he will be in little chewed itchy bits inside the cat, inside the Devil, inside hell.'

THE ENGAGEMENT RING

In the 1950s, Aunt Nancy lived in London. She had come over before the war to work, had become a nurse and through the war worked her way up to Matron. This was made possible by the fact she had attended a very good national school and had a primary certificate. She had worked through the blitz night after night, risking life and limb through danger, destruction, desolation and terrible scenes of blood, broken bodies and the terrifying screams and wails of the dying, that nobody should have to witness. She was twice decorated by the war office for bravery, leadership, efficiency and dedication. Through all of this she had acquired a beautiful BBC accent as well as a house in Tufnell Park and a little bit of snobbery as she moved in higher circles. She had been stuck on age twenty-nine for several years and her biological clock was ticking. On a seemingly casual summer holiday in Ireland she had renewed a teenage romance with Pat who had just reached two score years. Pat was a glamorous cattle jobber with a little hat on the Kildare side of his head. When he proposed she said yes but she wanted an engagement ring from Tiffanies in London. After all, she wanted to impress her London friends and show that she was getting a man of substance. This did not faze Pat as through wheeling and dealing in cattle and sheep, he had acquired great confidence, a good farm and a canny ability to access the thoughts of others, way ahead of his time. Psychologists would have envied his skills.

Pat went along with the price of a wagon-load bullocks in his pocket. On arrival in Tiffanies they were met by a dress-suited gentleman who bowed, shook both their hands and announced they were most welcome. He gave Nancy several brass rings just to get the right size. During this exercise the suited gent discreetly asked Pat what price range he was thinking about. Pat replied that he wanted a good ring with a tiara of stones.

At that time a good engagement ring could be got for £50, but Nancy meant to cut a dash before leaving the posh life.

'Would a £100 be about right?'

'Have you nothing better?'

'300?'

'Something better,' said Pat. 'Do you think we're beggars?'

'Would the 500 range be suitable?'

'I suppose,' Pat replied.

A tray of rings within that range was produced and after much fitting and discussion, Nancy made her choice.

'An excellent choice, if I may say so,' said the suited one.

At this stage, a lady arrived with coffee and biscuits on a very fancy tray. After the refreshments, the suited one handed Pat a little box containing the ring.

'Will the £500 be cash sir, or perhaps a guaranteed check?'

'Hold out your hand,' said Pat and when he did so, Pat hit it a mighty slap as if buying a cow and said, 'I'll give you £250 and not a penny more.' While every head in the shop turned their way and all stopped to watch, the suited one turned pale with pain, fright and awe. He stuttered, 'We, we, don't do discounts and why did you hit me?'

'I want to see the owner,' said Pat.

'I'll get the manager,' said the suited one, but the manager was already approaching fast.

'What seems to be the problem?' he asked.

Pat replied, 'Your man here asked me £500 for this ring and I bid him half, maybe I'll do a little better but first you'll have to alter your price.' The manager, who was very embarrassed, tried to usher Pat and Nancy into a side room but Pat would have none of it.

'We'll stay where we are,' he said. 'Or is it that you think we're not good enough for the gentry around here?' The manager stared.

'Well …?' Pat said, holding out his hand.

'Well, what?' asked the manager.

'What's your best price?' said Pat.

'400,' said the manager who was totally mesmerised. Pat saw his advantage, and surmised that this softie was no match for an Irish cattle jobber and five minutes later he had the ring for £300. Meanwhile, the other couples, mostly upper-class stuffed shirt types, looked with pity on Nancy, wondering why she had not run out of the shop in anger and shame. Who on earth would want to marry a boorish cad who would haggle over the price of an engagement ring? And what on earth were those ignorant peasants doing in an establishment such as this anyhow? Despite the apparent distain, there were many envious eyes cast at the fabulous ring, and one or two at Pat, especially by the females.

As Pat handed his little hat to the suited one, he displayed a shock of wavy black hair speckled by an experience of gray. With a flourish worthy of a nobleman, he went down on one knee and loudly asked, 'My beautiful, wonderful, darling Nancy, would you do me the great honour of marrying me?'

Nancy, who had watched the whole show in silent amusement, now replied, 'Yes, yes, yes!' and kissed Pat passionately on the lips to loud applause from all in the shop. She knew she was getting an able dealer who would be well able to keep her and their children in peace and plenty all of their lives. She also knew that the £200 saved would pay to sink a well and give her running water and a proper bathroom in her house years before the neighbours. How right she was. Both she and Pat also knew that the price of the house in Tufnell Park would easily buy the fifty-acre farm that was for sale adjoining his farm. Land in north Roscommon can be variable but their farm was on a hillside overlooking a bog from where they got their turf.

Although their children have long since flown the nest, except for the one who stayed farming with wife, children, grandchildren and great-grandchildren, Nancy and Pat are still living happily into their nineties, and she still tells the story with great gusto. I wonder if many of the other couples did as well. This is what they think of the banning of turf cutting:

No more we'll cut the turf in Gorry's lovely bog,
Now this edict came from Europe, the creators of the smog.
No foreign despot ever stopped us from providing fires of turf.
Now our autocrats have barred us, will they ever have enough?
No more we'll see sods slip from the swinging slane's bright steel,
Nor watch a shapely maiden, between the barrow shafts to wheel.
No more we'll boil the eggs in the kittle for the Tay
Nor hear the lark's sweet singing on a showery April day.
No more we'll hear the curlew wild calling on the wind,
Now the turf, the bog, the good times, must all be left behind.
No more we'll leave the baby in the horse's collar there,
Nor pause at twelve bells summons, for the bog to join in prayer.
No more sweet bog pipes nor smoke or spit upon bog coals,
Nor as it simmers up, say 'Lord have mercy on all souls.'
No more the healthy hunger that bog work can create,
Nor relish big bog dinners, without a smell of mate (Meat)
No more we'll see the stork/crane winging slow his lazy way,
Nor watch the diving snipe a bleating on an August day.
No more we'll see bog water, made sterile by the caoibh
Nor can we show our children, our tradition we must leave
No more we'll jump big bog holes from the high bank to the low,
Nor dig deep bog canals to let the brown bog water flow.
No more we'll build new kishes to traverse the big bog drains,
Nor build tents of sacks and sallies to protect us from the rains.
No more we'll see the donkey with the cleeves upon his back,
Nor walk the scented heather on the brown bog's beaten track.
No more we'll share the hearth with our children, dog, and cat,
Nor keep the clothes horse by the fire or dry anything like that.

No more we'll say the rosary before the night-time fire is raked,
Nor next morning eat the hot bread that was on the griddle baked.
No more ghost stories by the turf fire with the kettle boiling hot,
Nor your mother stirring porridge in the little skillet pot.
No more kissing lovely maidens by the turf clamp or the hay,
Nor hand holding through the heather at the closing of the day.
No more we'll see the pilibín with his crested lapwing head,
Now our turf fires all are quenched, we might as well be dead.
Now came another edict not all the bogs are banned,
Now you can cut in certain places so let us see your hand.
Now at last we'll get to work and let our skill be seen,
Now my aching back is hurting, we'll send for a machine.
No more we'll boil the eggs in the kettle for the tea,
Now we'll have them scrambled with wine and finger food you see.
No more we'll hear the curlew wild calling in the wind,
Now we have double glazing that we gladly hide behind.
No more we'll hear a mother tell her child to bring in turf,
Now in central heating comfort he'll show her how the net to surf.
No more we'll smoke the pipe it's just so bad for your health,
Now instead we'll snort a joint and display our new found wealth.
No more the horse's collar with the baby's cries and sobs,
Now the baby's in the crèche for both of us have jobs.
No more we'll see the shapely maiden with the barrow on the bog,
Now we'll see her in the gym or out on the road to jog.
Nor when twelve gives the summons we'll no longer stop to pray
Now instead we'll take our cue that this is a shopping day.
Now avoid for the flock of pilibins that are circling in the sky,
Nor don't you dare look up or they'll maybe fill your eye.
No more we'll go hand-holding nor will words of love be said,
Now we'll drink until we're langered then we'll both jump into bed.
No I don't like these modern times, they make me feel a great unease,
Nor are they aisy on an auld lad but May I just stay on here please?

POEM GLOSSARY

Caoibh – hard clumped bog plant
Kish – wattle bridge over bog drain
Griddle – flat baking iron
Pilibin – lapwing
Langered – drunk
Rosary – long night prayer
Angelus – short midday prayer
Horses collar – part of harness covered with a rug and used as a baby sitting-up cradle
Cleeves – large baskets.
Sally – flexible bog shrub that can be bent into a tent shape facing away from the wind
Aisy – easy

LONGFORD

PHILIP BYRNE

LONGFORD AND THE *TITANIC*

The *Titanic*, or more accurately the sinking of the *Titanic*, is perhaps the most famous story in all maritime history. There were over 2,200 people aboard RMS *Titanic* under the command of Captain Edward Smith when it sank shortly after 2 a.m. on Monday, 15 April 1912. The sinking claimed the lives of more than fifteen hundred people. On first examination there may seem to be little connection between that terrible disaster in mid-Atlantic and landlocked County Longford, but there is.

Emigration since the Famine years (1845–50) saw approximately 61,500 leave the county between 1851 and 1911. In 1912, 426 people left the county and of these, fourteen were passengers on the ill-fated *Titanic*. All fourteen from County Longford were single and under the age of thirty. Their stories form part of the folk tales of the county from the early years of the twentieth century.

All of those from Longford were third-class or steerage passengers. There are many tales of third-class passengers being kept below decks and crew members using violence to stop the inadequate supply of lifeboats being overloaded.

The passengers from County Longford were:

David Charters, Ballinalee
Ellen Corr, Moyne
James Farrell, Killoe
Kate Gilnagh, Killoe
John Kiernan, Fostra, Aughnacliffe
Philip Kiernan, (John's brother)

Denis Lennon, Carrickedmond
Thomas McCormack, Ballinalee
Agnes McCoy, Ballinalee
Alice McCoy, (Agnes' sister)
Bernard McCoy, (Brother of Agnes and Alice)
Katie Mullen, Killoe
Kate Murphy, Aughnacliffe
Margaret Murphy, (Kate's sister)

Seven young men and seven young women setting off on the adventure of a lifetime. Ellen Corr, at sixteen years of age, was the youngest of the Longford passengers on the ship. So how did they fare? Did they die, or did they survive?

DAVID CHARTERS (21)

Before leaving home on his great adventure, David was telling his parents, William and Marianne, and his siblings about the huge size of the ship. He walked from his front door to a point up the field that was almost three hundred yards away. The entire family were incredulous that any ship that large and made of steel could float.

Sadly, David lost his life. His death was only the start of tragedies that beset the Charters family. One brother died as a child undergoing surgery. Another was killed in the First World War. A third brother was killed by the IRA in 1921 as they believed him to be an informer. Yet another brother died of a brain haemorrhage, while their sister Ann died while giving birth to her baby.

ELLEN CORR (16)

Ellen was emigrating to her two sisters, who were already established in New York or Jersey. Her father, who was a small farmer, at 65 years of age was very much older than his wife Bridget (44) when the sinking occurred. Ellen survived the tragedy. However, she never spoke of what she had experienced on the night of the disaster for the rest of her days.

She arrived safely in America and found work as a waitress. She later married an Irishman, Patrick Sweeney. They had no children and Ellen died on 9 March 1980. She was the last of the Longford survivors to pass away.

JAMES FARRELL (25)

James was one of the heroes of the disaster who failed to survive. His body was recovered still holding his rosary beads. He was buried at sea with little or no ceremony on 24 April. It was the policy aboard the ship searching for bodies in the days following the disaster not to recover bodies that were badly decomposed or crushed, especially if they 'looked like Steerage passengers'. This was in sharp contrast to the treatment of the corpses of first- and second-class passengers, many of whom were stored in ice and placed in funeral caskets.

Three other Longford travellers – Katie Gilnagh, Kate Mullins and Kate Murphy – found their escape route blocked by a crewman at a closed barrier.

> Suddenly steerage passenger Jim Farrell, a strapping Irishman from the girls' home county, barged up. 'Great God, man!' he roared. 'Open the gate and let the girls through!' It was a superb demonstration of sheer voice-power. To the girls' astonishment, the sailor meekly complied.
>
> Walter Lord, *A Night to Remember* (1978)

KATIE GILNAGH (17)

Katie was saved, saved because of a lie. When she managed to get to the boat deck, she was told that the lifeboat where she stood was too full. Katie started crying and shouted, 'But I want to go with my sister!' The sailor in charge had a change of heart and allowed her into the overcrowded boat, even though she had no sister aboard *Titanic*.

Katie's arrival at the lifeboat was only possible because of the gallantry of two men – James Farrell as described above and another unknown man on the second-class promenade deck. When Katie reached the promenade deck, she had no idea how to get higher to the boat deck. There was a man on the deserted deck standing beside the rail looking out sadly to sea but making no effort to save himself. He allowed Katie to stand on his shoulders and this way she managed to climb to the boat deck.

Katie Gilnagh was wearing a small shawl on her head as she boarded a lifeboat. The shawl blew away and James Farrell of Clonee took off his cap and gave it to her. As he did so he shouted, 'Goodbye forever,' and that was the last she saw of him.

About a week before the ship sailed a travelling woman had called to the Gilnagh household. Katie's father was turning the old woman away when Katie demanded that the gipsy read her fortune. She paid sixpence for the palm reading. The old woman told her that she would soon be crossing water and there would be danger, but that she would come to no harm.

Katie returned to Ireland in 1962 for the fiftieth anniversary of the tragedy. The flight to Ireland was only her second time crossing the Atlantic. On the flight the calm voice of the captain came over the intercom of the plane. 'Good afternoon ladies and gentlemen, this is Captain Smith …' Katie was immediately very upset and frightened. In fact, she had to be brought to the cockpit to make sure it wasn't the same Captain Smith who had been in charge of *Titanic*.

JOHN (25) AND PHILIP (22) KIERNAN

John had previously emigrated and had become established in New Jersey as a barman in premises owned by his uncle. He had returned to the family home in Aughnacliffe to bring his younger brother Philip to join him in America.

By all accounts, John was a very handsome young man and before emigrating he had begun courting a neighbour's daughter, Margaret Murphy. When he came home, Margaret had a plan of which John was unaware. She hoped to marry John and travel with him back to New Jersey.

On the night of his 'American Wake' party before returning to America, Margaret and her sister Kate attended. At the party Margaret finally told John of her plan. John 'reluctantly agreed' and also agreed that her sister could join them on the journey. Farrell may have been unaware that Margaret's family knew nothing of her plan.

It was brotherly love that cost John and Philip their lives. On their way up through the ship John called on Philip to go on, that he would be there in a minute. As they reached the stairs, Philip looked around and didn't see his brother and started back for him. This was the testimony of Thomas McCormack, a cousin of the Kiernans.

Slightly later, Margaret was trying to get to a lifeboat when John appeared on deck, shouted to her and came running up. 'Here, take my life belt,' he said. He made her put it on and that was the last she ever saw of him.

Both John and Philip Kiernan were lost. One of the strangest incidents following the tragic sinking relates to their parents. Before John and Philip left home for America, they made a solemn promise to their parents, John and Catherine, that no matter what happened they would come home. Both were drowned but in the early hours of the morning of the sinking and at approximately the very time of the sinking, the parents of the two boys heard the latch on the door of their home being opened. They saw both boys come in and go up the stairs to where they slept in the loft. Sadly, in the morning both beds were empty. Later when news of the disaster reached Longford the parents understood that their sons had kept their promise to return.

DENIS LENNON (20)

This is a love story from the sinking. Denis Lennon, Ballymahon and Mary Mullen (18) from Clarinbridge, County Galway, were eloping to America. Denis worked in Mullen's thriving pub and general store in Clarinbridge. Denis and Mary had fallen in love and planned to escape to the New World and start their lives together.

Mary was still a schoolgirl attending Loreto Abbey boarding school in Rathfarnham, County Dublin. She had gone home for the Easter holidays and was supposed to be returning to Dublin by train. As the train left Oranmore, Mary's sister, Bridget, said she thought she saw

Lennon. The first indication that something was afoot was when the family received a telegram from the school saying that Mary had failed to return. Mary had indeed gone to Dublin but from there she took a train to Queenstown (Cobh) in the company of Lennon.

Mary's quick-tempered brother Joseph was a carter working in the Guinness brewery. He was also a heavy consumer of the same product! When Joe heard what had happened, he quickly put two and two together. He got a loaded gun and set out for Queenstown to shoot Denis Lennon, who had 'defiled' his little sister. However, when he arrived at Queenstown, *Titanic* had just set sail.

Both Denis and Mary were drowned. Joseph took to drinking in a big way and sadly drank himself to death. Her sister, Bridget, joined the Sisters of Charity.

AGNES (29), ALICE (26) AND BERNARD MCCOY (23)

When *Titanic* started to get into trouble, the three siblings dressed quickly and made their way towards the boat deck about five decks above them. When they arrived there, they were told by an officer there was no immediate danger and they were to return below. They began to do as instructed but when Agnes saw water rushing into steerage quarters they stopped. By the time they got back to the officer the girls were just in time to secure a place. Bernard was left behind and watched as the boat was lowered.

They feared that Bernard had drowned. When they had been in the lifeboat for about thirty minutes, they saw Bernard in the water struggling towards the boat. When he grabbed on, he was beaten on the hands with an oar to make him let go. He held on and was then struck on the head and shoulders by the sailor. Agnes flew into a blind rage and attacked the sailor, throwing him to the bottom of the boat. In the meantime, Alice helped Bernard aboard.

All three survived. Agnes became a servant employed by the famous actor Douglas Fairbanks. Agnes never married. Alice was twice divorced and had another long-term partner. Bernard developed a permanent stutter from the trauma of that terrible night.

KATIE MULLEN (21)

Katie shared a stateroom on the ship with her neighbour, Katie Gilnagh, and with Margaret and Catherine Murphy from Killoe, County Longford. It was the actions of James Farrell recounted earlier that enabled Katie to make her way on deck. She was the last person to be taken on the lifeboat on which she made her escape. She survived.

Years later she told her own daughter that the last she saw of James 'was of him kneeling beside his suitcase saying the rosary'. When Farrell's body was later recovered, he was still holding the rosary beads.

KATE (17) AND MARGARET (19) MURPHY

Kate and 'Maggie' ran away from home to join *Titanic*. Margaret left with the intention of marrying her neighbour, John Kiernan. The girls slipped away from home carrying all the clothes they could and went to the going away party at Kiernan's. There she told John she could not bear to wait while he got established in America and he reluctantly agreed to elope with her.

The girls' widowed mother, Maria, did not want her two daughters to leave her. She insisted they both stay on the farm and not abandon her. Margaret and Kate decided that they were going anyway. They hid their cases in the barn and began gradually smuggling clothes from the house to fill them. They did it this way, so their mother would not notice their packing.

Kate and Margaret both survived but, as already mentioned, John did not. Within two weeks of her arrival in New York, Kate met her future husband, Michael. In 1913, Margaret met Matthew O'Reilly from Cavan. O'Reilly was an undertaker and dance promoter. On their honeymoon they returned to Longford to make amends with her mother. Kate never returned to Ireland, having 'an extreme fear of water and flying'.

Another Longford resident who could well have been on that terrible list was James McGoldrick from Ennybegs, Killoe. Shortly before *Titanic* was due to sail from Queenstown (Cobh), James bought his third-class ticket for eight pounds and, like the others, prepared to make his way to the port to meet the great liner. However, two days before he was due to sail, he was unable to find his ticket.

He searched high up and low down, but no trace of the ticket could be found. In order to leave no stone unturned or any source of help untapped, he made his way to the church. There he asked the parish priest, Fr Tom Conefrey, to pray for divine intervention in his search for the errant ticket. Fr Conefrey told him to forget about the ticket and that all the hype about *Titanic* being the biggest ship in the world was just a publicity stunt. He told Tom there were many other ships crossing the Atlantic on which he could travel. Ominously he added, 'It may be all for luck that your ticket is missing.' James took the priest's advice and cancelled his passage.

How true Fr Conefrey's words were to prove. James McGoldrick eventually sailed from Queenstown on 27 April aboard RMS *Adriatic*. James was aged 30 at the time.

References

A Night to Remember, Walter Lord, Holt McDougal, Reprint, 2008.
Fireside Tales, Jude Flynn, Vol. 11, 2013.
The Irish Aboard Titanic, Senan Molony, Mercier Press, 2012.
From the Well of St Patrick, Dromard Parish, p.161, James P. MacNerney, 2000.
www.encyclopedia-titanica.ord
www.irishamerica.com/2012/03/the-irish-on-the-titanic
www.longfordlibrary.ie/Heritage/Projects/Longford-The-Titanic
www.titanic.com/titanic_passengers_residing_county_longford_ireland.shtml
www.longfordlibrary.ie/Heritage/Projects/Longford-The-Titanic/Longford-the-Titanic-03-LongfordDead.pdf
www.longfordlibrary.ie/Heritage/Projects/Longford-The-Titanic/Longford-and-the-Titanic-Schools-Education-Pack.pdf

THE CANNON CHAINS AND GUNNER MAGEE

The Battle of Ballinamuck was a seminal moment, not just in the history of the 1798 Rebellion but in the history and folk memory of the people of County Longford. The battle marked the end of the French expeditionary force under General Humbert, who surrendered himself and his troops after the battle. It also saw the slaughter of many Irish 'croppies', who were either summarily executed or simply pursued and cut down as they tried to escape the battle area. It is beyond the scope here to give a full account of the battle and the events leading to it but rather to give account of two episodes that have lived for over two hundred years in the folklore of County Longford.

The 1798 Rebellion began in May of that year and fighting quickly spread to many parts of the country. On 22 August, a force of about a thousand French troops, under the command of General Humbert, landed at Killala Bay, County Mayo. The French were quickly joined by the rebel Irish force. They had great initial success by defeating the British at Castlebar. Indeed, so quick was the British retreat that it became known as the 'Castlebar Races'.

The French and Irish rebels planned initially to make for Ulster but, hearing incorrectly that the midlands were under rebel control, left Castlebar on 4 September and headed from Mayo, through Sligo, into Leitrim and towards Granard. This was a gruelling forced march. The French–Irish force were being pursued by British troops led by General Lake, who were following in their rear with a force of fifteen thousand men. Lord Cornwallis, meantime, was leading a large force north-westwards to intercept them. General Humbert was aware of the danger of being encircled by two large enemy forces. He therefore decided to make a stand and give battle from a defensive position of his choosing.

By 7 September the Franco–Irish force had reached Cloone, County Leitrim. Here they rested for the night.

At Cloone in fair Leitrim they rested,
For two days then Dublin they struck,
And mounted on the eight of September
The hillsides of Ballinamuck.

The French officers rested at the home of William West, a rich Protestant farmer. In the folklore it is said that Mr West showed great hospitality and showered his guests with food and drink of the best. They overdid it on the drink and as a result overslept next morning, the morning of 8 September, the fateful day of the Battle of Ballinamuck.

In their haste upon waking, they were unable to find the chains that were needed to haul the artillery pieces and limbers that would be so needed in any upcoming battle. Vital hours were lost searching for the chains while all the time they knew that the advancing British to their rear were closing. The conclusion was that the chains had been stolen during the night.

There are many theories and stories about what happened to the 'stolen chains'. One finger of suspicion pointed to West who, it was said, had stolen the vital chains and thrown them down a deep well. Other members of the West family and their servants also came under suspicion. A more innocent explanation is that, knowing the importance of the chains to the artillery, the chains had been brought into the house when the French arrived on the evening of the seventh and covered with hay.

In the darkness and panic of their oversleeping nobody could find the chains, nor remember where they had been hidden. It was also said that after the troops left Mr West eventually found the chains and dropped them into a well because he was afraid. He would be accused of their theft if they had been discovered on his property. Another suspected of their stealing was 'a wretch' called Neary, who had originally been employed by Mr West.

Whatever the cause, the fact was that the chains were gone, and valuable time had been lost. Time that might have allowed the French and Irish to reach and defend from the town of Granard, a naturally excellent defensive position. Necessity is the mother of invention, and the guns were manhandled with ropes. Progress, however, was slow, and the pursuing British were getting ever nearer. In order to maintain speed some of the artillery pieces, their limbers and ammunition were dumped into Keeldra Lough. The result was that only two cannon were in the passion of the Franco-Irish troops as they approached Ballinamuck.

General Humbert knew that he could not reach Granard and so decided to halt and give battle to the English, who were approaching on two fronts. The location he chose was Ballinamuck. He drew up his troops on the high ground around the village. The main force of pike men was placed on Shanmullagh Hill to the north-east. The rest of his troops, including the two cannon under the charge of Gunner Casey and Gunner Magee, were positioned on high ground, south-east of the village, commanding the road leading from Cloone from where General Lake's force could be expected. The guns were deployed at the Black Fort near Gaigue.

The two field pieces they had were six-pounders with smooth bore and were loaded from the front or muzzle. This weapon was greatly liked by Napoleon, who himself had originally been an artillery officer.

Gunner James Magee had originally been a member of the Royal Longford Militia (a British force) led by the Earl of Granard. It is thought that at some stage in his career he had been a member of the Royal Irish Artillery Regiment, where he would have learned his trade as a gunner. It was not uncommon for members of local militias to have been trained in gunnery by the Royal Irish Artillery Regiment.

For reasons that seem to remain unclear, both Gunners Casey and Magee decided to desert the Longford Militia and join the rebels after the Battle of Castlebar. They simply turned their redcoats inside out and became, as would later be seen, a very valuable asset to the rebel cause. When the battle started at about 8 a.m., the artillery on both sides fired on each other. Eventually a shell, or more rightly, a cannon ball from a British gun smashed Gunner Casey's gun and put it out of action. This increased the morale of the British and they rallied.

Gunner Magee always referred to his six-pounder as 'Aunt Kate'. Aunt Kate spoke loud and clear that day. Tradition has it that a 'chain ball' from Gunner Magee's gun halted the British progress. A chain ball is two cannonballs joined by a length of chain. When the cannon is fired the balls spread out to the length of the chain and fly parallel to the ground. The taut chain could carry off men, horses and heads to great effect.

Magee fired a second 'chain-ball' shot and this hit a British ammunition limber, which exploded. Before long Magee's ammunition was running low and tradition has it that he had all the bits of metal – bolts, pans, stones and anything else at hand – loaded into the muzzle of his cannon and fired. This had the effect of 'canister', effectively turning a cannon into an oversized shotgun. This also had a significant impact on the British.

Magee was in the process of reloading the cannon when its carriage was hit by an English cannonball, which broke the right wheel and rendered the gun useless. In order that the gun could fire again, several rebels lifted the heavy bronze cannon on to their shoulders and physically aimed it at the enemy. Magee fired the cannon successfully, but the recoil killed those holding it.

By about 9 a.m. the French surrendered their swords and the officers and men were well treated as prisoners of war. The Irish knew there would be no such terms for them. This was especially true for Gunner Magee, who would not only be seen as an enemy but as a traitor. Accounts say that Magee remained at his shattered gun, grabbed a pike and fought the advancing enemies until he was overpowered and taken prisoner. He was given a drumhead court martial, sentenced and hanged.

Many of the other rebels were captured or hunted down as they tried to escape through the fields and bogs around Shanmullagh Hill. Those that were taken prisoner were brought to Jack Griffin's house in Coilte Craobhach. The first to be hanged was General Blake, the Irish Commander, who was hanged from the raised shafts of a two-wheeled cart. Blake was buried in Tubberpatrick graveyard, just off the road to Arva. They then began hanging the rest of the prisoners. There were so many of them that the British troops were getting exhausted with the task. They decided to pick victims by a lottery. If a man drew 'life' he was released but anyone who drew 'death' was hanged.

The Irish that were killed that day were all buried in pits by the roadside. The English dead weren't buried at the battlefield but were loaded on to carts and taken away.

Ballinamuck and the defeat of the French and Irish force effectively marked the end of the Rebellion. The Rebellion had lasted from 23 May until 8 September 1798.

While Saint Barbara is the patron saint of gunners in every country, the Artillery Corps of the Irish Army is the only arm of the Defence Forces to have an historical figurehead. That figurehead is Gunner James Magee for the enduring values of 'respect, loyalty, selflessness, physical courage, moral courage and integrity'.

References

'Traditions of 1798: The Battle of Ballinamuck', pp.393–95, Pádraig Mac Gréine, *Bealoideas*, Vol. 4, No. 4, 1934.

https://www.militaryheritage.ie/wp-content/uploads/2018/11/Gunner-Magee-Defender-of-Arty-Corps-Values.pdf, Brigadier-General Paul A. Pakenham (retd), Sept 2018.

The Battle of Ballinamuck, pp.1–7, James O'Neill, National Graves Association.

Killoe, History of a Longford Parish, pp.125–37, Revd Owen Devaney.

Undaunted by Gibbet and Yeos, pp.2–43, Des Guckian, 1998.

NFC S225: 144–5, NFC S758: 438–41, NFC 1858: pp.42–42.

MEATH

RICHARD MARSH

GARRAWOG

I've never come across a story like this in 30 years of storytelling and research. It is a fine example of a community embracing a traditional local story in its present-day culture. Tierworker is in north-west County Meath on the Cavan border.

Her name was Maura Gargan, also called the Cailleach Geargain, but she is known as Garrawog in the story.

'It was said that she lived at Tierworker, some place about the foot of Tierworker Mountain,' Michael Gaffney of Relaghbeg, Mullagh, Kells told collector P.J. Gaynor in 1941:

> She was going to Mass in the old church at Moybologue. She told her servant man to get her a blackberry. He refused, as everyone went fasting to Mass in those days. She got down off her horse and plucked the blackberry herself. And when she ate it she ate the man and the horse. St Patrick was sent for, and only he killed her by throwing his staff at her she would have eaten the congregation.
>
> I used to hear it said that where St Patrick slew Garrawog, one part of her was buried in the hollow of the road near Mick the Brock Gargan's. (This would be on the road from Relaghbeg to Tierworker, and which passes the ancient cemetery of Moybologue.) There are big flags of stone in the road at the place where she (or a quarter of her) is said to be buried. It was stated that St Patrick said she would rise again when nine times nine, or it might be 199 or 999, generations of Gargans had been taken that way for burial at Moybologue. [Some say when 999,999 Gargans had walked over the spot. One version has the woman change into a "ferocious black swine".]

And I remember when I was a little boy seeing funerals of Gargans leaving the road when they came near to the spot and going into Sheridan's field and coming out on the road again further on. They were afraid that if they crossed the spot she would rise again. They said that another part of her went into Clugga Lake.
(NFC 792: 259–61)

A separate account says that another quarter of her went up into the air and another east into the sea. Sheridan's field is just across the road from the new cemetery.

'John O'Donovan in *Ordnance Survey Letters Meath* (1836) made a few guesses at the meaning of the town/townland name, "Teevurcher" on his map: *Taobh Urchair* – "side of the great cast or throw or for practicing missile throwing", "land of great tillage", "Murcher's house". *Taobh* literally means "side", but it is also used for "site", and "site or place of the cast" ties in with Patrick's throw of the crozier, though the story may have come about to explain the place-name, as many of the Dindshenchas yarns do. Kathleen Cooney of Tierworker told me that *Taobh an Urchair* refers to an old tradition of holding sports competitions on Tierworker Mountain: "There was a traditional fair, and at the fair there was missile throwing or skittles, and it was known for tournaments of skittles – the place of the missile throwing."'

THE BACHALL ÍOSA

Garrawog was a powerful witch or demon, and so a more powerful weapon was needed to defeat her. What better instrument than the staff that Jesus had carried?

On His travels, Jesus stopped one time on an island in the Tyrrhenian Sea (an arm of the Mediterranean west of Italy) and was given hospitality by a young married couple. He blessed their house and said that they and the house would remain young and new until Judgment Day. He left His staff there, telling them that St Patrick would drop by in a few hundred years to collect it. Just before he came to Ireland as bishop, Patrick visited the island and found that same couple, as young as ever, with old and decrepit children and grandchildren, and they gave him the staff.

This was the famous Bachall Íosa, which found its way into many – often irreverent or sacrilegious – hands down through the centuries. Gerald of Wales said in the twelfth century that it was the most famous and potent of all the saints' croziers in Ireland, and St Patrick used it to banish poisonous reptiles. It was moved from Armagh to Ballyboghill in County Dublin, thence to Christ Church in Dublin in 1173 and preserved there until 1538, when it was stripped of its gems and gold covering and publicly burned in High Street by the Archbishop of Dublin, George Brown.

CLUGGA LAKE

Clog, the Irish for 'bell', or *clogán*, 'small bell', could be the origin of the name of the lake, which is at Relaghbeg south-west of Tierworker. It was drained in the 1990s and has nearly disappeared. Teddy McCabe of Tierworker told me: 'If you got out there and peered your eyes down in the valley, you might see a puddle of water. That's Clugga Lake.'

St Patrick founded a church in Moybologue, and in penal times the bell was removed and thrown into Clugga Lake, according to Barney Gargan of Tierworker:

> And every seven years that bell was heard ringing below in the lake. The late James Reilly, of Annacloo, who died about forty years ago [before 1941], often said that he heard the bell ringing in the lake and that there was always an interval of seven years between each time it rang.
>
> (Collector P.J. Gaynor NFC 792: 454)

> Long years ago there was a man buried in Moybologue graveyard, and because he had done something that made him unpopular his body was lifted and left outside the graveyard gate. The police came and buried it again. It was lifted a second time, and was buried again. But the third time it was lifted it was carried away, and I used to hear the old people saying that it was thrown into Clugga Lake.
>
> (Daniel Lynch, 69, Leitrim, Mullagh, Moynalty. Collector P.J. Gaynor, 1941 NFC 792: 408–9)

Folklorists of the future will undoubtedly find it a fascinating challenge to work out the mythological significance of the demon Garrawog, the bell of St Patrick's church, and a 'riz' body all ending up in Clugga Lake.

(NFC is the National Folklore Collection at University College Dublin.)

THE GORMANSTON FOXES

The gist of this tale was told to me by one of the guides at Newgrange, who had lived all her life in the area. She was a bit vague on the details.

The Preston family arrived in Meath from Preston in Lancashire in the fourteenth century and soon became prominent 'Old English' Catholics. The senior male is a viscount; the title Viscount Gormanston was awarded in 1478 as the premier viscountcy in Ireland.

The story of the Gormanston foxes has been spread far and wide by students from Gormanston College, the Franciscan secondary school at Gormanston Castle near the border of County Dublin. It is also part of local oral tradition, and has found its way into collections of folklore and legends. But little-known first-hand reports by reliable witnesses raise an eerily charming legend to the status of family history.

The 1926 *Complete Peerage* sums up the story in the entry for the Preston family of Gormanston Castle: 'When the head of the house dies, and for some days before, the foxes leave all the neighbouring coverts, and collect at the door of the Castle.'

Everyone who has heard the story knows the reason for this. At some unspecified time in the distant past – some say the seventeenth century – a Viscount Gormanston rescued a vixen and her young litter from the hounds during a hunt. In gratitude for this act of kindness, when the viscount died, all the foxes in the district gathered on the lawn of the castle and howled with grief. The foxes did not attempt to molest the farmyard fowl, and the dogs of the house left the foxes in peace. This ritual continued for many generations.

In fact, that was the 12th Viscount, who died in 1860, according to Eileen Gormanston (Eileen Butler Preston), wife of the 15th Viscount. In her memoir, *A Little Kept* (1953), she says that when she was ill with a high fever following the birth of her first child, her nurse told her there were two animals larger than cats sitting under her window. Lady Gormanston said, 'Oh, I hope they're not foxes,' and told the legend to the nurse, who quickly assured her that 'the one thing they most certainly were not was foxes, and that, in any case, they had now run away.'

Following the death of Jenico William Joseph Preston, the 14th Viscount, in October 1907, the April 1908 issue of *The New Ireland Review* carried statements by members of the Preston family and household staff.

Mrs Lucretia Farrell, daughter of the 13th Viscount, said:

> On the day before my grandfather, Jenico, 12th Viscount Gormanston, died, the foxes came in pairs (an unusual thing) into the demesne from all the country round; they sat under his bedroom window, which was on the ground floor, and howled and barked all night, although constantly driven away only to return.
>
> Next morning we found them crouching about in the grass in front and around the house. In those days there were many hares in front of the house, and the foxes merely wandered through them and the same amongst the poultry; and even when driven away they only crouched down before one.

Lady Gormanston said:

> At the death of Edward, the 13th Viscount [in 1876], the foxes were also there. He had been rather better one day, but the foxes appeared, barking under the window, and he died that night contrary to expectation.

The coachman, Anthony Delahan, described his experience on the night of October 28th, 1907, after the 14th Viscount died in Dublin earlier that day:

> At about 8 o'clock, I saw two foxes in the chapel ground and five or six more round the front of the house and several more in the cloisters, which were circling round in a ring, crying all the time. I saw them continuously from then till about 11 o'clock when I went to bed.

Richard Preston, son of the 14th Viscount, reported what happened two nights later:

> At about 10 p.m., I went down to the chapel at Gormanston Castle to watch by the remains of my father ... From the outside came a continuous and insistent snuffling noise, accompanied by whimperings and scratching at the door ... It suddenly flashed across me that these must be the foxes. I accordingly went to the side door of the chapel and opened it suddenly. The night was very dark, but from the many candles within the chapel there flashed a broad beam of light through the wide open door. In the very centre of this beam of light, sitting on the gravel path within four feet of where I stood, was a full grown fox. Just in the shadow, sitting close up against the walls of the chapel, was another. ... Neither of the two which I saw attempted to move until I left the chapel and took a step towards them. They then *walked* quietly off into the shadow. I returned to the chapel, closed the door, and went across to the other door opposite the altar. As soon as I opened it I saw two more foxes, one walking across the door about nine or ten feet away, the other sitting against the wall so close that I could have touched him with my foot. ... the noise of whining and sniffling was that of a considerable number ... It continued without intermission till 5 a.m., when it ceased suddenly.

Elizabeth, Countess of Fingall, said in her memoir, *Seventy Years Young* (1937), that the foxes were already in mourning at Gormanston before word came from Dublin that the viscount had died. Her husband was hunting that day and a man told him he might as well go home: 'Every fox in Meath is at Gormanston.' Another account says that foxes also mourned at the house in Dublin where the viscount died.

Jenico Edward Joseph, the 15th Viscount, served in the First World War. His wife, Eileen, received a letter saying that he had been killed in action, but she didn't believe he was dead, as the foxes had not put in an appearance at the house. A few weeks later, she learned there had been a mistake, and her husband was still alive. The foxes gathered at Gormanston for him when he died in 1925, as they did for Jenico William Richard, the 16th Viscount, who was killed at Dunkirk in 1940.

John Campbell-Kease (*Tribute to an Armorist*, 2000) reports:

> A distinguished Irish lady, who was living near Gormanston at the time, told me that one of the villagers came into her parents' house one morning in June 1940 and said, 'Something has happened to Lord Gormanston, the foxes were barking all night long.' The news that the 16th Viscount had been killed in action in France came through shortly after.

The present (17th) Viscount, Jenico Nicholas Dudley Preston, succeeded to the title at the age of seven months. The Gormanston family crest shows a fox 'pleasantly passant', and in the coat of arms is a fox 'aggressively rampant'. The Preston family sold the property to the Franciscans, and it has been a secondary school since 1954.

LOUTH

DOREEN MCBRIDE

ORIGIN OF THE RIVER BOYNE

I got this story from Michael Scott who tells a good yarn and writes beautifully.

The River Boyne arises gradually from bogs and marshes at the foot of a hill the ancients called 'Sidh Nechtain'. It runs for a short distance between County Kildare and County Offaly before running into County Meath. It continues in a north-easterly direction past Clonard, Trim and Navan before sweeping past the ancient burial tombs in the Boyne Valley and on to Oldbridge in County Louth before flowing through Drogheda and into the Irish Sea at Invra Colpa, which is between Mornington and Baltray.

Boann was 16 years of age, very beautiful, spoilt and headstrong when she was forced to marry Nectain. She didn't like him much. He was old and grizzled and not much fun. She was bored. He kept leaving her, going out on his own and telling her she couldn't come.

'Why can't I come?' she kept asking petulantly. 'Why do I have to stay at home while you go out enjoying yourself? I'm bored, do you understand? BORED!'

'Be reasonable,' said Nectain, trying to be patient. He found his young wife, with her constant demands, a bit of a pain. He had married her for political reasons and was disappointed in her. He had hoped his young wife would have been a help, but all she did was complain. He was fed up with her demands and her vanity and pride.

'Boann, I've told you before, you simply can't come. You know my family were chosen to guard the magic well. The Tuatha De Danann blessed its waters with their magical powers for the use of the people of Erin. Sadly, powerful chieftains and kings became greedy and grew rich by charging for use of the waters. The result was terrible. The people rose up in revolt and the druids took the situation into their own hands. They decided one honourable family should care for the well and its magical waters; misuse had caused its water level to sink dangerously low so it could only be used during times of plague. My family were proud and delighted to be chosen. We are the only people allowed near it. Looking after the well is a very responsible job. What I have to do is serious and dangerous.'

'Why can't I be treated with the respect I deserve? After all, I'm married to you so I'm a member of your family. I should be allowed to visit the well,' Boann complained.

'That's true, to a certain extent, but your blood is different from my blood. It would be very dangerous for you to go anywhere near the well. Our children will carry my blood and be able to go. You can't and that's that.'

'So I'm to be used as breeding stock to provide keepers for that stupid old well? My children will be able to go into places where I'm not allowed to venture. That's unfair and stupid,' Boann snapped. 'Everyone knows the well is just a hole in the ground surrounded by smoothly rounded stones somewhere in the middle of the forest. You're making a fuss over nothing.'

'That's not true. The well isn't just a simple hole. A crystal wall was built around it in the past and an ornate wooden cover overlaid with gold placed on top of it to keep a single drop of the precious water escaping.'

'Now stop girning. You know my brothers and I have to make obeisance to the well at full moon. Content yourself and get on with your spinning.'

Boann was furious, but felt it wise to hide her feelings. She smiled, sat down by the roaring fire in the great hall and started spinning.

'Woman's work,' she thought. 'I hate woman's work. I'm as good as any man. Why should I sit here meekly spinning while my so-called lord and master swans off into the forest? I'll find out where he's going. I'll follow him. I'll visit the well.'

Boann had studied enough magical lore to know that magicians visiting ancient places of power have to be spotlessly clean. Bad spirits and malignant influences are attracted by dirt and can attach themselves to it. She watched sourly as Nectain purified himself, removing all metals, washing in the spring running beside his fort and changing his clothing.

When Nectain came to say goodbye, Boann lowered her head modestly so her ash blond hair shone in the firelight.

'Huh,' she muttered, 'I bet there's not much magic left in the well anyway. I bet it's just a useless pool of water.'

'That's not true,' Nectain replied. 'My family have guarded the precious waters of the well for many generations. They have not been misused. Now the magic is stronger than ever.'

Boann waited patiently until Nectain and his brothers had left, then followed them through the ancient forest. She realised leaving the track would be dangerous at night, because she might trip over an exposed root, fall and break a leg. She followed the track carefully, deep into the heart of the wood, and was disappointed when she came out the other side. Nectain and his brothers must have turned off somewhere, but where? She decided she had no chance of finding the well by herself and the best thing she could do was to get back to the fort before her husband returned. But she felt more determined than ever. She was not going to be beaten. She would visit the forbidden well, but she must find out more about it. She kept questioning her husband and he enraged her by refusing to answer.

'I've heard that anyone drinking the well's magic water will live forever. Have you ever drunk from it?'

'Why would I want to do that? I've seen all I want to see, done all I want to do. Now I'm just looking forward to being released from this life's troubles. I look forward to entering the Otherworld. I'm 40 years of age, old, gnarled and ancient. I've had enough of this world and I'll be glad to leave.'

'How can you say you have had enough? You haven't done anything but guard that stupid old well. You've never even left the valley. Have you never longed for adventure? To see more of life? To have fun?'

Nectain shook his head. 'No, I think they're foolish notions. You should be content with what you've got and make the best of it. It's silly to go looking for greener fields.'

'Well, I think you're an old stick in the mud. I want adventure. I'm bored here in this backwood of a forest. I can see nothing but trees, trees, trees and more trees. I can hear nothing but the rustle of leaves. I want life, laughter, music. I want to dance, sing, have fun. Please take me to the well.'

Boann got up and danced around the room. Nectain sighed. He should never have married her. She would never be content; she would always search for an impossible dream.

She grabbed his wizened hand. 'Please, please, please take me to the well.'

'I can't. It's forbidden. I've told you, the well must be treated with respect. It's dangerous.'

'But I would treat it with respect.'

'You're a woman. Women mustn't go near the well. Only men from my family are allowed to approach it.'

Boann was determined to follow her husband and his brothers when they next visited the well. When the time came, she donned a long dark cloak and slid silently into the darkness behind them. She knew they would suddenly disappear off the familiar track, so watched carefully. They didn't notice the shadow behind them. Clan Nectain moved silently through the ancient forest, while Boann kept as close to the group as she dared. She noted carefully where the men put their feet.

'There're bound to be booby traps along the way,' she thought. 'That's what Nectain means when he says it's dangerous.'

At one point, the men took an extra long step over a gnarled root. She followed and shivered as she glanced down. What she thought was a root was in fact a spiked bar. At another point the men left the path. Boann followed but looked carefully to see if she could find out why they had avoided that particular place. It was a pit hidden under a covering of leaves and grass.

It was almost midnight when Clan Nectain reached the magic well. Boann watched from a distance, feeling very disappointed. She had thought the well would be beautiful, with shining crystal walls and a lovely golden covering. It looked very ordinary. The crystal walls looked dirty and the gold skin covering the wooden cover was shabby, peeling off in places and covered in moss. She watched as her husband and his brothers moved around the pool. They were obviously carrying out some ancient ritual.

'Mumbo jumbo,' she thought, 'I thought Nectain had more sense than to believe in that kind of rubbish. There's nothing to that silly old well. It's much ado about nothing. It's not dangerous. It's just an old useless ruin, like my husband.'

The men ended the ceremony by lowering a polished wooden cup into the depths of the well. Each brother drew out a cupful of water and ceremoniously poured it on the ground. There was a flash of light. The brothers bowed towards the well, backed out of the clearing and vanished down the path.

Boann kept hidden behind the trees until they had disappeared from sight, then walked firmly up to the well, looked at it and walked three times in an anti-clockwise direction round it.

'Have Nectain and his brothers spent their entire lives watching this boring old well?' she thought. 'They're fools. Absolute fools.'

She stopped and ran her hand over the golden cover. Mosses and lichens were growing on it, hiding the ancient complicated pattern. She ran her hand over the design, tracing loops, curves and spirals. The sixteen stones circling the clearing behind her suddenly sprang to life and began to sparkle and glitter as they burned with white fire. Boann had her back to them and didn't see what they were doing. She roughly shoved back the well's cover and gazed down into its murky depths.

'Huh,' she muttered, 'I can't see anything there. It's a dead loss. I wonder what the water tastes like? Would it make me live forever? It's worth a try.'

She took the wooden cup and lowered it down, down and down into the depths of the well. Eventually she heard a splash as the cup reached the waters and she began to pull it up again. It was very heavy; surprisingly heavy for such a small cup. Her arms and shoulders became sore with the effort of pulling and pulling and she was out of breath by the time it reached the top. She breathed a sigh of relief and took a sip. The water was like nothing she had ever tasted. It was icy cold and oily. It hit the back of her throat and burnt its way down her gullet like the strongest mead. She liked it and drank the whole cupful.

'The men were crazy throwing this on the ground,' she thought. 'This is great stuff.'

She threw back her head and laughed as the effects hit her. She was no longer exhausted. She felt the magic water rushing through her body, making it strong, warm and impervious to the chill air of night.

'That really was *uisce bestha*, the breath of life!' she shouted in triumph.

The sixteen standing stones that had been set to guard the sacred well lumbered into life. Each was as tall and as wide as a man. They were monsters, and they lumbered noisily towards Boann. She whirled around at the sound and screamed. The stones then formed a circular wall around her and closed in on her, forcing her into the well. She screamed as she fell. The crystal walls caught her scream and sent it out into the forest as a terrified wail. Leaves trembled on branches, ancient timbers groaned and rasped, and the very forest shook. The well exploded and the crystal rocks and standing stones shattered and tumbled as a column of silver water erupted, knocking out Boann's eye and disfiguring her face before slicing through the forest towards the ocean. It left a trail of devastation in its path, swallowing men, animals, and whole communities on its mad journey to the sea. Those who were awake at the time caught a glimpse of a wild-haired woman in the column of water, which was christened the River Boyne.

There's still magic in the water. If you sit quietly by the River Boyne and drink in its beauty, you may feel its healing power.

THE BIRTH OF CUCULAN AND NEW GRANGE

In the past, New Grange was called Brúg na Bóinne. It is where the sun god Lugh lived in his enchanted castle and where, according to folklore, Cúchulainn was born before he moved to Dun Delgan (Dundalk) This is one of Granny Henry's stories, although she didn't mention what she would have referred to as 'naughty bits'. (They came from Cecile O'Rahilly's word-by-word translation of Táin Bó Cúalnge, a manuscript originally written about 1100.)

'Your Majesty's one irresistible smasher,' exclaimed one of the laughing group of women surrounding King Conor.

'Aye, you can say that again. He's irresistible, as I know well,' giggled another, who had had too much to drink, 'but is this one wee bride who won't follow the custom by sharing the king's bed on her wedding night?'

'Do you think I'm so hard up that I have to bed my own sister?' snarled the king.

'Sire, we know grooms are grateful to you for breaking their wives in so they can enjoy a happy marriage. It's very hard work. You don't enjoy it. You do it for the sake of the kingdom and derive no pleasure from performing your duty.'

King Conor uttered a shriek of laughter as he took his place at the top table beside his sister Dechtire and her new husband King Sualtim. He lifted a golden goblet filled with mead, gulped a mouthful, then lifted his glass and proposed a toast.

'*Slanté*,' he shouted, while holding the shining goblet aloft, 'Here's to Dechtire and Sulatin. May their cess never go sour and may all their troubles be little ones.'

He turned towards Dechtire. She looked pale and strained.

'How's about ye?' he asked fondly.

'Fine,' she responded without enthusiasm, 'I'm delighted to strengthen an important treaty enabling Ulster to remain at peace. I know that's important to you and to the kingdom.'

King Conor looked worried. He loved his sister dearly.

'I wish you looked a bit happier,' he said. 'Come on, pet, cheer up. Sualtin's a good sort. He worships the ground you walk on. He'll be good to you. He's dead on.'

Dechtire smiled wanly, glanced towards her new husband and felt sick. He was so uncouth. His beard was matted with grease and his rough, calloused hands were filthy. He grinned, exposing inflamed gums with broken teeth. He grabbed her and planted an enthusiastic kiss on her lips. She tried not to shudder as his stinking breath hit her. She avoided it by wrapping her arms around him and putting her head against the rough texture of his chest. She glanced down and saw, with annoyance, the greasy stains his hands were leaving on the shimmering folds of her silken wedding dress.

'Ugh,' she thought. 'I can't stand much more of this. How will I cope with him in bed? It doesn't bear thinking about. I've got to get a breath of fresh air or I'll die.'

She pushed firmly against her new husband's muscular chest. He held her more tightly.

'You're not trying to escape, are you darling?' he jested.

'No, of course not,' she responded, 'I've got a call from nature. I'd better go outside before I act in a childish fashion.'

'Too much excitement,' laughed one of the women, 'has a bad effect on the bladder.'

'You could say that.'

Sualtin let her go. She walked gracefully out the door and fled out through the high circular earthen ditches with their sturdy wooden fences, which surrounded the fort and into the welcoming gloom of the forest. She breathed a sigh of relief.

'I wish I didn't have to face the horror of a wedding night,' she thought. 'I wish I could stay here in the clean fresh air. I wish I had a little romance in my life. I wish I was a serving girl who could marry whoever who she liked.

'Oh dear, it would be a help if I even liked Sualtin, but I can't stand him.'

A black cloud of despondency hung over her soul. She gave herself a mental shake, attempted to cheer up and whispered. 'Come on,

Dechtire. Sualtin's not all bad. He's good-natured and very generous. Conor's right. He'll be kind to you. You're too fussy. He can't help having horrible black hairs sticking out of his nose and red rough horny hands. Ugh,' she shuddered at the idea of what those hands might do on their wedding night. Then she squared her shoulders and began to walk firmly back to her wedding feast.

'I might as well get on with it. There's no escape,' she muttered aloud, as she walked towards the edge of forest.

The sun shone brightly, lighting the leaves and casting shadows on the bright ground.

'Why can't you escape?' asked a melodious manly voice.

Startled, she looked around the clearing.

'Dechtire. Over here, come on. Over here,' a voice called softly from some bushes at the edge of the forest. She thought she was imagining things and continued walking slowly back to the fort.

'Darling, listen to me,' whispered the voice. 'Look behind you.'

Dechtire turned and saw a tall, handsome stranger with a long, golden beard and heavy gold torques around his neck and arms. She looked at his merry smile and sparkling blue eyes. He was a genuine hunk.

'Who are you?' she gasped.

'Lugh.' came the quick reply.

'Lugh, the Ss-sssssuuuun God?' she stuttered.

'No less,' smiled the stranger. 'And I love you. Will you marry me and come to live with me in my enchanted castle, Brúg na Bóinne?'

'I can't do that,' whispered Dechtire. 'I don't know you.'

She shivered with desire as Lugh took her in his arms. They felt so nice, so different from the rough hug of her husband. *If only. If only …*

'If only what?' asked Lugh.

'What? Have you read my thoughts?'

'Yes. We could be so close, so happy. Come, run away with me.'

'I can't do that.'

'Why not?'

'My brother's delighted I've agreed to marry Sualtin. He wants Ulster to prosper in peace. If I run away with you, there'll be a war.

The birds led them across County Armagh (Slieve Fuad), by Ath Lethan, by Mac Gossa, between Fir Rois and Fir Ardae (Ardee).

Dusk fell and Conor began to look for somewhere to spend the night. He spotted lights shining through the gloom. The Men of Ulster walked towards them and discovered a beautiful castle. They went up to the door, which opened immediately, and they were amazed when guards greeted each one of them by name and invited them in.

That was a great night, that was. The craic was mighty. The Men of Ulster enjoyed the food, the wine, music, dancing and the company of beautiful women.

Their hostess appeared strangely familiar. Conor kept staring at her. It couldn't be, could it? Then he realised it really was Dechtire, but Dechtire as he'd never seen her before. He got up, went over to her, smiled, held out his hand and asked for a dance.

'Are you really my little sister?' he asked as they twirled about the floor.

'None other,' she replied.

'Please Dechtire, come home with us,' he pleaded. 'We miss you terribly.'

'Can't you see I'm really happy? I love being here.'

'Please Dechtire, please come home.'

'This could be dangerous,' she thought. 'Conor's as stubborn as a mule. He'll never give up on the idea of wanting me to go back with him. He could annoy the Shee. That could be life-threatening. I can't let that happen.'

She looked up into her brother's eyes.

'Poor Conor,' she thought, as she placed a couple of her soft fingers against his lips.

'Hush,' she whispered, 'keep your counsel. Anything else could be dangerous. I'll think about it.'

Conor smiled, 'You do that, dear. Think about it and remember how much we love you.' Dechtire planted a quick kiss on his cheek, before returning to her husband.

That night, King Conor fell into a deep, contented sleep, believing his dear sister would find a way to return with him. He thought she must have wanted to see him. She must have sent the birds to lure the Men of Ulster south. Their hosts acted as if they had been expected. He was warm and comfortable as he fell asleep and it was a great shock when he awoke in a clearing in the forest. The rain was coming down in stair-rods and he was soaked. He stood up, amazed. What had happened? Where was his warm, comfortable bed? Where was Dechtire?

The men woke one by one. There were questions on every lip. Where had the castle gone? Why had it disappeared? Why were they in the middle of a forest clearing in a howling gale with the rain pelting down?

'Shush,' whispered King Conor. 'We must be patient. Did you recognise Dechtire last night? I think she intends to join us. We must be patient and wait for her.'

Dusk fell and Dechtire did not appear. Suddenly they heard a baby crying and searched their surroundings. They finally found the wee mite in a basket hidden among the willows. Conor lifted the baby up and cuddled it. He was delighted.

'This baby is a dead ringer for Dechtire,' he said, 'She must intend coming home with us. I think we should stick around a while longer.'

They waited until it was dark but Dechtire didn't come. Eventually, the Men of Ulster decided the best thing they could do was return to Emain Mach, bringing the baby with them.

Sualtim was delighted when he saw the baby.

'This child,' he declared, 'could have been my son. Look at the wee dote. He's the spitting image of Dechtire. I'll bet she's sorry she can't come to live with me. She loves me and knows I'm very lonely without her so she's sent her wee baby to keep me company. I'm going to call him Setanta, son of Sualtin. He's dead on. He'll grow up to be a great warrior, so he will, I feel that in my bones.'

GALWAY

RAB FULTON

ENDA AND BRECAN

Often overlooked in the telling of Irish wondertales are the accounts of the saints, who were a wild and passionate bunch who could zap friend and foe alike with blasts of magic, as Enda and Brecan often did. For more about them, check out T.J. Westropp's 'A Study in the Legends of the Connacht Coast, Ireland', in Folklore, *Vol. 28, No. 2 (1917).*

The Aran Islands were once ruled by a great pagan chief named Corban. When rumour came that something untoward had been witnessed in the sea, Corban made ready to hurry out from his fort. As he prepared himself he demanded answers from his retinue, but none of his ministers, warriors, poets or druids would admit to knowing what precisely had been witnessed that morning by the fisherfolk.

'One of you must know. I can see the fear in your eyes. Tell me.'

His wife spoke up: 'A fisherman saw a rock floating on the water.'

'So? Islands move, why cannot rocks?'

'There was a man on it in the garb of a Christian monk.'

Corban laughed. 'Only one, that's barely enough skin to make a belt.'

Corban's wife did not smile. 'This intruder may not be so easy to flay.'

The great chief looked at his wife. She was the perfect companion and match for him in all things: war, politics, art, feasting and, above all else, humour. Now she stood before him, her expression grave. She gripped the long handle of her sword, but her hand trembled and her knuckles were as pale as bone. Corban felt a chill of fear quiver in his belly.

After the druid made a sacrifice and called on the protection of the ancient deities, Corban and his court set off for the coast. They reached their destination that afternoon but did not go directly down on to the sands. Instead, the group waited at a field while Corban took a moment to stroke and admire his twenty beautiful horses. After kissing the brow of a grey stallion, the chief left the horses and walked to the shore. A great gathering of whispering men, women and children were already there. Over their heads could be seen the neighbouring island of Inis Meáin, and beyond it the distant cliffs of the mainland, stark and majestic in the sunlight. As the entourage stepped on to the shore the crowds quickly moved aside. Soon, Corban saw for himself the great dark rock resting on the beach, and before it, a grim-faced monk.

The great chief spoke to the Christian: 'I am Corban, chief of all this land. Climb back on your stony vehicle and leave, whilst you may.'

'I am Enda,' came the reply. 'I care nothing for your position. I once had power and wealth beyond your dreams. I renounced it all for the greater riches of Christ's love. I come today to bring the one and true message of God's light to the people of these islands. So now I ask you to leave. Whilst you may.'

A scarlet rage filled Corban. Raising his war axe he ran at Enda. His warriors raced beside their lord, weapons raised. Enda stepped forward and the warriors suddenly saw their opponent's eyes. Never had they beheld such power and such anger in a man. With a joint cry, Corban's men dropped their armaments and fell onto the sands. But Corban and his wife were not so easily broken. On they came, their rage greater than their terror.

Enda was unconcerned. He held up his arm and pointed over Corban's head. Screams then erupted from the field above the bay.

Corban and his wife turned to see their beautiful horses convulsed with terror. The creatures were leaping, kicking and screaming in torment. Some fell to the ground and rolled as if trying to beat out invisible flames. Then, in an instant, all the beasts turned and galloped towards the sea. The sand burst upwards in a stinging cloud as the creatures thundered across the beach. The sea churned and spat as the creatures rushed into the waves. But the cold water did not end the creatures' torment. They swam further out, still neighing in terror.

'Save my horses!' begged Corban.

'Only if you swear to leave the island,' demanded Enda.

'I swear.'

Enda lifted his arm and the madness left the horses. Calmly, they swam to Inis Meáin. True to his word, Corban, his wife and his court left their homeland on the evening tide and never returned.

Following his victory, Enda began to build the infrastructure that would allow for the worship of the one true God. In contrast to the islanders' former pagan masters, Enda lived an austere and diligent life, and demanded the same from the monks who joined him. Places of worship were built, including the first Irish monastery at Killeaney; rules for monks were enforced; and the new religious rites were propagated. Yet Enda was not a man skilled in the craft of conversion. He was a living exemplar of the terrible and harsh power of his God, but he failed to give proof of his divinity's joy and love. Reluctantly, Enda sent word to the mainland asking for the assistance of monks with a talent for winning over the hearts and minds of pagans.

The new monks were led by one whose humour and joy, it was said, not only won souls to Christ but sent a shiver of fear through the most terrible of demons. Brecan had arrived in Enda's domain.

Soon the laughter and affability of Brecan and his followers brought many of the islanders into the embrace of the Christian faith. They openly discussed their new faith and the joy of conversion, but they also voiced their disdain for the island's grim abbot. Brecan understood, though, that Enda's severity was the hard foundation without which Christ's Church would never be built. Brecan therefore gathered his followers and led them in a procession to Enda's monastery. There he knelt before the abbot and asked if he could become his pupil. When Enda accepted, Brecan turned to his followers and declared, 'Abbot Enda is now my teacher and leader in all things. If you love me you will also commit yourself to be led and taught by our wise and selfless brother.' This the Christians of Aran did. But Enda was still not satisfied.

'Brother Brecan,' he said. 'What rewards we may have earned will be given to us in Heaven, not on earth. However, I would be a weak master if I did not give some recognition for your endeavours. Word has come to me that there are some who believe that I have dominion over too much of this island and that more land should be given to new monks. This is what I propose: a week from today I will say mass here in my monastery, and you shall say mass in yours. When we have finished, you will journey to my monastery, and I to yours. Where we meet will become the border between your territory and mine.'

A week later, the two rivals performed mass in their respective monasteries. Enda's ceremony, as usual, was a slow, stoic and considered affair. Brecan, by contrast, shortened his mass and was no sooner finished than he climbed on a donkey. His followers cheered in anticipation. Word came to Enda that Brecan was already on his way, but the abbot refused to hasten his mass. Instead, he prayed to God and asked for His assistance.

It was a windy day, but dry and clear, and Brecan's journey should have been easy. But the ground beneath his donkey turned to mud and the creature sank into the brown sludge up to its knees. Brecan's journey stalled. Enda arrived an hour later and asked if Brecan accepted the boundary. Brecan said he did so, at which the mud vanished. Enda was satisfied at his victory, whilst Brecan was amused that he had been defeated by a jest.

From the conflicts and disagreements of these two holy men a perfect synthesis of struggle and joy arose, reflecting the harshness and the beauty of the islands they had brought into God's light. For millennia unmeasured the mass and weight of these islands had mitigated the rage of the ocean beyond Galway Bay. With the arrival of Enda and Brecan, the rocks became the frontline against Satan and his demonic host. The Christian settlement on Aran would be replicated across Ireland and Scotland; the sons of kings and nobles would embrace its teaching and discipline, and pass that knowledge on to the wider world.

THE LAST OF THE SUPERHEROES

While a lot of the Irish myths involve great battles and acts of heroism, there are also quieter, more poignant tales, and it should be no surprise that one of those tales involves lovers fleeing westward to the lands around Galway Bay and Connacht.

Fergus Fionnliath was a Galway chieftain renowned for his contempt for all living creatures. One day a messenger came to him from the great warrior Fionn Mac Cumhaill, captain of the Fianna warriors. Beside the messenger stood a great hound. 'Fionn requests that you look after this bitch until such time as he comes to collect her. Mind her well as she has life growing in her belly.' So it was that Fergus, the hater of all men and beasts, was forced to accommodate another mouth and another heartbeat in his household.

The chieftain's inclination was to beat and starve the creature, but he was afraid of Fionn's wrath. Instead, he treated the bitch with cold respect, which she repaid with warmth and affection. Over the weeks and months Fergus began to show more interest in the dog's welfare. He fed her from his own hand, let her sleep in his own bed chamber, and took her for long walks through the woodlands of Galway and down to the shore, where she ran along the sand and splashed in the glittering waters of Galway Bay. He tended her all through the night and morning of her labour, and was filled with joy when two pups spilled out, blinking and whimpering, into this world.

However, the love that Fergus felt was merely the unforeseen outcome of a jealous Immortal's jest. For the bitch was in truth a great noble woman named Tuiren who had been betrothed to Lollan, a Fianna warrior from Ulster. Prior to the engagement Lollan had a romantic understanding with an Immortal, Uchtdealb of the Fair Breast. It was she who had turned Tuiren into a hound. To compound Tuiren's misery she had then, in the guise of a messenger, given the bitch to Fergus, who she expected would be a most miserable and cruel master.

Tuiren was the aunt of Fionn Mac Cumhaill and when he heard she was missing he threatened Lollan with destruction. Lollan in turn confronted Uchtdealb of the Fair Breast, who confessed her actions but excused them as being the result of her passion for Lollan. Lollan agreed to wed the Immortal if she transformed Tuiren back into her human shape. However, Fionn decided that Tuiren's offspring would not be allowed their true human form. Rather, he ordered that they remain as hounds and that they would live with him.

The hounds were given the names Bran and Sceolan and, as Fionn's loyal companions, they were to become as renowned as any of the Fianna warriors. As to what Tuiren thought of her children being denied both a mother's love and a human form, there is no record.

For all his bravery Fionn, like many an Irishman before and since, had a confused and vexatious relationship with women. He was attracted to feisty, clever, fabulous women, but was perplexed by their refusal to do exactly what Fionn wanted them to do. The gathering of years, grey hairs and wrinkles did not bring him any greater understanding and empathy for the fairer sex. If anything, the disconnection between the reality and Fionn's ideal of femininity became more pronounced with every passing year.

It was in old age that Fionn's trouble with women reached its bitter climax. Like many a noble, the captain of the Fianna understood the need for constantly improving one's position in society, and so it was a moment of great joy when the High King of Ireland, Cormac Mac Art, agreed to Fionn marrying his daughter Grainne, a woman with hair as wild and red as a summer blaze, and with a passion and intellect to match. She agreed to the marriage but at a great celebratory feast her gaze fell on one of Fionn's young warriors, Diarmuid O'Duibhne. And as she looked at him, he turned and looked right back at her.

Later, with the guests drugged or drunk, Grainne and Diarmuid made their escape. And where else would a pair of young lusty miscreants flee to, but the hills and woodlands overlooking Galway Bay? Enraged by the treachery of his betrothed and his vassal, Fionn gathered together a great army of Fianna warriors from across Ireland. Bran and Sceolan too were set on the scent.

On the south side of Galway Bay, in the dark and thick woods of Derry Bo, Diarmuid sought protection from his foster-father, Aengus Og, a lord of the Tuatha de Danann and the brother of Finnbheara, King of the Immortals of Connacht. Wise in the ways and the passions of men, Aengus sought to bring an end to the episode before humiliation and anger turned into bloodshed and sorrow. He briefly succeeded in separating the lovers by magicking Grainne southwards to Shannon River and opened negotiations with Fionn and Cormac Mac Art.

Yet sometimes a story has its own dynamic and, try as they might, participants can do nothing to prevent the outcome. Fionn's fury burned ever brighter. His warriors and even his loyal hounds feared the outcome. In their own ways the men and beasts of Fionn tried to send warnings to Diarmuid, but every such attempt only added kindling to the blaze of their captain's hatred. As for Grainne and Diarmuid, they were reunited and, on the banks of one the rivers feeding into Galway Bay, finally became lovers.

Hunted to the death, the two fled onwards, from the woods in what is today Lawrencetown, westward along the hills and cliffs overlooking the southern shores of Galway Bay. The land before them grew ever narrower until the land was no more and they found themselves facing the dark and restless waters of the Atlantic, stretching on westwards to the end of everything. From this very final fingertip of the known world they looked around, seeking escape. To the south they could see the distant islands off the coast of Kerry, but the lands and waters there were black with warriors and mercenaries. Looking eastward to the route they had already travelled, all they could see was a throng of soldiery, seething like angry ants pouring from their nest to fight an intruder.

Only northwards, across the stretch of Galway Bay, was there any hope. The great mountains of Connemara remained, as yet, untamed by men, being the home of giants, Immortals and only the rare group of men and women. At the place known ever since as Diarmuid and Grainne's Leap they made a desperate jump northwards. But their strength was greatly reduced and the distance too great; the lovers fell short.

They landed in the middle of Inis Mór, the island that stretches a third of the way across the opening of Galway Bay. Inis Mór was the home of a great chief, and the lovers knew it was only a matter of time before he would send his warriors to capture them. Near the present-day village of Corruch, Diarmuid and Grainne made a bed of flatstones and lay down to watch the sun tumble bleeding into the waters of the Atlantic. In their hearts they had already accepted this would be their last evening together. The morrow would bring separation and death.

But death did not come for them, not yet. For Fionn suddenly called off his hunt. It may have been the wisdom of his years that finally tempered the Fianna captain's rage, or perhaps the fear of angering Aengus Og the Immortal foster-father of Diarmuid, or losing the patronage of Cormac Mac Art the royal father of Grainne. Perhaps it was enough to have the prey trapped: killing them would blemish Fionn's reputation; freeing them would add lustre.

Grainne and Diarmuid were allowed to live in peace in Sligo. There they had children and lived a good life. Yet as age tightened its hold on his limbs, so jealousy tightened its grip on Fionn's heart. He contrived for Diarmuid to be mortally wounded by a boar, then refused to save him. With the death of her beloved helpmeet, Grainne's spirit was finally tamed and she married Fionn. Yet his victory was short-lived.

It came to pass, not many years later, that Fionn and all his warriors gave battle to a host that outnumbered them sixty to one. Three generations of Fianna fought that day: white-bearded ancients, beautiful long-limbed men and eager smooth-chinned boys. All fell in the slaughter.

In sorrow the Immortals took the heroes' bodies and buried them, and to this day the Immortals have refused to say where the remains of the Fianna lie.

KILDARE

STEVE LALLY

DAN DONNELLY, THE KING OF THE CURRAGH

I wish to dedicate this story to Seamus McCormick, founder of the Sacred Heart Boxing Club, Newry. For he taught me to stand tall and face my fears with courage and dignity.

Also the Sculptor Aidan Harte who created the controversial sculpture of the Pooka Horse, created a magnificent sculpture of Dan Donnelly in 2021.

THE BALLAD OF DAN DONNELLY

Come all you true-born Irishmen wherever ye be,
I pray you give attention; and listen unto me;
It's of as true a story as ever you did hear,
About Donnelly and Cooper that fought at Kildare.
'Twas on the third of June, my boys the challenge was sent o'er,
From Britannia to old Granua to raise her sons once more,
To renew their satisfaction, and their credit to recall;
So they were in distraction since bold Donnelly conquered all.
When Granua read the challenge, and received it with a smile,
You had better haste into Kildare, my well-beloved child,
It's there you will reign victorious, as you have always done before,
And your deeds will shine most glorious all around Hibernia's shore.
The challenge was accepted, and those noble lads did prepare,
To meet with Captain Kelly on the Curragh of Kildare.
The Englishmen bet ten to one that day against poor Dan,
But such odds as these would never dismay the blood of Irishman.

When these two bully champions they stripped in the ring,
They faced each other manfully, and to work they did begin,
From six till nine they sparred on, till Danny knocked him down,
Well done, my child, Granua smiled, this is ten thousand pounds.
The second round that Cooper fought he knocked down Donnelly,
But Dan had steel likewise true game, and rose most manfully,
Right active then was Cooper and knocked Donnelly down once more
The English they all cried out, the battle you may give o'er.
The cheering of those English peers did make the valleys sound,
While their English champion kept prancing on the ground.
Full ten to one they freely bet, on the ground whereon they stand,
That their brave hero would soon deceive their boasting Irishman.
Long life to Miss Kelly, she recorded on the plain,
She boldly stepped into the ring, saying, Dan, what do you mean?
Saying, Dan, my boy, what do you mean, Hibernia's son, says she,
My whole estate I've bet on you, brave Donnelly.
When Donnelly received the fall after the second round,
He spoke to Captain Kelly, as he lay on the ground,
Saying, do not fear, for I'm not beat, although I got two falls,
I'll let them know, before I go, I'll make them pay for all.
I'm not afraid, brave Donnelly, Miss Kelly she did say,
For I have bet my coach and four that you may gain the day;
You are a true born Irishman, the gentry well do know,
And on the plains of sweet Kildare this day their valour show.
Donnelly rose up again, and meeting with great might,
For to surprise the nobles all he continued for to fight,
Cooper stood on his own defence, exertion proved in vain,
He then received a temple blow that reeled him on the plain.
Ye sons of proud Britannia, your boasting now give o'er,
Since by our hero Donnelly, your hero is no more;
In eleven rounds he got nine knocks down, besides broke his jawbone
Shake hands, says she, brave Donnelly, the battle is our own.

Anonymous

Growing up in Kildare I had heard enigmatic tales about the great boxer Dan Donnelly from the old-timers. I was always fascinated and when I heard that his arm was kept somewhere in the Curragh, this drove my curiosity even further. People talked about him like one would speak of a fictional superhero or a brave character from some film epic.

Who was this Dan Donnelly and why was and is he so revered both in Kildare and boxing folklore? Like Mohammed Ali, 'Sir Dan' was not only a champion of sport but a champion of the people. This is his story.

Dan Donnelly (March 1788 – 18 February 1820) was a pioneering pugilist and was Ireland's first home-grown boxing heavyweight champion. In 2008 Donnelly's name was entered into the 'International Boxing Hall of Fame' under the category of 'Boxing Pioneers'.

He was born into a poor Dublin family who lived in the city's violent and deprived docklands. His father was a carpenter and found it very hard to make ends meet due to the fact he had seventeen children and suffered from very poor health. It is speculated that he suffered from bronchitis, so the breathing in of sawdust combined with the extreme physical labour meant that he was often incapable of holding down the job.

With little or no income, the Donnelly family were always just one step away from the workhouse. Poverty pervaded Dublin at the end of the eighteenth century and Dan, like may other children of his day, went to work in his father's trade as soon as he was old enough.

Little did Dan know that the shadow of political revolution would come looking for him. In 1803, a group of Irish nationalists, including Robert Emmet, Thomas Russell and James Hope, made an attempt to secure Ireland's independence from the United Kingdom. The revolt failed and, despite going into hiding, Emmet was captured, tried and executed in Dublin by hanging and beheading for the crime of high treason on 20 September 1803.

Donnelly, realised he lived in a country that had no one to represent its people and that they were regarded as second-class citizens. The country was in desperate need for someone to come along and give the British a black eye. Dan was very proud of Ireland and its people; he wanted to give the Irish a sense of pride and self-respect at a time when it was badly needed. He hated nothing more than unfairness and to see advantage being taken of the weak and vulnerable. He was a proud man with high morals and principles and no lion could display more fury than Dan Donnelly when he witnessed what he considered to be blatant bullying.

Dan was not an easy man to get a rise out of and he would do whatever it took to bring peace and harmony to an otherwise potentially violent situation. On the rough Dublin streets he was constantly goaded to fight due to his great athletic stature, but when pushed too far he would make short work of his tormentors. After a while Dan got a name as a fine street fighter and defender of those weaker and more vulnerable than most. In fact, he became a bit of a celebrity amongst the people in his locality.

On one occasion, upon hearing the screams of a young woman down at the dockside area where he lived, Dan went to investigate and found two sailors attacking a girl. He witnessed them throw the poor girl into the River Liffey, so he dived in after her and pulled her out, saving her life. Unluckily for the exhausted Dan the thugs were waiting for him when he climbed out. They grabbed him, attacked him with stones and kicked him. His arm was so badly damaged that one would have thought it impossible that he should become Ireland's greatest boxer of his time. Fortunately for Dan, he was found by some good people and taken to Dr Steeven's Hospital (which still stands to this day beside St James' Gate, where Guinness is produced and opposite Heuston railway station). He was treated by the renowned surgeon Dr Abraham Colles, best known for his *Treatise on Surgical Anatomy* (1811).

Colles was well known for his compassion towards the city's poor and when he heard about the great act of selfless courage that the young Donnelly had performed he promised to do what he could to save the arm.

On first seeing the injury Dr Colles was sure that he would have to amputate it; but he decided to try to save the limb and with artistic precision and delicate dexterity he mended Donnelly's arm. When he was done, he affectionately put his arm around Dan and said he was nothing short of a 'Pocket Hercules'. Dan Donnelly was to be another one of Dublin's poor to thank the great Kilkenny-born doctor for his skill and kindness. I am sure Donnelly would have been knocked out again if he knew the magnitude of the man who had saved his arm. For Abraham Colles came from a long line of surgeons and he was twice president of the Royal College of Surgeons in Dublin. Widely acclaimed as a medical researcher and graphic lecturer, one of his papers on the fracture of a forearm bone was so highly acclaimed that the term *Colles Fracture* is still used to this day all over the world. But then one could argue that Colles would have passed out himself if he knew he had saved the arm of the future heavyweight boxing champion and legend of the sport.

Dan was to become the people's champion and a hero to those who could not fight for themselves. There are many stories in regard to this fact and one that stands out involves an old neighbour of his in Dublin, who had died in terrible impoverished conditions.

This neighbour was an elderly lady who lived on Townsend Street and, like sweet Molly Malone, she died of a fever and no one could save her. Because everybody was so terrified of being infected by the contagious disease, not a single soul would come forward to claim or remove the body of the deceased. When the bold Dan heard about this he was disgusted at the inhumanity of it all, especially knowing that the old woman in question was a kind and giving soul who would have gone out of her way to help any of her neighbours. So he took it upon himself to go to the woman's house and lift the remains. He wrapped her body in a blanket and put her over one of his broad shoulders. With that, he proceeded to take her corpse to a local churchyard. When he got there, he found some gravediggers in the process of digging a fresh grave. Dan announced that wished to put the woman's body into the new grave. The gravediggers were not at all pleased with this and dismissed him as a madman.

He looked at them firmly and told them if they did not step aside, they would be occupying the grave and went on to say that this was a land of equality and that this woman had as much right to buried in this grave as anyone. The gravediggers stood back as Donnelly grabbed a shovel from one of them and proceeded to bury the woman.

Donnelly was nearly 6 feet tall, and with a powerful, physical build. He weighed almost fourteen stone and had the heart of a lion. Fearless, strong and brave, Dan knew he had the makings of a great fighter. Ironically he was not comfortable with this, as it went against his principles and his disregard for violence. His strongest trait was his outgoing, friendly and sociable personality, and his strong sense of right and wrong. He had many friends and was very popular with all those who knew him. But, human nature being what it is, others around him saw this as a threat and a challenge and felt he should be taken down a peg or two.

There was an incident that took place when Dan was in his early twenties, while having a drink with his sick father, Joseph Donnelly, by the docks. Joseph took a fit of coughing. A brutish sailor who had just come off a boat saw this and began to mimic and berate the poor man. Dan begged the sailor to show some respect and leave his father be. According to the writer Patrick Myler in his book *Dan Donnelly 1788–1820 Pugilist, Publican, Playboy* the sailor replied by saying, 'Any cheek from you, me young bucko, and I'll teach you a lesson in respect.' Dan replied, 'I have no desire to fight you, but if it's what you want, then I'll not back down.' The sailor ran at Donnelly with a terrible roar, but Dan did not budge. He met the madman with a powerful right-hand punch. He broke the sailor's nose but, with blood streaming down his face, the sailor got to his feet and came at young Dan again. A terrible fight took place, lasting for over fifteen minutes, until the sailor could take no more and muttered the word 'enough' through bloody, swollen lips.

It was not long before word got out about Dan and how he dealt with the bully. The violent gangs and hard men of Dublin were intrigued by this new scrapper in town. They were also interested to hear that he was doing what the local constabulary could not do in regard to keeping the streets safe from their kind.

There was one particular character who was considered to be the best boxer in the city and had yet to be beaten. He was not too happy with all the great praise that Dan was getting. It seemed that in every bar and tavern he frequented he heard tall tales about Donnelly's exploits. So he decided that he would have to put him in his place. He toured through the city streets and went to all the haunts where he knew Dan frequented, announcing that he was demanding to face Dan in a fight. When Dan got word of this he declined, as he did not see himself as a man who would fight for the entertainment and sport of others. When the other man heard of Dan's reply he scoffed and deemed him a yellow-bellied coward with no guts. This was said in front of Dan's family and friends. Dan was furious and agreed to fight the man in order to save his honour. It was then announced that a fight would take place along the banks of the Grand Canal in Dublin. The people of the city were full of great excitement at the news of this epic event.

When the two combatants met by the canal, Dan tried his best to talk his opponent out of this foolish display of aggression. However, the other was not interested in such cowardly talk and threw the first punch. At first Dan did not engage, dancing around the ring, avoiding punches and throwing none himself. This caused the audience to become frustrated and hurl abuse at him. What the audience did not realise that this was a brilliant tactic, as Donnelly was tiring out his opponent and he made a fast, powerful attack in the sixteenth round. He knocked his opponent to the ground, after which he was unable to get to his feet. Donnelly was declared the new Champion of the City. After that there were no more challenges and Donnelly was more than happy with this.

Meanwhile in an English tavern, a wealthy Irish nobleman called Captain William Kelly overheard English pugilists talking with affiliates of what was known as 'The Fancy' (affluent dandies who supported and sponsored boxing during the eighteenth and nineteenth centuries). Kelly was horrified to hear them poking fun at Mother Ireland and her brave children, stating there was not a courageous man amongst them. They also said that they had gone to Ireland and issued open challenges to the best pugilists there, but no one accepted. What would one expect from a nation of conquered cowards?

Furious at the slander of his native land, Kelly was determined to find a fighting Irishman to take up the challenge. His search eventually took him to Dublin and to Dan Donnelly. Kelly went with his friend Robert Barclay Allardice, a Scotsman, who had heard of this fine young fighter. Allardice was better known as Captain Barclay. He was a renowned long-distance walker and trained many great pugilists. They were told that their man would not come easy as he was very much against the idea of fighting. When they arrived in Dublin they did not have much trouble finding their quarry at the carpenter's yard. But as expected, Dan Donnelly was not interested in fighting. He apologised to the two men for wasting their time and explained that he was a man of peace. But Kelly did not wish to return to England without a fighter who would prove those English dandies wrong. He tried to win Donnelly over by telling him how he would follow in the footsteps of Ireland's great warriors and mythical heroes such as Cuchulainn and Finn McCool. He told him of the epic battles and conquests that ancient Ireland was so famous for and now through Dan they could bring back this sense of pride and deference that had been lost by the Irish people after so many years of oppression. Kelly told Dan that he would bring fire back into the bellies of the Irish people and there was also a fair few bob to be made out it too. Dan was silent and then told Kelly he would think about it for a while.

He came back with: 'Gentlemen, I shall first return to you my sincere thanks for the great dependence you have on my country. The honour you have bestowed on me shall ever be cherished in my bosom. To appear before a multitude of spectators on a plain is wholly against my will, yet my country claims my support.' Dan then clenched his fists and raised his right arm, quivering with the passion of a man about to go into battle and he made this oath: 'I owe no spleen to Great Britain, but the man of any nation who presumes to offer insult to my country, this arm, while my life blood flows, shall defy.'

Kelly and Captain Barclay were impressed with the fine and noble answer that Donnelly gave them. They promised to train him and give him the best advice and expertise at their disposal. While training under Barclay, Donnelly earned his keep by looking after the cows at Calverstown Demense in Kildare. (Donnelly's initials were supposed to have been carved on the rafters at Calverstown House, but there is no sign of them now.)

Dan was to have his first major fight under the patronage of the eccentric Captain Kelly in the Curragh of Kildare. The bout took place on 14 September 1814 in a natural amphitheatre called Belcher's Hollow. Dan was up against a well-known English prize-fighter at the time, Tom Hall, who had been touring the country, teaching and demonstrating the art of boxing. By 1 o'clock there were thousands of people milling around the hollow, which had been roped off.

The art of boxing was very different to what it is now, with no real regard for the safety and wellbeing of the fighters. Fights would carry on until one of or both of the opponents were too weary and injured to continue. There were no rules against dirty tactics and just about anything went in regards to bringing the other man down. Fighters were allowed to jump on each other, bang their opponent's heads off the hard wooden corner posts, hold each other in headlocks, pull hair, ears, noses, etc. It was a vicious and unforgiving sport, and was more like a form of street fighting. The only redeeming thing about it was, unlike today where you have a ten-second countdown, back then you were allowed thirty seconds but once they were up, you were out.

For the first part of the fight between Hall and Donnelly, Hall proved to be the stronger opponent and he drew first blood. This was very significant, as bets were made on the basis of who would draw first blood in a bare-knuckle fight. What Hall did not know was that Dan was utilising his trademark tactic of lulling his opponent into a false sense of security and wearing him out at the same time. When Hall realised this and became aware of Donnelly's awesome strength and stamina he began to use a tactic of his own. Every time Donnelly went to deliver a killer blow Hall would drop down on one knee. This would allow him a thirty-second rest. Dan became very aggravated with this cowardly tactic and when Hall went down yet again on one knee, Dan lashed out and caught him on the ear. There was a gush of blood and Hall stated that Donnelly had cheated and should be disqualified. But the onlookers disagreed with Hall. Hall refused to fight on, saying that Donnelly had fouled him but Donnelly was declared the victor. The fight ended in some controversy, but to the Irish people, he was the champion.

After this victory 'Belcher's Hollow' was re-named 'Donnelly's Hollow'. Dan became an Irish champion in having done what so many other Irishmen before him had failed to do: 'stick it to the English oppressors' and live to tell the tale.

After this fight, Dan, fuelled by the admiration and loyalty of his fans, was full of confidence. So sure was he of his fighting ability that he stopped sticking to the strict training programme that Captain Barclay had laid out for him. In fact, he put his time and effort into a completely different activity; enjoying the high life. Dan was to be found in every bar, tavern and inn, being bought drinks and treated like a true superstar. What young man would not love this?

In an effort to curb Dan's drinking, Kelly and Barclay set up a wide circle of spies to keep track on Dan and keep him away from the taverns and bars. Dan eventually realised that Kelly and Barclay had his best interests at heart, so he complied with their regime. He knew, deep down, that the invaders loved to see an Irishman drunk, for that was a great and effortless way to keep him in his place, unable to think or fight for himself. He therefore returned to Dublin where he was greeted with more jubilation. After this Dan went back to work at the carpenters' workshop and resumed some sort of normality.

Dan's reputation as a fighter was to be immortalised in the summer of 1815. That same year Ireland was in a terrible state of affairs and powerless in the face of the mighty British Empire. Britain's navy was the most powerful in the world and its empire was growing stronger and greater by the day. The Duke of Wellington had recently conquered Napoleon Bonaparte at the Battle of Waterloo and Ireland was seen as an embarrassment and a nuisance, a blemish on the well-polished crown of mad old King George III. In fact, Arthur Wellesley, better known as the 1st Duke of Wellington or the Iron Duke, was born in 6 Merrion Street, Dublin in 1769. It was a common occurrence that he would receive jibes and dubious enquiries regarding his Irish birthplace. He would always reply, 'Being born in a stable does not make one a horse'.

It was going to take something or someone spectacular to raise the profile of Ireland and her people. Dan was the man for the job. Dan was their only chance to maintain some respect and dignity. The perfect opportunity for Dan to help his beloved Ireland rise from the ashes of oppression was about to come knocking at his door.

While Dan was working at the carpenters' workshop in Dublin he got word that two men wished to meet him in a local tavern. Something in Dan's bones told him that this was going to be significant, so he agreed.

He went to the tavern and ordered himself a drink; not long after, two unusual-looking men arrived to meet him. One of the men was an African-American who introduced himself as Tom Molineaux. He introduced his comrade as George Cooper. Molineaux explained to Donnelly that they were in Ireland together on an exhibition tour, teaching the art of boxing. Molineaux went on to inform Donnelly that they had been told by a reliable source that he was the best boxer in Ireland and that he would like to challenge him. Donnelly did not answer straight away and he took time to think about the offer. It was a great honour to be sought out by such great fighting men, but Donnelly did not see much of a challenge in Molineaux as he had already been beaten by Cooper. Donnelly told him he did not wish to fight a conquered man but he was willing to challenge Cooper if he was up for it. Molineaux was angered by this dismissive answer and began to insult Donnelly, calling him all sorts of terrible names. Cooper intervened to calm his comrade and happily agreed to Donnelly's challenge by shaking his hand. Sadly, Molineaux fell into a deep decline after this; he felt that a fight with Donnelly would have helped his profile – which was far from impressive. He had already been beaten by Tom Cribb for the English title and then defeated at the hands of Cooper. Molineaux already had a serious drink problem and the demons of his time as a slave on a Virginia Plantation, combined with defeat and rejection, proved to be too much. He fell ill while touring the west of Ireland in 1818 and died from liver failure at 34 years of age.

Dan's supporters were delighted to hear that he was going into the ring with Cooper. A native of Stone in Staffordshire, Cooper was a formidable fighter with a fierce reputation and was fondly known amongst the Fancy as 'The Bargeman', because he worked as a labourer on the canal barges. He was of gypsy origin and was rated as one of the greatest prizefighters of his time. Cooper would punch hard and fast with both fists and he was renowned for his 'one-two' technique, as well as being an expert at blocking and countering punches. Bill Richmond, an African-American pugilist who settled in England, said he was, 'the best natural fighter I have ever worked with'. The one thing that stood against Cooper as a fighter was his contempt for training. Then again, Donnelly was not overly enthusiastic about training either. He claimed he was doing well by limiting himself to just twenty-five glasses of whiskey a day in preparation for a fight. Although this was a far-fetched boast, Donnelly did prefer the taverns to the training ground. Kelly and Barclay made sure that Dan was kept on close watch and made sure he trained well. And Donnelly always complied in the end, for he knew that it was all for the greater good and he was determined to beat Cooper.

The fight was to take place on 13 December 1815 at the now newly christened Donnelly's Hollow at the Curragh of Kildare, the same place where Dan had beaten Hall. On the day of the fight there was an estimated 20,000 people from all over the country gathered to witness this historic event. The air was filled with excitement and fervour as bets were placed and Cooper was the favourite to win with odds of 10 to 1. It seemed that the Curragh of Kildare was the only place to be.

But George Cooper did not hold the same enthusiasm for the day. Not only was he made to feel unwelcome by the baying crowd but he was bamboozled by the organisers. Cooper had originally been told that the winner received £100 and the loser £20, but not enough cash was raised and now the victor would only receive £60 and the loser nothing at all. Cooper stated that he would not go through with the fight and sat for an hour while the organisers discussed the matter with him. There was a fear of a riot breaking out if the fight was cancelled and when Cooper realised he was up against 20,000 furious Irish people on their own turf, he thought it wiser to just fight the one man as originally intended and the bout went ahead.

Cooper arrived in the ring to polite applause but when Sir Dan made his appearance the roar and applause from the throngs of people could be heard for miles around.

The fight began with some basic sparring and then Donnelly landed the first punch to Cooper's neck. This was greeted by great cheers from the crowd. In retaliation Cooper applied what was known as 'the cross-buttock move'. This was a wrestling tactic and involved getting in front of Dan, throwing him over his hip and sending him crashing to the ground, winding him severely.

By the fifth round Dan was looking like he was going to lose. However, it was at this point that 'Miss Kelly', Captain Kelly's sister, intervened. She told him that she had put her entire fortune on the fight and would be left penniless and destitute if he lost. This appealed to Dan's chivalrous nature and he found the strength to carry on. It was also said that Miss Kelly slipped him a piece of sugar cane to replenish his strength. As she did this she was supposed to have uttered these words: 'Now my charmer, give him a warmer!' After this, the waning Dan revamped his mettle and the fight started to go in his favour.

By the seventh round Dan was fighting well and landed Cooper on the ground with an unmerciful jab. He then jumped on his chest, winding the poor English fighter beyond what seemed like any possible recovery. But Cooper did come back; he was a beast of a man and seemed truly unbeatable. But in the eleventh round, after twenty-two minutes of ferocious battling, Donnelly broke Cooper's jaw with a powerful punch and took him out. The fight was declared finished and Dan declared the overall champion. The cheers from the crowd could be heard for miles around as the people hailed the 'King of the Curragh'.

After the fight Dan marched up the hill to his carriage, some of the ecstatic fans ran behind him and dug with their bare hand at the footprints he left in his wake. The footprints are still there today, leading from the monument erected in his honour at Donnelly's Hollow, and are known as 'The Steps to Strength and Fame'. People regularly visit the site and can walk in the footsteps of Dan Donnelly.

Once Dan was in his carriage he ordered the driver to take him straight home to Dublin and not to hang around for the celebrations in Kildare. This was because he had squandered all his winnings after the last fight, and it had left him penniless. But when he arrived in Dublin there was a huge welcome for him. He was taken around the taverns of Dublin to celebrate his victory. The most outstanding part of these celebrations lay with his mother. As Donnelly was carried through the streets of Dublin on the shoulders of his adoring fans, his mother led the procession with one of her breasts bared. She slapped it and exclaimed, 'There's the breast that suckled him; there's the breast that suckled him!'

After the fight, Dan's winnings of £60 only lasted five weeks. He realised that he needed steady work, as fighting was an unpredictable and dangerous way to earn a crust and popularity did not keep food on the table.

Dan was offered a very attractive career as a publican by a wealthy timber merchant, more than likely his boss at Connery's timber yard. Although there were many pubs in Dublin it seemed like a good business move to have a famous sportsman as the landlord. Dan's tavern was on Poolbeg Street, near Townsend Street where he grew up. The bar was so busy that the staff had no time for breaks in the first three months of it opening. Dan married the girl that he had been courting for a long while and she helped run the bar, while his mother took care of the kitchen. As far as getting back into the ring was concerned, Donnelly vehemently declared that he had no interest at all, for now his place was as a good husband and businessman. However, Donnelly's heavy drinking and constant disappearance started to take their toll. He was squandering money and when he was not present, the punters who came to see him went to the other bars which he frequented, taking their business with them. Dan's poor wife and mother were left to run the show and they were too busy and physically incapable of stopping non-payers and troublemakers. The business suffered and it was not long before it fell away and Dan was left in debt and despair. The only way out was to return to the ring.

However, Dan's reputation as a fierce fighter frightened potential English contenders from coming over to Ireland to fight him and Cooper stated that an English fighter would be made to feel very unwelcome by the Irish mob. He assured them that they would do all in their power to make sure that their man won. This meant that Dan would have to go over to England to fight, which was something that he did not want to do.

He made a few more failed attempts to run bars, but all he did was run up more debt. In the end he succumbed and went to England for fight his third and final fight on 21 July 1819. He defeated Tom Oliver in thirty-four rounds on English turf, at Crawley Down in Sussex. After this final victory Dan stayed on in England, spending all but £20 of his winnings. As he left to return to Dublin he was stopped by a bailiff and handed a writ for £18, for money he owed to Jack Carter, an old sparring partner. He left with just £2 to his name.

There is a famous story of how Dan almost became a knight. After his win against Crawley, he met with Prince Regent, later to become King George IV. When introduced, the prince stated, 'I am glad to meet the best fighting man in Ireland'. Dan replied, 'I am not that your Royal Highness but I am the best in England'. The prince was very amused by this and took an instant liking to the brash young Irishman, bestowing a knighthood on him there and then. There is no hard evidence of this but it is a great story and he was fondly known as Sir Dan by his followers and some of the decadent dandies amongst the Fancy who respected his ability as a pugilist.

On 18 February 1820, Dan Donnelly died in his own pub, Pill Lane Public House. This was the only tavern he had left. A few days earlier he complained of feeling 'dull and heavy' but he just put it down to playing football and having a cold. He decided to take a stroll, thinking some fresh air would make him feel better. But this proved too strenuous for him. He was shivering and weak and returned to the tavern and went to bed. His wife was very worried to see how much his condition had worsened by the time she locked up for the night. The next day she called the doctor, who said that Dan was in a fatal condition. She would not believe this because her Dan was stronger than any other man in the land; he had never been sick before or if he was he would never show it nor complain. However, Dan had not taken care of himself; he drank to excess and would not eat food for days, only consuming whiskey and porter. He would sleep outdoors in the rain and on hard stone floors of cellars and barns if he was too drunk to make it home. It was also said that Dan had exerted himself with hard training and drank so much 'water' that he had suffered from 'Hyper-Hydratio', a form of water intoxication.

The night before his death, Dan went into convulsions and his wife asked him if she should get a priest. Dan agreed. The priest came and gave him the last rites. At one o'clock in the morning on Saturday 18 February 1820 Dan died in his weeping wife's arms. According to Patrick Myler's book *Regency Rouge, Dan Donnelly his Life and Legends* (O'Brien Press, 1976), Dan's last words to his wife were: 'I have been given so much and I have done so little'. He was only one month shy of his 32nd birthday when he died. Despite his self-depreciating last words, Dan Donnelly will always be remembered as a hero of the Irish people.

In 1979 a Blue Plaque was erected in Pill Lane, Dublin, commemorating the place of his death. In the Curragh of Kildare a stone obelisk was erected in 1888 in the centre of Donnelly's Hollow with the immortal words 'DAN DONNELLY BEAT COOPER ON THIS SPOT 13 DECEMBER 1815' in relief text on the stone surface.

Dan was buried for a brief period in the ancient 'Bully's Acre' cemetery in Kilmainham, Dublin, but his body was dug up by graverobbers and sold to an unscrupulous surgeon named Hall. The surgeon removed the corpse's right arm and returned the rest of the body for reburial. Dan Donnelly was only one of many victims of the body-snatchers. Judging by a report published in *The Lancet* in 1830, Bully's Acre was a playing field for the students of Dublin's medical schools:

> An abundant supply is obtained from the burial ground … there is no watch on this ground and the subjects are to be got with great facility.

Eventually the arm was preserved in red lead paint and sent to a medical college in Edinburgh, Scotland. Here it was used by students to study how the human arm operated. The arm then somehow ended up in a Victorian freakshow, travelling round Britain as part of a circus.

In the early twentieth century it finally got back to Ireland and it became the property of a Belfast bookmaker called Hugh 'Texas' McAleavy in 1904, who displayed it in his pub. McAleavy fell out of love with the macabre exhibition and had it put in his pub's attic where he told his staff not to enter as Donnelly's ghost was there. Eventually Dan's arm got back to Kildare, to the town of Kilcullen, in the 1950s, where it remained on show for forty-three years in the Hideout pub, which belonged to Jim Byrne. He decided to recreate the fight between Donnelly and Cooper at the Hollow in the Curragh.

The arm then travelled to America, where it went on display and then ended up in the Ulster American Folk Museum in Omagh Northern Ireland. It then found its way to the GAA Museum in Croke Park, Dublin, before returning home again. The arm is a grisly shadow to what was once the larger-than-life character Sir Dan Donnelly. Legend has it that he had the longest arms of any boxer and his reach was colossal.

One thing we know for sure, despite Dan's roguish and wayward sensibilities, he had the heart of a lion. When Ireland's people were at their lowest and there seemed to be nothing left to raise their broken spirits, Dan Donnelly stood up and gave the country a sense of pride and integrity that was thought to have died out with the ancient warriors of Erin.

Crawley Common's the place, and who chanced to be there,
Saw an Irishman all in his glory appear,
With his sprig of shillelagh and shamrock so green.
When in sweet Dublin city he first saw the light,
The midwife he kicked, put the nurse in a fright,
But said they, upon viewing him belly and back,
'He's the boy that will serve them all out with a whack,
From his sprig of shillelagh and shamrock to green'.

He thought about fighting before he could talk,
And instead of a go-cart, he first learned to walk,
With his sprig of shillelagh and shamrock so green,
George's Quay was his school, the right place for good breeding,
Where the boys mind their stops, if they don't mind their reading;
There Dan often studied from morning till dark,
And could write, but for shortness, like making his mark,
With his sprig of shillelagh and shamrock so green.

At his trade, as a chip, he was choice in his stuff,
None pleased him but what was hard, knotty and tough,
Like his sprig of shillelagh and shamrock so green,
Nor to strip for his work would he ever refuse,
And right hand and left he the mallet could use,
Length and distance could measure without line or rule,
And a flooring was famous without any tool
But his sprig of shillelagh and shamrock so green.

Whenever he arrogance happened to meet,
No matter in whom, he took out the conceit,
With his sprig of shillelagh and shamrock so green.
To the best of all nations that crossed Dublin bar,
Dan was ready at tipping a mill or a spar,
The hot-headed Welshmen served out by the lot
And cut up their leeks small enough for the pot,
With his sprig of shillelagh and shamrock so green.

Hall and Cooper went over with wonderful haste,
On the soil where it grew, they were longing to taste
Of the sprig of shillelagh and shamrock so green.
On the plains of Kildare 'twas proposed they should meet
And Donnelly wished to give both a good treat;
Yet so such things as Hall, gallant Dan never stooped,
But he took the stout Cooper, and Cooper well hooped,
With his sprig of shillelagh and shamrock so green.

And as Irishmen always politeness are taught,
He the visit returned, and to England he brought
His neat sprig of shillelagh and shamrock so green.
With the good-natured stranger the English seemed shy,
And Cooper no more fickle fortune would try;
But at last the game Oliver entered the field
And, though on his own soil, was soon forced to yield
To the sprig of shillelagh and shamrock so green.

With his kind English friends, he'll again just to please them,
Soon meet, and if troubled with money, soon lose them,
With his sprig of shillelagh and shamrock so green,
But if John Bull is wise, he'll from market hang back
And keep all the corn he has good in his sack,
As to him the next season no harvest will bring,
For, like hail, Dan will beat down the blossoms of spring,
With his sprig of shillelagh and shamrock so green.

THE DEVIL AT CASTLETOWN HOUSE

Growing up in Kildare, I went to school in Celbridge and I was always interested in Castletown House, a big stately home with a strange aura about it. The house was built by William 'Speaker' Conolly (then Speaker of the Irish House of Commons) in 1722. The Conolly family were well-known for building other fine pieces of architecture around Kildare. During the Great Famine they commissioned 'Conolly's Folly' or 'The Obelisk' to generate work for the starving. 'The Wonderful Barn' was also built to store food.

William 'Speaker' Conolly had a hunting lodge built on top of Mount-Pelier Hill in the Dublin Mountains in 1725. After his death in 1729 the lodge lay unused until it was bought by Richard Parsons, Earl of Rose, in 1735. He turned Conolly's lodge into 'The Hellfire Club'.

This became a place of demonic practices and extreme debauchery. And, indeed, it is said that Auld Nick himself decided to pay a visit. In fact, it seems that the Devil may have made several visits to Castletown House. I found this story in a great little book called Irish Ghosts *by J. Aeneas Corcoran published by Geddes & Grosset in 2002.*

Castletown House was inherited by William Conolly's nephew, who married Lady Anne Wentworth, daughter of the Earl of Stafford. One day she saw the figure of a tall man standing in the upper gallery, who proceeded to walk down a nonexistent staircase, past a big window, taking little steps as though each stair was quite shallow. He paused and laughed, a high, cold, arrogant laugh, as though he were the rightful owner of the place, mocking the people who lived there.

Ten years later, a staircase was built in exactly the location in which Lady Anne had seen the figure. More than twenty years after that, Lady Anne's son, Thomas Conolly, now the owner of the house, was walking in the garden with his wife, recalling the strange story of what his mother had seen in the hall. A few days after that, he was out riding with the Kildare Hounds. Many of the hunt gave up and went home, for the fox was proving to be tricky and elusive. Only Conolly and a handful of others were left, when he noticed that a newcomer seemed to have joined them. Mounted on a fine black horse that looked as fresh as if it had just come out of the stable door. The rider was a tall fellow, dressed in grey, with great thigh-boots.

'Good day to ye,' called out Conolly. 'A poor day for sport, though.'

The man merely grinned, showing large, discoloured teeth, then set his horse to the slope of the hill and went galloping up. At that same moment, the hounds began to bay, as if they were closing in on their prey. Conolly followed the horseman up the hill, but when he got to the brink, he reined in, astonished. The hounds were not to be seen, but the stranger stood there, dismounted from his horse, and with the bloody carcass of the fox held in both hands high above his head. He grinned again at Conolly, then lowered the fox's body to the level of his mouth, and in one swift bite with his great teeth, cut away the brush. Dropping the carcass he held it out to Conolly, still grinning.

The young squire of Castletown turned away in disgust, but the man then spoke: 'Conolly, if you will not take the brush, will you offer me a cup of something hot in your great house?'

The Conollys had always maintained a tradition of hospitality, and Thomas did not refuse, though there was something about the man, his leering smile, and his high voice, that turned his blood. 'There is hot rum punch at my house for all who want it,' he said.

The stranger entered the house at Conolly's side. Conolly saw him pause and survey the great entrance hall, and the staircase that came sweeping down from the gallery, past the window, and he heard a sound of hissing laughter escape from the man's lips. The stranger took a chair by the fire, and stretched out his legs, but when a servant came up, to help take his riding boots off, he waved the man away.

'Leave me be,' he said. 'I am sleepy and don't choose to be disturbed.'

He closed his eyes and appeared to settle down for a comfortable nap. Coming more closely to get a good look at him, Conolly was amazed to see that the stranger was as hairy as an animal. Coils of hair matted on the backs of his hands and more emerged at his cuffs. Tufts of coarse hair sprang from his ears. Beginning to have suspicions, Conolly told two of the servants to take off one of the sleeping stranger's boots. As they cautiously worked it off, a thickly haired leg appeared, terminating in a great black hairy hoof.

Hastily, as all the company retreated from the fire, Conolly sent a man to ride for the parish priest. As the priest arrived, the stranger awoke, glanced at his feet and saw one boot had been removed. With a snarl he rose up, and placed himself against the mantelpiece, right in front of the roaring fire, and laughed the same high-pitched, spine-chilling laugh that Lady Anne had heard all those years ago in the same room. The priest, as terrified as anyone, mumbled an incantation, but it had no effect except to provoke further demoniac laughter. At last, the priest in desperation threw his missal at the figure. It missed its target and struck the mirror above the fireplace, which shattered. But, at the threat of being touched by the holy book, the figure leapt high in the air and vanished, leaving only a greasy boot in the room, and a great crack in the stone fireplace.

THE STORY OF CASTLETOWN HOUSE IN CELBRIDGE

This is another version of the story given to a young person at Rathcoffey School over eighty years ago by John Brilly of Rathcoffey, Donadea. He had heard it several times from the old people around him. This story was collected by The Irish Folklore Commission in University College Dublin.

There was a gentleman living in Castletown House, Celbridge named Conolly. He was a very bad and wicked man. One morning he was going out to hunt. As he was mounting his horse, he said he would ride against the devil or get the fox's brush.

On leaving his own house a strange gentleman saluted him and accompanied him to the Liffey Bridge at Celbridge, where the hounds met and from where the hunt started. Conolly was supposed to have had a splendid horse. Still he was unable to get away from the man who kept following him. The fox was eventually caught and killed.

Conolly and his new friend were the only two who were there at the time and they were about to draw lots for the brush when the stranger agreed to give it to Conolly. Conolly invited his friend home to dinner. James Graham, the head groom, was ordered to take care of the stranger's horse.

After dinner the guests played a game of cards and the stranger was winning every game. A card fell on the floor. Conolly stooped down to pick it up and he noticed a cloven hoof instead of a foot on the strange man. Conolly called his servants and attendants and tried to get the stranger out of the house, but they failed. He sent his carriage for the RIC but they too were unable to get the stranger out of the house.

All the animals in the outhouses burst their doors and raced madly through the yards. Conolly sent for the Protestant minister of the place, but the stranger just laughed at him. He remained there for two days.

The gardener asked Conolly if he would go for the priest. Initially Conolly refused but at last he gave in and went himself for Father Kenny of Celbridge. When the priest arrived at the house he found the devil in a room burning up in a great fire.

The priest prayed for a long time and the devil disappeared through the hearth stone, leaving behind a large split in this stone.

The priest, Father Kenny, only lived for nine months afterwards.

THE DEVIL AND TOM CONOLLY

I found this little masterpiece of 'folk-art' in the 1911 edition of the Kildare Archaeological Society Journal, *p.415, under the chapter entitled 'Ballads and Poems of the County Kildare'. The piece is entitled 'The Devil and Tom Conolly: An Eighteenth Century Legend of Castletown'. The author goes under the strange title of 'A Broth of a Boy (Russell)'.*

The ballad is based on Tom 'Squire' Conolly's encounter with the Black Earl of Hell. The terminology and turn of phrase is unique to the period and there is a good balance of humour and horror alike. The poor fox is referred to as 'Reynard' (an old folkloric name for the red fox or trickster) and the Devil as 'Auld Nick', giving the piece a sense of familiarity and empathy with the characters. You will notice that certain words are missing; this was common at the period so as to not cause offence or controversy to the family this ballad is based on. The Ballad first appeared in 1843 in The Dublin University Magazine, *Vol. xxii, p.677 and was reprinted among 'The Kishoge Papers' in 1877.*

It is a brilliant piece of work that conjures up so much wonderful imagery and excitement, creating the archetypal great fireside tale.

'A southerly wind and a cloudy sky.
What a beautiful day for the Scent to lie!'
Says a huntsman old, with a very keen eye,
And a very red nose, to a whipper in by,
As he sits on the back of a very spruce hack,
And looks with delight on a beautiful pack
Of foxhounds as ever yet ran a track.

There were Howler and Jowler and Towser and Yelper
And boxer and pincher and Snarler and Skelper.
But Alas! And Alack! That it rests to be said,
That the last of the pack is some eighty years dead!

And the huntsman that sat on the back of the hack,
Died very soon after the last of the pack,
Having kept up the chase by good humour and mirth'
'Till Death one fine afternoon ran him to earth.

Rest to his bones! He has gone for aye,
And the sod lies cold on his colder clay;
He lists no more to the deep-mouthed bay,
Nor wakes the hills with his 'Hark Away!'
But never did a man with a hunting-whip rack
That I'd back at a fence against red-nosed Jack.

The cover is reached, and a better array
Of sportsmen it never has seen than to-day.
'Tis as gallant as all Ireland could yield:
The horsemen to all kinds of devilment steeled,
The best of the senate, the bench and the bar,
Whose mirth even Petty and Coke couldn't mar.

Bright spirits! Regarded with pride by a race
That loved Genius unmasked by Stupidity's face;
Nor fancied that Wisdom high places should quit
If she flung round her shoulders the mantle of wit!
The hunting-cap triumphs today o're the wig,
The ermine is doffed for a sportsmanlike rig;
But enough of the horsemen: the nags that they ride
Are as noble as horsemen might ever bestride;
In bottom or speed, few could match them indeed,
And if put to the pound wall of Ballinasloe,
There are plenty amongst them, who would never look,
'No!'

But the best mounted man at that gay coer-side
Is honest Tom Conolly, Castletown'a pride;

And mirth and good fellowship beam in his eye,
Such a goodly collection of guests to descry;
For guests shall be all, in Tom Conolly's hall,
Who keeps 'open house' for the great and the small;
And none who takes share in the fox-hunt today
Ere midnight from Castletown's mansion shall stray.

Right warm are the greetings that welcome the squire,
As he rides up-but the entire preamble will tire;
Besides that the hounds through the brushwood are dodging,
And making inquiries where Reynard is lodging;
Some snuffing the ground, with a caution profound;
Some running and poking their noses all round;
And now of the whole not a vestige is there,
But a number of tails cocked up in the air;
And now there's a bark, and a yelp, and a cry,
And the horsemen are still standing anxiously by;
And some of the pack
Are at length on the track;
And now there's a shout!
Sly old Reynard leaps out.

'Hold hard! Don't ride over the dogs!'
What a scramble!
Away go the hounds in the wake of the fox!
Away go the horsemen thro' brushwood and bramble!
Away go they all, o'er brooks, fences and rocks!
Afar in the plain, they are stretching amain:
Each sinew and nerve do the gallant steeds strain,
While the musical cry of the fleet footed hound
Is ringing in chorus melodiously round,
And the horseman who rides at the tail of the pack
Is a very tall gentleman, dressed all in black!

Away! Away! On his restless bed
His wearied limbs let the sluggard spread,
His eyes on the glorious morning close,
And fancy ease in that dull repose!
Give me to taste of the refreshing draught
Of the early breeze, on the green hill quaffed!
Give me to fly, with the lightning's speed
On the bounding back of the gallant steed!
Give me to bend o'er the floating mane,
While the blood leaps wild in each thrilling vein!
Oh! Who that has felt the joy intense,
To tempt the torrent, to dare the fence,
But feels each pleasure beside give place
To the manly danger that waits the chase?

Onward still – 'tis a spanking run
As e'er was seen by morning's sun!
Onward still, O'er plain the hill
Gad, 'tis a pace the Devil to kill!
A few of the nags it will puzzle, I trow,
To ride at that neat bit of masonry now.
Steady there, black fellow! – over he goes;
Well done, old bay! – ho! The brown fellow toes,
And pitches his rider clean out on his nose!
Eighteen out of fifty their mettle attest,
There's a very nice view from the road for the rest.

And now the 'boreen', with that rascally screen
Of furze on each bank – by old Nim, that's a poser!
There's the black fellow at it – 'Gad, over he goes, sir!'
Well done, Conolly! Stick to the brute, you dog!
Though he does seem old Beelzebub riding incog.
Ha! The third fellow's blown – No go, doctor, you're thrown,
And have fractured your 'Dexter Clavicular' bone;
Gad, here's the Solicitor-General down on him:

Who could think that he ever had got wig or gown on him?
Cleared gallantly! But sure, 'tis plain common sense,
Bar practice should fit a man well for a fence.
Five more show they're good ones, in bottom and speed;
But that tall, strange, black gentleman still keeps the lead!

Ha! Reynard, you're done for, my boy! At your back
Old Jowler and Clinker come, leading the pack;
Ay, close at your brush, they are making a rush;
Come face 'em old fellow, and die like a thrush!
Well snapped, but won't do, my poor 'modereen rue!'
That squeeze in the gullet has finished your breath;
And that very black horseman is in at the death!

The very black horseman dismounts from his steed
And takes off Reynard's brush with all sportsman-like heed;
Then patting the nag, with air of a wag,
Says, 'This is cool work, my old fellow, to-day!'
At which the black steed gives a very loud neigh;
And it is odd indeed, neither rider nor steed
Seems one whit the worse of their very great speed;
Though the next four or five, who this moment arrive,
Their horses all foaming, themselves all bemired,
Look beyond any doubt all heartily tired,
As they think, 'Who the deuce can be this chap in black,
Who has ridden all day at the tail of the pack?'

The group has come up with the stranger the while,
Who takes off his hat to the squire, with a smile,
And hands him the brush, with an air most polite,
Expressing his joy at transferring the right,
Which only the speed of the hunter had won
To him who had shown them so noble a run
And whose name, he would add, he had heard from a lad,
As a toast through all Ireland for humour and fun.

'Gad, sir,' says the squire,
'Whether most to admire, your politeness or daring I'm puzzled to say;
But though I've seen hunting enough in my day,
All I've met with must yield, to your feats in the field.
I trust I at least can induce you to dine,
And your horsemanship pledge in a bumper of wine;
And if longer you'll honour my house as a dweller.
All I promise you is you'll find more in the cellar.'

'Thanks Tom! I beg pardon, I make so d___d free,
When a man of your thorough good nature I see!
But excuse it'.
'Excuse it my excellent friend!
'Tis the thing of all others I wish you'd not mend;
None but good fellow had ever the trick.
But your name by the way?'
'Mine? Oh, pray call me Nick.'

'Very good, there's a spice of the devil about it!'
'A spice of the devil! Ay, faith, who can doubt it?
I'm dressed by the way in his livery sainted;
But they say the old boy's not as black as he's painted;
And this clerical suit ___'
'You're no parson sure come?'
'Ah, no pumping on that, my friend, Conolly ___mum!
This clerical suit, faith, though sombre and sad,
Is no bad thing at all, with the women, my lad!'

'Well done, Nick, on my life, I'll look after my wife,
If you came in way.'
'Gad,' says Nick with a laugh.
'To look after yourself, would be better by half'.
'Look after myself!' says the squire
'Lord! Why so? You've no partnership, sure, your namesake below?'
'No,' says Nick with a squint, 'I mean only to hint;

But I'll do it more plainly, for fear of mistake,
If we play at blind-hookey, be d____d wide awake'.
Then with laughter and jest, Honest Tom and his guest
Ride along, while their humour is shared by the rest,
Who vow, one and all, Master Nick to install,
As the prince of good fellows; and just at nightfall
They reach most good-humour'dly Castletown Hall.

'Tis a glorious thing when the wintry sun,
Ashamed of himself, has cut and run;
When the drizzling rain falls thick and fast,
And the shivering poplars stand aghast;
No sight abroad, but landscape bleak,
No sound, save whistle, and howl, and creak;
'Tis a glorious thing, in the dismal hour,
To be snugly housed from the tempest's power,
With a blazing fire, and a smoking board,
With all the best things of the season stored!
Not costly, mind, but good plain dinner,
To suit the wants of an erring sinner.

But enough, to their dinner the hunting folk sit!
With silence displaying more wisdom than wit.
But with dessert, wit begins to assert
His claims to attention; and near to its close
Takes the field while old wisdom goes off in a doze.

Then after a couple of bumpers of wine,
Ye gods, how the urchin commences to shine!
While, as for the stranger, his feats in the field
To his feats at the table unspeakably yield;
In drinking, in laughter, in frolic and jest,
He seems but the sun who gives light to the rest;
And after a while, when the squire begs a song from him,
He sings for them this, which grave folk will think wrong of him:

A fig for philosophy's rules!
Our stay is too brief upon earth,
To spare any time in the schools,
Save those of Love, Music and Mirth:
Yes! Theirs is exquisite lore
We can learn in life's summer by heart;
While the winter of gloomy four score
Leaves fools in philosophy's art.
Oh! Surely, if life's but a day,
'Tis vain o'er dull volumes to pine;
Let the sage choose what studies he may,
But Mirth, Love and Music be mine!

What a fool was Chaldea's old seer
Who studied the planters afar!
While the bright eye of woman is near;
My book be that beautiful star!
The lore of the planets who seeks
Is years in acquiring the art;
While the language dear woman's eye speaks
Is learned in a minute by her!
Then surely if life's but a day,
'Tis vain o'er dull volumes to pine;
Let the stars be his book as they may,
But the bright eye of woman be mine.

The chymist may learnedly tell
Of the treasures his art can unmask;
But the grape-juice has in it a spell
Which, is all of his lore that I ask.
In gazing on Woman's bright eyes
I feel all the star-student's bliss;
And chemistry's happiest prize
I find in a goblet like this!

Then fill up, if life's but a day,
What fool o'er dull volumes would pine?
Love and Mirth we can learn on the way,
And to praise them in music be mine!

'Hip, hip, hurrah!'
How they're cheering away.
'Hip, hip' They're growing uncommonly gay,
'Hip 'tis a way we've got in the' 'Hic-hiccup'
Lord! What a deuce of a shindy they kick up!
But at length they have done,
And drop off, one by one,
From their chairs, overcome by the claret and fun:
And at a quarter to four
All lie stretched out on the floor,
Enjoying in chorus a mighty fine snore;
While still to the claret, like gay fellows, stick
The warm-hearted squire and his jolly friend Nick!

There's a cooper of wine by Tom Conolly's chair
And he stoops for a bottle
At what does he stare?
My fine lad, you're found out!
There's the cloven foot plainly as the eye can behold.
'Cut your stick master Nick, if I may make so bold!
'Pon my life, what a jest, to have you as a guest.
You toping by dozens Lafitte's very best!
Be off sir, you've drunk of my wine to satiety.'

'No thank you,' says Nick; 'Tom I like your society,
I like your good humour. I relish your wit,
And I'm d____d but I very much like your Lafitte.
You may guess that your wine, has more bouquet than mine
And I'll stay, my old boy, in your mansion a dweller,

While a drop of such claret remains in your cellar!
I've my reasons for this, but 'twere needless to state 'em,
For this, my dear fellow, is my ultimatum!'

Tom rings for the flunkies: They enter, 'What now?'
He looks at Old Nick, with a very dark brow
And says, while the latter complacently bears
His glance 'Kick that insolent rascal downstairs!'
At their master's behest, they approach to the guest,
Though to kick him downstairs seems no joke at the best;
But when they draw near, with humours leer
Nick cries 'My good friends, you had better be civil.
'Tis not pleasant, believe me, to deal with the Devil!
I'm that much-abused person so do keep aloof,
And, lest you should doubt me, pray look at my hoof'.
Then lifting his leg in the air most polite,
He places the cloven hoof full in their sight,
When at once, with a roar, they all rush to the door;
And stumbling o'er wine-coopers, sleepers and chairs,
Never stop till they've got to the foot of the stairs.
The parson is sent for, he comes, 'tis no go,
Nick plainly defies him to send him below:
With a comical phiz, says he'll stay where he is,
And bids him be gone, for an arrant old quiz!
Asks how is his mother, and treats him indeed
With impertinence nothing on earth could exceed.

A pleasant finale, in truth, to a feast,
There's but one hope remaining, to send for a priest;
Though the parson on hearing it, says 'tis all fudge,
And vows that he never induce Nick to budge.
Still, as 'tis the sole hope of getting a severance
From Nick. The squire sends off at once for his reverence,
And would send for the Pope, if he saw any hope
That his power could induce the old boy to elope.

Father Malachy, sure that for Nick he's a match,
Doesn't ask better sport than to come to the scratch;
And arrives at the hall, in the midst of them all
While the frightened domestics' scarce venture to crawl:
And learning the state of affairs from the squire,
Says he'll soon make his guest from the parlour retire,
If he'll only agree, to give him rent free
A plot for a chapel; but if he refuses,
Master Nick may stay with him as long as he chooses.
'A plot for a chapel!' Tom Conolly cries
'Faith, I'll build one myself that will gladden your eyes,
If Old Nick cuts his stick.'

'That he shall double quick, if you undertake to stand
mortar and brick.'

'Agreed!' says the Squire; so the priest takes his book,
Giving Nick at the same time a terrible look
Then th' Exorcism begins, but Old Nick only grins,
And asks him to read out the 'Table of Sins';
'For between you and me, Holy Father' says he
'That's light and agreeable reading, you see,
And if you look it carefully over, I bet,
Your reverence will find you're a bit in my debt!'

At an insult so dire, Father Malachy's ire
Was aroused in an instant; so, closing the book,
He gives the arch-rascal one desperate look,
Then, with blessed precision, the volume lets fly,
And hits the arch-enemy fair in the eye!
There's a terrible yell that might startle all hell!
A flash, and a very strong brimstony smell!
And, save a great cleft, from his exit so deft
Not a trace of the gentleman's visit is left;
But the book, which was flung, in his visage was clung

To the wainscot, and sticks so tenaciously to it,
You'd fancy some means supernatural glue it;
And his reverence in fact finds it fixed to the mortar,
To the wonder of all, a full inch and a quarter!
Where the mark of it still to this day may be seen,
Or if not, they can show you where once it has been;
And if after that any doubts on it seize you,
All I can say is 'tis not easy to please you.

The delight of the Squire I, of course, can't express.
That 'tis boundless indeed you might easily guess
The very next day, he gives orders to lay,
The chapel's foundation; and early in May,
If in his excursions Nick happened to pass there;
And it stands to this day, slate, stone, mortar and brick
By Tom Conolly built, to get rid of Old Nick.

Since the period that Nick got this touch in the eye,
Of displaying his hoof he has grown very shy;
You can scarce find him out by his ill-shapen stump,
For he sticks to the rule: 'Keep your toe in your Pump!'

DUBLIN

BRENDAN NOLAN

THE HA'PENNY BRIDGE

The River Liffey has had many bridges thrown over it. Most of them carry both people and wheeled traffic, but a few are for pedestrians only.

With an abundance of bridges now available, we do not think about how we would cross the river if the bridges weren't there, these days. Earlier citizens and visitors crossed over the river using fords when the tidal river was at low tide. Then walls were built to lessen flooding as port commerce demanded a hard standing be provided at the water's edge. The odd bridge was built to convey materials to the other side. Here and there, ferries took people from one side to the other and there was a commercial charge for doing so. A number of ferries operated from the Temple Bar area on the southern side of Liffey Street and on the other.

Crow Street Theatre, the chief theatre in the city, lay on the southern side of the city. Many people crossed over to attend its productions. Then a proposal was made to replace seven ferries with a single-span metal bridge at the Bagino Slip. It would exact a toll for its use in crossing over.

An Alderman Beresford and William Walsh joined together to erect the bridge as a commercial enterprise. It opened for business in 1816 and was formally named Wellington Bridge, but was known to most Dubliners as the Metal Bridge, at least in its early days. Arthur Wellesley, 1st Duke of Wellington, had just defeated Napoleon Bonaparte at the Battle of Waterloo, so it seemed appropriate to call the bridge after him. Wellesley was born in a fine house on Merrion Street and was the only Dubliner to be elected Prime Minister of the United Kingdom.

The bridge was the only pedestrian bridge on the Liffey until the Millennium Bridge was opened upstream in 2000. It was cast at Coalbrookdale in Shropshire in England. The right to exact tolls was set for a period of one hundred years from 1816. Paying tolls to cross the relatively short span was subject to some resentment among the populace and any way that could be used to circumvent the toll was to be applauded by the common man.

The adjacent Bachelors Walk and Ormond Quay were populated for many years by the city's auction rooms. People brought their household goods, including beds and wardrobes to be sold at auction there. Those that wanted these second-hand goods came to bid for them. It made this a very busy area of the city, with milling masses of people either collecting or depositing all kinds of merchandise into and out of a myriad of premises along the quays. In the evening, theatre goers crossed the bridge along with ordinary folk going about their daily lives as best they could.

The story of the pair of tinkers who took exception to paying the toll in pursuit of their trade is a battle of wits and triumph, and is not unlike the history of a wonderful night on the town. Some claim to recollect all the little events which lead up to the climax of the story, but few can recollect their order or the exact time they occurred, which makes all the difference to their value or importance.

The toll had been set at a half penny, of which there were some 480 in an Irish pound of the day. But it was still more than the tinkers would pay. After a while, the crossing came to be known as the Ha'penny Bridge, as well as its official name of Wellington Bridge and its unofficial moniker of the Metal Bridge. To confuse matters even further, the present-day official name for the bridge is the Liffey Bridge.

In its original form, the bridge had a space at either end where a person stepped through a turnstile to pay the toll and then proceeded across the bridge. In those very early days, a toll taker collected the ha'pennies of crossing pedestrians of all classes and creeds. It was thus when the pair of travelling tinkers arrived at the crossing. The tinkers, or workers in tin and travelling menders of metal household utensils, repaired and replaced objects made of tin on the spot, usually at the person's residence or place of business.

They were just some of the many artisans to be found on the streets of Dublin at this time. Bread firms employed men who drove two-wheeled horse carts to deliver freshly baked breads and confectionary to the shops and houses in the city. Laundrymen, wearing uniforms and caps, delivered and collected laundry in the days before the domestic washing machine replaced such activities. Coal men carted coal for the city's coal merchants on four-wheeled lorries. The tolling of the bell on an independent bellman's lorry showed he had coal for sale; when it was silenced he was finished selling for now. Vegetable sellers and fishwives passed by, on their way from the city markets. Newspaper sellers called out the headlines of the day to attract buyers to the paper. In the midst of this hubbub, our pair of tinkers, Johnny and Paudge, approached the toll taker in their most civil manner.

The busy keeper heard the murmur of two voices, where only shortly before he had been listening to the sleepy, hissing, grating sound of a scissors-grinder's wheel as the sturdy Paudge sharpened up knives for Molly, a passing fishwife who had a nice smile and dancing eyes and curled hair worn to her shoulder to show she was not spoken for yet. Charming as she was, Paudge made sure she paid over the few coins agreed for the work, before she walked off pushing her cart with the day's offerings laid out for sale for the crowds to examine.

Where Paudge had been working, he was now standing beside Johnny who was the spokesperson for the pair of them. Johnny was a taller figure than his partner. He wore a dilapidated chimney hat on his head which stood out among the flat caps of the working Dubliners who were passing by. He touched his hat respectfully as he approached the toll man. He asked how much the price of crossing the bridge might be for a working man that did not earn very much at all, and who had earned even less this week past. The keeper said it was a half penny, as everyone that had any business on the bridge well knew. He looked past Johnny to where Paudge stood with most of their paraphernalia strewn about his person. They travelled light for their work was itinerant and they had no use for heavy tools and had no horse or pack animal to carry it for them.

Paudge tipped his own hat at the keeper to show he was part of the transaction, but he was content to allow the others to discuss the matter between them, as men of commerce might. Johnny asked if there was an allowance for someone crossing on foot. 'It's a pedestrian bridge,' the busy keeper snapped back at him, all the while watching that nobody slipped past without paying their fair share. Was there any discount if two people crossed over at the same time and did not return? It was well known that tinkers could not keep still, and it would be unusual for one to return over a bridge once he had gone to the bother of crossing over to the other side, in the first place. To make the proposition more attractive, Johnny told the keeper that some day they would be back again and would most certainly use the bridge once more and would pay the toll all over again on that occasion. 'The toll is a ha'penny,' the keeper replied sternly, to show that he would speak civilly to anyone for a time, but beyond that, he was a busy man.

Johnny stepped away after giving thanks to the man for his forthright answers. He and Paudge then wandered away a little from the bridge to appear as if they were no longer interested in crossing over. In fact, they did so only to regroup and review the situation now that the reconnoitre had been completed. There were other ways of crossing the Liffey. Other bridges did not require any payment at all, but the challenge was there now and Paudge and Johnny were determined to cross over the Metal Bridge. They were equally determined they were not going to hand over the full amount demanded. For if they were not natives of the city, they were natives of the country and deserved to be accommodated in their travels as much as any local person might be.

They waited until the flow of people had risen up once more and the keeper was busier than he had been all morning. Paudge stepped forward and asked a question of the toll taker. 'Do you charge anything, Sir, for luggage, or for what a man may carry over on his back?' he asked. The keeper looked at the well-built man in front of him. Paudge was festooned with all the tools of his trade, and held the sharpening wheel in a maw of a hand. The wheel looked like the plaything of a privileged child in a nursery in one of the big houses of Dublin. The keeper responded saying that there was no extra charge for luggage over and above the half-penny toll, but that it must be paid. 'Thank you Sir', said Paudge and he stepped back a little to hunch down. To the toll taker's astonishment he saw Johnny come running along the path to leap up on the back of the crouching man. Paudge straightened up. His thick arms held Johnny's skinny legs as safely as if they were bolted together. His hands held their tools and equipment, Johnny's hands held the rest and away they went for the toll bridge like that.

When the toll taker tried to stop them, Paudge reminded him that he had said there was no charge for luggage and poor Johnny, having taken faint, was now his burden to carry across the bridge. As he moved on Johnny dropped the single ha'penny piece into the hand of the astonished toll taker. 'God bless you Sir,' said a contented Johnny as the pair crossed the bridge. 'We'll see you the next time we are in Dublin. It surely is a fine bridge you have, God bless it and all who cross over it.' And with that they were gone.

DEAD CAT BOUNCE

Who knows what goes on in a cat's mind? They pay lip service to man, but leave as soon as the call comes from their kin, day or night. They return when it suits them and devil a one knows what transpired while they were away.

There is a story that is told in many ways and in many countries of a man that witnessed hordes of cats burying the king cat, with a great torch-lit ceremony one pitch black night. Often, when the story is told in the presence of a cat, he will listen attentively to the end of the tale where the king cat is declared dead. Then, the formerly silent animal attacks the teller or races away declaring itself to be the new king of the cats.

A story is told of a meeting of cats on the road near Tallaght in County Dublin. They were there, it was said, to elect a new king. In the suffocating darkness, a man, with drink on him and in charge of an ass and cart, drove through them. He killed so many cats that locals swept barrowfuls of them off the road, the next morning. The now sober man did not sleep for weeks afterwards for fear the watching, hating cats would tear his throat open in revenge if he fell asleep. His only solution was to buy a pair of terriers that he loosed on the cats until they were dispersed to the four winds. Whatever evil eye had been placed on him for killing cats, with the wheels of his cart, was finally sent away to another parish. What happened to him when the dogs grew old and slow and the descendants of the vengeful cats returned we do not know. But ever afterwards he walked with a permanent twist in his neck from looking over his shoulder. If he saw a big buck cat on the path ahead of him, he always crossed the road to be away from it.

Another man in the county of Dublin had cause to wonder at the mortality of cats. He wondered how many lives a cat really had after what happened to him on the high descent down a steep hill in the valley of the Liffey. Clem lived all his life in the valley not far from Dublin City. To get to the nearest town he had to climb up one hill, pushing his bicycle by the saddle and walking freely beside it. Once there, he freewheeled down the far side to the shops and the bookies in the nearest village.

When he was out of puff from pushing the old black Raleigh bicycle with the well sprung Brooks saddle on it up one hill, he freewheeled down the other side without bothering with brakes at all. This was no major decision to make for the bike had no brakes at all left on it. The brake block shivered and shuddered and eventually ceased to greet the rim of the wheel at all. In any case, Clem leaned into the corners mightily on the way down and took the entire width of the road when necessary to gather speed on a sharp bend. On the odd day when he slowed his descent, he leant backwards and rubbed the side of his boot on the rim of the front wheel to slow down. Such was the way he progressed and no harm ever came to him over it. He even had time to whoop at people he knew as he whizzed past them on his way downhill.

One day, a neighbour woman asked him to drown a dead cat for her. The cat was a family pet, she explained, and she did not want to throw it away herself in her grief. Clem was a little taken aback, for he had only called in to see if she knew whether the milkman was on holidays or not or had someone stolen the milk from his door early that morning. He suspected the neighbour herself to be the milk thief, but would never say so. At one time, it was perfectly acceptable to drop animals into the river, where they floated away as a passing treat for local water rats. The woman was an old friend of his departed mother so he agreed.

You would think it would be an easy task, to peg a tied plastic bag with a dead cat inside it into the river, but no. Every time Clem approached the river bank, there was someone about, and this stayed his hand, for he did not want to be seen throwing dead cats about the place, for he too was aware of the strange confraternity that made cats the unsettling presence they are, when they take a mind to watch your every movement. He did not want to be the target of vengeful cats, lurking along the dark road at night. When he tried to dispose of the cat under the cover of darkness, there was always a constant steam of cars coming along the road with their headlights on. So, he brought the cat home and left it in the back scullery of his house in the red fertiliser plastic bag while he waited for a better time to present itself. It stayed there for a few days while he forgot about such considerations in favour of a more pressing matter, that was, the form of three racehorses that were running on Saturday in three different races.

If he placed a bet on the first, with the winnings going onto the second, and the winnings of that being placed on the third horse, and if that horse won, he would have a small fortune to vex him with the spending of it. He discussed these matters with knowledgeable men in the run up to the event. Those that mooned it with him, over a glass or two at his home, were Christian enough not to mention the pervasive smell of recent death hanging about the house. Clem eventually noticed it on the Saturday of his big betting coup, for he could not avoid it any more. It was a powerful smell and if the rats from surrounding townlands had not yet arrived to feast on the desiccated cat, it was only because they had sent invitations to their cousins to join them and they were waiting for them to arrive to begin the festivities.

Clem was faced with a dilemma. He needed to get to town to the bookies to place the first bet as soon as possible, but it was obvious the dead cat had outstayed its welcome. It might not be safe to leave it here in his house, for a passing stranger might call the Garda to report the scent of a rotting body. Clem was not sure, but he thought there might be a rule about keeping unburied bodies on your premises for too long. He would do away with it now. No time like the present.

He pumped up the tyres of the bike to achieve more speed. He tucked his trousers into his tan socks and zipped up his good green anorak so that it would not cause counter momentum by filling with air on the descent. When he was ready, he walked out to the road with the bagged cat in one hand and his Raleigh bike in the other. Just as he was about to lob the burden into the flooded river, he saw the cat's sorrowful owner coming down the road towards him. She thought the cat was gone long before and here it was inside a bag swinging from Clem's hand. Clem unzipped his jacket just enough to stuff the stinking cat inside, next to his clean canary-yellow shirt, before the neighbour passed by with a sweet if sorrowful smile with her head to one side like it was burdened with sorrow on the one side.

The time was, by now, very close to the off in the first race. Clem threw caution to the wind. He threw his longest leg over the bar of the bike and away with him towards the town and the bookmakers. He remembered there was a builders' skip on the way into town and he wondered why he hadn't used it for disposing of his charge before this. If he kept the jacket zipped, people might think he had put on weight and was filling out the jacket more than he used. He pedalled fast and was sweating with his excess baggage and the excitement, and the exertion of rushing along to his certain fortune by the time he crested the hill. He peddled as fast as he could between the tops of the two hills and then let her freewheel down the road on the other side. Clem knew he was faster when he allowed the machine to gather its own momentum. Besides, he needed his feet free to double as brakes if something came amiss.

It was then that a strange and disturbing thing happened. The cat made its move. Clem had just rounded the final chicane, when he felt a movement above his hips and below his perspiring chest. The three racehorses together could not have sweated as much as Clem did when he felt movement. The dead cat slid its way out of the bag onto his lap as if he were sitting down. In that moment, Clem thought the frozen blood of the cat had warmed up and it had used one of its nine lives to come back to torment him. He tried to slow down as best he could, with his shaking foot, but his foot brake missed the wheel and ploughed straight into the tumbling spokes. This pitched Clem straight over the handlebars and onto the road's cold hard and ugly surface.

It was assumed afterwards that the cat they found under him had run out in front of Clem to be killed. But they said also that the suicidal cat had saved Clem's life as Clem bounced on the dead cat on his descent to earth. Clem had to have sixteen stitches put into his face to draw it back together. The Raleigh bike with its Brooks saddle was wrecked. The cat was dead for the second time, though someone threw it into the skip afterwards so it might have just been sleeping or even playing a game with Clem, much as a hunting cat will play with a mouse it is about to kill.

And what of the treble wager that Clem was racing to and almost lost his life over? Well the first horse lost and the accumulator bet didn't work out, as a result. It stopped dead there and then. No win, no second wager. Because Clem never got to the bookies, he still had his wager in his pocket when he came home from hospital. For ages afterwards he retold the story to anyone that asked him how he had acquired the scar on his face where he had been stitched. But as the wound faded, so too did the questions, and Clem went back to normal life on his replacement bicycle. However, neighbours wondered if the fall had not affected his head in some little way. He had always been an uncomplicated man, but now neighbours said he seemed to want to stop and talk to any stray cat he met on the road. People said he seemed to be trying to explain something to the cat, but that couldn't be right, could it? For who talks to cats in daylight anyway?

CLARE

RUTH MARSHALL

INCHIQUIN LAKE

NEVER DISTURB A WOMAN AT HER KNITTING

Before there was a lake or a castle or anything else there, there used to be a hurling field where Lake Inchiquin is now. Boys used to come from all around the area to play hurling matches there. So one day there was a big crowd of lads playing hurling, and they began to quarrel when one of them had hit another. The one said the other tripped him up on purpose, the other denied it. Voices were raised and fists would be out next, as the quarrel got louder and louder.

There was an old woman who lived in a cave on the side of Clifden Hill. She was sitting there working at her knitting, and minding her own business, when the sound of the boys' fighting caught her attention. She got up from her rocking chair, and with her knitting under her arm, she went marching down to see what the cause of all the noise was. Finding the boys still fighting with each other, she shouted at them crossly to stop it at once.

When the boys paid her no heed, and just kept on with their sport, the old woman took out one of her knitting needles and stuck it deep into the ground. When she pulled the needle out again, up sprang a well full of water. It spouted up into the air, and ran bubbling over the ground, rising higher and spreading further until it covered the whole field.

That was how Inchiquin Lake was made.

CONOR O'QUIN AND THE SWAN MAIDEN

If you pass by any of County Clare's many lakes, you will often see a party of swans gracefully taking their ease on the still waters. When they fly over the lakes, it is surely one of the most beautiful and haunting sights, with the sound of their wings beating echoing through the air, it is easy to picture the sad story of Conor O'Quin who met with a beautiful swan maiden on the shores of Inchiquin Lake near Corofin.

There was a young chief, Conor O'Quin, who lived near Inchiquin Lake.

One day as he was out walking near an old stone fort by the lake, he saw a large number of swans swimming on the lake, heading in towards the southern shore. As he watched them, the swans stretched their necks, shook out their wings and walked ashore. There they seemed to grow taller, and removing black hoods and feathered dresses, became a group of graceful young women dressed in thin white shifts. These girls danced and chattered there at the lake's reedy edge. One girl sat on a rock to comb her black hair, and turned her face in O'Quin's direction.

O'Quin had never seen such a beauty before, and he was immediately smitten. The girl, when she noticed the man watching her, took up her feathered dress and flew off over the water, the other swan-girls behind her in graceful flight.

O'Quin could not get the face of this beautiful swan maiden from his mind. He took to wandering down by the lake each day in the hope of seeing her again. Three times he caught a glimpse of her as she sat on the rock by the water's edge combing her dark hair. Each time he approached she would quickly pull on her hood and feathered dress and take flight.

One day however O'Quin, now consumed with love for the swan maiden, had a plan. He rose early and hid himself behind some scrubby trees and bushes near the water's edge and waited for the swans to come to shore. When they did, he watched them shake off their feathered dresses and hoods, biding his time, waiting only for the right moment to make his move. As his beloved lay down her black hood, O'Quin quickly grabbed it up and held it fast. This time the swan maiden could not escape him.

He asked her to marry him and come live with him in his grand house.

She tried to dissuade him. 'You would be better to marry one of your own kind,' she said. But O'Quin would not be put off. He asked again, stressing the depth of his love for her. At last she agreed to become his wife, but she named three conditions to her consent. The first condition was that the marriage must remain a secret; the second, that he must never invite an O'Brien into their house; and third, that he must not engage in games of chance.

O'Quin agreed at once, and swore that he would tell no one about his lovely bride; that he would never invite an O'Brien to the house; and that he would neither gamble nor play cards. He thought these conditions a small price to pay for the love of his life.

O'Quin scooped her up into his arms and carried her back to the grand house. There they lived happily together for many years. As time went by two children were born, and as they grew, all seemed well in the world for Conor O'Quin.

One day, O'Brien of Leamanagh and some of the other chiefs of the area decided to hold a tournament nearby at Coad. There would be horse races, and great sport was promised. O'Quin's wife begged him not to go, but when he insisted, she pleaded with him to accept no invitation to dine, nor to invite anyone to dine at their house. O'Quin gave her his solemn word and set off for the races at Coad.

In the excitement of the day, he quite forgot his promise. He invited O'Brien to dine with him and the chief came with all his retinue to O'Quin's house. O'Quin's wife prepared a glorious feast and served it up on the finest of dishes, but she spoke not one word. While O'Brien and his party ate their fill, entertained by her foolish husband, she took up her swan gown and put it on, along with her black hood. She carried her children, one under each arm from their beds, and then slipped away down to the shores of the lake, and was never seen again in human form.

Not knowing about his loss, O'Quin played cards with O'Brien after dinner. He wagered his house and lands and lost it all to Tadg O'Brien of Coad. O'Quin was a ruined man. Having broken his promises, he had lost all that he held dear: his wife, family, house and lands, all gone in one foolish, thoughtless night. They say O'Brien gave him a place to build a small house and he lived out his days there, a sad and broken man.

I can see him still wandering the shore on Lake Inchiquin in the hope that his beloved swan maiden might one day return.

THE FAIRIES' DANCE IN GLENDREE

Between the villages of Feakle and Tulla, sits the lovely glen known as Glendree. Some would tell you that the name means 'valley of the druids', others say it is 'valley of enchantment'. Yet again, it may be named for the fairy folk who lived there, and some would say that dwell there still.

I lived there myself for a short while, when my son was just a toddler. Staying in a house without running water, we each day collected water from the stream that ran past the house for the washing, and brought drinking water from a spring in the field across the road. We hung the washing on the hedge or the bars of the gate to dry in the sunshine of that late summer. The bohereens were bordered with rough stone walls, framed by the bright fiery oranges and reds of montbretia and fuchsia and the creamy lace of meadowsweet. My few months in Glandree was a magical time in my life: a time of in-betweens. The end of summer, the beginning of a new way of living. I was there to take respite, to lick my wounds and prepare for life as a single parent. Life with a young child was simple, and it was magical, as I have found it always is, in those strange gaps in life when the everyday and the otherworld seem closer than usual. Fairies seemed to be there in abundance, and they are never far away when I visit friends who live there now.

Here is a story about two lads who lived in Glendree in centuries past:

Long ago, there lived in Glendree two boys, John Maher and Tim Clune. In their early days going to school, they were fast friends. As they grew to become young men they learned to sing and dance and play music. They were known as the sport of the place and were invited to all the big dances.

After a while Tim got married to Mary, a lovely handsome girl, and the young couple settled down in a little house in Glendree. However, sadly Tim's young wife died one year later, which brought a cloud of sorrow and gloom on the place. Now there was no more fun or dances for poor Tim. His good friend John called round often and tried to bring him some cheer, but to no avail. Tim had no interest in cards or music or sporting. By the time another year had passed John got sick himself and before long he died. Now poor Tim was all alone, without his wife and his closest friend. He was a broken man, wandering about the roads and fields aimlessly. No one could reach him, he kept his own company and had time for nobody, just lived alone in that fine little house.

Those were dark days for Tim, but there came a day in one year's time after, that Tim took a strange notion, and went to Tulla to meet his old friends. They were happy to see him out and about and spending his time in company. They fetched out a bottle of poitín, and Tim drowned his grief for that one day with a glass or two.

Later, as he was coming home, just as the night was growing dark, Tim took a short cut home by what was known as Helly's Fort. Just as he was about to climb over the stile, there he met his old friend John, standing as if he'd been waiting for Tim. Tim was afraid to see what must be the ghost of his old friend, and thought to run away.

But John called out to him, 'Tim, I never did you any harm in life, nor will I now I am dead. If you come with me now and I tell you, you will enjoy the best night you ever had in your life! Don't you remember the many good nights we had together?'

Tim paused a while and pinched himself. If this was a ghost, it seemed friendly enough. He said, 'John, old friend, or spirit, or whatever you are, what do you plan to do with me?'

TIPPERARY

AIDEEN MCBRIDE

THE PIPES OF FORTUNE

John O'Neill was born in 1777 in County Waterford, and came to live in Carrick-on-Suir where he worked as a shoemaker. His treasure trove of stories, which he collected from around that area, was published in 1854. It is a wealth of folklore, with some of the best leprechaun stories I have ever come across. This is one of those stories that shows how an entire village came together to raise a 'foundling'.

Darby Milligan was a foundling. He had been found on the side of the road as an infant. The whole village had been involved in his upbringing, each of them taking a turn to house him, feed him, clothe him and teach him, from the most well off of the community to the poorest, and all considered it a privilege to be able to do anything for the wee fellow, for Darby had that type of a disposition that pleases you to please him.

He had taken a strong liking to music and used to follow Tim the piper around learning bits from him and he seemed to show promise on the pipes. So much so that when Tim died the community got together to get the money to buy Tim's pipes from his widow and start Darby off. Darby was very grateful and he played for anyone who asked him. He played at the fairs and crossroads too, sometimes just to please himself, and people would throw him a few coins. Now Darby had never had money before, but now that he had a few coins he found himself wanting more.

He was playing one day on a stone up on the fields when a little man suddenly appeared to him. He was dressed in a green coat and he had bright red hair. Darby stopped playing.

'Oh play on,' said the little man.

Darby played on.

'You are a good player,' said the little man and he took out a new shiny penny, 'Here's a penny for you and there'll be one for you under that stone every time you play here. But mind now, a penny for a tune and don't you ever take the penny without first playing the tune.' Darby took the penny and the little man disappeared. Darby looked at the penny for a while, then he put it in his pocket and played another tune. When he finished he looked down at the stone, there was another shiny new penny. He put it in his pocket and played another tune. He sat there for the evening playing tunes and pocketing pennies. By the time he went home he was too tired to play for the neighbours.

The following day he spent the whole day on the stone, playing tunes and pocketing pennies. By the end of the day he needed to find somewhere to hide his store of pennies. He did the same the following day and, realising he had been nearly two days playing and not a proper bite to eat, he went to get a meal. No one would touch his pipes where they were so he left them on the stone and went or get something to eat.

When he returned there were the pipes, playing themselves and a couple of pennies peeping out from under the stone. Darby was tempted to pocket them for himself but he remembered that he had to earn every penny he got. He took up his pipes, ignored the other pennies and played a tune himself. When he had finished he picked up the new penny he had earned.

So it went on, day after day, Darby played to no one but the stone and earning his pennies. When it rained he built a shelter over the stone, then walls and eventually a house was built around the stone. He had a great deal of money and could afford fine things (a new shiny penny went a long way in those days). He got married to a girl from the next town and settled in with his wife in his house and, in time, had a couple of children. In the night when everyone was in bed, Darby would sit on the stone and play away for his pennies.

Darby had never been a drinker – there used be a saying, 'as drunk as a piper, as sober as Darby Milligan' – but he kept a bottle in the house to be sociable. It happened that in entertaining his guests and his wife's family he grew to like the stuff and began to drink more and more. Soon it got to a stage that you couldn't tell whether he liked the drink more or his money.

One night he woke from a drunken stupor to see his pipes playing themselves on the stone and a couple of shiny new pennies peeping out. Without thinking he reached out and took the penny. A penny he hadn't played for. Suddenly everything went cold and dark. There was his house, wife, family, everything, gone! Darby was alone with just his pipes on the stone in the middle of the field as it had been the first day he met the little man. He cursed himself, his stupidity and he cursed the drink. But what good could that do him now? Darby felt too ashamed to go to anyone who knew him the way things were so he just walked on, away from the stone.

He travelled on till he could go no more. He was cold and hungry but loath to play the pipes as he blamed them for his bad luck. Still he realised he had the means to make a decent living in the playing of the pipes and that alone was something to be grateful for. He shed a few tears remembering his wife and children and then took up the pipes and began to play a sad mournful tune. As he did he felt a weight lift off of him. Out of the corner of his eye he noticed a movement and looking down saw hundreds of little eyes peeking up at him. He smiled, the first smile in what seemed like ages, and played a merrier tune, the little people danced. Darby looked and there beside him was the little man with the red hair who had given him that first penny. He was smiling.

'Well Darby,' he said, 'You're not a bad sort, and when you're sober you're an industrious fellow, but the drink did you no favour nor your miserly ways. You should have shared more and kept less. I'll tell you what though, we'll give you a second chance. Take yourself home now and leave off the hoarding and drink.'

Darby was very grateful. He hurried home and as happy as he was to see the house where it had been, he was happier again to find who was inside it. Mind you, his wife and children couldn't understand why they were getting all the hugs and kisses. Darby was a more generous man after that, and he often had the neighbours around for a few tunes, just a few tunes though and the whiskey stayed corked in the bottle.

Sources

Will Handerhan the Irish Fairyman and Legends of Carrick by John O'Neil (1854)

KNOCKSHEGOWNA

Knockshegowna is a townland in County Tipperary, not far from Ballingarry as you travel towards the Laois border. Its translation is Cnoic Shí Gabhna, *'Hill of the Fairy Calf'. Well, there has to be a story in that, and there is.*

Close to the top of the hill at Knockshegowna there is a pasture area, a lovely place enticing to any herdsman to pasture his cattle or sheep. But that area had once been a fairy spot before human kind had come to live in the area.

Now, the fairies were getting fed up with the mournful sound of cattle lowing on one of their dancing grounds and they plotted as to how to rid the spot of the cattle, sheep and herdsmen. How better of course than to frighten away the men in such a manner so as they wouldn't return, and would spread the word to others not to venture near the spot either.

So in the night, once the cattle were settled and easy and the herdsmen wrapped in their cloaks, the fairy queen came and danced. As she danced, she changed her form from one hideous frightening being to another. First she was a horse with the wings of an eagle and the tail of a dragon, then a little man with a lame leg and a bull's head, then a great ape with duck's feet and a turkey tail. I could go on all day about the shapes she shifted herself into. And she made noises, terrible frightening noises, hisses, howls, hoots, screams, neighs and cackles, as was never heard in this world before.

The poor herdsmen covered their faces and cried to all the saints of heaven for help but it was no use. A puff of the fairy woman's breath moved their cloak from their faces, and, try as they might, they could not look away for they were rooted to the spot for the duration of her dance. The hair of their necks rose and their teeth almost fell out from chattering; the cattle were driven into a mad frenzy from fear and the poor herdsman were rooted to the spot till dawn came and the sun rose over the hill.

The poor cattle were pining away from night after night of disturbed rest and there seemed no end to the accidents. Each night there was sure to be some accident or other, a cow falling into a pit, or into the river and getting maimed, hurt or even killed. And the herdsmen, well the farmer had gone through so many herdsmen by this time it was hard for him to find another, no one wanted to herd on Knockshegowna. The farmer offered double, then treble, then quadruple the money for the herding of his cattle, but not a man could be found who would go through the horror of facing the fairies.

The fairies rejoiced in the success of their efforts, and with the herd thinning and the herdsmen afraid to set foot on the land the fairies came back in numbers, gambolling and dancing on their green.

The farmer was greatly troubled for he had his bills to pay and a landlord who looked for rent. If he couldn't pasture his herd on the land what had he? Everyone he had asked had refused to bring the herd up to Knockshegowna. Who was left to ask?

One day while walking deep in thought the farmer met Larry Hoolihan. Larry was a piper and a good one at that, an equal to his piping was not known for fifteen parishes. With a few drinks inside him, Larry feared nothing; he would defy the devil himself, face a mad bull, even fight single handed against the whole fair. Larry met the farmer this day, saw he was troubled and asked him what was wrong. The farmer told Larry of his misfortunes.

'What am I to do Larry? No one will herd my cattle. How am I to fatten the cattle enough to get a decent price for them?'

'If that's all that ails you,' said Larry, 'worry no more. It would be a fine thing if I who was never afraid of any man should be afraid of a fairy no bigger than my thumb.'

'Mind what you say,' warned the farmer, 'You don't know who's listening, but if you can stay with my cattle for a week on the mountain you'll never want for anything again.' A bargain was struck and that evening as the moon was rising Larry took his place on Knockshegowna to watch over the cattle. As soon as he was settled on a comfortable rock out of the wind and cold, he took out his pipes and began to play.

It wasn't long till the fairies made their presence felt. He heard them laugh and one say, 'What, another man disturbing the peace of our fairy ring? Go show him Queen what happens to men who disturb our peace,' and with that Larry heard a rustling and felt a wind on his face and when he looked up he saw a great black cat poised above him, the cat leapt and became a salmon in a bow tie before him.

'Go on jewel,' said Larry, 'If you dance I'll play,' and he played his best and she turned first from this and into that and then from that into this, but it was not having the desired effect on the new herder. He just continued on playing, and meeting her movements in the rhythm and mood of his music. She decided to try a new tactic and changed into a new white calf, gentle and calm – or so it seemed. The calf fawned and lowed, great big brown eyes on her and moved closer to Larry hoping to catch him off guard but Larry was not to be fooled by the fairy's tricks. As soon as the calf was close enough he downed the pipes and leapt on her back.

Now as you look westward from the top of Knockshegowna you can see the River Shannon flowing 10 miles away. The fairy calf, seeing this as a great opportunity to better Larry, took a great leap and in one bound landed on the other side of the river. Larry fell from her back onto the soft turf, he looked up at the calf and, looking her in the eye, said, 'By my word! Well done. That was not a bad leap – for a calf!'

The fairy queen gave up, she resumed her own shape.

'You're a bold fellow Larry,' she said. 'Will you go back as you came?'

'I will,' said Larry, 'If you'll let me.' She turned into a calf again and Larry got on her back. In one bound he was back on the top of Knockshegowna again. The fairy queen took her own shape again and addressed Larry.

'You've shown much courage Larry,' said she, 'so much so that I promise that as long as you tend the herds here, we will not harm or disturb you. Go and tell the farmer this and if ever we can be of assistance to you, you need only ask.'

The fairies kept their word and for as long as Larry herded there on the top of the hill he was never harassed or bothered by them. He watched the herd on the hill and played his pipes and the farmer was true to his word. He had a room built for Larry in his house, fed him and clothed him and paid him well. Larry was a constant presence on Knockshegowna till his death, and he was buried in the valley of Tipperary. Whether the fairies returned to the hill after that or not I couldn't tell you – you might have to visit the hill top on a clear night to find out.

Sources

Fairy Legends and Traditions from the South of Ireland by Thomas Crofton Croker (1825)

LAOIS

NUALA HAYES

THE RED FAIRY OF GRANTSOWN

The old woman or the red fairy – the 'cailleach' in the Irish language – appears in many of the stories in County Laois and the surrounding counties. She is a force to be reckoned with and is not always depicted kindly.

Eileen Ahern, who told me a version of this story, is originally from Newcastle West in County Limerick, but she lived for forty years beside Grantstown Lake, which is in the southern part of County Laois, near the parish of Aghaboe, in the region of old Ossory. (Laois Oral Archive, CD.1.)

The Great Famine was a traumatic time for the impoverished Irish people and, understandably, the scarcity of folklore from this time reflects this. This story is sometimes called 'The Fairy's Revenge' and is part of John Keegan's collection of stories.

Grantstown Lake is a beautiful place and it's now very well known as a fishing lake. It is popular with visitors from England, Scotland and, of course, many parts of Ireland, who fish mainly for eel, perch and pike.

In springtime the lakeside explodes with daffodils, hyacinths and bluebells, as well as the waterlilies that bob on the water. There are birds of all species there, including swans, which appear every year in the spring. Their arrival is taken as a sign of good weather. The swans leave when winter comes. The area around Grantstown is very popular for hunting fowl but the local gamekeeper will give you short shrift if he catches you shooting pheasants or other wild game.

But it is said that there was a time when there was no lake there at all, when instead there was a lovely fertile valley with wild flowers, daisies, primroses and bluebells in abundance. In the middle of the valley was a beautiful spring well, gurgling up from the centre of the earth, which was so deep that people believed there was no bottom to it.

Overlooking the valley was a simple little cabin, where Moya Liath, or Grey Mary Slattery, lived with four little children: three little boys and a *girsha* (a little girl). They weren't her own children, but the children of her daughter, Rose, who was dead and buried with her husband in the churchyard of Bordal not far from the valley.

Summer came and there was nothing to eat. The potatoes had failed, the corn was blasted, the cattle had died of distemper and no food could be had in the valley for love nor money. Moya had tried everything to feed the children. She boiled nettles and weeds and grass and whatever else she could lay her hands on. But the children cried and whinged because they were starving. One evening in July, when the sun had sunk behind the mountain, Moya sat at the door, trying to comfort the children, wiping the tears from their eyes and the snot from their noses. '*Dá fhaide an oíche, tiocfaidh an lá …*' (However long the night is, the day will come). They had no idea what she was talking about.

As she spoke a shadow crossed the door. Moya looked up and she saw a strange-looking little woman in front of her. Crooked and wrinkled, with hair as grey as Moya's, she wore a crimson cloak and her hair was tied up with a blood-red scarf. Moya had never seen her like before.

'Good evening,' she said, as she walked into the cabin.

'*Bail ó Dhia ort*, the blessings of God on you,' Moya replied.

'Save your breath to cool your porridge. Keep your blessings. I never asked for them,' the little woman replied.

'I wish I had porridge,' said Moya. 'If I had, I would find breath to cool it and to say a prayer for the good of my neighbours too!'

'Are you a good neighbour?'

'I think I am,' said Moya.

'I've no pot to boil my supper. Will you lend me yours?' the woman asked.

'I will, with a heart and a half, for I've no supper to boil.'

'Thank you, Moya,' said the woman. She grabbed the pot, which was full of water from the well for the children to drink at night.

'Can I ask you where do you live? I've never seen you around these parts before.'

'No matter where I live,' said the woman. 'The pot will be back to you in the morning. I give you my word. Goodnight!' As she turned from the door, she turned around suddenly. 'And let none of you look after me! If ye do, I'm warning you, I'll smash this pot into smithereens.' With that, she disappeared from their sight.

Next morning, Moya was up early to forage for some edible greens for the children's breakfast. 'Oh, I forgot about the pot,' she said out loud. 'That old hag never brought it back.'

'You're a liar, Moya Liath!' came the voice of the old woman from behind the door.

Moya opened the door and there was the pot, full to the brim with steaming stirabout porridge. There was a big yellow lump of delicious-looking butter melting in the centre.

She called the children down and in no time at all they emptied the pot. By the end of the day, their smiles had returned.

That evening, as the sun went down, the little red woman came back and borrowed the pot, with the same warning: 'Don't be looking after me now!' Next day, the pot of beautiful porridge topped with more golden butter was glistening in the sun outside the door.

This went on, day after day, for a week, and by the end of it, there wasn't a better-fed or happier family of children in the whole of Ossory.

One evening, the strange little woman appeared as usual. This time she said, 'Moya Liath, after tomorrow night, I'll be troubling you no more, for my time here has come to an end. I have orders to move. But I thank you for your neighbourly generosity.'

'My generosity!' Moya cried. 'What will we do without yours? What will become of us now and the hunger and sickness raging all over the country?'

'*Dá fhaide an oiche, tiocfaidh an lá*,' said the old woman, as she swung the pot away again.

'She's a quare little woman,' thought Moya. 'Well, if she's leaving soon, I've nothing to lose.' She looked out the door, her eyes following the figure of the old woman. 'I'll see where she is going at least, if nothing else.'

You can just imagine Moya's surprise when she saw that the little woman headed straight for the well in the middle of the valley. She raised the wooden lid and got into it, pot and all!

'I knew it. I always suspected she was a fairy and I was right!' said Moya.

Next day was a bad one for Moya. Her mind raced all day. The fairy woman was to visit for the last time. What would she do without food for the children after that? Then, as quick as a flash, an idea came to her. 'Well,' she thought, 'I have nothing to lose, have I?'

The sun was setting when the little red woman appeared again. 'This is my last time asking for the pot,' she said. 'I know you won't refuse me.'

'Indeed I won't. But I've no water for the night for the children and I've nothing to carry it in only the pot. So sit down there by the fire and I'll hop out for a drop from the well. I'll be back before you know it!'

The little red woman sat by the fire and Moya hobbled over to the well with the pot. She lifted the lid and filled the pot with water. She fastened the wooden lid on top and made the sign of the cross over it.

'Now,' she said to herself, 'my guess is she won't be able to lift it. If she can't, I'll make her promise me a bag of gold as long as my arm and a bag of meal that would flatten an ass.'

'What's keeping you?' the old woman shouted from the house. 'Will you be there all night?'

'I'm coming,' said Moya. 'Just get me that basin from under the dresser to keep the water in.'

The old woman grabbed the pot and set off with it as usual. Moya watched from the door as she got to the well and stooped to lift the lid, then she heard her raise a cry loud enough to wake the dead in the graveyard!

'Moya Liath! What have you done?' she screeched 'Raise the lid and let me into the well or you'll rue the day you ever set eyes on the red fairy of Grantstown!'

'I will,' said Moya. 'I will, if you promise me enough oatmeal to last a year and enough gold to put me and my seven generations nine days' march before poverty!'

'Is that what you say?' shouted the old woman in a voice that would shake a mountain.

'It is indeed, *a chara mo chroí*!' said Moya.

'Well then,' said the fairy. 'If I can't get into the water, the water will come to me.' She plucked a white hair from under her red scarf, muttered some words over it, flung it into the air and gave a whistle which echoed over the valley and the grey ruins of the Fitzpatricks' castle.

At that instant a thundering, gurgling sound was heard from within the well and the water burst through the lid with a terrific crash, then flowed furiously and spread itself across the valley in no time. The red woman disappeared. Moya ran as fast as her legs could carry her. She grabbed the children and dragged them up the hill to a place of safety as the water rushed and filled the valley and covered the well and the house and everything she had.

Next morning, when Moya came back to look for her cabin, a wide expanse of water met her eyes and the lovely valley was covered from that day to this with the bright waters of Grantstown Lake.

But the red woman wasn't finished yet. Scarcely had the flooding stopped when a mighty whirlwind blew up and swept over the lake, sweeping away everything in its path, levelling houses, towers, cornfields and trees, all belonging to the Fitzpatricks and the O'Moores.

After a day and a night, the storms ceased and the skies cleared and the sun shone on the lake and showed it as clear and as silver as glass. Then the waters were found to be teeming with fish of various shapes and sizes, all edible and delicate to the taste. The people of the area fished them and ate them with relish.

The fairy tempest had also blown in flocks of fowl which appeared throughout the lands of Laois and Ossory; birds more beautiful than any that had been seen in the area before, with red, green, blue and gold plumage. They were so tame that they would sometimes fly in the doors of houses, ready to be plucked and eaten! Moya lived to a good age and her grandchildren, when they were grown, told this marvellous story to their children, who have passed it on to us.

The plague ended and hunger disappeared and the good lands of County Laois became well known for their wealth and abundance right up to the present day.

THE TALES OF JENNY MCGLYNN

*Jenny McGlynn (*née *Dunne) lived in Mountmellick, County Laois, all her life. She told me about the rambling houses in the bay area where she lived after she was married to Tom McGlynn, and the cottages in Manor Lane, where she grew up, as Jane Dunne, and where stories of ghosts and the little people and the other world were part and parcel of her life.*

Jenny is the only person I met in Laois who claims to have seen the banshee.

I saw the banshee in the yard the night my mother died. My mother was dying and I was minding her. I thought I heard the gate opening. I was expecting my brothers home. I had let them go out for a pint. When I heard the noise I opened the door and looked out. As soon as I opened the door this white figure came right at me, she almost got to me and then went across the yard.

She was small and dressed all in white. I couldn't make out a face, just dark holes where the eyes should be. Of course I stiffened with fear. I wasn't able to take in a lot.

Of course I bolted the door and I went back into Mammy's room and I sat down on the bed with her and didn't leave until my brothers got back.

That was on a Saturday night.

On Sunday morning my neighbour came in. Her name was Mrs Fitzgerald, God rest her. She said, 'Did you hear herself last night, under your mother's window? She was roaring the place down.'

I heard nothing, never heard a sound.

About seven o'clock on Sunday evening, Mammy took a bad turn and within an hour, she was dead. It didn't register with me straight off it was the banshee I saw, but I knew then that it was her.

There would have been a lot of noises heard on Manor Lane, where I grew up. We were the middle house on the lane. You'd hear men marching and strange lights coming out from among the trees.

Not glow-worms. Lights. Like a ball of fire. The banshee is supposed to walk the lane at night. In those days, it used to be pitch dark. There are a few lights there now. I was never afraid going up in the dark. Never afraid.

But I'd never be out during the dead hours, between twelve o'clock at night and three in the morning. I'd either be home before twelve or wait until after three. Those are the hours where you leave the dead to go about and you don't want to be in their way.

I believe there are evil spirits as well as good spirits still on the land. I do believe it.

My father used to work on a farm. He used to come down a laneway about half a mile long. He was due to be home at half past six, but he was delayed. He was coming down the lane at five past twelve when the bike was pulled from under him. He couldn't cycle it and it was held solid. It was only released at three o'clock after he had been pulling away, wondering what was holding it.

When he came into the light of the house, he fainted out cold. I remember that well. He was a strong man, my father.

NIGHT-TIME ENCOUNTERS

There was another man who used to drink a lot. He lived up the lane.

At that time there was a little river with no wall. You could fall into it easily. His mother came out looking for him one night. He was lying on the bank of the river with his hand out, saying, 'Give me your hand and I'll pull you out!' The mother had a habit of carrying holy water with her and she sprinkled the water on her son to get the devil away from him. A blue light came up from the river. The man sobered up and walked home with his mother.

My husband Tom was a great storyteller. He told all kinds of stories. He used to work at Bórd na Móna and one night when he was coming home in the dark from working a night shift, he saw lights on the bog.

Thinking they were the lights of the town, he followed them. But he realised he was going the wrong way. He then changed direction, but that was the wrong way too. Then he realised the only way to get out of it was to take off his coat and turn it inside out. He continued to wear it that way until he got back on a track. He did come home with his coat inside out. I was waiting up for him to give him his supper.

I thought he'd been to the pub, but he hadn't.

Some of the stories I heard were old wives' tales, but some were true. I do believe in spirits, I do. You have to believe in spirits. If you didn't, you couldn't believe in God. That's my belief anyway.

Some people are born to see things and others can't. My own daughter could see, from the time she was a baby. We'd be coming down the road in the dark and she'd pull me out into the light. She would have seen this particular man. My mother then told me that there was a man who used to live around that spot and he was supposed to have sworn that he would stay on his land, dead or alive. My daughter could see him, but I couldn't.

THE RUSHEEN

The fairy rath we had up the bog lane was called the Rusheen. But it was burnt down. The man who burned it down had no luck afterwards. The poor unfortunate chap was deranged and he hanged himself after. He hanged himself and was saved, then a couple of years later, he poisoned himself.

People weren't afraid of the rath at all. As long as you didn't take anything out of it, you'd never have any harm befall you. But if you took a stick out of it, anything could happen. My father-in-law used to tell this story:

THE TREE AND THE WHIP

'A man cut a branch off a sally tree to herd his cattle. He didn't think twice about it and he was herding them out on to the road. When a little man came up and handed him a cow's tail and said, "There's a whip for your stick!"

'The Rusheen was a gorgeous and peaceful place. There was a centrepiece; it was soft like velvet and there'd be a ring of daisies all around. And a little tree, like a chair, with a cushion of moss in the fork. There were three branches coming out of this cushion. I often sat on it when I was a child and we'd be there playing. And as an adult, when Tom and I would go walking, we used to go around it. We always went to that same spot. It was a lovely place to be. No matter how windy it was out along the bog, when you'd go there, it would be warm. There wouldn't be even a breeze through the trees.

'And you could hear music. I often heard music. I often looked around to see if there was anyone playing or if there was someone with a radio. It was Irish music. You couldn't make it out, whether it was one instrument or more. The music was just there, but you couldn't make it out. We didn't ever use the word 'fairy'. It was the 'little people'.

If you didn't cross them, they wouldn't cross you. You respect them, they'll respect you. Do harm on them and they will do harm on you.

A bride would have to wear a patch of red with a darning needle on it so she wouldn't be taken. Because the fairies had no blood, not like the human race. If they saw blood, they'd run away. They don't have any blood, so they don't die. They won't go to heaven.

The same with a baby. My mother-in-law used to say, if the child got too cross, 'That's a changeling'. So they would put something red near the child to protect it. I don't remember that in my family, but my mother-in-law used to say, 'That one's taken'. I think she really believed in it, she did!

The little people never cursed or swore and to change the child back, they used terrible language in the room where the child was. They didn't curse or swear at the child, they just used bad language in the room where the child was. I can't use that language, but they'd be effin' and blindin' and eventually the child would quieten down. It would terrify a child. Wouldn't it? Even at my age, if I hear an argument and bad language, I get into the corner, and I'd be terrified!

There was an old lady, used to live in Manor Road. She was very old and we used to call into her on the way home from school to get her water or go down for bread for her. Some days we'd go in and she'd say, 'Shh, don't stir, they're dancing there on the hearth.'

You see the ashes would be spinning there on the hearth. You'd see them spinnin' around, like the whirlwinds you'd see on television. She'd be sitting there watching them dancing. We could see the white ashes from the turf and we were innocent enough to believe her.*

---

* Laois Oral Archive, CD.9.

WICKLOW

BRENDAN NOLAN

A CURE FOR BALDNESS

Judy was a Murrough girl who married Davy Brian, a thatcher, and took to the roads of Wicklow with him to follow his itinerant craft. The coastal wetland of the Murrough extends for about 15km along the coast from Newtownmountkennedy down to the pier at Wicklow harbour, but the pair soon moved into the hills where most of the work was to be found. A thatch lasted in best condition for about four years on a house, so there was always some thatching work to be had in the glens.

Judy's father had outlawed her for marrying Davy, for he didn't think much of him as a son-in-law or as a provider for his daughter. However, Davy was happy enough with Judy, and she with him, and they got along well enough. Davy swore she brought him money in a dowry, but no one ever saw much sign of it in the time that followed.

In any case, Davy was a well-known liar who liked nothing so much after a day's work but to sit down with fellow travelling tradesmen to swap lies and tell tall stories. So well did he tell his tales that the house he was in used to fill up with people anxious to hear lies told about impossible situations in which Davy allegedly found himself.

He told a story one night of a walking-woman he met who had a cure for baldness. Now, it was a curious fact that bald heads were not to be seen that much in the countryside. It was not that they were not there, it was that they were hidden under the hats or caps that everyone wore, since long ago, in the outdoors. The only way to know if a man was bald was to attend the same church as him and to see what happened when he removed his cap on the way into worship. For males were not allowed to have their heads covered at Mass, while women were not allowed to have their heads uncovered at Mass, such were the mysteries of religious observance in Ireland at one time.

And because the men wore caps or hats all week while the Wicklow weather beat into their faces and gave them a permanently tanned appearance, their little round skulls were as white as their behinds on the day they were born, for no sun ever shone on them. Some deniers trained stray strands of hair to go from one side of the skull to the other in the vain hope that people would not notice the arid desert over which it travelled. They were fooling no one but themselves.

Even so, few others had the gaucheness to remark on hair-dos that vanished under headgear as soon as the outside air was encountered, once the celebrant had blessed everyone and told them to go away in peace, for now.

On this particular night, a wandering schoolmaster who went by the name of Mr Saul, or Fr Saul, was staying in the same house as Davy and Judy. He might have been a priest left over from the days when the saying of Mass was prohibited, though that seemed unlikely given that prohibition had been done away with from 1829 or thereabouts and Davy was explaining this cure for baldness some 100 years later.

The man might have been a failed priest who at one time was in the full flow of a vocation but became a civilian once more, now taken to wandering the roads teaching reading, writing, prayers, Latin and history for a living as he passed along.

When he was not teaching he worked as a casual labourer in the fields. There were others besides the tradesmen who tramped the same roads. Labouring men who hired themselves out, as required, were known as spalpeens, though if you were to call such a man by that name you were likely in the early stages of a clash that might leave you badly injured or with something loose inside you that shouldn't be so.

Workers in wood were known as hedge-carpenters and they walked the roads as well. They made everything from chairs to sit on, to the wooden spokes of a cart, though such jobs would often take seven days to complete and they were paid *2s 6d* (a half-crown) per day. There were eight half-crowns to a pound in the old money and these were hard to come by, as everyone knew. The weekly wage for a herd on Powerscourt Demesne at that time was twelve shillings for a week's work; there were twenty shillings to a pound.

On this storytelling night, while Davy was accepting a small libation from the man of the house, he allowed the floor to go to Saul.

In honour of Judy, Davy's wife, Saul recalled that the Vikings founded towns at Waterford and smaller communities at Arklow, and Wicklow, as well. Many exotic goods were brought into Ireland from Britain and Europe, he said. Shipbuilding was also an important industry along the coast, as you might imagine, he said, for wooden boats could be built on a sloping shore and pushed into the sea as soon as they were ready to float away.

There were many benefits for people living in the countryside near these new seaside towns. The inhabitants of these new towns needed food to eat, and timber to make houses and ships. Farmers who lived in the hinterland were only too glad to supply the townspeople with food and timber, he added, as if he had some personal knowledge of their relationships.

He did not mention whether or not the same Vikings, whose credo it was to take what they wanted at any time, actually paid for goods received or simply accepted such things as tribute from a frightened populace.

'It was the old walking-women that brought the knowledge of such things around the country', interrupted the now lubricated Davy, to take the story away from his wife's people and forebears, for there was no way of knowing if any fraternisation between the races had occurred. He did not care to dwell on the possibility that Judy's father might be some part Viking and might now be sharpening an axe on the way to searching for his daughter on the high roads of Wicklow.

The schoolteacher was nonplussed; he didn't know whether Davy was agreeing with him or suggesting that his talk was woman's talk, or whether he was being challenging for superiority.

He made the mistake of pausing for clarification and that was the end of him, for Davy was away with the cure for baldness that he had heard from a woman of the roads down near Greenane one winter's night long ago. It was her contention that women did not go bald, for a good reason.

Davy asked if any of the company had ever seen a bald woman. He asked in the same way you might enquire if anyone had heard a banshee calling for them. People were only too happy to shake their heads and affirm that they had never seen nor heard tell of anyone who had ever seen a bald woman.

Davy explained that this was as a result of headgear.

'Women,' he said, in the manner of a well-travelled man who had made a study of baldness, 'wore hats that were a fit for the shape and size of their heads, whereas men wore hats that would stay on in a gale from the sea or a storm in the mountains, or both.'

This was a practical matter, for a man could not spend his days pursuing hats and caps all over the place when he was working. That was to the detriment of a fine harvest of hair upon the head, Davy said.

People now looked to Tom Cullen in the corner, who had only known hair on the crown of his head for a few short years before he went prematurely and permanently bald, as did all the men in his family. They looked to his cloth cap, which even now in the heat of the indoors of the cottage was as firmly ensconced on his head as were his flaming eyebrows over his rheumy eyes.

But Tom said nothing as he wondered to himself when he had last worn a cap loose enough to let the breeze from the soft bog cross his scalp. He couldn't remember when that might have been, but he asked the thatcher what he was getting at, so he could arrive at a conclusion by which he could measure his own baldness. Perhaps, on the days when he was alone on the hill with the sheep, he might leave the cap off and see if any hair would grow on his bare head.

'Well', said Davy in a lowered voice that induced the listeners to lean in to listen with more attention to him. Even the wandering priest found himself turning his head so his ear could come closer to this piece of information. He would travel on tomorrow and if he had a cure for baldness he might give up teaching Latin grammar to wild Wicklow kids who'd rather be out on the hills than listening to him and his declensions. Curing baldness would probably be easier on the spirit.

Davy drew something from his pocket and showed it to the gathering crowd. Three straws sat side by side in the palm of his hand.

'A bald man need only to burn three straws like these and then rub the ashes in the bald place and hair will grow', he said, with the air of a man sharing the secret of serenity.

'Does he need to leave the cap off, so?' asked Tom Cullen.

'It would help, but it is not compulsory', said Davy as he stood up to throw the three straws into the fire, where they were instantly immolated with a sizzle and flair, to the bewilderment of the astonished watchers.

'It's a skill', said Davy. 'You need to watch out for the walking women and ask them for three such straws. From such a companion I learned that skill', he said as he prepared to retire for the night.

And not for the first, nor the last time in their life, did people study Judy and wonder if she was the fount of Davy's wisdom and storytelling abilities.

For who knew what abilities the Vikings had left with the people of the Murrough and the coast of Wicklow, where it faced the known world.

It was enough for the thatcher and his life's companion that they wondered at all.

DERRYBAWN COW

It seems that Fionn Mac Cumhaill left his mark everywhere he went, not least in Wicklow and in Glendalough in particular, long before the better-known St Kevin came along to say his prayers there.

Kevin is said to have arrived in Glendalough in the sixth century and to have founded an early Christian monastery by the dark waters of the mountain lakes. After the saint's death the place attracted not only a large number of ecclesiastics, but also a lay population seeking solace and personal contentment.

Not surprisingly, a town of sorts grew up in the area, with many people moving to work and trade there. The remains of a number of stone churches, an intact round tower and crosses can be seen by the modern visitor.

However, the story of the Derrybawn Cow does not concern saints or prayers, though there is an element about it of matters unknown to man.

Glendalough is a glacial valley formed during the Ice Age which, as everyone knows, was some 20,000 years ago. It is known as the glen of the two loughs, or lakes, which were created when the ice melted away and people began to swim and sunbathe once more. Millions of years before that, a collision of continental plates resulted in the formation of the Wicklow Mountains, but there are few people alive now who remember that day.

On the southern side of Glendalough, Lugduff Mountain towers over the Upper Lake, Mullacor is midway between Glendalough and the next glen, south at Glenmalure. The oak-footed Derrybawn sits quietly above the spot where, in present times, visitors park their cars. And where, in 1835, stood a smelter house and ore-grinding mill associated with an ore extraction and processing site from Glendalough mines.

An old man who was born in nearby Glenmalure said in the late 1990s that he had a number of children and they all went to California, with what he could give them. Once there, they bought a bit of a field. However, when they put in the plough, it stuck fast. Perplexed, they looked underneath it, and there was fine gold stretched within the earth, said the emigrants' father. He said that his children were made rich, and that their daughters were riding on fine horses with new saddles and elegant bits in their mouths. Yet not a ha'porth did they ever send home to their father in the hills. For his own part he wished that the Devil might ride with them to hell. And maybe he did, for a father scorned is an angry father.

But the story told by Máirín Ní Broin, who attended Glendalough school in the years 1934–38, took place long before a car park or visitors' centre was envisaged for the glen.

A break in the strata in the mountain of Derrybawn, which is composed of mica slate, is called the Giants Cut, mainly because one part has sunk many feet below the other. However, local lore states that the defile was caused when Fionn Mac Cumhaill was in an angry mood one day and smote the mountain with his sword, creating the division in the hill that anyone can see to this day.

At the base of Derrybawn Mountain sits a bullaun stone, a granite stone with a single conical basin and curved sides. It is known as the Deer Stone, from an old story that a deer shed its milk in the basin for St Kevin to drink.

Sometimes it is hard to know where fact and folklore blend and the fanciful story takes over from the prosaic everyday.

According to a story recorded midway through the twentieth century by Máirín Ní Broin of Glendalough school, there was once a man who owned a herd of cows and who had seven sons, none of whom had gone out to America to find gold or buy a field there. The family grazed the cows around Derrybawn. As was the custom of the day, the man hired a boy to herd the animals for him on the hills and especially around Doire Bán, Derrybawn. All went well for a time until the man noticed that one particular cow gave more milk than the others. He wondered why this should be and asked the boy if he knew any reason why this cow should be yielding more. But the boy could not give a reason that made any sense to the animal's owner. So he instructed the herd boy to pay particular attention to that animal so that they could reflect on why it was producing more profit than the others after its daily grazing on the hillside of Derrybawn.

Well, the boy was as perplexed as anyone else as to why one animal was producing more milk than the others. He watched for a few days and could see no difference between them. Then he decided on an old herds' boy trick: he would follow the cow's tail all day and leave the others to fend for themselves, for as long as it took.

Next morning, when it came time to lead the animals out onto the grazing area, he stationed himself behind the particular cow and watched to see which way she went. To make doubly sure, he held onto the animal's swishing tail before it started to move.

It ambled along at first and then picked up a shambling pace until it reached a trench, which surrounded a place that had been fortified at some stage in times past. According to the story gathered by Máirín Ní Broin, the mound was called Round Mote. The herd boy watched as the cow leaned in and began to lick at something that the young boy couldn't see.

He pushed the protesting cow away from whatever was taking its interest so much that it would leave the herd to graze alone in the rocks.

There are some things that you are glad you find and there are others you would be just as glad you never had to come across.

The boy peered closer at what was before him. He wanted to be sure of what was there, as he didn't want to appear foolish when reporting back to his employer on this favoured cow's secret.

For there in front of him was a pair of human feet, not the sort of thing a traveller might expect to find on the hill on a day's ramble, much less a terrified herd boy carrying out his employer's instructions.

The feet were bare white flesh, the feet of a person and not of a skeleton. Nicks and cuts visible on the skin showed that the owner of the feet had not favoured the wearing of shoes overmuch in his life, a common enough situation in the Wicklow of the time. People at that time did not begin to wear boots until they were 20 years of age, when their feet were supposed to be grown full-sized.

It is said that people in the olden days did not have bad feet as a result. Any corns or the like that appeared were cured with bog water. Those afflicted with chiropodial problems worked in the bog with bare feet for a few days, as a cure. It was said that James Kearney of Cryhelp, 3 miles east of Dunlavin, did not wear boots until he was 60 years of age. The people who knew him said he died in hospital of old age.

All this was known to the herd boy; but he had never in his short life heard tell of a pair of feet talking to a living person, which was what was happening now. Or at least that was what he thought; but in reality it was a voice in his head, or in the air, that he heard.

The voice told him to take the rest of the body of which the feet were the only part he could see and to bury it in consecrated ground. He stood stock still in pure shock, as it was clear to him that he lacked the physical prowess to lift a body, carry it elsewhere and bury it, even allowing that the priest, the authorities and his employer would allow him to do such a thing.

So, he drove the cows home once more and told his employer what had happened.

The man retraced the boy's steps to where the feet still lay. Satisfied with his preliminary investigation, the man went to the priest and asked for permission to rebury the lost soul in consecrated ground, to which the priest assented, not quite knowing how the feet and body had come to be buried in the mound in the first place.

The man asked his seven sons to go with the herd to where the body was hidden. They were to dig out the remains and bring them to the space in the graveyard specified by the priest. However, according to the story, one son refused to participate in the sad ritual. He told his father that it had nothing to do with him and he would not go with his brothers and the herd to the Mote. The father instead urged the others to carry out the wishes of the poor soul who had spoken to the herd boy.

Three days in five bring rain across Wicklow's mountains, it is said, but prolonged rainstorms are rare. Nonetheless, the wet slopes of sedges squelched underfoot as the silent men transported and interred the body in consecrated ground, as requested.

The objecting son took his hounds onto Derrybawn as his brothers intoned a silent prayer below in the graveyard. Those who know the tale said that he felt justified in himself that he had followed the correct course. Until, that is, his hounds turned on him and sprang at his unsuspecting body. They were not long about tearing him to pieces, for these were hunting dogs, used to tearing flesh from a living body.

His grieving brothers found but little evidence of his passing when they went in search of him on the mountain of Derrybawn above silent Glendalough.

The cows resumed milking, neither one nor the other exceeding her sisters in production. No matter what fate had befallen the missing son, he never returned to create problems for anyone minding cows on a Wicklow hillside.

CARLOW

AIDEEN MCBRIDE & JACK SHEEHAN

EILEEN KAVANAGH

There is something magical about the county of Carlow, something in the water maybe that causes so many handsome people to come from that county. So is it any wonder then that one of the most beautiful airs to come from Ireland was written in praise of a Carlow woman?

Eileen Kavanagh lived in Poulmonty Castle down in the very southern tip of County Carlow. Cearbhaill O'Daly was a harpist, he travelled around the country composing and collecting songs. He was very good at it too: you might say he sang for his supper. Cearbhaill's journeying brought him to many of the castles and forts across the country, and he was welcome in all of them. Now it would be no surprise to discover that he had his favourites among them; there might be one that appreciated his music more than another, or one was more generous with their food and drink. But the favourite Cearbhaill had was not for reasons of food nor drink nor appreciation, but for the presence of a pretty face. Cearbhaill's favourite of the castles was Poulmonty Castle, because there lived Eileen Kavanagh.

Now Eileen Kavanagh was just as fond of Cearbhaill's visits to the castle as he was. Over the course of his visits they had fallen in love, but the Kavanaghs were not pleased with the match. Cearbhaill could not bring to the family the connections or status which the Kavanaghs hoped to achieve through Eileen's marriage. He was a wandering minstrel, and as good a musician as he may be that was not the life the Kavanaghs – who for centuries were the Kings of Leinster – had in mind for their daughter. Their complaints were made known to Cearbhaill and he left, hoping to improve his fortune and so return to claim Eileen. In the meantime the Kavanagh family went about convincing Eileen that Cearbhaill had no love for her and that he had left to marry another. Eileen was heartbroken, but eventually she agreed to marry the suitor her family had picked for her, though she did not love him, and never would, not as she had loved Cearbhaill.

The day before the marriage was to take place Cearbhaill learned of what had happened, and rushed to Carlow to Eileen. On the way he stopped in a quiet place not far from the sea and composed a song. He headed then on for Poulmonty Castle where the wedding feast was about to take place. Heavily disguised and unrecognisable even to those who had known him well, he entered with his harp – a harpist is always welcome at such events, don't you know?

It was Eileen herself who called on him to play, though she did not know who he was, and so he took up his harp and began to play. His fingers brushed lightly across the strings, and all the love he felt for Eileen he poured into that song he had composed for her and sang to her now:

'*An dtiocfaidh tú no an bhfanfaidh tú? Eibhlín a Rún*'
'Will you come with me or will you stay Eileen my love?'

As the music played Eileen raised her head, recognised her love through the song, and answered,

'*Tiocfaidh mé ní bhfanfaidh mé …*'
'I will come I will not stay …'

Cearbhaill answered:

'*Céad mile fáilte romhat Eibhlín a Rún …*'
'A hundred thousand welcomes to you Eileen my love …'

It is said that that was the first written reference to the Gaelic welcome now so common to hear.

Needless to say that night Eileen was reunited with Cearbhaill, she left her home and family and they eloped to have, we hope, a long and happy life together.

Some say the Cearbhaill O'Daly in this story is the famous poet from Clare who died in 1404, which would place the story around the 1380s; others say he was the brother of Donagh More O'Daly, a chieftain in Connaught in Elizabethan times, which would make it 200 years later. But all sources agree that the story behind the song is that of an elopement of two young lovers kept apart by the girl's family.

The song became very popular in England and Scotland, the Scots writing their own version where it's the lady who sings to her love called 'Robin Adair'. It has been mentioned and referred to in numerous articles and fictional stories, even in *The Diary of Samuel Pepys*. The song was sung during intervals in Shakespearean performances and in Smock Alley all through the 1700s. Handel himself is reported to have thought the air so lovely that he would happily have swapped all his great works to have been the composer of the tune. Today it is still a great favourite and sure why not, it is a lovely tune and isn't its story ever repeating?

EIBHLÍN A RÚN

Sheolfainn féin gahmna leat Eibhlín a Rún
I'd herd the cows with you Eileen my love
Sheolfainn féin gahmna leat Eibhlín a Rún
Sheolfainn féin gahmna leat
I'd herd the cows with you
Síos go Tír Amhalghaidh leat
Down to Tir Amhalghaidh with you
Mar shúil go mbeinn I gcleamhnas leat Eibhlín a Rún
In hope I'd become engaged to you Eileen my love

An dtiocfaidh tú no an bhfanfaidh tú Eibhlín a Rún
Will you come or will you stay Eileen my love
An dtiocfaidh tú no an bhfanfaidh tú Eibhlín a Rún

Tiocfaidh mé 'sní bhfanfaidh mé
I'll come and I'll not stay
Tiocfaidh mé 'sní bhfanfaidh mé
I'll come and I'll not stay
Is ealóidh mé le mo stór Eibhlín a Rún
And together we'll run away Eileen my love

Céad mile fáilte romhat Eibhlín a Rún
A hundred thousand welcomes to you Eileen my love
Céad mile fáilte romhat Eibhlín a Rún
Céad mile fáilte romhat
One hundred thousand welcomes to you
Fáilte is fiche romhat,
Welcome by twenty to you
Naoi gcéad míle fáilte romhat Eibhlín a Rún
Nine hundred thousand welcomes to you Eileen my love

THE MERMAID AND THE KING'S SONS

In 1934, Pádraig O'Thuathail took his ediphone to Hacketstown to record stories. There he met James Coleman, from whom he recorded story after story, each even more spellbinding and fantastic than the one before. This is one of the stories James told that night. There are a number of 'rambling houses' or 'storyhouses' around Carlow where people still gather to tell stories, recite poems and sing songs, keeping this great tradition alive today.

There was once an old king and a queen, often there was and often there will be. They were happy enough but for the fact they had no children. One day the old king was fishing out on the sea when he caught a fish, but as soon as he pulled it aboard it turned in to a mermaid.

'Go and fish further down the shore,' she said, 'there you will catch another fish. Give this to your wife to eat and she will bear a son.'

So the king released the mermaid and went to fish further down the shore, and as she had said he caught a fish. He took it home to his wife and in time she had a son. All was well but the king began to grow uneasy about only having one son, so he went fishing. Again he caught the mermaid who again told him to fish further down the shore. And again he caught another fish.

He brought this home to his wife and in time she bore him a second son and all was well for a time, but then the king began to grow uneasy again and wanted a third son. He went to the sea shore and caught the mermaid, and again she told him to fish further down, but this time she asked, 'When this third child of yours comes to the age of 21 will you give him to me?'

The king promised he would.

As before, the queen in time gave birth to a third son.

Now as the boys grew the king would take the first two out hunting with him, but never the third son. As he got older the youngest son wondered about this, so he asked his mother why it was his father would take his brothers but never him out hunting. The queen did not know but she asked the king. The king told them all the story of the mermaid and the promise.

When the youngest son heard the story he waited no longer but, determined, headed out to find his fortune. He travelled further than I can know or you can tell till he came to a forest and there he rested. The next day he passed a hawk, a deer and a hound fighting over which would get to eat the carcass of a dead horse they were standing over. The young man intervened and with his knife cut the carcass in to three parts: the body he gave to the deer, the two hind quarters he gave to the hound and the remainder he gave to the hawk. The animals were grateful and as he was leaving the deer said, 'Pull three hairs from my tail and whenever you want you can turn into a deer.'

The hound said, 'Pull three hairs from my tail and whenever you want you can turn in to a hound.'

And the hawk said, 'Pull a feather from my tail and whenever you wish you can turn into a hawk.'

Well, the young man travelled on another little bit, but then he thought he would like to fly like a hawk. No sooner had he voiced the wish than he turned into a hawk and flew through the skies over fields and woods till he came to a high tree, from which he cold see a light in the distance. He headed for the light.

That night he stayed on the roof of the house and the next day entered the kitchen. There was a girl there who took the hawk and put him in a cage and fed him. After a time, he would open the cage and come out to talk to the girl. One day he showed himself in his human form and told her that he'd marry her if she'd have him. The girl went to her father to ask if she could marry the hawk.

'How the devil,' says the man, 'would a hawk marry you?' But the young man showed himself in human form and the father was happy for them to be married. For seven or eight years he lived there with his wife, and then he returned to his home and his father.

The king and queen were delighted to see their youngest son again, and the next day the father took his son hunting with him. At one stage they saw a hare start up.

'I wish I was a hound,' says the young man, and he turned into a hound and chased that hare, but the hare ran down by the sea shore and as soon as he was within reach of the waves the mermaid jumped out, grabbed him and pulled him into the sea.

The wife was distraught and went to see an old witch who lived nearby to find out if there was anything she could do.

'There is something you can do,' says the old witch. 'Tomorrow, take this gold ball down by the sea and the mermaid will show you his head.'

So the following day the wife took the golden ball the witch had given her and went walking with it by the sea, spinning it on her hand so as all could see it. Sure enough the mermaid put her head out of the waves and she wanted the golden ball.

'First show me my husband,' said the wife, and the mermaid raised his head out of the water. The wife was satisfied and gave her the golden ball and returned home to the witch.

'Tomorrow,' said the witch, 'take this fiddle which spills gold out the sides down by the sea and ask the mermaid to show you as far as his knees.'

So the next day she walked down by the sea playing the fiddle which played beautiful music and spewed gold out either side of it as it did. Sure enough the mermaid raised her head and nothing would do but for her to have the fiddle too.

'First let me see my husband as far as the knees,' said the wife. The mermaid raised the young man out of the water and the wife could see all of his head and shoulders down to his knees; she was satisfied and handed over the fiddle and returned to the witch.

'All is well,' said the witch, 'now tomorrow take this wheel which spills gold on all sides, and this time ask her to show your husband on the palm of her hand.'

The wife did as the witch said and she took the wheel down by the sea. The mermaid wanted it and asked what the wife would take in return.

'Show me my husband standing on the palm of your hand,' says she.

The mermaid did, but as soon as the young man was raised out of the water on the palm of her hand he wished he were a hawk and flew away. The mermaid was enraged and grabbed the wife in vengeance, but the hawk turned into a deer and trampled the mermaid in the water, forcing her deeper and deeper and further from the shore, then he took his wife home and they were bothered no more by her.

KILKENNY

ANNE FARRELL

THE ROSE OF MOONCOIN

If you have ever stood in Croke Park, or indeed in any hurling pitch, in County Kilkenny or elsewhere, when a Kilkenny hurling team took to the field, you will understand what I mean when I say that this lovely ballad has huge power. Once the first chords of 'The Rose of Mooncoin' are played, the whole attendance seems to gel and become one. Even the supporters of the opposing teams find it hard to resist.

The story of how this ballad came into being is simple and easy to understand and I will tell it to you the way I know it.

A long time ago, when Ireland was occupied, many good and bad things happened. One of the good things, which swung in that balance, was that there was an education available even in the small village of Mooncoin. Granted, it rested with the whim of the English Crown. Sometimes the Irish were permitted to have schooling and sometimes it was prohibited under pain of death. Imagine that state of affairs.

The time I am telling you about was just after one such prolonged banning of schools, and brave people were beginning to teach children openly. One of the terrible things happening at that same time was that the 'Tithe Act' was still being enforced.

Under the Tithe Act all the local people were bound by law to pay tithes or dues to the local Protestant clergy. People were very poor and some of the tithes demanded were absolutely destroying those who had little or nothing to live on already. So there was a lot of unease in almost every corner of the country, let alone in County Kilkenny.

This is how things fell out in Mooncoin. A man called Henry Murphy moved into the area in or around 1800. How he came there is not recorded, but he must have been a good man for he set up a school nearby in Carrigeen (little rock). He was the principal there for a good long while and his son, who was called Watt, which was probably short for Watty or Walter, decided to start up another school in the village of Mooncoin. I am told that it was in Chapel Street near the halfway mark, but I have no way of knowing now, no more than anyone else.

To return to my story, Watt was a scholarly man and given to writing the odd piece of poetry. Indeed, he followed the path of the bards of old who could wither a man with satire.

Now, Watt was well aware of the hardships suffered by the locals under the demands of the Tithe Act, and nothing would do him only to put his pen to paper. Didn't he write a blistering poem about the landlords, they being the ones who enforced the law.

If we had the words of it today wouldn't we use them, and we to be pitied with the impositions being made on ourselves.

The poem was read far and wide and, while some saw the justice in it, others took it very personally indeed, and the upshot of it all was that Watt was severely taken to task and his meagre wage, as principal of his little school in Chapel Street, was stopped forthwith. You see, his school was under the patronage of the Church, as were many other small schools just started at that time, and upsetting the gentry was not something they could support.

The position of the Church itself was precarious, with Catholic Emancipation finally granted, against much opposition, and written into law in 1829. The last thing they needed was for a school under their patronage to be seen as a hotbed of anti-establishment activity. Bless us and save us, couldn't young Watt, the schoolmaster, be turning out rebels under their very noses?

It must have been very difficult for him to survive, but I think he had great support from the locals. Nor indeed did he take the lesson to heart, for his pen was never far from paper, and it seems he was the author of a piece of prose about the Battle of Carrickshock also, and so became known as 'The Rebel Poet'.

Time was moving on for Watt and he was not yet married. He had a little house in Polerone, not too far away, down near the banks of the

River Suir. Watt was a scholarly man and liked nothing more than to engage in debate, so when a new neighbour moved in nearby he was pleased to find it was a man of the cloth with a good education.

His new neighbour moved into the rector's house, which was located beside Polerone Church. In spite of his previous denunciation of the Tithe Act, he became very friendly with the neighbours and in particular he got on very well with the daughter of the house, Elizabeth. To be honest he became infatuated with the beautiful Elizabeth, who was also fondly called Molly. Now she was almost thirty-six years his junior, he being around fifty-six and she only twenty years growing, as they say.

Sure, who are we to judge? She was well educated, and they had common interests, so it was often they would walk out along the banks of the river, talking and discussing this and that, reciting favourite poems, and occasionally writing them as well. Her father was not long in the district when he was made aware of Watt's poetic satire. Weren't some people tripping over themselves to tell him? Human nature is a strange thing entirely.

Elizabeth was, by all accounts, a handsome young lady, and there were many who would have wooed her if it were not for her apparent attachment to the rebel poet Watt Murphy. It was clear now to see that Watt and Elizabeth were more than fond of each other. Whether Watt approached her father with the request for her hand or not is not known, but there was a terrible disagreement, and even though Elizabeth loved Watt and didn't care about the age difference, her father would have none of it.

She was only twenty years old and so, by the old custom, was under his parental control. He moved swiftly, despite her pleas, and the assurances of Watt that he would love and care for her. Elizabeth was put on board a boat in the port of Waterford and sent to England in 1848.

Watt was left broken-hearted.

I know what you are thinking now, 'Couldn't he have followed her?' Times were different then, and where would poor Watt get the money to follow her, even if he knew where she was gone. Also he would be in trouble as she was still under her father's protection, being only twenty.

Watt turned to the pen again. It was his only comfort now. He poured his heart into this beautiful ballad and called it 'The Rose of Mooncoin'.

How sweet 'tis to roam by the sunny Suir stream,
And hear the dove's coo 'neath the morning's sunbeam.
Where the thrush and the robin, their sweet notes combine,
On the banks of the Suir that flows down by Mooncoin.

Flow on, lovely river, flow gently along.
By your waters so sweet sounds the lark's merry song,
On your green banks I'll wander where first I did join
With you, lovely Molly, the Rose of Mooncoin.

Oh Molly, dear Molly, it breaks my fond heart,
To know that we two forever must part
But I'll think of you, Molly, while sun and moon shines
On the banks of the Suir that flows down by Mooncoin.

Then here's to the Suir with its valley so fair
As oft times we wandered in the cool morning air
Where the roses are blooming and lilies entwine
On the banks of the Suir that flows down by Mooncoin,

Flow on, lovely river, flow gently along
By your waters so sweet sounds the lark's merry song
On your green banks I wander where first I did join
With you, lovely Molly, the Rose of Mooncoin.

Watt took many a lonely walk by the banks of the River Suir, but never again was he to meet his darling Molly, the love of his life. Their companionship was of the rarest kind, and even in these enlightened times it would probably be frowned upon.

There is no information on what became of the lovely Elizabeth, whether she too mourned the loss of a precious friendship or went on to find a new love.

Broken-hearted Watt lingered in Polerone and passed away some ten years later. He was laid to rest nearby in Rathkieran cemetery.

This ballad has been adopted as the Kilkenny GAA anthem. It was a good choice given the wealth of emotion it stirs up in the manly hearts.

THE LAST FITZGERALD IN CLUAN CASTLE (CLONAMERY)

There is a story about Cluan Castle which often makes me wonder if animals really do haunt certain areas where they once lived.

In the late 1600s the man who was in charge in Cluan Castle was Edward Fitzgerald. He made the mistake of taking the side of King James II and subsequently forfeited his lands. Apparently he was one of the better landlords at that time and was known for his love of music and in particular he liked to play the harp. The harp would have been the clairseach or Irish Harp and, when played by a Master Harper it could raise the listener to the heights of bliss or break their hearts with a lament.

Even when this castle fell into ruin, locals would still point to the window where he used to sit and play his harp. It must be a grand gift to have.

It is hard for us to understand how things worked all that long ago but, as owner of large tracts of land, Edward had in his care many tenants and retainers and in time of strife he could call on them to support him, or whomsoever he followed, onto the field of battle. He had been raised to this way of life and had often taken his people far from the banks of the River Nore to fight against different foes. At one time he took them as far north as Meath and they were engaged in the Battle of the Boyne.

Behind all this soldiering he was a man with responsibilities and probably should have given more thought to his own business in Cluan. Life then was so different that we can only guess at the pressure he felt and it is likely that he had good people left behind to manage his estates.

Well, when he took off to join in the Battle of Aughrim, with his own men gathered around him he probably felt relatively safe and relaxed. Aughrim was to be a journey of a similar distance across country as he had previously undertaken, and he probably had that terrible failing which sometimes besets the young, he thought himself invincible.

Whatever he thought, the poor man, he always must have expected to come back to his own family.

The Battle at Aughrim was to go down in history as the last battle fought on behalf of an unworthy king. The Irish had been used as battle fodder in their mistaken trust in James II. In the heat of the battle Edward Fitzgerald came off his war-horse and engaged the enemy with his sword. His horse-boy was a young lad, green to the field of battle, and his task was to hold and have the horse ready for his Lordship at any point in the engagement with the enemy. The battle raged around him and he was at his level best holding the fine strong animal.

As you would expect, he was in due course separated a bit from his master and when the terrified lad realised that the battle was being lost he must have been in dread and terror. By all accounts Cromwell's mounted troopers were trained to advance in a boot to boot close formation and not to engage in individual pursuit unless given a command to do so. It must have been a terrifying spectacle to see the mounted enemy advance like a great killing machine across the field of battle.

Whether he heard his master call out to him, to bring the horse, or not, no one can say now for the noise on a field of battle is a terrifying thing. Can you imagine the shouts and challenges, the screams of the dying, the neighing of the frightened horses and over all this the clash of swords and the raucous calling of the ravens who followed the battles then.

The boy must have been terror struck and there to his hand was a means of escape from what he must have perceived to be certain death. The big war-horse strained and pulled against him and then perhaps, because he was only a lad, he could no longer see where his master was, he took the only option for him at that moment and leapt to the stirrup and into the saddle and away, away from the terror behind him.

With no war-horse to take him to safety, Edward Fitzgerald must have felt the first surge of real fear. The plunging hooves of the retreating army all mixed up with men running and the enemy troopers cutting through them, intent on slaughter would have been enough to break a stronger man. Edward was no weakling, but he was disadvantaged in that he still wore his boots and spurs. He never expected to be on foot at a moment of flight. Indeed he most likely never expected to be fleeing the battlefield in the first place.

Edward Fitzgerald was a man like any other and it is said that in the full retreat by the Irish, finding himself horseless, he ran with the rest to get away from the mounted foe. His attire marked him as an important enemy so he was a target from the word go. I expect it never occurred to him to cast off his finery as he ran so he could mingle with the less notable, so having run for a time probably almost to a safe place, he was caught up by a mounted enemy and struck down, mortally wounded, by one of the Williamite troopers.

As the Williamite army swept through and on after the fleeing Irish two of his followers found Edward among the slain and it is said that they wept firstly for the loss of The Harper and then for their leader.

On the morning after the battle his war-horse was found standing outside the stable in Castle Cluan and it was only then that his family and retainers knew the battle had been lost and that they, themselves, were now in mortal danger from William of Orange and his followers.

What became of the boy is not known except that there are several tales about how he brought the war-horse home and fled in great sorrow from the place which had been home to him.

I came upon this following ballad during my research and thought you might enjoy it.

There stood beside the winding Nore
A castle fair to see;
It was the home of the Geraldine,
And a gentle knight was he.

But now a hoary ruin it stands
Beside the winding Nore,
All lonely, and all desolate
A hundred years or more.

An' though its woods each year grow green
And the clear Nore flows on,
Yet Cluan's tower shall ever be
A ruin grey and lone.

Cluan's lord was a true knight –
He fell amid the slain,
The first in fight for his king's right,
On Aughrim's bloody plain.

Two summer nights scarcely past
Since that last fatal day,
When Cluan's lady mourning sat
For her good lord away.

Oh! heavily and wearily
She sits within her hall
And startles often as if she heard
Her good lord's wonted call.

She sits beside her baby boy
As quietly he sleeps,
And recks not of the woes for which
His tender parent weeps.

And now she listens eagerly,
For hark! there comes a sound
Of footsteps, and her anxious eye
Is looking all around.

The sound grows loud and nearer
Along the well-known track –
Can it be true that her good lord
Is well and safe come back?

'Ho varlets all! Wake ye in haste,
And on your lord await –
I hear the stamp of his good steed
Without the Castle gate.'

Thus did she speak in ecstasy,
And well did all obey,
And quickly did the gate unbar
Ere yet began the day.

Down came the lady Eleanor
All trembling for joy,
And brings to welcome back his sire,
Her sleeping infant boy.

But oh! it was a dismal sight
To see the good steed there,
When Cluan's lord had not come back
To greet his lady fair.

Oh! Is he a prisoner to his foes,
Or fallen in the fight?
Or why comes back his gallant steed
In such a woeful plight?

Why stands he thus impatiently
Without a curb or rein?
There's blood upon the saddle-bow
And foam upon the mane!

'Oh, woe is he!' the lady cried,
'Sure this must bode of ill!
'To see those ruddy drops of blood,
My very soul doth chill.'

In vain they looked, they searched in vain
Around both tower and tree
But the last lord of Cluan's Hall
They never more shall see.

One summer day of dread and doubt
Had scarcely passed away
When a youth rode up in fearful haste
With looks of wild dismay.

'Oh! noble youth wilt thou not bide
To speak one word to me –
What means this look of wild despair,
Or whither does't thou flee?

'I am the lady of this tower.
You may find shelter here –
For friend or foe, which e'er you be,
Thou shalt have nought to fear.'

'For friend or foe, which e'er I be,
With thee I cannot bide –
A woeful tale is mine to tell,
And one I fain would hide.

'Our rightful King has lost his crown –
And all our hopes lost we –
Nought now is ours, and the proud foe
Exults in victory.

'I saw thy lord fall by my side
Amidst a heap of slain,
While swiftly flew his gallant steed
Across the battle plain.'

Thus having said, he turn'd his rein
No more she heard him speak;
The tears were falling from her eyes,
And pallid grew her cheek.

And well might she both wail and weep
To leave her kin and home –
Her lovely tower to seize upon
The ruthless foe is come!

And though its woods each year grew green
And aye the Nore flows on,
Yet Cluan's tower shall ever be
A ruin grey and lone!

Before I found this story my daughter had a very strange experience one night coming from Kilkenny on to Carrick-on-Suir. At one point of the road she swore that as she drove a great horse with a flowing white mane galloped alongside her car for a long stretch of the road. She felt no fear and it was as though the horse was taking care of her. Then just as suddenly as he appeared he was gone. Perhaps the ghost of the gallant war-horse still gallops towards home.

WEXFORD

BRENDAN NOLAN

THREE GEESE

Wexford folklorist Patrick Kennedy told the following tale of wandering geese and a wife who was nearly buried alive:

A tailor and his wife lived alone in a small cottage. They had no children but had lived a quiet and contented life for many years – until one day they had a difference of opinion over the number of geese marauding around their small garden.

The wife declared that there were at least a hundred geese trampling down their crop of oats and demanded that her lazy husband do something about it. He husband, who was busily pursuing his tailoring trade, pointed out (not altogether unreasonably) his good wife had less to do than he; but, rather than engage in an argument he knew he could not win, he rose with a sigh and headed out to deal with the reported invasion.

He stepped into the bright sunlight and was brought up short – all he could see was a pair of geese. One, two. This he reported to his wife (though perhaps he would have been better off not saying anything). Challenged, his wife amended her hand to fifty geese; but the tailor said he wished he was as sure of receiving 50 guineas as he was sure there were only two geese in it. She then declared that there were forty geese there, destroying the oats, as sure as there was one.

Giving up the argument on whether there was two, forty, fifty or a hundred, the tailor drove away the geese and went back to his tailoring, thinking all was well. But, when dinner came, after his wife had tumbled out the potatoes for him, placed a noggin of milk and a plate of butter before him, she went and sat in the corner by herself. With a dramatic gesture, she threw her apron over her head and began sobbing loudly.

The surprised tailor implored her to come over and take her dinner. But she was adamant there had been at least a score of geese in the garden when he had insisted there were only two, and that she would not sup with him until he owned to the truth. He stubbornly maintained that he owned to the truth, that there were two geese there and that was that.

The die was cast and the wife, instead of taking to the bed, made a shake-down for herself to lie on and would not gratify the tailor by sleeping in their high-standing bed beside him.

If the tailor thought a night's sleep would change her demeanour, he was mistaken. The following morning she would not rise, even after he had spoken kindly to her and brought some breakfast to where she lay. Instead, she asked him to go for her mother and relations; she wanted to take leave of them before she died. There was no use her living any more, not now all the love was gone from her marriage.

The tailor asked what he had done to bring their lives to this pass. His wife replied that he insisted there were only two geese in the garden when at the very least there could not be less than a dozen. She demanded he acknowledge the truth and not to be an obstinate pig of a man, and to let them be peaceful again.

Instead of giving her any answer, the tailor walked over to her mother's house, and brought her back, with two or three of her family, to take up the struggle on his behalf. But whatever way words were exchanged, she near enough persuaded them that her husband was to blame.

The tailor was called and was addressed by his declining wife before the assembled mediators. She said that if he didn't intend to send her to her grave, he should speak the truth and agree that there were three geese there; though she persisted in her assertion that there were six, at the very least, present. The annoyed tailor refused to yield – there were but two. At that, his wife told them all to go home, and on the way bid Tommy Mulligan prepare her coffin. He was to bring it to the house at sundown.

It's not everyday that someone orders their own coffin to be brought to their wake; but thinking that doing so might give her a fright, her kinspeople went to Tommy Mulligan and brought back a coffin he had readymade for someone else that was not quite dead yet. It was so new there were fresh shavings in the bottom of the box. Once it was in the house, the tailor took a wood auger to it and drilled some air holes in the coffin lid, just in case.

Meanwhile, the gathered women ordered the men out so they could wash the 'corpse', as was traditional. The tailor's wife waited until the men were gone before she gave tongue to the women – how dare they think she wanted or needed washing? If she chose to die, she said, it was no concern of theirs; if anyone attempted to lay a drop of water on her, she would lay the marks of ten nails on their face.

Just the same, washed or unwashed, she was persuaded to get into the coffin, as a corpse might do. A clean cap and frill was put around her face and her skin was attended to with sprinkled flour to give it a deathly pallor.

But while she was alive and not yet dead, the tailor's wife would have the last word on her appearance and when she saw her face in the mirror she took a towel and scrubbed the flour from it, restoring her rosy cheeks. She bid her husband be called in, and gave her sister and mother a charge, in his hearing, to be kind to the poor man after she was gone. However, she once again turned to the subject of the three geese and, without a word, the tailor put on his hat and walked out.

That was that. Evening came, and candles were lit, tobacco and pipes were laid out for mourners, and the night-long conversations commenced. They followed the usual themes and the poor undead woman had to listen to a good deal of conversation not to her liking. They discussed the cause of her death and the evidence that could be seen of it on her blotched skin (even though the corpse looked very well). They discussed her auld bitter tongue and the opinion was expressed that the tailor would bear her loss with patience. That he was a young man for his years – he didn't look forty – and he could have his pick of the village women. They tried to recall who it was that the tailor used to walk out with on an odd Sunday evening, before his marriage, and if that friendship could be resurrected within a few weeks of the funeral?

All this time the tailor's wife's blood was rushing around her veins like a herring caught in a net; but she was determined to die, out of spite, and she neither opened her eyes nor her mouth.

A broken-hearted tailor, in his misery, came up after some time and, leaning over her, whispered to be done with the foolery. If she would but say the word he, as her husband, would send all the people away about their business. But until he would admit that there were more geese in the garden than he claimed, his wife would not move and, giving up, the tailor went and sat in a dark corner of the room until dawn broke.

He made another offer next morning, just as the lid was being put on the coffin and the men were about to hoist it on their shoulders; but not a foot she would move unless he would give in to the three geese, which he would not.

They came to the churchyard, and the coffin was let down into the prepared grave. The tailor slid down to the coffin on his backside and, stooping to speak through the auger holes in the lid, he begged her, even after the holy show she had made of herself and himself, to give up the point and come home. All he got from her was the same question.

Every man has his breaking point and the tailor seemed to have reached his. He clambered up out of the grave, and began to shovel soil like mad down onto the coffin that he had lately stood upon.

The first loud rattle that the soil made on the bare lid nearly frightened the life out of the not dead woman. She shouted out to let her up, let her up, that she was not dead at all. She would even agree to there being only two geese if they would just let her up.

But the enraged tailor said it was too late; people had come from far and near to the funeral and they shouldn't be losing their day for nothing. So, for the credit of the family, he told his wife not to stir, and down went the soil in showers, for the tailor had lost his senses and who could blame him?

The bystanders, tiring of the sport, would not let the poor woman be buried against her will; so they seized the tailor and his shovel and restrained him. When his madness was checked, and he looked around at the concerned faces of the assembled crowd, he gave a low moan and collapsed on the ground in a dead faint.

When his wife stepped from the coffin, the first sight she saw was the tailor lying there, without a stir in him. A mischievous neighbour proposed to her that she should let the tailor be put down in her place, and not give so many people a disappointment after coming so far to witness a burial. But the dead woman, now full of love for her marriage and understanding husband, was having none of it. She roared and bawled for the poor tailor to come to life, promising that if he did she'd never say a contrary word to him again while she lived. The tailor was brought around; but it took a good while for him to come around to looking his wife in the face after that.

Ever after, whenever a sharp answer came to tongue, the memory of rattling clods on a coffin and of the three geese that were only two after all came to mind, and her words were checked.

For such is the way that a tailor minds his own oats.

CROSSING THE WATER

Stories have always been told of travellers finding their way blocked by a river or lake and having to obey the crossing protector or pay a ferryman for safe transport to the other side. The most famous perhaps is the Styx, a river in Greek mythology, which formed the boundary between Earth and the Underworld, or Hades. Charon, the ferryman, transported the souls of the newly dead across this river into the Underworld. Placing a coin in the mouth of the deceased paid the toll to cross the Styx, which led on to the entrance of the Underworld.

But that was a long time ago. A more recent ferryman was involved in a conversation with a number of legal bigwigs about crossing the Barrow to get to the other side. Among their number was the splendidly named Caesar Colclough.

In 1797, Colclough lived at Duffrey Hall, in the western section of the county, about 80 miles west of Enniscorthy. His family had extensive estates in the south of the county and were reputed to be among the more liberal Anglicans of the area, though he actively opposed the encouragement of insurrection in the county.

One day, a number of legal gentlemen of the Leinster circuit were waiting on the Kilkenny side of the ferry at Ballinlaw on the Barrow for a favourable moment to cross to the Wexford side. A storm was blowing and the river was angry. The ferryman was fearful for the safety of the crossing, but lucrative briefs lay on the other side of the river to be dealt with. The venture was worth the risk, agreed the legal eagles. Among the barristers was Colclough, who carried with him at all times on his journeys a pair of valued saddle bags. While the rest were hesitating, like timorous bathers with one toe in the water, Colclough impatiently flung his travelling bags onto the ferry and jumped aboard.

Charles Kendal Bushe, who later became a judge, recalled that while the shivering ragged boatman pointed out the danger inherent in casting off for the other side in such conditions, Colclough dismissed his fears with the cry: 'You carry Caesar and his saddle bags,' a reference to Julius Caesar and a similar reported occurrence from the days of the Roman Empire. Whether or not the boatman of the day was as familiar with Caesar and his Roman pronouncements as the story suggests, the saga was to take a more profound twist.

As they headed away from land, the full force of nature came to bear on the boat. The boatman rose to his element on the water, while Colclough the learned barrister was most definitely out of his.

Colclough began to cry on the Lord for protection on the waters in this storm on this day. But, the boatman said, he should not be praying on that side if he pleased; it was the other lad he ought to be praying to, in this situation. An alarmed Colclough asked what lad the boatman meant. 'What lad?' shouted the boatman into the searing wind, 'Why, sir, the auld people always say the Devil takes care of his own, and if you don't vex him by praying the other way, I really think, sir, I have a pretty safe cargo aboard on this present passage.'

And so it proved, for the boatman landed his charge safely on the other side and Colclough went on, in 1805, to be appointed Chief Justice of Prince Edward Island, one of the Atlantic provinces of Canada. His salary was £500 per annum, a sum that would have provided more than a few coins to compensate any ferryman for crossing stormy waters.

Someone who did indeed prevent people from passing her position beside a Wexford stream was the ghost of Petticoat Loose, and her story was recalled in the 1950s by eighty-five-year-old farmer John O'Neill of Ballinglee, to folklorist Jim Delaney of the Irish Folklore Commission.

Some Irish roads cross over streams and sometimes streams cross over roads; it all depends on the terrain and whatever is most convenient. Most times, a bridge of sorts takes man and beast dryshod over the water. However, in this particular place where Petticoat Loose appeared, the stream crossed the road. That was enough in itself to cause a traveller to pause on his journey, for we will all seek a way around or over water rather than splashing straight through it.

The fearsome ghost challenged all men that approached and demanded they call out their name to her. Dire consequences followed if the wrong name was given. It was known locally that if a challenged man jumped across the stream safely, she had no powers over him and he was safe. But if he did not manage that feat and the name he gave was the name she sought, then his end had arrived.

She had killed no less than three men up to the day that the man in the story hove into view. As it happened, his name was John and she soon made it clear to him that she only killed men named John.

John used all his reasoning to persuade the mad woman not to take away his life: he told her of all the good deeds he had done, and all he would do in the future if she would allow him pass her by without harm. When that did not impress her, he told her he was the son of parents and the parent of sons himself, and that he was a brother and a cousin and an uncle and any other relation he could imagine might lead her to a change of heart.

It did not persuade her from her declared intention of killing him, however. He offered her riches he did not possess to change her mind;

but earthly riches impressed her less than his family responsibilities or his good works.

In the end, he sank to his knees and began to cry with outstretched hands, begging her to let him go. If she did, he said, he would return to her on the following night. He wanted to make peace with his family, he claimed, and his neighbours, his debtors and his creditors before his life ran its course. He promised he would return on the morrow to continue their conversation. This stratagem is well-known to the folklore of many lands; when a condemned man agrees to return in a day, or a year and a day, or some other agreed time-span, to be murdered having dealt with his duties in the time allotted.

She agreed to allow him to go and return on his word on the next day, when she would take his life. A trembling John crossed the stream and hurried to find a holy man, a priest, to advise him on what to do. The priest listened and asked questions and listened again, and finally he advised John to return and to keep his word to Petticoat Loose, lest he lose his own immortal soul, with his integrity compromised, for not keeping his word.

John returned on the agreed day. But this time while he spoke to her he remained on the safe side of the stream and did not jump across. Petticoat Loose was mad at that and said he promised to return. John replied that he had returned; but he had not said on which side of the water he would stand. He said he had a question to ask her: why did she kill only men named John?

She said she had killed an unbaptized child and had sinned against St John. However, she did not say which St John or why she wished to take the life of any man called John who came to her spot by the water's edge as a consequence. Try as he might, John could get no more from her and so returned to the priest to tell him what had occurred, and what he had learnt from his encounter with the mad woman called Petticoat Loose on the road beside the stream.

The priest called a meeting of all the priests that he could find and they sat and sat and sat for three days and three nights, discussing what they should do about this woman who had sinned against St John.

They were of the opinion, finally, that the killing of the child had left her soul in limbo and brought her to the place on the road where it must have taken place, and where she waited to take away the life of yet another victim. They decided, eventually, that they would banish her to a small island in the bay of Youghal Harbour in the neighbouring county of Cork. But, when she heard this, Petticoat Loose said that if they banished her, by whatever prayers and incantations they used to do so, she would wreck every ship that passed by the island.

The priests met again and decided instead to send her to the Red Sea, for it was the mouth of Hell, they believed, and there was no coming out of there for Petticoat Loose or anyone else banished there. This they did and she was never heard of again, according to farmer John O'Neill of Ballinglee.

However, another version of the same story as related by Kathleen Ronan of New Ross, a pupil in the Mercy Convent, in 1938 to teacher Sister Ni Mhaoldomhnaigh, said the victims were the mother and father, and two children (one without baptism), of Petticoat Loose herself. She herself died soon afterwards and on a dark night, not long after her death, her ghost appeared to a man riding by who took her up on the horse, as was the custom of the day. As soon as she settled on its back, the horse staggered under the sudden weight. The man remarked that he had never noticed the horse stagger like that before. She replied that the horse never carried such a weight of sins on its back before.

The man made her dismount and he journeyed home. In the morning he found the horse was dead. He mentioned the matter to a priest, who later visited the spot on the road where she had been left down. Petticoat Loose appeared in front of him and said she was here to kill any man who passed by.

He asked who sent her and she replied the Devil had sent her from Hell. She told the priest she was there for killing her mother and her father. He replied she could be shriven for that. But when she said she had also killed an unbaptized child, the priest said it was the killing of the child that had cursed her and banished her for ever.

So there she stayed; she may be there yet, waiting beside the stream that crosses the road in County Wexford.

WATERFORD

ANNE FARRELL

THE TUNNEL BENEATH THE RIVER SUIR?

We were often told that long ago, in troubled times, and there were many such times in Waterford's history, the merchants and clergy got together and decided it would be a great idea to dig out a tunnel under the River Suir. The idea was that if those in the city needed to get away from a besieging enemy they could cross over through the tunnel and come out in the grounds or indeed inside in the abbey on the Ferrybank side and vice versa.

The location of the tunnel entrance in the city was never specified except that some believed it came up near Reginald's Tower and some that it came up near Christ Church Cathedral.

Whether they had the technology to do such a thing or not is debatable but it was widely believed that it was not only possible but was done.

The further addition to this story was that, during the 'Troubles', someone discovered the entrance to the tunnel and started into the depths with some companions. They had little light and were scared witless in case the River Suir would come down on top of them and there were spiders and cobwebs the like of which they had never seen before. Also there were scurryings and half-seen movements all around them and the air was musty and damp.

They decided to turn back, all except one, who, despite warnings from his companions, chose to carry on investigating. Well, need I tell you, the story goes, that he was never seen again and no one dared to investigate any deeper into the tunnel. But a dog did once run down it and came back with a human bone. So they say. No name was ever even suggested to go along with this mysterious disappearance nor did any of us ask, for fear it might be someone we knew.

We were always told that there were rats down there as big as dogs and they would surely eat a man let alone a youngster.

The following account of the same tale was told by an old man who seemed to know more than he should but when we questioned him he tapped the side of his nose and said 'I'm saying nothing'. But this is what he told us.

There was a young man once and his name was Murphy. He came from the right side of the bridge, as they say, meaning Ferrybank. There was another name for Ferrybank once; it was called The Slip because of all the shipbuilding that went on there. Young Murphy was interested in all things mysterious and spent a lot of time with his head in books.

It was no wonder then that he stumbled upon a tale which was to stir him up to take action eventually. This was no foreign or fanciful tale, as far as he could tell, and it was entirely possible. Waterford had been invaded and besieged many times so the secreting away of valuable items of Church and State was common practice and he was sure that not all of it had been recovered yet. Sure didn't people who hid things often get killed, and he was right in that.

He spent some more time trying to get a look at old maps and records held by Waterford Corporation, on the pretence of writing about history, so no one paid much mind to Murphy and his comings and goings. If they did notice him they called him The Professor and smiled.

Three weeks into his research he withdrew from the public eye and appeared content to live his life with his head in a book.

But Murphy's heart was all of a flutter. He had found a mystery on his own doorstep and only he could put the pieces together. He lived alone since both his parents were lost to TB, which was rife at the time. In the quiet of his own kitchen, as the sunset, he lit the oil lamp and brought it to the table. His next step was to remove a very old piece of vellum from between the pages of his book. This he had appropriated during his perusal of the old maps in the Corporation's oldest files. He fully intended to give it back, when he was finished with it. He would slip it back into the old leather pouch, covered in dust and cobwebs, down at the side of the press, and no one would ever know it had been out of the room.

Now all he had to do was make it correspond to the Waterford he knew in his time. The river still flowed in the same manner so it shouldn't be hard, but which building was which now was another problem.

There was no bridge marked on the map but Reginald's Tower was clearly indicated. So was Kilculliheen Abbey on the other side of the river and another place, further back. The church, marked with a cross had to be Christ Church, or maybe the Friary. There were one or two other squiggles which were smudged and could not be made out at all.

He spent a long time studying the old map and trying to interpret the directions written in faded ink at the side. He was sure the map lead to buried treasure. He was positive it led to hidden artefacts, maybe golden chalices or other items of immense value. Why else would there be a big X marking different places. Everyone knows that X marks the spot. He decided that he needed someone to confide in. It was too big a responsibility for him to take on alone and if any digging or heavy lifting needed to be done he was not suited to that kind of labour.

Now you and I know the way of secrets. If more than one person knows you might as well take out a full page add in the *Munster Express* or the *News & Star*. Word got around quite quickly that Murphy had found a treasure map and he might need a little bit of help. This was a cause for jeering, for no one thought very highly of 'Murphy the Book'. Only Flynner, who was always on the outside of things looking in, much the same as Murphy himself, agreed to meet with him and take a chance it might be genuine. The others waited and watched.

There was no electric light then so Murphy gathered his candles and matches and even got a little Tilly Lamp for an emergency. It was early in the evening when he started out on his adventures. He was to meet Flynner down by the Boat Club and they would bide their time and slip over the Abbey wall into the graveyard, when no one was looking, and following the directions on the map they would unearth the buried treasure.

The plan seemed sound but the first thing Murphy noticed was that there seemed to be an awful lot of lads hanging around the Boat Club. Eventually he got fed up waiting – the map was burning a hole in his pocket – so he gave Flynner the beck and the two of them walked back up the lane, as though they were going home, and they slipped in the gate of the Abbey instead.

Murphy thought his heart would leap out of his chest, so excited did he feel. Flynner kept looking around and was very jumpy, starting at every sound. He had never been in a Protestant graveyard before, sure anything could happen. They got to the shelter of the abbey wall and checked the map again. They stepped out the paces as best they could from the riverside of the graveyard. It was getting darker by the minute and the overhanging trees didn't help with all their rustling and shadow casting.

They were intent now on their adventure and were more than a little disappointed when they came to a flat table-like gravestone each time they counted. They sat on it and wondered where they went wrong and decided to count again. The sounds in the graveyard were increasing and there was a rustling and movement all around them.

The Tilly Lamp had to be lit this time so they wouldn't fall over anything as they paced and counted. As the wick took light, both of them nearly jumped out of their skins. A loud scraping sound echoed around the graveyard and birds fluttered, away out of the trees above them. Flynner gave a little croak and his hand gripped Murphy's arm.

'Did you hear that?' he gulped.

'Probably a slate coming off the roof with the birds', whispered Murphy.

'Yea, yea, that's what it was.' Flynner let go his arm and they began to walk forward, counting softly. Two seconds later Murphy let out a yell as he back pedalled into Flynner. The Slab had been lifted and now sat askew across the grave. 'Oh heart of God we're finished altogether', gasped Flynner. Sounds of movement came from all around them. Soft rustling like feet walking, whispers, and something that sounded halfway between a giggle and a scream.

Murphy, thinking on his feet, grabbed Flynner and the two of them went headlong into the uncovered grave. If whoever owned this grave was out and about then the safest place to hide was inside. They could hide in it until the daylight came, he reasoned. But he was not going to meet any ghosts walking around that night. All went quiet and by the light of the little Tilly Lamp they saw that they were not in a grave at all but the start of a tunnel of some sorts. Just as they made this discovery they heard the stone slab being shoved back in place above them.

Terror gripped them and they shouted and screamed and hammered but all they heard was laughter echoing back at them. When the first wave of terror passed they decided that they might as well see where the tunnel would lead to; maybe they could escape at the other end.

It was dank and musty and seemed to lead them down and down. Here and there water dripped and pooled. The little lamp began to flicker and its light dwindled slowly. Clutching each other, all thoughts of the treasure gone, they began to move, step by careful step, stumbling and weeping with fright as strange gurgling noises seemed to come from all around them.

Something brushed against Murphy's leg and he screamed. He thought he heard another scream echo way back behind him. They dared not stop. Flynner took the lead now and they lighted one of the little candles from his pocket. It flickered alarmingly and the air was thick around them. Prayers began to come involuntarily to their lips.

The prayers were interspersed with curses for their own stupidity. Fear of death dogged every step. The water seemed to be getting deeper now and was up almost to their knees. Flynner dropped the candle as something fluttered past his head. With chattering teeth and shaking hands they somehow managed to light another stub of candle.

'It has to come out somewhere', said Murphy. 'It just has to.' Ten more steps and the water seemed to get less again and they were climbing up, and up a gradual rise. If anything the air was worse here and the skittering and movement seemed increased.

Thinking that they might never see God's good light again they struggled wearily on. Sometimes they had to climb over old timbers and mounds of earth to get past. When Flynner banged his head on the roof of the tunnel they stopped. They listened. Faint noises came to them.

'Footsteps, and voices, can you hear them?' Murphy cried out in relief.

It took them another fifteen desperate minutes to find a way out. They came out in a church crypt but they could see a crack of light up the steps and they ran, stumbling, towards it. When they burst forth from the crypt there were screams and shouts of alarm from the group gathered there.

They didn't care. They were safe. The guns on the table didn't scare them. Nothing would ever scare them again.

The cold feel of the revolver pressed to his cheek somehow steadied him. He smiled and smiled. Flynner giggled like a child and hugged the man with the gun.

It took them a long while to make sense to the people around them. Murphy handed them his map with the X marks the spot on it and another candle was lit so everyone could see it clearly.

Some men took candles and guns and went back down through the crypt. Nothing anyone could say or do would persuade either Murphy or Flynner to go with them. Someone gave the two lads a swig of whiskey. Never having had it before it went straight to their heads and both slumped quietly down against the wall.

It was a long time later when someone knocked twice on the room door. The party who had gone down the tunnel were back. They were grim-faced and dirty. They had found their way through they said, across under the river and scared a group of young men and women half to death.

The jokers had slid the slab off the grave and never checked inside it in the dark so when Murphy and Flynner disappeared into it they slid the stone over as a joke intending to move it in a few minutes but when they did move it the two lads had vanished. Then before they could decide who to call, up came a group of armed men from the same grave. Terror was the name of the game.

In the days that followed they were sworn to secrecy and now lived in darker world than they had known before. They never spoke about what happened that night and no one else did either. The fact that their hair had turned grey over night was noted but not commented on. Speculation about a tunnel was forgotten and those who knew left it so.

AN BÍDEACH

This story is an interpretation of a story by the first President of Ireland, Dr Douglas Hyde. I got this version from Master Storyteller, Liam Murphy of Waterford, who had adapted it to suit his own place. I hope I can do it justice.

The *Bideach* lived with his mother on the peninsula of Rinn an gCunach, across the bay from the town of Dungarvan. From birth he had never grown any more than eighteen inches and his mother had reared him in cotton wool, tended to his every need and reared him without the benefit of school. She was probably afraid, the *cratur*, in case anyone might step on him.

The *Bideach* never went far from the house but, even in his thirty-ninth year, he was happy as a sunbeam. He had never been to church, chapel or meeting, or to the town of Dungarvan. His mother warned him to 'beware of the women of that place, the way they might look at you and, heaven forbid, that they might wink at you'. His mother repeated her warning, 'Beware of the women of Dungarvan, if they wink at you.'

One day, shortly after his thirty-ninth birthday, his mother had to go into Dungarvan to make arrangements. She prepared porridge, meat sandwiches, lemonade and sweet tea and as she set off in the ass and cart she again warned the *Bideach* to stay and to speak to no one, no matter who called. He promised and promised, and why wouldn't he, and he living in the lap of luxury. When the mother was out of sight he settled down in comfort and stretched out in the sunbeams dancing through the windows, such was his delight, until a dark shadow crossed the sky and fear leapt to his heart as down the grassy boreen to the cottage came a tall dark man of bad temper, astride an *asal beag dubh*, a little black ass. He beat the ass and urged it forward

'Don't buckle under me now', he cried as they turned into the yard and he cried out 'Come out this instant, *Bideach*. Come out now.'

How did he know the *Bideach*'s name? I tell you this, some people know a lot more than they let on, and the tall dark man of the Formoire knew more than his prayers.

'Come out *Bideach* or it will be the worse for you.'

The *Bideach* shook with fear and went to hide behind the pot in the hearth.

The tall dark man kicked in the door and strode in across the flags of the floor.

'Where are you my little *Bideach*? Come out now like a good little man or it will be the worse for you. Come out.'

The *Bideach*'s little heart was crossways in him, from fear; there was no escape. He looked this way and that, and the only daylight he could see was between the tall dark man's legs. Without waiting to think, he made a dash for the door, straight out between those gigantic legs. The man was not expecting this, and as he tried to grab at the flying figure of the panic-stricken *Bideach*, scooting out between his legs, didn't he trip himself up and came crashing down. Sprawled across the flagstone floor he fell, splitting his head on the hearthstone.

The *Bideach* had won clear, and shot out the door into the sunlight beyond, panting and gasping until he thought his heart would pop out through his little jacket. He stopped at the far wall of the garden and realised that he was not followed. Hands on his little knees he rested for a few minutes and there was still no sign of the man.

Though still in fear, curiosity got the better of him and he gathered his courage again and crept back up to the broken door. Oh, mile a murder, what did he see? Only the long fellow stretched across the floor and his head in smithereens against the hearthstone. His first thought was for his Mammy. She will kill me, look at the state of the place, and she after telling me not to let anyone in. What will I do, what will I do at all? The door is broken and a dead man in around her kitchen.

Now, in all this world, the only thing the *Bideach* feared was that his Mammy would be upset. So gathering strength from somewhere deep inside his little chest, he grabbed the long fellow by the two legs and pulled and pulled until he managed to drag him out over the broken door and around the side of the little house, where his Mammy wouldn't see him when she came back from Dungarvan. He might mend the door, in time, when a voice spoke beside him.

The poor little *cratur* nearly leapt out of his skin, the fright he got.

'Well done *Bideach*, well done. You did a good deed this day to rid me of that torment from off my back.'

Try as he might, in his fear, the *Bideach* could see no one but the *asal beag dubh*, who was indeed speaking to him.

'Don't be afraid', said the ass. 'Don't be afraid for I am a prince of old Ireland, trapped by a curse in the body of this ass, by the tall dark man of the Formoire, and if you can do just one more favour for me, I can be set free and go back to helping my father, the king. If you do this one thing for me now I will reward you beyond measure or pleasure.'

Still in a dazed state, the *Bideach* found himself up on the back of the *asal beag dubh*, going like the March wind across the country, until they arrived at the Penitential Island of Lough Derg.

'I will be released from my curse if you can go around this island, from shrine to shrine, on your knees, and pray for me and the poor souls who need our prayers. Do this deed tonight and in the morning I will be restored and your reward will be waiting for you at home.'

As trusting as ever the *Bideach* did as he was bid, and, even though his knees were cut and blistered, he completed his task. He was greeted by a warrior prince who said, 'Close your eyes and you will be back home, back home in your yard at Rinn an gCunach. Down your boreen will come the Herd of Plenty led by a golden sow. Climb up on that sow's back and put your hand into her right ear and a silk purse will be your reward, a silk purse from a sow's ear, which will never empty, no matter how much gold you take from it.'

In the shudder of the wind the *Bideach* found himself back in his mother's house. There was no sign of the tall dark man and the door stood as good as new, with no sign of any damage. The *Bideach* let out a long breath and just then, down the *boreen* came the Herd of Plenty. They were thundering towards him and he knew that the only chance he had of getting up on the golden sow's back was to make a run for the little wall by the gate. He made it just in time and took a flying leap and landed safely. Sure, to a little man, like himself, the pig's back was a great place to be. He climbed up until he could put his little hand into her ear and sure enough he drew out the silk purse of plenty, just as he had been told.

Such was his delight that when his Mammy came home, shortly afterwards, he told her the whole story. Well wasn't she delighted herself, bless her, and why wouldn't she? And such is the way with money and them that have it, the name of the *Bideach* spread far and wide. His generosity was legendary, and people travelled the length and breadth of Ireland to call at the *Bideach*'s house, and they never went away wanting.

It is said that St Patrick called when he was building the cathedral in Ard Macha, and went away with a *flúirse* of gold.

Now we come to the sad part of the story, and isn't there often a sad turning in our own story too? The *Bideach*'s mother died and was buried with a High Mass of bishops and clerics, and in his sadness and loss the *Bideach* resolved to go to the town of Dungarvan, as he had never been there when his mother was alive. Sure, he forgot the dear woman's warning and he delighted in the women of Dungarvan, who did wink at him, and tickled him under the chin as well. He soon cheered up and fell head over heels in love with a girl with summer eyes, golden laughter and a wink that would charm even the hardest heart. Before the harvest was ripe they were inseparable, and under a warm harvest moon they married and settled down in Rinn an gCunach.

The *Bideach* was never happier and he lavished fistfuls of gold on his new wife and his purse never grew less. They spent days whispering in each other's ears, and at night she would nibble the *Bideach*'s ear and tell him how wonderful he was.

In the first chill of winter she stopped her nibbling and whispering and began to make demands. 'If you loved me you would let me take the purse with me to the town of Dungarvan, where my friends could see how much you love me and trust me.'

Sometimes she would snap at his head, and bit by bit the *Bideach* relented and in the end he gave his wife the purse, to shop on her own. She hugged him in delight and rushed to show off in the Square in Dungarvan, buying bolts of material and expensive folderols and filligree gee gaws and fripperies of every colour. When the time came to pay for her treasures she took out the purse, the silk purse of plenty, and plunged her hand deep into it and took out only a handful of stones. She recoiled in shock and howled in rage, as time and again, only gravel fell from her fingers. She rushed to the *Bideach* and attacked him.

'You have shamed me before the world and the town of Dungarvan. Made me a laughing stock and a mockery. Put it right at once!'

The poor *Bideach*, who was indeed poor now, put hand into the purse and got only stones. The magic, like love, was gone out the window. A chill struck his heart as his wife turned on her heels and walked out of his life forever.

'I should never have married you, you little maneen, you little *Bideach* you. Me mother was right; small men are useless.' With a chill in his heart the *Bideach* took to his bed. His sadness and loss broke his little heart. With his last remaining breath he took the purse and hurled it up into the stormy south-west wind, which carried it away in towards Waterford.

Where it landed no one saw, but the story goes that a Tree of Plenty grew up on that spot. Many have searched for it, to no avail. To this very day some people who hear this story believe that their lives could be changed, if only they could find it, as if a story could change anybody's life anyhow.

LIMERICK

RUTH MARSHALL

JOAN GROGAN, BEAN FEASA

Just as County Clare has Biddy Early, renowned as a wise woman throughout the whole country, so County Limerick has Joan Grogan. She lived in West Limerick, near the Kerry border, and had a reputation as a healer and seer. Here are some of the stories told about her and her abilities.

HOW JOAN FOUND HER POWER

Joan Grogan was born in a small, modest house in the townland of Athea, near the border with County Kerry. She seemed happy enough, was a lively child, and there was no sign in her early years of any particular ability that would set her apart from others. She grew up among the girls and boys of the district, and joined in their sport and play like any other girl.

When she was around 20 years old she set off with a crowd of other young people to a wake. It was already dark when they set off and the group stayed close together, laughing and joking on their way. But when they crossed a stream the party split, some leaping across quickly and racing ahead while others took their time crossing the water. So none of them noticed that Joan was missing. The first and faster group just thought she was coming up behind with the other party; while the second group thought she had gone ahead with the first.

By the time they all met up again at the wake, they noticed that Joan was not among them. They thought little of it, laughed at how each had thought she was with the others. 'She must have decided to go home early,' they said, or 'Joan probably changed her mind and went to see her auntie.'

No one was concerned that Joan was not with them, nor thought any harm had come to her. But the next morning, there was a very strange story on everyone's lips, telling what had befallen Joan Grogan. Joan herself had no memory at all of that night, from setting out with her friends for the wake until she woke up in the strangest of places. She awoke in the morning out of a deep sleep, but was as surprised as anyone might be to find herself sitting up on the roof of her own house, up on the top of the chimney pot! How she had got there she couldn't begin to wonder, but because she herself laughed at the absurdity of it, everyone else treated it as a strange joke.

After that night Joan began to have epileptic fits from time to time. She had also suddenly developed a kind of second sight, for now she knew things about other people that no one else could have known. When she was having a fit, Joan would somehow travel out of her body and see things that she had no way of knowing. Some began to fear Joan for the strange power she had and they called her a witch. But to others, she was a wise woman who could help them with cures for diseases of man and beast.

The news of her abilities spread and people came to her from far and near for help. Joan found that she could bring on a fit or trance at will by drinking a little whiskey. When she visited the house of a sick person, she would often tell the woman of the house to go and open the door and hold out her apron. Then a sprig of herbs would fall into the outstretched apron. When these were boiled in goat's milk, they were given to the patient to drink.

They say that Joan cured several people whom the doctors had given up as hopeless cases, and once she even raised a man who had been dead for twenty-four hours and he lived for a further five years after that!

MEAT FOR THE TABLE

As often happened to women with knowledge of healing, the priests took against Joan, claiming her powers came from an evil source, and warned people to stay away from her. They went so far as to excommunicate Joan, although she was welcomed back into the fold before she died.

When Joan was visiting a neighbour one day, there was only a few potatoes and a jug of buttermilk when the family sat down for dinner. Joan said aloud, 'It is a pity there is no meat for your dinner.'

'You are right there,' said the man of the house. 'It is indeed, but what can we do?' Joan went up and opened the back door. She held up her apron stretched between her two hands. The next thing you knew, there was a joint of roast beef came falling down into her apron. Joan brought the joint of meat to the table, saying, 'Here is a fine joint of meat for your dinner!' and with that, she left the house, so that they could enjoy their meal. The meat was hot, as if it had just come out of the oven, and the aroma was rich and made their mouths water. But not one of them would touch so much as a mouthful of it, no matter how delicious it smelt. When Joan had gone, the woman of the house took the meat outside, threw it away across the fields, where none of their animals could find it, and left it there for the crows or foxes. Perhaps they had listened to the priest when he spoke against Joan in the church on Sunday, but they did not trust the source of the meat and were afraid to tempt fate by eating it.

A CURE

Joan worked at one time for a man in Glenamore. In the house there was a young man who suffered with polyps in his nose. When he asked her could she find a cure for him, she put herself into a trance, and whilst she was 'out of herself' she spoke to those present and gave them instructions on what to do for the cure.

She told a woman in the house to go out and milk a certain goat belonging to her master, which would be found at the top of the boreen near the house. She said she must watch out, for the goat would get its leg twisted three times, and try to spill the milk. Joan told her that if the milk should be spilt three times the cure would not work. She said that if any of the milk were saved, it was to be boiled and certain herbs to be sprinkled in it. She told them where to find these herbs, which was on the bed where the patient usually slept.

The woman went out and did as Joan instructed. She milked the goat, and the milk was spilt twice, but saved the third time. She found the herbs lying where Joan had said and put them in the milk to boil. The drink was given to the young man and he recovered completely.

Joan would tell the woman of the house to watch the pot well as she boiled the herbs in the milk, as the colour of the leaves could foretell the fate of the sick person. If the herbs should turn green, the patient would surely recover; whereas if the herbs turned brown, then they would die.

STOLEN BUTTER

Home-made butter is yellow as gold and every bit as precious. People used to steal a neighbour's butter, if they could. They would put a piseóg on it: a spell of some kind, that would mean your butter would go to them, and you would have none, despite all your work at churning.

Joan Grogan was sent for one day by a farmer's wife. Day after day, despite hours of churning, she could not turn her milk into butter. Everyone believed that someone, perhaps even a neighbour, had put a charm on it and was stealing away their butter.

Joan arrived, and having drunk her glass of whiskey, she fell down writhing on the floor. When her limbs became still, she lay on the floor, her face as pale as if she herself had died. Then suddenly she sat bolt upright and began to give orders that they should now start the churning. While they were busy with churning, Joan called for the sock of an iron plough to be brought into the kitchen and set on the fire to heat.

Despite all the best efforts of the woman of the house and her maids, busy at the churn, still the butter would not come.

Joan called out, 'Now, it is time, you need to be watching that house up on top of the hill.'

Joan took up the fire tongs, removed the plough sock from the fire, and plunged it into the churn. Steam filled the dairy, with the sizzling sound of hot iron in cold liquid.

The woman and her maids ran outside to watch the house up the hill. And what did they see but the neighbour woman running out of her own door, waving her hands in the air, her feet stamping. They could hear her screaming, 'Stop it! I beg you, make it stop! I swear I will give you back every bit of butter I took from you, if you will just stop burning me!'

It was the neighbour on the hill who had been charming away the dairy woman's butter. But now that Joan had exposed her for her trick, she kept her word and gave the dairy woman two big firkins of good butter, and she never interfered with the butter-making again.

WELL, WELL, WELL

There were two men digging in a garden. After a time they needed to take a break and have a bite to eat. Once they had eaten, the pair sat down to take a smoke of their pipes. One of the men fell asleep on the ground, while the other took up his spade again and returned to his work.

Suddenly the sleeper was rudely awakened by a blow to the head. He sat up with a start and, seeing a big stone close by, accused the other of hitting him with the rock. 'If I did, I did not know I did,' said the other man, who had simply been working away. The man had not seen the stone at all.

Later that night, back at his home, the man complained of a terrible pain in his head. His wife sent for Joan Grogan to come and help.

Joan put herself into a trance, and then she told the man that it was the ghost of a dead man who had struck him. She gave detailed instructions of what he must do to restore things to a balance again.

He was to visit three holy wells; he was to walk round each well three times; he was to take a handful of mud from each well, place it on his side, and then return it carefully to the spot it had come from. She also told them to give three alms for the good of the man's soul that had harmed him and for the good of the man's soul that did him good.

The man's family did all that Joan instructed. The man was so unwell that he had to be carried on a table to the first well. By the time he visited the second well, he was able to be brought in an ass and car.

The man's health continued to improve and he rode to the third well on his own horse.

They had done all that Joan had said, and the man was feeling quite well again. How she knew, they never learned, but Joan Grogan came to the door, and told them, 'You have still to give the alms. I warn you, the cure is not complete until that is done too.'

When that was done, the man was back to his old self again, thanks to Joan Grogan.

THE PLACE OF SKULLS

A man and his nephew lived near Newcastle West. One day the nephew grew sick. The doctor could find no cure so the man called to Joan Grogan for her help. It was late in the evening when he knocked at Joan's door.

'Who is this from the place of skulls, knocking at my door?' called Joan. She had seen that the uncle lived next to the churchyard, where the grave diggers piled any unearthed bones on the walls of the monastery ruins.

The man told her of his nephew's sickness. Joan listened and then told him he must follow her instructions to the letter, if his nephew was to live. He agreed.

She told him he was to go to the ruined church at the stroke of midnight on the Friday night following the next full moon. He was to take a skull and bring it home with him. He must scrape small shavings from the skull into a small pot of water and bring this to a boil over the fire. All the time he was doing this he was to speak aloud the name of the person who he wished would die instead of his nephew seven times.

When such instructions are given, usually it is the name of a sick or elderly person, close to death, that is spoken. Someone who is grateful for their end to be hastened. But not so, in this case.

The uncle discussed the matter with his own son and with his agreement, he spoke the name of his son's wife as the one he wished would die in his nephew's place.

Whatever the morality of this particular cure, the nephew recovered, and lived to a great old age, without ever knowing the price of his recovery. The uncle died suddenly a year to the day after his visit to the place of skulls and his own son died the following year.

Sources

'How Joan Found Her Power', 'Place of Skulls': NFCS 485: 309–11. Mr Sheehan. Collector: William Danaher, Gortnagros, Athea, County Limerick.

'A Cure': NFCS 491: 260–61. Mrs N. Riordan of Monagea. Collector: Mary Ahrerne, Monagea, Newcastle West, County Limerick. Scoil: Monagea (C).

'Well, Well, Well': NFCS 480: 386, Glin Girls School, Glin, Limerick. NFCS 485: 309–11. Mr Sheehan. Collector: William Danaher, Gortnagros, Athea, County Limerick.

SEAN O'HEA AND THE WOMAN IN THE WHITE DRESS

Sean O'Hea was a piper, and there was hardly a dance tune that he could not play. Whenever he played, the people present could not control their feet. First they would be tapping at the ground, but it wouldn't be long before their legs carried them up and dancing despite themselves.

Sean and his wife Judy lived in a small cottage at the foot of the hill of Knockadoon, overlooking Lough Gur. Whenever there was a wedding, or a christening, or any other kind of gathering, a message would come asking Sean to play his pipes. Sean was always rewarded well for his playing, so himself and his wife were never short of money, but lived comfortably enough in their cosy little home.

One evening in late summer Sean was out walking around Knockadoon, checking on the cattle. He was taking his ease, enjoying the mild August evening, the gentle breeze, the light reflecting from the lake, and the beautiful scenery all around him. All was well in his world, with nothing to disturb him. When he heard a voice behind him, he turned, and there was a lovely young woman all dressed in white.

'Good evening to you, Sean O'Hea,' she said in a soft, sweet voice that sounded to Sean the way honey tastes.

'And good evening to you too, miss,' said Sean. 'Can I help you? Have you lost your way? Are you looking for somewhere?'

'It is yourself, Sean, I was looking for. I have come to fetch you to play your pipes at a ball tonight.'

'Aha, is that so?' said Sean.

'You can be sure there will be a generous reward if you choose to come with me.'

'Is it far I'd have to go?' asked Sean. 'Only my wife Judy would be mad with me if I am away for too long. Sure, she would be so cross she would not smile at me for seven days or more!'

'It is not so far, Sean,' said the lady, 'but perhaps it is best that you go and ask your good wife first before you come with me. I will wait here for your return.'

Sean made his way home and told Judy about the lady in white. Judy was not keen and tried to dissuade him from going.

'I do not think you should go with this stranger, Sean. Let me tell you, I had a strange dream this morning and it has left me afraid that something bad will happen,' said Judy. 'I dreamed I was making my way home from old Nellie's, having fetched some starch, and didn't the starch turn as yellow as gold? And on the road home, there was a fine lady in a carriage throwing up two gold balls with one hand and catching them in the other. All the time she was looking down at me with a mocking sneer on her face. I was so afraid that I woke shaking and in a fever. I don't know what it means, Sean, but it surely was a warning.'

'Away with you, Judy!' said Sean. 'You made your tea too hot and too strong last night. It was only a dream, and there is no harm in that. She promised she'd pay me well. I must go now, for the lady will be getting impatient waiting for me so long.'

What Sean did not know was that the lady in the white gown was none other than Áine, the queen of the Munster fairies, and the ball was to be in the fairy palace of Knockfennel.

Saying goodbye to Judy, Sean tucked his pipes under his arm and made his way back to the spot where the lady in white was now sitting in a magnificent carriage, drawn by two fine grey horses. She opened the carriage door and bade Sean to join her inside. When he had climbed in and settled beside her, the horses trotted off along the road.

As the carriage wound its way along the narrow lanes, not one word was spoken between them. Sean did not know what he could have said to such a fine lady, and she herself just sat and smiled, with a faraway look in her eyes. Soon they were travelling along wide avenues lined with tall trees heavy with fruits, and the perfume of sweet scented roses wafted in the air. At last they stopped before a grand mansion. The doors were open and Sean was led into to the ballroom.

What a sight it was! Gentlemen in frock coats embellished with golden braids bowed to him. Ladies in wide satin gowns with low necklines curtseyed before him. Tall mirrors stretched from floor to ceiling and the lights of a hundred golden candelabras were reflected there.

A tall glass full of a golden drink was brought for Sean, and he downed it in one. It was an unfamiliar taste, fiery but sweet. 'Will you make sure ye have a good measure of the "cratur" for me in the morning before I go home!' he said. Then he sat himself down in a gilded chair and made ready to play his pipes.

That whole company was up and dancing straight away. The small, the tall, the fat, the thin, the strange and the beautiful, every one of them was on their feet. Sean played tune after tune, the whole night through, without a rest. His eyes were on the lovely young women as they whirled and reeled around the room, a fine colour in their cheeks. But now and then he had the strange thought, while he was playing, that he saw shoals of fish gazing in at him through the large windows of the ballroom. He wondered then, perhaps he was not in fact just some miles from home along the road, but instead in the palace of Gearóid Iarla, beneath the enchanted lake? But never mind that, still he played on and on, and all the good folk danced, and laughed and never took a rest the whole night long.

At last his hostess brought Sean his glass of the 'cratur'. He laid down his pipes, and took his drink. As soon as the music stopped, the dancers, exhausted, retired to their beds. But before they disappeared, each of the dancers placed a golden guinea into Sean's hat.

The lady in white came to Sean then, and handed him a small purse. 'It is a *sparán an tsallainn*, a bag of salt, that will never be found empty,' she explained. 'Thank you for your playing, Sean O'Hea. I told you there would be a grand reward.'

Sean thanked her, and then, exhausted himself from the whole night's piping, he fell into a deep sleep.

When Sean awoke, the sun was already high in the sky. He was cold and stiff and, rolling over, he found he was lying out on the damp ground. He sat up, rubbed his eyes, and looked around. Where was he but up on the top of the Suidechán Bean Tíghe, and all his golden coins were nothing but dry gold-and-copper leaves!

He unfastened the strings and opened up the purse. Inside, he found that the lady in the white dress had kept her word, and the purse was still full of salt. At least Judy would be grateful for that, for salt, after all, is the one thing that makes everything taste good.

Sean had been known all around as a piper, but after that August night, he had another claim to fame. Now he had a fine tale to tell by the fireside of a winter's evening.

Sources

'Sean O'Hea and the Woman in White': NFCS 517: 8. Owen Bresnan, Lough Gur, Limerick. Ballinard (B) School.

KERRY

GARY BRANIGAN &
LUKE EASTWOOD

THE SIEGE OF SMERWICK AND THE DOWNFALL OF THE GERALDINES

The reign of Elizabeth I was one of the most tumultuous periods in Irish history, resulting in the conquest of the whole country, something that had never been achieved previously. The Fitzgeralds feature heavily in Ireland's Norman and post-Norman history but their entanglement in the Catholic counter-reformation ultimately led to their demise. The earthworks at Smerwick above the harbour are still there, one can almost imagine the terrible battle, standing at the site and looking down at the sea, where English ships bombarded the headland. The fall of the Geraldines (the Fittzgerald clan) was only a prelude to a desperate struggle for control of Ireland that unfolded in the two decades after these events.

The Fitzgeralds or Geraldines, Earls of Desmond, and the Butlers, Earls of Ormonde, were two of the most powerful families in Ireland since the Norman invasion; they maintained an intense rivalry down through the centuries that sometimes spilled over into bloody warfare. This bitter feud was effectively ended by the second Desmond rebellion and the subsequent demise of the Geraldine dynasty, but the conclusion did not happen overnight.

Following the first Desmond rebellion, led by James Fitzmaurice Fitzgerald, Fitzmaurice was pardoned but stripped of his lands as punishment. His cousin, the earl, also evicted him from rented land, leaving him effectively in poverty.

In 1575, Fitzmaurice fled to France and began seeking the assistance of Catholic powers in Europe, eventually making his way to Rome to petition Pope Gregory XIII for help. After securing modest assistance, an abortive invasion occurred in 1578 that subsequently led him to return to Rome, seeking further support.

The following year he departed from Spain with a small force of Spanish, Italian and Irish troops, and made his way via the English Channel. He captured two English vessels en route, before arriving at Dingle Harbour in mid July.

On 18 July 1579, the party relocated to Smerwick Harbour at Ard na Caithne, further west on the same peninsula. Here they took advantage of a long disused Iron-Age fort, Dún An Oír (fortress of gold), to establish their garrison, creating new earthworks on the promontory.

With the assistance of papal commissary Nicholas Saunders, Fitzmaurice declared a holy war on Elizabeth I at Dingle with much ceremony, calling upon Ireland to rise up against the heretic queen, who had been excommunicated in 1570.

Fitzmaurice's forces numbered roughly 100 men, and although two more Spanish galleys arrived soon after with a further 100 troops, it is clear that without raising support his rebellion would have been easily crushed.

Irked by the English authorities undermining Desmond's power, John of Desmond and his brother James entered the fray on 1 August with the assassination of two English officials in Tralee. Having secured some support from relatives, Fitzmaurice himself was only to play a small role in the war and, having travelled north into the province of Connacht to raise further support, he was killed in a skirmish with the Burkes after his men foolishly stole some horses from his cousin Theobald Burke.

The rebellion was now well underway and leadership was left to John of Desmond, who took over much of south Munster, raising some 2,000 men. In response, the English Lord Deputy brought 600 troops to Limerick, joining forces with Sir Nicholas Malby, Lord President of Connacht, and his army of over a thousand.

Up until now the Earl of Desmond, Gerald Fitzgerald, had stayed out of the conflict and had even given up his son as a hostage to guarantee his loyalty, but strictly on the condition that his lands not be attacked. After the plundering of Geraldine territory and the demand that the earl hand over his castle, the situation changed. Gerald refused to leave Askeaton Castle and, despite assurances from the English, he was declared a traitor, which left him with no choice but to enter the war on the side of the rebels. In November of that year he sacked Youghal in County Cork, escalating the conflict to all-out war and imploring Irish lords to defend Ireland and its Catholic faith.

In July 1580, following the rising of the O'Byrnes in Wicklow, the English sent a new army of 6,000 men under the new Lord Deputy, Baron Arthur Grey. After an initial humiliating defeat at Glenmalure, Grey marched his men south into Munster to support the English forces there, unleashing a campaign of terror that would be long remembered.

Pope Gregory, whose hand was stoking the fires of war across Europe, intervened once again in Ireland. Having failed to convince Philip II of Spain, who had his own difficulties with the Dutch and Ottomans, to invade Ireland, the Pope secured ships to transport a force of around 700 Spanish, Italian and Basque troops under the command of Sebastiano di San Giuseppe.

The Papal army arrived in Smerwick Harbour on 10 September 1580, joining the small force at Dún An Oír before heading inland to join the Earl of Desmond, John Desmond and Lord Baltinglass. However, the English had somehow gained knowledge of the invasion and, with a force of around 4,000 men, Lord Grey and the Earl of Ormonde marched to cut them off.

Meanwhile, a naval blockade provided by Sir Richard Bingham prevented them leaving by sea to join the Irish rebels elsewhere. Trapped in the Dingle peninsula, Giuseppe was forced to retreat to Smerwick and make what they could of the defenses at Dún An Oír.

In October, Grey took his forces as far as Dingle and waited for supplies and eight cannons to arrive by sea with Admiral Winter at

Smerwick. With the Papal forces trapped by the English on one side, the sea behind them and Mount Brandon on the other, Grey was in no hurry. When the artillery finally arrived on 5 November, preparations began for the siege, which started two days later.

Hopelessly outnumbered and remorselessly pounded by three warships in the harbour and many artillery pieces on land, the rebels stood little chance in a fort consisting mainly of earthworks. Despite this, they held out for three full days, although Giuseppe rather cowardly tried to bargain with Grey by releasing three local allies to the English. The three men, including a priest (Fr Laurence Moore) were horrifically tortured to no avail, before being used for target practice as the siege continued.

Finally, on 10 November, the defenders could take no more and surrendered to Grey's terms, which were apparently that they would be spared. However, Grey, in his report to Elizabeth I, maintained that he had demanded an unconditional surrender and 'that they should render the fort to me and yield their selves to my will for life or death'.

Regardless of what was actually agreed, what happened afterwards is well known. The commander, Giuseppe, along with twelve of his men, emerged from the fort with their flags rolled up and presented themselves to Grey. English troops were sent in to establish that the defenders had indeed laid down their arms and to secure and guard the munitions. Once the fort was secured, the 600 or so troops and the few accompanying women were taken to the place that has since earned the name of the Field of the Cutting (*Gort a' Ghearradh*) and executed one by one. The severed heads of the slain were apparently buried in the field where a monument stands today, while their bodies were thrown over the cliffs into the sea below.

After the massacre at Smerwick, the tide turned very much against the Desmonds and their rebellion. The coalition began to fall apart, although the war of attrition dragged on for another two years, with Desmond's supporters being killed or falling away with the offer of a pardon. In early 1582, John of Desmond was engaged by English troops and killed at the River Avonmore, his head sent to the now infamous Lord Grey.

Grey's brutality was notorious, but he had still not been successful in defeating the Geraldines. Possibly because of his cruel methods, Grey was recalled to England. The Fitzgerald's arch enemy the Earl of Ormonde replaced him as Lord Deputy, continuing on with the war that left much of Munster bereft of people, crops and livestock.

By the winter of 1583 the Earl of Desmond stood alone, with only a handful of supporters following him into the Slieve Mish mountains to elude English troops. It was here at Glenagenty that Gerald met his end. Desperate and hungry, he had stolen a few cattle from the Moriarty clan and supposedly mistreated the sister of the clan chief. Owen Moriarty and his men caught up with the earl at a small cabin, where he was killed and beheaded.

In return Moriarty received 1000 pounds of silver, a vast fortune, and Gerald's head was sent to Elizabeth in London, while his body was strung from the walls of Cork city for all to see. His title and all the Geraldine lands were confiscated by the English crown. Attempts to revive Desmond fortunes and the Earldom soon after were a failure and so the once powerful Geraldine dynasty came to a sad and miserable end.

MARIE ANTOINETTE AND RICE HOUSE

Dingle town is a place that is full of history, and it was almost home to one of France's most famed historical figures. I have visited the house on several occasions, and it is still in use by the local council and other bodies. It is located at the top of the Main Street and is easily accessible, although it is not currently used as a tourist attraction. One can only hope that it will one day be restored to its former appearance, at the time that the Rice family prepared it for this illustrious visitor. Of course, unfortunately the French queen never arrived, but the house remains, keeping alive the story of her would-be saviour and his attempted rescue.

Marie Antoinette is possibly one of the most well-known queens in world history, but her connection with the town of Dingle is a piece of Irish history that is hardly known outside of Kerry. A plaque erected on the wall of Rice House in 2010 by Dingle Historical Society was unveiled by the Austrian Ambassador to Ireland. Apart from this small commemoration, there is little to acknowledge the rescue attempt that could have saved the French queen's life, which was just one of several such failed plans to rescue her.

The plan to save her was organised by James Louis Rice, the son of 'Black' Tom Rice, who was a successful wine merchant from Ballymacdoyle, close to Dingle town. Tom had built up extensive connections with traders and vineyards throughout both Spain and France. James, born in 1730 into a Catholic family, was educated at the Irish Pastoral College in Louvain, Belgium as there were few educational opportunities in Ireland due to penal laws against Catholics. James did well in Belgium and even began studying for the priesthood at the Franciscan seminary in Louvain. However, he abandoned his studies and went on to join the Irish brigade of the Austrian (Hapsburg) army, becoming a cavalry officer, and was later made a Count of the Holy Roman Empire by the Austrian Emperor Joseph II, who he had met and befriended at military academy.

Rice even gained a seat on the Emperor's privy council and was one of the trusted soldiers honoured with escorting Joseph's younger sister, Marie Antoinette, from Vienna to Versailles in May 1770 to join her new husband, Louis XVI of France. James remained in Paris, in service of the royal family, but retained his contacts with his friend Emperor Joseph into the 1780s, while the situation in France deteriorated in the run-up to the revolution in 1789.

After the death of Joseph II, his younger brother Leopold became Emperor of Austria and it was his support, and that of his sister for the French monarchy, that led to France declaring war on Austria in 1792. Louis XVI was separated from Marie Antoinette and their two remaining children, who were themselves imprisoned in the tower of the temple in Marais. At the behest of Leopold, James Rice began planning an audacious attempt to rescue Marie Antoinette – or Maria Antonia as her brother would have called her.

The plan was to bribe the guards at the temple and take her and any other members of the royal family by carriage and a relay of horses to Nantes. From there, a merchant ship, owned by the Rice family business, would take them to Dingle. The Rice family went so far as to furnish rooms in their Dingle home in readiness for the Bourbon monarchy, although the plan was to eventually send them to London and then on to safety in Vienna, with her brother Leopold, the Austrian Emperor.

Rice enlisted the help of Thomas Trant, a man from Ventry serving with the Irish Brigade in France, William Hickie, from Ballylongford, and Count Waters of Paris, who was married to his sister, Mary Rice. Although the plan went off well initially, Marie Antoinette, who was held separately from her husband and two children, refused to leave her family and so the escape had to be abandoned.

After the abolition of the monarchy, Louis XVI was tried, found guilty of treason and executed at the guillotine in January 1793. After Marie's transfer to the Conciergerie, a final rescue attempt, which became known as the Carnation Plot, was attempted, but unfortunately also failed. The former queen, in failing health, was executed in October of that same year.

James Rice was able to escape from France and moved to London, after which he served in the allied forces, which consisted primarily of Britain, Austria, Russia and Spain, in the first of the French Revolutionary Wars. This conflict was known as the War of the First Coalition, which ended in 1797 with the humiliation of Austria by the French.

In the late 1790s, Rice returned to his native Ireland and settled in Limerick, during which he witnessed the United Irishmen's rising of 1798 and the emergence of Daniel O'Connell as a political force. He died at the age of 61 in 1801, as Napoleon continued his rise to power and eventual victory in the War of the Second Coalition.

Count James Louis Rice's death was widely reported, both in Ireland and across Europe, having become quite a hero among monarchists during those turbulent times.

Rice House, which was built in the 1750s, came into the possession of the Catholic Church and was used as a presbytery, but it eventually came into the ownership of *Údarás na Gaeltachta*. A subsequent plan to redevelop and sell the house came up against considerable opposition, due to what would have been the effective gutting of the interior with additions and modernisations of the exterior. Most of the original features of the house, including the rooms prepared for Marie Antoinette, were still in excellent condition, leading to a campaign to keep the historical building in its near-pristine state.

Largely due to the work of the Rice House Alliance, planning permission was revoked and the house became a listed building in 2004. It was then sold to a local businessman from Dingle, and today Rice House is home to Kerry Education and Training Board and, albeit partially modernised, thankfully still retains its unique features and period character.

CORK

KATE CORKERY

GOIBHNIU THE WONDER SMITH AND THE COW OF PLENTY

Off the far end of the Reen Peninsula and in sight of Dursey lies a small, steep-sided island called *Oileán Aolbhach* (Crow Island). Here, it is said, Goibhniu, the wonder smith of the *Tuatha Dé Danann*, kept his forge. The *Tuatha Dé Danann* were a divine race of people who inhabited Ireland long ago. They were the people of the Goddess Danu and they were said to be very gifted in arts, crafts, music and magic.

In the *Lebor Gabála Érenn*, it was written that Goibhniu was 'not impotent in smelting'. Small praise indeed for this gifted smith who forged weapons for the gods – magical weapons that never missed their mark, whose every wound was fatal. He was quick at repairing splintered spears and broken swords at the first Battle of Moytura and afterwards he even crafted a remarkable, fully functioning arm of silver for King Nuada, whose entire limb had been brutally severed in battle.

From his island forge, Goibhniu also tended to the needs of passing ships. As son of Esarg (the thrower of axes) and brother to Credne (the bronze worker) and Luchta (the carpenter), Goibhniu was part of a renowned mythological family of craftsmen. Their descendants went on to be absorbed into popular culture in characters such as the Gobán Saor, the master builder who features in folk tales from all over Ireland.

Many tales are told not only of Goibhniu's great skill and craftsmanship, but also of his huge generosity and hospitality. He brewed his own special beer and provided a great ale feast at which his guests, instead of getting drunk and disorderly, got protection from old age and decay.

Goibhniu was the proud owner of an extraordinary cow, the *Glas Ghoibhneann*, endowed with an inexhaustible supply of milk. They say on the day this white and green bovine creature appeared up out of the sea, Goibhniu made a halter for her and from the moment he put the halter round her neck, she was faithful to him ever after.

This magnificent cow had a very independent nature. She could jump 60 miles from Crow Island in an instant and walk the length of Ireland in a day's grazing but she would always return home in the evening. She gave milk generously to all who came to her and no one went away hungry.

Everyone who saw her admired her and envied Goibhniu his magical 'Cow of Plenty' – especially Balor of the Evil Eye. This tyrant of the demonic *Fomorian* race had been banished to Tory Island, but was forever leading cattle raids around the coast. His evil eye, which had the death poison in it, was usually covered up, but his seeing eye was envious and avaricious – always on the lookout for anything he could steal.

He wanted the *Glas Ghoibhneann* and sent one of his messengers out at night to capture her. Goibhniu was fast asleep, but awoke just in time to catch the thief trying to lead the cow away. Goibhniu managed to grab her tail and pull her back, but the thief escaped with the halter.

It was hard to mind the *Glas Ghoibhneann* after that. There was no holding her without the halter. She was liable to wander off anywhere and never return. Goibhniu struggled to keep an eye on the cow as well as run a busy forge. Ships would stop by for repairs, giants would call in to have their razors sharpened and of course the warriors of the *Tuatha Dé Danann* were forever in need of something.

One day, a young champion, Cian, son of renowned royal physician Dian Cécht, came to the forge to get a sword made. 'Can you make me a long, keen-edged death biter?' he enquired.

Goibhniu said he could, so long as Cian would guard the cow while he worked. Cian was happy to keep an eye on the cow, who was grazing outside, while his new weapon was being forged. After a while, a young red-haired boy came up to Cian and told him that Goibhniu needed him to come inside, as the sword was almost ready.

'But who will look after the cow?' said Cian.

'I will,' said the boy with a cheeky wink.

Cian abandoned his post and in no time the boy (who was really Balor in disguise) was making off towards the shore with the cow.

Goibhniu was furious that the animal had been kidnapped so quickly. Cian was ashamed that he had been so easily tricked and promised he would waste no time in retrieving the *Glas Ghoibhneann*.

Cian swiftly made his way to the foggy shoreline, where he came upon a grey old man seated in a small boat.

'Old man, can you row me as far as Balor's island?'

'I can, if you swear to give me half of whatever you get there.'

'You have my word. I will share anything with you – apart from the halter of Goibhniu's cow,' said Cian.

'I will not ask for that,' said the man.

In spite of the great age of the oarsman, the smallness of the boat and the strength of the wind and tide against them, it seemed to take no time at all for them to reach the rocky shore of Tory Island.

'You have helped me, old man. I have nothing but my cloak to pay you with.'

'Let us swap cloaks,' said the old man. His voice was hushed. The wind had dropped. His eyes shimmered as sun pierced through the mist and his old brown cloak took on all the colours of the sea and sky. 'Take this, my son. It will cover you as night covers the earth. Beneath it you will be safe. You will move unseen and doors will be opened to you.'

The cloak fell about Cian in long folds. He knew there was magic in it. He stepped ashore and turned to thank the old man, but he could see him no more and the boat was gone. Cian was alone in this strange, wild place. Wrapped in the hooded cloak he headed inland until he reached a dark fortress surrounded by fierce *Fomorian* soldiers. Seen by no one, Cian slipped through the gates and bravely made his way to the court of Balor of the Evil Eye. He then removed the cloak, bowed low before the infamous tyrant, and asked if he could be of service.

'What service can you offer me?' growled Balor.

'I can make whatever you wish grow on the land.'

'Can you make apple trees grow even in this rocky soil?'

'I can.'

'What reward would you ask for that?'

'I would ask only for the halter of Goibhniu's cow.'

'I will give you that,' said Balor, who had always envied accounts of apples growing on other islands.

Cian was given a bed for the night, and he set to work early next morning as Balor's gardener. He spent the day planting apple trees and searching the island for any sign of the *Glas Ghoibhneann*. He walked far and wide but found nothing. At dusk, just as the light was fading, he caught sight of a white marble tower stretching up from a remote cliff edge.

It looked deserted, but as he approached, the entrance door swung open and he found himself inside. He tiptoed past a room full of sleeping maidservants and mounted a spiral staircase to the uppermost room, where he beheld the most beautiful woman he had ever seen.

She was sitting at a loom, looking out to sea and singing. Her voice was like silver. Cian stood still, enchanted.

She stopped singing and asked, 'Who is there that I cannot see?'

Cian dropped the cloak, and Eithlinn (the imprisoned daughter of Balor) beamed with delight as she recognised the vision of her dreams.

Night after night, Eithlinn had dreamt of such a one as Cian, but her cruel father had denied her the right ever to set eyes on a man, confining her to a lonely life in this secret tower. Eithlinn welcomed Cian as the long-awaited sweetheart destiny had chosen for her. They fell in love instantly and sank into each other's arms

Cian and Eithlinn spent many secret nights together in the tower after that. Within months, a child was born to them. He was so bright and beautiful they named him Lugh ('light'). By now apples were appearing on the trees. Cian's work was done, but Balor had no intention of parting with the halter. He pretended it was missing and sent his servants to hide the halter in Eithlinn's secret tower.

The servants were astonished to hear a baby crying from the top window. Druids had foretold that the invincible Balor could only ever be slain by his own grandson. This was why his beautiful daughter had been forbidden to marry or ever bear a child. If the baby were discovered, he would immediately be put to death.

As the servants returned to their master, Eithlinn feared for the life of her baby boy.

That evening Cian arrived at the tower with a branch of apples. 'The first apples are for you!' he said, presenting them to Eithlinn.

'And the halter is for you, my love,' she said, tears welling up in her eyes. 'You must take this now and go. And you must also take our son with you.'

With trembling hands, she gave away her child. Cian took the baby and the halter and wrapped the cloak about them. He bid a sad farewell to Balor's daughter and headed for the dark waters. A boat was there before him and the old man in it. They were a short time crossing.

'Do you remember our bargain?' said the old man

'I do,' said Cian, 'To give you half of whatever I got on the island. But I only have the halter and the child'.

'I had your word on it.'

'I cannot give you the halter,' said Cian.

'Therefore I will take the child,' said the old man. 'And I will have him fostered and brought up like my own son.'

'Then take back your cloak, old man,' said Cian, 'and protect my child.'

As the old man took the baby in his arms, Cian wrapped the cloak around them, and when he spread it out it had every colour of the sea in it and a sound like the waves when they break on the shore. The old man was beautiful and wonderful to look at. With beaming face and twinkling eyes, he lifted the little sun god aloft and said, 'Cian, son of Dian Cécht, you will not regret this for I am Manannán Mac Lir, god of the sea. When you see your son Lugh again, he will be riding on my mighty horse, Aonbharr, and no one will bar his way on land or sea. Now take farewell of him and may gladness and victory be with you.'

Cian stepped ashore and watched as Manannán carried the child away in a boat that was shining with every colour of the rainbow, as clear as crystal. It went without oars or sails, with the water curling round the sides of it and the little fishes of the sea swimming before and behind it.

Cian set his face towards the forge on Crow Island where Goibhniu was waiting. As he arrived with the halter in his hand, the *Glas Ghoibhneann* emerged from the sea and stood calmly before them. Unrestrained, she had plunged into the waves and swum all the way back to her rightful owner. Goibhniu put the halter on his Cow of Plenty and from then on she was content to remain nearby. He turned to Cian and smiled.

'May everything you undertake have a happy ending.'

'The same wish to yourself,' said Cian.

And there was gladness and friendship between them ever after.

Over the years, the baby grew up to be Lugh, the shining sun god, who fulfilled the druid's prophecy and put an end to the tyrant Balor. He destroyed the power of his grandfather's evil eye in one well-aimed slingshot. Then he removed Balor's poisonous head and placed it on the crook of a hazel tree on *Carn Uí Néid* (Mizen Head).

His victory is still written in the stars. As well as shining bright as the sun by day, Lugh is said to re-appear above Mizen Head in the sky at night. From sunset to sunrise, 'Lugh's Chain' can be seen like a comet rising up from the west and blazing across the night sky towards the east.

Also, on some clear nights, locals from Dursey claimed to have seen a fire alight on *Oileann Aolbhach* (Crow Island), where they say Goibhniu, the wonder smith, occasionally returns to resume work at his forge.

Sources

'Goibhniu the Wonder Smith and the Cow of Plenty', IFCS 274: 185, NFCS 274: 473.

'Tales of the Glas Ghoibhneann', NFCS 375: 148.

'The Cow of Plenty' in Ella Young's *Celtic Wonder Tales* (Floris Books and Anthropomorphic Press, 1910).

'Goibhniu – Mythical Smith of the Tuatha dé Danann' in Dáithí Ó hÓgain's *Lore of Ireland* (The Collins Press, 2006), p.277–78.

THE *CAILLEACH BHÉARRA*

The *Cailleach Bhéarra* (the Hag of Beara) was one of the most ancient and all-pervasive deities of the pre-Christian world. As a powerful Celtic goddess, she symbolised the many aspects of female strength. Like Mother Nature, it was said that she not only gave the land its shape and fecundity, she also changed her own shape with the turning of the seasons, ruling the cold grey winter months as a weather-beaten hag and welcoming in the spring as the fresh-faced goddess of the new corn. Sometimes in autumn she manifested as a hare running from scythes at harvest time.

She embodied youth and age – the fertile young woman and the dried-up old crone. Like the earth, she continually renewed herself with the patience and resilience of one who has seen it all, lived through many joys and hardships.

The *Cailleach* was also regarded as the goddess of sovereignty who had the power to confer kingship only on those men she deemed worthy to rule. Sometimes in her ugly-hag guise, she would set out to seduce potential leaders to test if they had sufficient insight to recognise her hidden beauty and worth – and the judgement to see the true nature of things and to rule wisely. She is sometimes considered to be synonymous with other Celtic goddesses, but the *Cailleach* is the one who has outlasted them all.

Down through the centuries, people marvelled at her great age and many attempts were made to ascertain exactly when she was born. Was she older than the 'Great Eagle at the Forge' that spent 300 years sharpening his beak on an anvil until it was worn down as thin as a pin? Was she older than the 'Otter of the Rock' who spent 300 years rubbing his back on a stone until he had worn a hole through it? Was she more ancient than the 'One-Eyed Salmon' that lost an eye on the coldest day that was ever recorded in living memory? By all accounts, on that extremely cold day, as the salmon was leaping out of the river, the water froze over. Between his leaping and landing, a bird pecked out his eye. Blood trickled out of the socket and melted a hole in the ice big enough for the salmon to slip back under the water and live long enough to tell the tale.

Nobody knew the answer, but it was believed that the *Cailleach* had survived the Ice Age, the Stone Age and the Bronze Age and was still thriving. Over time, she became less identified with her role as nature goddess and queen of sovereignty and took on the mantel of archetypal old woman of Irish folklore, giving rise to the widely used phrase, 'He/she is as old as the *Cailleach Bhéarra*'.

Stories of the *Cailleach* as an old woman abound all over Ireland and Scotland as she was said to have wandered far and wide, driving her cows before her, dropping rocks from her apron as she went, leaving cairns on the hillsides and lakes in the valleys. For the most part, she moved stealthily and kept her distance from the rest of humanity. A wiry independent figure, she put up with no nonsense from anyone and many were afraid to go near her, but when they did they heeded her wise advice, especially on the best methods of threshing and harvesting.

Oral tradition remembers her both as 'Shaper of the Land' and as wife of the sea god, Manannan Mac Lir. Although she travelled far and wide, her beloved abode was in the wild primeval landscape of the Beara Peninsula.

Due to her great fondness for cattle, she was often referred to locally as Boí (the Cow Goddess) and her home was on a little island called Inis Boí off the tip of the peninsula. Others referred to her simply as the *Sentainne* (the Old One). She was the *Cailleach Bhéarra* (the Hag of Beara) whose extraordinary long life was a source of widespread fascination.

A visiting monk once tried to calculate her great age by having his servant count all the discarded bullock bones she had thrown away and left in a big pile up in her attic – one for every year of her life. But he took so long to complete the task that the monk got fed up and went away none the wiser.

In her young days, the *Cailleach Bhéarra* is said to have outlived many lovers and husbands, all of whom died of old age. She is believed to have had fifty foster children on Beara alone and to have thrived through seven periods of youth until her children and grandchildren were peoples and races. The *Corcu Loígde* maintained she was the ancestress of their sept (clan) and the neighbouring *Corca Dhuibhne* claimed she was the foster mother of theirs.

People gave accounts of her two sisters, the Hag of Iveragh (*An Cailleach Bholias*) and the Hag of Dingle (*An Cailleach Daingin*) who lived on the neighbouring peninsulas. She kept a close eye on them. Even from 20 miles away, her eyesight was sharp enough to see what they were up to and she would often shout a warning across the water if a cow of theirs had wandered off too far.

Her own magnificent bull, the Bull of Conaire (*Tarbh Conraidh*), was sometimes the cause of the distraction. Every time he bellowed, any cow within hearing distance got pregnant and calved within a year. He once tried to swim across a creek after a cow, so the *Cailleach Bhéarra* struck him with a rod and turned him into a rock in the sea that ever after was known as Bull Island.

Another time, the Dingle Hag decided to bring the *Cailleach* a gift. She tied a rope around a piece of land and attempted to drag it south to present to her sister. It split in two at the Iveragh Peninsula and the islands of Scarriff and Deenish were left in that place. And they are still there today.

When asked how she managed to live so long, the *Cailleach* answered simply:

> I never eat till I'm hungry. Never lie in bed after I wake.
> I never let too much cold or heat get to my head or feet.
> I never carry the dirt of one place to another as I travel.
> I thrive on the riches of the sea – dulse, wild prawns, salmon.

When asked how long more she would live, she answered prophetically:

I will not live to see this land have
forests with no trees;
flowers with no bees;
and no fish left in the seas.

The *Cailleach's* matriarchal wisdom was much quoted and although she was feared by many, people continued to have respect for her. However, when Christianity came to Ireland, attitudes changed. The *Cailleach's* reluctance to bow to the new religion or to take the veil of a nun led to her being viewed with suspicion and the defiant old woman became an unwelcome outcast in Christian society.

There are varying accounts of how the *Cailleach* eventually died. Medieval literature claims that St Cumaine Fada blessed a veil and put it on her head and, after that, age and infirmity came upon her and she passed away peacefully.

In Beara, the local story, set in Christian times, goes like this: the *Cailleach* was a thieving, scoundrelly old hag without religion or conscience. What she didn't make off with, she spoiled and destroyed. Some vented their anger at her. Others fled in fear.

She used to go north inland into the glens and south to Whiddy Island and gather up all before her. She caught salmon that no one else could catch and gathered all the seashore food she wanted on Whiddy. On her way home to Ballycrovane one day, she saw the holy man Naomh Caitiairn sound sleep on a hillock. Lying next to the saint was his magic staff. She searched through his clothes for anything she could steal and then mischievously made off with the staff. A cripple was watching this and he shouted at Naomh Caitiairn, who woke up with a start. The saint called out after the *Cailleach* as she ran away. He followed her and caught up with her in a place called *Ard na Caillí* (the Hag's Height) in *Cill Chaitiairn* (Kilcatherine). He grabbed the staff from her hand and turned her into a bare grey stone, a lump of rock overlooking Coulagh Bay at the western end of the Beara Peninsula. She was stuck there in that spot for evermore, with her back to the hill and her face to the sea.

There she remains to this day, the most enigmatic of all antiquities related to the goddesses of Ireland, a geological oddity, consisting of an extrusion of metamorphic rock, appearing completely natural, even though no other rock of any similar geological structure can be found within the whole south-west region.

Legend says the *Cailleach Bhéarra* has lived as long as the oldest rock and contains within her all ages and seasons. Turned to stone, she embodies the spirit and strength of the land, as she patiently awaits her husband, Manannan Mac Lir, god of the sea, to reclaim her.

As she waits, she has time aplenty to reflect on her long, eventful life, as is set out in this ninth-century Irish poem:

THE HAG OF BEARE

Ebb tide has come for me;
My life drifts downwards
Like a retreating sea
With no tidal turn.

I am the Hag of Beare,
Fine petticoats I used to wear.
Today gaunt with poverty
I search for rags to cover me.

Girls nowadays
Dream only of money.
When we were young
We cared more for our men.
Riding over their lands
We remember how, like gentlemen,
They treated us well;
Courted, but didn't tell.

Today every upstart
Is a master of graft;
Skinflint, yet sure to boast
Of being a lavish host.

But I bless my king who gave,
Balanced briefly on time's wave,
Largesse of speedy chariots
And champion thoroughbreds.

These arms, now bony, thin
And useless to younger men,
Once caressed with skill
The limbs of princes!

Sadly my body seeks to join
Them soon in their dark home –
When God wishes to claim it
He can have back his deposit.

No more love-teasing
For me, no wedding feast:
Scant grey hair is best
Shadowed by a veil.

Why should I care?
Many's the bright scarf
Adorned my hair in the days
When I drank with the gentry.

So God be praised
That I misspent my days!
Whether the plunge be bold
Or timid the blood runs cold.

After spring and autumn
Come age's frost and body's chill:
Even in bright sunlight
I carry my shawl.

Lovely the mantle of green
Our Lord spreads on the hillside.
Every spring the divine craftsman
Plumps its worn fleece.

But my cloak is mottled with age.
No, I'm beginning to dote –
It's only grey hair straggling
Over my skin like a lichened oak.

And my right eye has been taken away
As down payment on heaven's estate.
Likewise my left,
That I may grope to heaven's gate.

No storm has overthrown
The royal standing stone.
Every year the fertile plain
Bears its crop of yellow grain.

But, I, who feasted royally
By candlelight, now pray
In this darkened oratory.
Instead of heady mead

And wine, high on the bench
With kings, I sup whey
In a nest of hags:
God pity me!

Yet may this cup of whey,
O Lord, serve as my ale feast –
Fathoming its bitterness
I'll learn that you know best.

Alas, I cannot
Again sail youth's sea;
The days of my beauty
Are departed and desire spent.

I hear the fierce cry of the wave
Whipped by the wintery wind.
No one will visit me today,
Neither nobleman nor slave.

I hear their phantom oars
As ceaselessly they row
And row to the chill ford
Or fall asleep by its side.

Flood tide
And the ebb dwindling on the strand.
What the flood rides ashore
The ebb snatches from your hand.

Flood tide
And the sucking ebb to follow!
Both have I come to know
Pouring down my body.

Flood tide
Has not yet rifled my pantry,
But a chill hand has been laid
On many who in darkness visited me.

Well might the son of Mary
Take their place under my roof tree,
For if I lack other hospitality
I never say 'No' to anybody –

Man being of all
Creatures the most miserable –
His flooding pride always seen
But never his tidal turn.

Happy the island in mid-ocean
Washed by the returning flood
But my aging blood
Slows to final ebb.

I have hardly a dwelling
Today on this earth.
Where once was life's flood,
All is ebb.

AUTHOR BIOGRAPHIES

MADELINE MCCULLY

Madeline McCully spent many school holidays in her great-aunt's cottage in Donegal listening to stories and songs at the Ceildhe Nights. She developed a love of storytelling and has won several awards, enabling her to travel abroad to gather folklore and tell stories.

Madeline co-designed an award-winning website, www.derryghosts.com, in 2001 and since then has written four books: *Haunted Derry*, *Derry Folk Tales*, *Haunted Donegal* and *Haunted Antrim*. Madeline has taken part in several festivals at home and abroad, bringing stories, song and music into her sessions. She has taught storytelling in schools, libraries, hospitals, community centres and prison, and has broadcasted on radio and TV.

BILLY TEARE & KATHLEEN O'SULLIVAN

Billy and Kathleen began their collaboration after meeting at the Sidmouth Folk Festival over fifteen years ago. Kathleen is a highly regarded traditional Irish singer. She recorded and toured solo, as well as being the vocalist in a 'trad' band for eight years. She teaches Irish song and is also an accomplished poet.

Storyteller Billy was born and raised in Ballycarry. Starting an early career as a stand-up, Billy has appeared in acting roles on theatre stages, radio, TV and the big screen, having worked with Danny Boyle and Ken Loach. Billy plays harmonica and jaw harp.

Together, Kathleen and Billy have become Ireland's foremost story and song duo and co-authors of a successful book of Antrim folk tales.

DOREEN MCBRIDE

Doreen McBride was a teacher who found a year's secondment to the Ulster Folk and Transport Museum a life-changing experience, because it filled her with a desire to record folklore and local history. She took early retirement and became a folklorist and international award-winning storyteller.

Doreen has featured in many TV and radio broadcasts, including The Late Late Show. She has written numerous books, had short stories and plays broadcast on BBC Radio Ulster. Her play *The Funeral's Off* was given a professional reading, directed by James Grieve from Paines Plough, London, in the Bryan Friel Theatre, Belfast.

FRANCES QUINN

Frances Quinn is from Armagh, where her family have lived for many generations. Like a lot of people in Ireland, she grew up in a story tradition and as a young girl became familiar with some of the ancient stories. The old stories remain her foremost interest but she now has a keen interest in folklore of all kinds and countries.

As an actor she has worked throughout the UK and Ireland in radio, theatre, TV and film; and as a storyteller she has been recorded on radio and television and has toured in the US.

She has a general arts BA from University College, Dublin and a BA in languages from Queens University, Belfast. In 2017, she received an award for her contribution to storytelling at the Tommy Makem 10th Memorial Concert.

STEVE LALLY

Steve Lally has been working as a professional storyteller for twenty years and has written four best-selling books on Irish folklore.

He has collaborated with such noted artists as David J of gothic rock legends Bauhaus and Bill Drummond of the band KLF. He has been performing at the Electric Picnic music festival in Ireland since 2023.

Steve has been the resident storyteller at The Belfast Royal Victoria Hospital for Sick Children since 2013, as part of the Read for Good organisation. He continues to bring the ancient art of storytelling to a wider and alternative audience in the twenty-first century.

JOE BRENNAN

Joe Brennan has been telling stories and holding workshops for over fifteen years, having worked in radio and as a teacher previously. He has worked across Ireland and travelled widely, bringing the joy of his telling to a wide range of audiences and cultures. He has performed at many storytelling festivals, including Cape Clear and FATE. Joe has travelled to festivals in Norway, Belgium, the US, Austria, Egypt and Romania. He is the author of *Donegal Folk Tales* published by The History Press, which was chosen as the Read Donegal book in 2014. He is the organiser of Ramelton Storytelling Festival and also a children's playwright.

SUSIE MINTO

Words spoken and written have been Susie's high calling. Her writing career began in 1975 in print journalism and then public relations. Oral storytelling as an artform came into her life in 1998 and a whole new world opened up.

In 2003–04 she was employed by Grampian Association of Storytellers in north-east Scotland to conduct an oral history project in the Howe o' the Mearns district of old Kincardineshire, now south Aberdeenshire. This Lottery-funded work resulted in the publication of *The Butcher, the Baker and the Tablecloth Maker*, an audio DVD and a supporting booklet.

In 2004 Susie moved to the Republic of Ireland where she expanded her work as a storyteller, performer, workshop facilitator, teacher, creative writing group facilitator and oral historian.

In 2011–12 she was employed to conduct an in-depth oral history project for Cadolemo, a collective of Orange Lodges in the counties of Cavan, Donegal, Leitrim and Monaghan in the Republic of Ireland. She interviewed 66 people ranging in age from 14 to 96, spanning 100 years of Ireland's social history during and long after Partition. The collection of over 80 hours of recorded material remains in Cadolemo's care and most of the material has not yet been published. In 2014 an abridged collection of interviews with 22 of the contributors was edited and arranged by Susie Minto and published in paperback by Cadolemo Ltd under the title, *The Forgotten People of Ulster: Stories of Orangeism South of the Border*. The publication was funded by Towards Understanding and Healing. Stories from the book are available digitally here: https://accounts.ulster.ac.uk/repo24/collections/show/162/.

In August 2018 she contributed a chapter to *My Camino Walk #2* published by Writing Matters Publishing.

Since 2014 Susie has been living in Scotland, at the Findhorn Community in Moray, where she occasionally performs as a storyteller and runs creative writing groups.

GARY BRANIGAN

Gary Branigan is an historian, tour guide and writer whose previously published works include *Ancient & Holy Wells of Dublin*, *Fountains of Dublin* and books in The History Press' Folk Tales series.

TONY LOCKE

Tony Locke was a professional storyteller and member of the Storytellers of Ireland. He grew up listening to the tales of his grandfather, who was also a storyteller. Tony had a degree in heritage studies and also wrote and presented his own radio show for Westport Community Radio. He authored *Irish Ghost Tales* and *Tales of the Irish Hedgerows* for The History Press.

JOE MCGOWAN

Joe McGowan is a native of Mullaghmore, County Sligo. Born on the family farm, he worked there in his early years until emigrating to the US in the 1960s. Shortly after his return to Ireland in the '70s, Joe became aware of the accelerating pace of change in the Irish countryside and decided to record the old lore before it vanished completely. For many years he has been dedicated to preserving Ireland's disappearing traditions and customs.

Joe's books are inspired by countless nights spent listening to the stories of the older generation augmented by meticulous archival research. His publications include: *Echoes of a Savage Land*; *A Bitter Wind*; *Constance Markievicz, the People's Countess*; *Co. Sligo Famine Book*; *Inishmurray: Island Voices*; *The Hidden People*; *Sligo: Land of Destiny*; *Inishmurray: Gale, Stone and Fire*; *Even the Heather Bled* and *A Fairy Wind* CD.

P.A. WATSON

Pat Watson is a professional storyteller and writer who has appeared regularly on Shannonside Northern Radio. His previously published works include *Original Irish Stories*, *60 Lyrical Yarns* and *Dean Kelly School Memories*, a social history. His website is www.roscommonhistory.ie.

PHILIP BYRNE

Philip has been telling stories and training Irish tour guides in all aspects of the country's heritage for many years and has a great love and respect for its folklore. Philip tells stories on a regular basis as a 'resident storyteller', as well as appearing at many other functions and festivals throughout the country. The stories in this anthology are taken from his previous work *Longford Folk Tales*.

RICHARD MARSH

Richard Marsh visits schools in Ireland as a storyteller through the Writers in Schools scheme funded by the Arts Council, and travels elsewhere to share Irish legends and folk tales. His nineteen published books include *The Legends and Lands of Ireland*, *Tales of the Wicklow Hills*, *Irish King and Hero Tales*, *Spanish and Basque Legends*, *A World of Tricksters* and *Hellhounds and Hero Horses: Beasts of Myth and Legend*.

He was, for many years, a freelance contributor to Sunday Miscellany and other programmes on RTÉ Radio One. As a Legendary Tours guide, now retired, he took clients to places where the legends happened and told them on location. Meath was his most popular tour. His website is www.richardmarsh.ie.

RAB FULTON

Rab is the host of the world-famous Celtic Tales storytelling show, which takes place in Galway City. For more information visit: https://www.eventbrite.ie/e/celtic-tales-storytelling-show-tickets-503373151647.

He is also an author, lecturer and co-host of the Irish podcast 'The Celtic Tales Chronicles'.

Follow Rab on Instagram @celtictalesgalway

For more information visit: celtictalesgalway.com.

BRENDAN NOLAN

Brendan Nolan was a storyteller of wide experience who produced and presented Telling Tales, the access radio programme for writers and storytellers. He wrote and broadcasted more than ninety stories of his own, mostly light-hearted tales. He was a Dubliner, who travelled throughout Europe telling stories.

RUTH MARSHALL

Ruth Marshall is a storyteller, poet and arts and heritage facilitator who has lived in Ireland since 1986. She wrote and performed environmental puppet plays with Dandelion Puppets until her son's birth in 1989, which also saw the birth of her storyteller self. Ruth works with all ages and abilities, from preschool children to retired older people, facilitating creative writing and personal development groups.

As a storyteller, Ruth visits schools through Heritage in Schools and Poetry Ireland's Writers (and Storytellers) in Schools schemes, and is a regular contributor to the Clare Museum education programme. She spent several years as a heritage tour guide on Scattery Island, County Clare. Ruth is also a practitioner of sound healing using the power of the voice.

Ruth's books include *Celebrating Irish Festivals* (Hawthorn Press, 2003), *Clare Folk Tales* (2013) and *Limerick Folk Tales* (2016) for The History Press, and her poetry is published in journals and anthologies across Ireland and the UK.

AIDEEN MCBRIDE

Aideen McBride, daughter of Jack Sheehan, grew up hearing her father's stories. She now works professionally as a storyteller, telling stories through English and Irish in schools, libraries and festivals across the country. She also has a great interest in collecting stories from Ireland and other cultures.

NUALA HAYES

Nuala has had an eclectic career as an actor, storyteller, sometime folklore collector, and Independent Radio Producer.

She trained as an actor with the Abbey Theatre, and was a member of the Abbey Company for five years. She was involved in Theatre in Education and founded TEAM, a touring company for schools. She played the part of Máire, in the first Field Day production of Brian Friel's great play *Translations* in Derry in 1980 and played the title role of radio agony aunt Frank Byrne in *Dear Frankie* by Niamh Gleeson, which toured theatres across Ireland.

Her interest in oral storytelling began in the early 1990s when she founded Two Chairs Company with musician Ellen Cranitch to explore stories with music. She was artist in residence in County Laois in 2002 where she collected and recorded many of the local stories, which resulted in a radio series and film, entitled *Tales at the Crossroads*.

She has been involved in story recording projects in the Midlands and also on Cape Clear Island, off the West Cork coast. She has organised and curated many storytelling gatherings and festivals including Scéalta Shamhna, the first Dublin Storytelling Festival and the Farmleigh Festival of Story and Song. Nuala enjoys collaborating with musicians and artists, including the harper and composer Anne Marie O'Farrell, the clarinettist Paul Roe, and the visual artist Rita Duffy.

Nuala is presently exploring the stories of the renowned Irish storyteller from the Blasket Island, Peig Sayers, many of whose stories were collected by folklore collectors from across Europe and are stored in the National Folklore Collection in UDD, Dublin. Some of these stories have never been translated to English. She is collaborating with author and folklore scholar Éilís Ní Dhuibhne, on the project.

JACK SHEEHAN

Jack Sheehan (1932–2018) lived his whole life in the area where he was born in Bagenalstown, County Carlow. He always had a great interest in local stories and the characters who told them. He, in turn, was a great collector, teller and creator of stories.

ANNE FARRELL

Anne Farrell was born into a family of storytellers. She hung on to every word of the tales her father told on the dark evenings in Cloone, County Kilkenny. She brought the same joy to her own children as she filled their imaginations with stories from far and wide. Her storytelling took her on journeys to Wales, America and Newfoundland where she captivated audiences with her tales. Her collections of folk tales live on as a fitting memory of a beautiful and talented lady.

'Storytelling is a delight to the soul for it shifts and changes like the wind.' (Anne Farrell)

LUKE EASTWOOD

Luke Eastwood was born in Scotland but moved to Ireland in 1999, he lives in County Kerry and is co-author of *Kerry Folk Tales*. He is also the author of ten other books, including *Samhain: the Roots of Halloween*.

Luke has had a varied career as a journalist, graphic designer, professional musician, horticulturist and civil servant. He is currently the editor of *Pagan Ireland* magazine and writes for a number of magazines and websites around the world on history, social issues, environmentalism and spirituality.

KATE CORKERY

Kate Corkery is a professional storyteller, with a background in language teaching and theatre and is author of *Cork Folk Tales*. Based in London, Kate's role as Storyteller in Residence at the Irish Cultural Centre was recognised with a Fringe First Award for 'outstanding work in regenerating the art of storytelling in today's society'.

A passionate believer in the power of storytelling in education, she is a founder member of 'Everyday Magic' and of 'Spud and Yam'. Kate has travelled far and wide with her stories and has appeared at many festivals throughout the UK and Europe.